THE LAND OF
MANGO SUNSETS

THE LAND OF MANGO SUNSETS

Dorothea Benton Frank

**Doubleday Large Print
Home Library Edition**

WM

WILLIAM MORROW
An Imprint of HarperCollins*Publishers*

THE LAND OF MANGO SUNSETS. Copyright © 2007 by Dorothea Benton Frank. All rights reserved. Printed in the United States of America. No part of this book may be used or reproduced in any manner whatsoever without written permission except in the case of brief quotations embodied in critical articles and reviews. For information address HarperCollins Publishers, 10 East 53rd Street, New York, NY 10022.

ISBN: 978-0-7394-8465-4

**This Large Print Book carries the
Seal of Approval of N.A.V.H.**

In loving memory of my mother

In the Dream of the Sea

I call you from the open water
surrounding us, speaking
across divided lives.

I call you
from the waves
that always have direction.

Where strings of morning glory
hold the dunes in place,
I call. In winter,

when wind pours
through cracks in the walls.
Inside, I call

although my voice
has been silent
and dissolving.
In sand
pulled back

into the body

of the sea,
from the blue
house build on sand

balanced at the edge
of the world
I call you.

Drowning stars,
shipwrecks, and broken voices
move beneath the waves.

Here, at the open
center
of my ordinary heart

filling with sounds
of the resurrected,
in the dream

of the sea,
I call you
home.

—Marjory Wentworth

ACKNOWLEDGMENTS

Special thanks to my dear friend Marjory Heath Wentworth, South Carolina poet laureate, whose spectacular words enrich mine. We are all so proud of you, Marjory, and I am particularly honored to offer one vehicle to share your glorious talent, that of a *living American woman,* with readers everywhere. Bravo!

To my New Jersey literary friends, the geniuses: Pamela Redmond Satran, Deborah Davis, Debbie Galant, Benilde Little, Mary Jane Clark, and especially Liza Dawson, who knows why. Huge thanks for your support and your friendship, which I value more than you could know. And my love to all the members of MEWS, which is run by the indefatigable Pamela Redmond Satran, who keeps the four-hundred-plus writers who live in the Montclair area informed on all issues pertinent to the fun and games of a writing life.

To my South Carolina literary friends who constantly inspire me with their endless wit and the choir of their authentic southern voices: Josephine Humphreys, her sommelier husband, Tom Hutcheson, Walter Edgar, Anne Rivers Siddons, Sue Monk Kidd, Nathalie DuPree, Jack Bass, Tom Blagden, Barbara Hagerty, Robert Rosen, Mary Alice Monroe, William Baldwin, Robert Jordan, Roger Pinckney, and especially to the sainted one, Cassandra King, who most of you know is the long-suffering wife of my favorite old grizzly bear, Pat Conroy, who gave me the courage to write and continues to explain the publishing world to me, one drop of ink at a time. To Jack Alterman, for my youthful author photo and for his photographic genius in general.

To Gerald Imber, M.D., my plastic-surgeon pal, who has yet to make me resemble Jack Alterman's work, who is fabulous, hilarious, a genius, and an artist, but who will not give you free plastic surgery unless you are the pope or something, or Oprah, who, as I understand it, doesn't need it or the charity, and let me assure you I have sucked up to her in other acknowledgments with zero results. To the other real people who appear in this book— Kathy and Mike Rumph, Woody, Elizabeth and Caroline Wood, and my other two favorite doctors: George Durst, M.D., and Gordon Ferguson, DDS—huge thanks, and, folks, if their characters act out of character for them, it's my fault, not theirs. And as always, to the out-of-state belles—Rhonda Rich, Mary Kay Andrews, Patti Callahan Henry, and Annabelle Robertson—love y'all madly

Again thanks to my agent, Gail Fortune, for years of friendship and excellent guidance, and all best wishes to Gail's partner, John Talbot, a heckuva guy.

To the William Morrow dream team, beginning with my fearless and brilliant editor, Carrie Feron, whose truly stellar thoughts and suggestions were invaluable in shaping this entire work—Carrie, darlin', if they like this book, make sure you take a large chunk of the credit! Thank you for everything! And to Jane Friedman, Michael Morrison, Lisa Gallagher, Brian McSharry, Virginia Stanley,

Carla Parker, Michael Morris, Michael Spradlin, Brian Grogan, Donna Waitkus, Rhonda Rose, and Lord knows, to Tessa Woodward—whew! Thank you over and over! And to the marketing and publicity wizards—Debbie Stier, Ben Bruton, Buzzy Porter, Pamela Spengler Jaffee, Lynn Grady, and Tavia Kowalchuk—huge thanks! I curtsy to Liate Stehlik and Adrienne DiPietro from Avon, to Rick Harris in the audio division, and to the visionaries, Tom Egner and Richard Aquan, for my gorgeous covers.

To Debbie Zammit—what can I tell ya? We're still alive! Thanks for everything, especially the endless hours of scrutiny, your wonderful friendship, and your humor that saved many a day. To Ann Del Mastro, Mary Allen, George Zur, and Kevin Sherry—you know how much the Franks love all of you and appreciate your keeping our mother ship afloat in so many ways. And to Penn Sicre, my friend of many years, for taking the leap (we hope!) from page to screen with *Plantation.*

And to the booksellers—especially Patti Morrison, Avery Cline, Emily Morrison, and every last soul from Barnes & Noble in Mount Pleasant, South Carolina; Tom Warner and

Vicki Crafton of Litchfield Books in Pawleys Island; Jennifer McCurry of Waldenbooks in Charleston; Andy and Carrie Graves of Happy Bookseller in Columbia; Frazer Dobson and Sally Brewster at Park Road Books in Charlotte; and to Omar Dowdy and Larry Kirshbaum, my old friend and new friend—huge hugs and kisses to you, one and all.

Special bowing and scraping to my wonderful cousin Charles "Comar" Blanchard Jr., whom we adore for who he is and to whom we owe enormous gratitude for everything he does.

Obviously, the bulk of all my thanks I should place at the feet of my wonderful, brilliant, handsome husband, Peter, and our two gorgeous, outrageously funny, and smart nearly adult children, Victoria and William. We are so proud of you and I thank you for understanding this crazy career of mine and always rolling with the insanity with such warmth and love. I love you all with all I've got. But back to Peter for a moment—hey, Pete? You're number one! (Inside joke.) Seriously, I love you and thanks!

And to my readers? I thank you again and again for all your nice e-mails, for coming out to book signings, and for being so great in every way. Your generous words of support keep me going in the tough moments and I mean that from the bottom of my heart.

THE LAND OF
MANGO SUNSETS

PROLOGUE

We called it the Land of Mango Sunsets.
None of the old islanders knew what we
meant by that, as they had only ever heard of
mangoes. Bottled chutney perhaps, but that
was about the sum total of their experience
with a food that was so foreign. But I knew all
about the romance of them from my earliest
memories of anything at all. My parents had
honeymooned in the South Pacific, which in
those days was considered a little reckless,
certainly titillating, and above all, highly exotic. Every morning they left their beds, still
half dreaming, to find a tray outside the door

of their bungalow. They would bring it behind the curtains of mosquito netting and into their bed. Still in their nightclothes, my mother's hair cascading in tendrils and my father's young beard stubble scratching her young complexion, they would burn away the sour paste of morning breath with a plate of sliced mangoes, dripping with fleshy sweetness, a pot of strong tea, and a rack of toast. From then on, mangoes were equated with love, tenderness, and hopeful beginnings, and we spent our lives looking everywhere for other examples of them.

On the island where my family had kept the same cottage for over one hundred years, there was a sliver of time late in the day when the sun hung in the western sky, after it stopped burning white and before it dropped into the horizon. For just a few minutes it would transform itself into a red orange orb. Wherever we were on the island, we would all stop to face it and my father would say to my mother, Look, Josephine, the mango sunset. We would wonder aloud about the majesty of the hand that shaped it. About heaven. About where our ancestors were and could they see us looking for them in the twilight. I believed that they could.

As if in a postscript, great streaks of red and purple would appear on some evenings and on others streams of light, burning through clouds, dividing the horizon into triangles of opalescent colors for which there are no words. The Land of Mango Sunsets was a force all on its own. And whether you understood mango sunsets or not, the ending of most days in the Lowcountry of South Carolina was so beautiful it would wrench your heart.

On Sullivans Island there was of a chorus of bird whistles and song to begin and end each day. On the turning of the tide there were endless rustling fronds brushing the air in a windy dance only they understood. And perhaps most important, there were the leathered but loving hands and peppermint breath of old people, always there to help. The pungent smells of salt and wet earth haunt me to this day because you see, before I could speak, I could smell rain coming, sense a storm, and knew enough to be afraid of fast water that would spin you away from life in an instant.

It was there on that island that I learned about the power of deep love and came to believe in magic, only to forget it all later on.

But years later, the struggle came to remember, a struggle worth the salt in every tear shed and the blood of every bruise to my spirit.

I was a very young girl then with an empty head, who knew little more than a nearly idyllic reality. I did not know yet about heartbreak and I was not old enough to have the sense to plan for a future or even to think of one. Wasn't that day enough? Yes, it was. When we were on Sullivans Island we lived from day to day without a care in the world, or so it seemed to me.

The story, this story I want to tell you, is all true. It may not always be pleasant to hear and I know that much of the time you won't agree with me and the things I have done. I was not always nice. But if you will indulge me just a bit, in the end I think you will see things a little more from my perspective. That's a large part of the point of this. Recognizing yourself mirrored in my mistakes won't be pretty, but perhaps it will keep both of us from making the same mistakes again.

I am on the porch now, rocking back and forth in Miss Josephine's rocking chair. In my ear, I can hear the lilt of her honeyed voice and feel the touch of her hand on my shoulder. She's telling me the same thing I am going to show you.

Things happen for a reason. You'll see what I mean. Think of all the times you have told yourself, Well, I wish someone had given me a clue. Or, Why didn't I see that coming? How could I have been so stupid? Or what's the point of trying? Those thoughts always occurred when you were about to learn a lesson in life.

I am older now and it doesn't matter anymore if someone thinks I am a fool. It makes me laugh because I have been a fool so often that if you could stack the occasions one upon another, they would reach the top of the sky and then spiral away into their own orbit. But I hope I am a fool no longer. If I catch myself falling back into my old ways, I would like to think I would just forgive myself, pick up, and carry on. I know now what matters.

Think of a heavy key chain and this story is one of the keys. Use it on the quest toward the happiness there is to be found in life on this wretched but beautiful earth. It's not the answer to everything, but it might help. Let's start at the height of my stupidity.

Chapter One

MANHATTAN—SOME TIME AGO

Dear Ms. O'Hara,
Your father was such a lovely man and this tragic loss will be felt by everyone who knew him for years to come. In my mind's eye, I can still see him cleaning my grill with a vengeance. That man surely did love a clean grill. Please accept my deepest and most sincere condolences.

There is the small matter of his rent for the month of January. Not wanting to be an additional burden at this terribly sensitive time, I will simply deduct it from his security deposit.

Although I am loath to broach this subject, I must notify you that the timely removal of his personal property will obviously impact the amount of money I am able to return to you.

Once again, please accept my profound sympathy.

Cordially,
Miriam Elizabeth Swanson

Making my way across Sixty-first Street, I checked that the stamp was secure and slipped the envelope in a mailbox. The weather was fast changing from cold and damp to a bone-chilling arctic freeze. My snow boots were tucked in my PBS member's canvas tote bag, just in case. I knew it was not very chic to be traipsing around Manhattan with a canvas tote bag. But the proud logo sent a message to all those people who enjoyed the benefits of Public Television but felt no compunction to support it even with the smallest of donations. The fact that people took without giving irked me. On the brighter side, I had always thought it would be great fun to be a volunteer in their phone bank during a campaign, to sit up there doing something so worthwhile as hundreds of thousands, perhaps millions of people, looked on. I had submitted my name as a candidate for the job many times, but I had never been called. Perhaps I should have sent them a more thorough bio with a more flattering photograph. Something youthful. Ah, me. Another disappointment. Another rejection. But what member of the human race didn't have unfulfilled little fantasies? Chin up, Miriam, I told myself, and trudged on.

The weather continued to deteriorate and Charles Dickens himself would have agreed that it was a perfect day for a funeral. Bulbous gray clouds lowered toward the earth and covered every inch of the sky. They were closing in and threatening to burst. It would surely pour snow or sleet at any moment. There was nothing I could do about the weather or my feelings of gloom brought on by a claustrophobic sky. After all these years in New York, I was as resigned to winter as I was to any number of things that fed my love/ hate relationship with the city. Anyway, where else was I to go? Live with my sons? No way. Live with my mother? Not in a million years.

I adjusted my muffler to protect my cheeks. At least I had written Ms. O'Hara a note, and despite the inclement conditions, I had been sure to get it in the mail. I couldn't help but pause to think there was something so lazy about people who abandoned fountain pens or pens of any kind in favor of the expeditiousness of e-mail on any and every occasion. Including expressions of sympathy. Believe it or not, I actually heard a story of someone receiving an e-mail telling of a close friend's death. Including a frowning emoticon, God save us. The reason I remember was that it was so completely absurd to me. And speaking of fountain pens, they now had a disposable variety available at all those office-supply chain stores, which to me defeated the purpose of using a fountain pen in the first place. Wasn't it about holding a beautiful object in your hands and feeling its solid weight? Its worth and the importance of its history? Remember when penmanship was taught in the classroom and its beautiful execution was prized?

But that is what the world has come to. Quick this and disposable that. To my dying day, I would remain a lonely standard-bearer in a world that continued to toss aside every inch of civility we have ever known. Handwritten notes seemed to have gone the way of corsages—their existence was rare. It just was the way it was.

I hurried along to the funeral service, tip-toeing inside the church and finding my seat next to my dearest friend and other tenant, Kevin Dolan.

"I have always loved St. Bartholomew's," I whispered to him. I removed my coat and gloves and, as inconspicuously as possible, settled in the pew. The service had already begun and I regretted the fact that I was late, even if it was only by a few minutes. In the steamer trunk of middle age, folded, packed, and wrinkled with one physical and emotional insult after another, perimenopause had delivered a measure of intolerance, even toward myself.

"Me, too," Kevin whispered back, and sighed. "Poor Mr. O'Hara. Whoever thought he would just drop dead on the crosstown bus? Just like that! Poof. Gone." He popped his wrist in front of him in a gesture that equated Mr. O'Hara's death with a magician's *now you see it, now you don't!*

"Hush," whispered someone in front of us.

We paused in silence in deference to the occasion and then couldn't resist continuing our recap of the fragile nature of life in the

Big Apple. That was the effect Kevin always had on me. In his presence I became a young gossiping washwoman, emphasis on young.

"Pockets picked and ID stolen," I added at a carefully calibrated low volume of clear displeasure. "Disgusting!"

"Five days in the *city morgue*? Dreadful! If I hadn't called his family . . ."

"He's lucky he wasn't eaten by rats. Thank heavens for dental records . . ."

"Who could believe he *went* to a dentist with his snaggleteeth?" Kevin said.

"Please. He was my . . ." said the woman in front of us, her shoulders racking with sobs.

Chastised for a second time, we were immediately quieted, but our eyes met over our lowered sunglasses with identical expressions of devilish curiosity. Did our Mr. O'Hara have a lover? Was this reprimanding woman in front of us Mr. O'Hara's tart? We shook our heads. Not possible, I thought, but knew we would discuss it later. Who had the strength and tolerance for relationships? Certainly neither of us did. Although I wouldn't mind if, on occasion, George Clooney found himself between my sheets.

I was wearing black, of course, and my

most provocative black felt hat secured against the wind with an antique onyx hat pin, thinking I looked rather smart. Kevin, bald as a billiard ball with his thick round tortoiseshell glasses, was impeccably turned out in a deep charcoal pinstripe suit. He smelled as luscious as he looked. His lavender silk tie was dyed to match his shirt, jacquarded in the tiniest of damask rectangles. If we kept our sunglasses on, which we did, an onlooker might have assumed we were a couple, which we were not. I was his landlady and he was what my grandmother used to call a *confirmed bachelor*. However, strict definitions aside, we were the dearest of friends.

Finally, the service reached its conclusion and the pallbearers carried the casket down the aisle. The bereaved family followed, leaning on one another, choking back tears. Even *my* heart made a little leap at their sorrow. It was bad enough that Mr. O'Hara had died in the first place. Why did his family have to suffer the added indignities brought on by living in New York City? In moments like that, I wondered why I had stayed in this godforsaken place for so long. I shrugged off the question as quickly as I had considered it.

It was depressing to think about it.

But wasn't depression an eager companion, lurking behind everything including Christmas? Long ago I had sworn off that sorry dark suitor with his cheap wilting flowers and his promises of commiseration. I was far better served by Kevin's company, a stiff cocktail, and a conversation with Harry, my bird who was so much more than a bird.

As we stepped out into January's afternoon light, countless tiny snowflakes swirled all around us. The steps of the church were partially covered in thin patches of white.

"Snow day," Kevin said drily.

"You're not going back to the office?"

"Please," he said. "I need a Bloody. Don't you? Funerals completely bum me out."

I nodded in agreement.

"Take my arm so you don't slip. P.J. Clarke's is right around the corner."

We made our way over to Third Avenue, huddling against each other for warmth. The raw air was so bitter that talking stung our teeth. Conversation was all but curtailed until we reached our destination.

Inside the restaurant we shook the snow from our coats and handed them to the coat-check girl. My hat had gathered powder in its rim and I took a moment to remove it, worrying that melted snow might discolor it.

"It's getting veeerry baaaad out there," she said, watching me as I placed my hat right back on my head. "Nice, uh, hat."

"Thank you." Apparently, she was unaware that hats worn during lunch were perfectly acceptable. And a highly desirable accessory in between salon visits, if you know what I mean.

"What does the Weather Channel say?" Kevin asked, slipping the coat checks in his pocket.

"Six to nine in the city and twelve north and west. And I gotta take the LIRR to pick up my kid from day care before six! It ain't easy, right? It ain't easy."

"Gracious!" I said. "Maybe you'd better leave a little early."

There came an onslaught of visions of an unswaddled toddler, stumbling through drifts, whimpering, shivering, wandering around blindly, searching for his desperate and harried mother, who trudged through snowbanks, rushing to her child's side, carrying a cooked chicken and fresh carrots in doubled plastic bags from D'Agostino's. Then I looked at her again—chewing gum, tight top, bizarre gold highlights strewn through her dyed black hair, and a chain on her neck that spelled out her astrological sign—what was I thinking? Cheap bling and Juicy Fruit. This was the kind of mother who would pull a hot dog from the freezer and throw it in her sticky microwave without the benefit of so much as a paper towel. I knew her type. This Scorpio would tuck juice boxes and dry Cheerios in the corner of her baby's crib so that in the morning she could sleep off the debauchery of her prior evening . . . not that I'm judgmental . . .

"Miriam? Come along, girl. Let's go to our table. You know, I don't think you heard a word I said, did you?"

I realized my breathing was irregular. "I'm sorry . . . I was just thinking . . ."

"About what?"

I took a deep breath to calm myself. "About how terribly fortunate I am to never have been in that poor girl's position. You know, forced to rely on day care while I slaved away in some underpaid menial job just to feed my sons?"

Kevin did *not* need to know every thought I ever had about little trollops and the bulging population of others like her.

"That's what I love about you, Miriam. You always remember to appreciate the good things Charles did for you as well." Kevin's smirk was too obsequious for my inner cynic.

"What? That lout? Oh please! I stayed home because Charles insisted and you know it. It was a sign of his success that his wife didn't have to work."

"The cad," Kevin said, changing political parties.

"The cad, indeed."

"A bit like having a plump wife in a starving African nation . . ."

I stared at Kevin and wondered if he meant to imply that my figure had become matronly. I sniffed at him.

"Miriam! Not you, dear! In fact, I was just thinking how you've become a rake! You're not doing some crazy diet, are you?"

"Please," I said, smiling and warming in the glow of his affection. "We know better."

The waiter took our order for Bloody Marys, home fries, and cheeseburgers. I was ravenous, and when the drinks arrived, I devoured the celery, crunching away at the stalk like a starving rabbit. Was I losing a little weight? Perhaps I was!

"So, how's work down at the Temple O'Couture?" I asked him.

Kevin had been in charge of all visual displays at Bergdorf Goodman for years. His windows, which received accolades and awards from all over the world, dictated the ultimate fantasies of others.

"How's work? It's the same old horse manure day in and day out. How do we make outrageously priced clothes designed for emaciated teenage Amazons seem appealing to middle-aged women of normal proportions who hope that a certain dress or a particular gown will ignite the long-absent spark in their spouse's eye?"

"Easy now, sweetheart. You're treading the shallow waters close to home."

"Oh, honey. I didn't mean you, Miriam, and you know it. I was speaking only in the most general of terms."

Kevin smiled and I was reassured that he had not meant me. Nonetheless, I spouted, "If there was such a thing as a dress that would bring Charles back to me, I wouldn't go near it. I can promise you that."

"And *I* wouldn't let you!"

"Hmmph. Thank you." I reached across the table and patted the back of his perfectly tanned hand. Where did he find the time to maintain a tan? Of course! He simply ran up to the Ciminelli spa on the seventh floor during his lunch hour and had himself sprayed with some bronzer. That was what he did. Probably. Well, I charged him so little in rent he had the resources for extravagances. In my world, I could barely afford a manicure once a week.

"Miriam?"

"Yes?"

"Honey? Are you upset about the funeral? You are so distracted today . . ."

"Oh, Kevin, I'm sorry. I just had another thought that if there was a dress that could make Charles bray at the moon like a donkey gone wild with regret, I might buy that one."

"He was a colossal fool, Miriam, and everyone knows it."

I looked straight in his beautiful blue eyes and thought how I loved him to pieces. They were the blue of the Mediterranean as I remembered the Mediterranean from the Charles Years, when there were no fiscal restraints. The good old days when I was naively uninformed of the facts.

The waiter reappeared with our food and asked if we cared for another cocktail. Of course we did. Wasn't it snowing? I downed the remainder of the one I had and thought, Golly, you surely did get a good measure of vodka at old P.J.'s, didn't you?

"Oh, to heck with Charles . . . did I tell you about the spring gala plans at the museum? You'll have to be my escort again this year, I'm afraid. My, this hamburger is simply beyond divine."

"There are still a few things worth living for, right? Pass the ketchup, please. Let's see . . . can I suffer another evening of champagne and foie gras by the side of the fabulous Mrs. Swanson? Hmm. I think I can!" He slapped the table. "When's the gig?"

"It's in May." We chatted about last year's event for a few minutes. The waiter delivered our drinks, I sipped a few times and felt my well of steely reserve beginning to evaporate. "I want to chair the decorations committee so badly I can smell peonies and sword fern every single time I think about it."

"There, there now, my Petal Puss, whom do we have to bribe?"

I giggled at his pet name for me. "Agnes Willis, the old stone-faced chair of the gala. Maybe she has a child or a niece who needs an apartment. I have to rent the second floor, you know. And quickly. What if Mr. O'Hara's family doesn't come for his things?"

"If they don't come in two weeks, we'll put them in storage and send them a bill. I can take care of that for you. And if you want, I'll throw a coat of paint on the apartment, too."

"Oh, Kevin! You're such a lamb! What would I do without you?"

"Well, for starters, you'd have to rent the third floor as well. You're not eating your potatoes. Do you mind?"

"Help yourself," I said, and slid my platter toward him. "Heavenly days, sometimes I feel like a character from a Tennessee Williams play."

"Hardly. Agnes Willis, huh? I think she might enjoy tickets to see the Bill Blass collection. Who wouldn't? Maybe I can help you with Madame Rushmore. Every stone has a fault line, doesn't it?"

Later, filled with hamburgers and the hope of a prestigious committee to chair and a wonderful new tenant living upstairs, Kevin and I made our way home through the snow. After I put on my snow boots. And Kevin had smartly brought his.

We had lingered over lunch as usual and it was getting late in the day. There were already about four inches on the ground at that point, and the snow was still falling as though it never intended to stop. The usual crowds of shoppers and tourists were down to a trickle of humanity, huddled in doorways and in small clusters waiting for a bus, stomping their feet to stay the numbness that only the very young did not feel. Taxis were nonexistent.

Familiar landmarks appeared different and we were unsure where the street ended and the curb began. No one had begun to shovel and we moved along with extra care. Nothing was more beautiful in the world than Manhattan hushed in a fresh blanket of pure white snow, even though part of me suspected it was radioactive. And here I was in New York all these years, now reduced to taking in boarders so I could hold on to my home, with two estranged sons in cockeyed relationships, a mother who had gone off the deep end, and an ex-husband who didn't want me anymore.

"What's going through your head, Miriam? You've got that look again."

"Everything. I'm middle-aged, Kevin. The game's half over and somehow I never got what I wanted."

Kevin stopped, turned to face me, and put his hands on my shoulders. "The past is the past, Miriam. You have to stop all this brooding. Seriously! It's got to stop! The looming question, my Petal, is what do you want now?"

I just looked at him and felt my jaw get tight as my volcanic bitterness grew. "I want to be vindicated from the guilt I feel. I want to be satisfied with my lot. All my life I conducted myself as polite society dictated, and look where it got me."

Kevin nodded, understanding exactly what I meant. We arrived at the front door.

"I'm going to run around to Albert's and buy us some veal chops and I'll pick up a great bottle of red wine. When I come back, we're going to make a plan. You set the table and think about this. It's time for you to break a few rules, Petal, because, you're right, following them didn't work worth a tinker's damn."

"Fine. That sounds good."

I opened the street door of my town house and picked up the mail from the floor. Then I stacked Kevin's mail on the hall table and opened the door to my part of the house. There on my coffee table stood Harry, my African gray parrot, who, at eleven years old, had matured into a very desirable room-mate.

"Charles is a horse's ass," he said.

"You're telling me?"

He followed me to the kitchen, hopped on my fingers, and I lifted him up to the top of his crate. Harry watched me as I dropped most of the mail straight into the trash. I gave him a small chunk of cantaloupe and he said, "Harry is a good boy."

"Yes, you are. You are a marvelous boy."

The message light on my phone was blinking. I pressed the play button and listened while I chose the least tarnished flatware for the table.

Hi, sweetheart! It's your mother. I left a message on your cell you can ignore. I just saw a weather report that you're having one dee-double doozy of a snowstorm! Just wanted to remind you to be prepared in case the electricity fails—water, batteries, logs for the fireplace? But then, I'm sure you think you know what to do . . .

There was no one like my mother. I mean, no one. Once the grande dame of Charleston, South Carolina, she'd flipped her chignon when Daddy died. Six months later, and to the utter shock of her known world, she sold our family's gorgeous home and all the contents I didn't want, moved to our funky old beach house on Sullivans Island, and became a hippie. She says she's not a hippie but I think the term accurately describes her lifestyle. Perfect for her, mortifying to me. She threw away an extremely enviable life to *live green,* whatever that is.

The next message was from my son Charlie, named for his father Charles, the horse's ass.

Mother? Ah, not home. Okay. Well, just checking in to be sure you're doing all right in this weather, but if you're out and about, you're obviously fine. If you need anything, gimme a shout. Um, okay then. We'll talk later . . .

Could he have said, *I love you, Mom?* No. He would never allow himself any overt display of affection. Especially toward me and especially after all that had transpired. But at least he still felt some obligation to his mother and I would just have to console myself with that miserly peanut.

The next three messages were solicitations and I erased them, saving the ones

from Mother and Charlie to remind myself to
return their calls. There was no call from Dan-
iel, my youngest, but it was no surprise. He
rarely called unless the earth moved in California or unless Nan got pregnant, and maybe
those two events weren't mutually exclusive.
I grinned at my own cleverness. They had
two precious little children that I thought were
God's gracious plenty. Nan had suffered
enough miscarriages for a miniseries on the
trials and tribulations of the reproductive system. The poor girl. Why she continued to attempt to have more babies, I could not begin
to fathom. Nan should only have known all
that I knew about the disappointments of
raising children. I was sure she didn't have a
clue.

I touched the corners of the packaged log
in my living room's fireplace with the long lit
match and watched the blue and purple flick-
ers become gold and orange flames as it
burned its way to life. The world was still re-
volving, the snow would come to an end
eventually, and somehow, I would be vindicated.

Chapter Two

GESUNDHEIT!

Dear Mrs. Willis,

How can I ever begin to thank you for coming to my rescue with a tissue this weekend? So thoughtful of you! The membership table is such fun, don't you agree? But with all the germs and flu that the visiting public and their crying toddlers in strollers bring around at this time of the year, I was so lucky to be near you when I sneezed. I do think they should leave their babies home with a sitter, but what can you do? This is what the world has become. In any case, how fortunate I am to be acquainted with someone who is ever at the ready! I do so hope our paths cross again soon. And I hope I shall have the opportunity to return your kindness.

Cordially,
Miriam Elizabeth Swanson

I sealed the envelope with a damp sponge, used my last special-edition Eleanor Roosevelt stamp, hoping to send a subliminal message that I was absolutely strong enough to chair the decorations committee. Call me Eleanor. I hate war. But no one knew how I emphatically despised the common indignities of the membership table. Good grief. Something had to happen to relieve me of membership duty.

Over the weekend, I had reminded Agnes Willis that I had some knowledge about flowers and branching materials. In the old days before Charles ran off with his whore, we enjoyed a nice friendship, sharing tables at events together, Charles; Agnes; her husband, Truman; and me. But once Charles's betrayal was exposed, I lost all my friends. And well, the unfortunate truth was that our serendipitous meeting did not unfold as gracefully as one might have hoped.

She sauntered by with her snooty clothes-hanger friends, choked by the tight folds of their Hermès scarves, wrapped to conceal their aging crepe. There was no doubt Agnes Willis was there to verify to them that her lowly minions she summoned with her irrefutable power had shown up at our lowly posts.

I looked up to her and said, "Oh! Mrs. Willis!"

She nodded to me. I was not about to be snubbed. I stood, careful to raise myself to my full height, and extended my hand to her sour-faced friend.

"Hello, I'm Miriam Swanson." I couldn't tell you what she said her name was for love or money. "Mrs. Willis? Aren't the flowers particularly spectacular this week? When my Charlie was a little boy he used to call them For Cynthia. I never had the heart to correct him."

I referred to the huge yellow branches of forced forsythia that graced the center of the lobby mixed with long white tulips, marsh grass, and exotic leaves from who knows where.

"Pardon me?" she said. "Oh, yes, they are, Mrs. Swanson."

Two of the ladies walked away, but the dour one said to Agnes Willis, "For Cynthia. How precious." She gave me a purse-lipped smile.

I thought, Oh, why don't you go eat a whole pizza, and don't you know that was when the pollen or the dust or some rogue virus overwhelmed my sinuses. I sneezed with the brute force of a longshoreman, thoroughly spraying them with nature's bounty. Agnes and her horrified friend stared me down as though I had just removed my panty hose and swung them around my head. But Agnes, still in possession of at least one gene of empathy, reached in her bag, flipped her wrist, and presented me with a tissue. I was completely demoralized.

"I'm going to the ladies' room," her friend said. "To bathe."

"I'm so sorry," I said. "I don't know what—"

"It's all right, dear," Agnes Willis said. Her eyebrows knitted in disgust and she put her hand on her friend's arm to delay her. "It could happen to anyone."

They walked away together and I heard

her say to her companion "she used to be married to Charles Swanson, you know." . . . yet again affirming to me that without Charles and his wallet, my social standing was greatly depreciated. She had not even bothered to whisper.

More than ever, I hoped Kevin would produce tickets for Agnes Willis to the Bill Blass fall show that was right around the corner. If I could be there as well, which was part of the plan Kevin and I had cooked up over dinner, perhaps it would provide the opportunity for me to remark on the flowers they would surely have in profusion. She might take the hint.

It was such a challenge and a frustration to remain a lady in the face of the endless stream of devaluations I endured. But that's what my mother had always said I should do. It was also hopeless to think that Agnes Willis would divine the real meaning of my remarks and then completely insane to hope that she would act in my favor. Why would she? Especially after I sprayed her and her friend with enough watery mucus to float the Staten Island Ferry. Gross. And, to be honest, what did she stand to gain by doing anything for me? Well, maybe a seat at Mr. Blass's show, but she didn't know that yet. I'd have to check with Kevin to be sure he didn't forget.

So, down to the corner I hurried and off went my thank-you note sealed with my dreams. I congratulated myself for not mentioning the committee assignments in my communiqué. Another thing my mother, the formidable Miss Josephine, had taught me about the art of written notes was to stick to the subject at hand.

It was snowing again, freezing and gray outside. I maneuvered around the slicks of ice and salt, wishing I had worn gloves for the short trip. Pulling my coat around me, I hurried home sighing and sighing. It seemed that the relentless winter tirade would stretch into May. Just the few steps to the corner and reliving my meeting with Agnes had been enough to make me want to indulge in an old movie and a good cry.

"Not me!" I said, resisting self-pity and unlocking the front door.

It took my entire body weight to close the outside door good and tight. Every door in the entire house needed to be planed, repainted, and rehung, but that was a job for the spring. In fact, the list of chores to be done and what they would cost frightened

me. Rightfully so. Even Kevin, good and generous with his time as he was, couldn't possibly see to them all. I worried about the
shallow steps that led to the second and third
floors. Over time they had begun to settle
and slump to the west. I worried about the
furnace and the chimneys and the gutters
and the roof . . . on and on it went. But I was
heartened by my decision to keep the first
floor for myself. I wasn't replacing the steps.
Listen, I wasn't exactly a little old lady, but I
wasn't getting any younger either.

I could hear Kevin's boom box streaming
Latin music from the second floor. He must've
been working on Mr. O'Hara's apartment. It
sounded like Sergio Mendes and Brasil '66.
How festive! Only Kevin would have the presence of mind to turn an act of drudgery into
something worth dancing through.

After several phone calls and polite warn-
ings that I would be forced to place his personal things in storage, Mr. O'Hara's family
rented a small van, drove in from Oyster
Bay, and claimed his property. As each day
went by, I became more anxious to rent the
space. After all, I had obligations to meet
just like the rest of the world.

I opened the door to my apartment. Harry

was sitting on the arm of my aging red-striped chintz sofa looking at me.

"Hi, Harry, my little feathered friend!" I said, throwing my damp coat over a club chair that had seen better days. "It's cold outside. And it's snowing again!"

He cocked his head to one side and stared at me.

"Charles is a horse's ass."

"Yes, he certainly is and Miriam loves Harry."

"I love you. Pretty Miriam!" Harry said, and whistled.

Of course I had trained Harry to say all the sweet things he said, but it still sounded nice, even if the flattery came from a bird. Unfortunately, Harry's words represented the vast majority of the compliments I received. I gave him three grapes as a treat. Organic, of course. Sometimes I thought Harry enjoyed a better diet than I did, except that I really had made an effort to buy organic when I could, another testament to my mother's power of suggestion.

"Come on, pussycat, let's go see what Kevin's up to."

He hopped on my fingers, we made our way up the stairs and swung open the door to Mr. O'Hara's apartment.

"It's just me, Mr. O'Hara!" Harry said, sounding exactly like me.

"Harry misses Mr. O'Hara," I said, and then realized that part of the far wall was an odd shade of green and that the window trim was some kind of orange. Kevin was wearing pre-splattered painter's overalls with a tight T-shirt underneath that accentuated his biceps. "What have you done here, Kevin?"

"Didn't you read Hop Along the obituary? Missed the memo, did you, Romeo?" Kevin turned the music down and his attention to me. "It's part of the plan, Miriam! So what do you think?"

"About the colors? Well . . . it's different, isn't it?" I let Harry down to walk around.

"It's very Key West . . ."

A Key West whorehouse, I thought. "Yes, it is," I said.

"Papaya and avocado and I'm thinking a splash of turquoise also—you know, just in bits of trim here and there to give it some pop . . ." Kevin's arms were flailing about as he justified his foray into the world of tropical psychedelic color.

"Who are we renting to, Kevin? What if they want beige walls? What if we rent to, I don't know . . . I mean, would a certified public accountant want to live with these colors?"

Kevin put his hands on his hips and stared at me in annoyance. "If they want beige, they can live somewhere else! I have made an executive decision, Miriam."

I didn't want to anger him because he had gone to a lot of trouble, so I said, "And what would that be, sweetums?"

"We're going to rent to someone who is younger than us. No more dead bodies. We need fun in our lives, girlie. And, in this house."

He was right about that and I agreed with him.

"Any potential tenants yet?" he asked.

"Yes, I'm actually seeing someone this afternoon at four."

"And who might this mysterious person be?"

"I'm not sure. He was an acquaintance of Mr. O'Hara, but I don't know anything about him, to tell you the truth."

"Miriam? You worry me. Just like that, you're going to let this man in your house? Our house?"

"Why, I hadn't even thought—"

"Honestly! We could wind up sliced and

diced into sushi on *Live at Five*! It's a good thing I'm home. I'll be in your kitchen making dinner in case anything seems peculiar to you, okay?"

"Well, he didn't sound like someone who would appreciate your handiwork anyway. These colors, I mean . . ."

"It's going to be very chic when I'm finished. Miriam? Sugar, I'm going to tell you something . . ." Kevin poured more fruit smoothie into his paint tray and ran his roller through it, squeezing away the excess.

"What's that?" I said, and Harry hopped back on my hand. I stroked his feathers.

He rested the tray and roller on the windowsill and leaned back against it, crossed his arms over his chest, and took a deep breath. I sensed an approaching lecture.

"You seem so somber, Kevin! What are you worried about?"

"Nothing! No, nothing at all, really! It's just that . . . look, Miriam. You have a fabulous apartment to offer. The kitchen is good, the bathroom is great—a big bedroom and living room, good light . . ."

"I'm aware. The point?"

"That it's also a privilege to live here. This

is a very smart address, Petal, and you know it. Let's be a little picky, okay?"

"Promise. I will. I've got to go call Mother. Tell her we're wearing sweaters and that we've got food—"

"I don't want to sound like Fred Mertz here. But, raise the rent, Ethel."

"Seriously? Yours, too?"

"Have you gone mad? No! The new tenant's!"

"Kevin, you know me. I think the quality of the tenant is just as important as the rent."

"Fabulous. When the furnace poops out, don't say I didn't warn you!"

"You're probably right," I said to placate him, and went to the door. "See you at four?"

"I smell condescension . . ."

"See you later. And, Kevin?"

"Yeah?"

"Thanks." I blew him a kiss and closed the door.

He was right about the furnace. At five o'clock in the morning, when it switched to its day cycle, it sounded like someone was crawling around inside the walls with a sledgehammer. It had been repaired and repaired, and soon it was going to expire. I knew it. Maybe I should consider raising the rent. I wasn't even sure what the going rate *was* for a one-bedroom apartment in my neighborhood.

"What are we going to do, Harry?" I said as I closed the door to my apartment behind me. "Perch?"

"Perch?"

"Okay, handsome." I put him on his perch in the kitchen and dialed my mother.

She picked up on the fourth ring, just as the recorded message on her answering machine was giving instructions.

"Hello?"

"Mother?"

If you're selling something, we don't want it . . .

"Let me turn this crazy thing off, Miriam. Hold on!"

If you want us to answer questions, forget it . . .

I heard something tumble and fall and then in the muffled distance of mother's efforts to quiet the offending machine, she said something like "dag blast it all to Hades!" Mother invented her own curse words, or like we say in the south, cusswords. To say *curse* is to actually curse and therefore ladies say *cuss*.

If you want . . . beep!

"All righty now! That's much better! Miriam? Are you still there?"

"Josie, Josie, Josie. That message of yours is pretty aggressive, don't you think?"

"That's *Miss* Josie to you, and no, it's not. If you knew all the fool phone calls I get . . . mol-asses!"

Read: Those asses!

"I'm sure that's so. So, Mother?"

"It's sixty degrees in South Carolina today and I can't for the life of me understand why you aren't here to enjoy it."

Mother always just jumped in and started telling me what was on her mind. She did this as though it was her duty to start up a conversation with a little dressing-down.

"Because then I wouldn't be here to attend Mr. O'Hara's funeral."

"He died?"

"He sure did."

"Why didn't you tell me?"

"Oh, really, Mother. What would you have done?"

"Well, I would've sent a card or something . . . how did he go?"

Mother had a morbid fascination with the final exits of others.

"He took the Fifty-seventh Street bus to paradise."

"Don't be cute with me, missy, or I'll cut a switch and come right to New York!"

I had to giggle at that. I could see her stripping the leaves from a thin branch and stuffing it in her tote bag. "No, seriously. He really did. He died on the bus. Heart attack."

"Mercy. Now what?"

"We cleaned out the apartment, Kevin is painting like crazy, and I'm interviewing a new tenant this afternoon. The snow seems to have stopped, so that's good. Maybe he won't cancel." I pulled back the window sheers and double-checked. A few flakes were coming down, but when I spotted a slice of blue sky I decided that they were from a roof or a branch, caught in a swirl of wind.

"*He*? Another man? Is this one a possibility for, you know . . ."

"Good grief! No! The last thing I need in my life is another man."

After all, but I wasn't bringing this up to her, I had married one and given birth to two more and somehow lost the affection of them all. It didn't matter what I left unsaid, my mother had an invisible umbilical cord from her brain to mine.

"Don't fret, Miriam. You are still their mother, and believe me, the boys will come around. As for you and men? People are not meant to be alone. You still have plenty of vitality left in you. Heaven knows, if I do, then you must!"

"Yes, but you're an original, Miss Josie."

"Oh, sure! Butter me up so I'll talk about something else."

"No. You really are. Besides, I'm not lonely. Anyway, no matter, Kevin thinks we should rent to a young person."

"Because Kevin knows you've become a dullard. A drip. B-o-r-i-n-g! And Kevin knows you need something to get your motor going . . ."

"I have to go, Mother. The doorbell is ringing."

"I don't hear anything. Maybe it sounds like that bird of yours is *imitating* the doorbell."

Busted.

"Well, he is, but the real one is ringing, too. I'll call you later this week, okay?" I hung up and looked at Harry. "Work on your doorbell voice, okay?"

"You got it!"

When I opened the door, there stood Kevin

loaded with grocery bags, and beside him was a very nice-looking middle-aged man. I felt my neck get warm.

"Mrs. Swanson?"

"Yes. Won't you come in?"

Well, I don't have to tell you that I thought he was perfect for the apartment. He chuckled when he saw the color of the walls and said he would repaint them at his own expense. Then I saw him staring at my legs. Kevin saw him staring, too, and I could tell from Kevin's bristling body language that he didn't like him at all. I took a deposit check and his cell-phone number and told him I would keep his check, that I had two other possible candidates to see on Monday, and that I would let him know. But I'll admit, I did practically let him think the place was his.

Kevin was furious with me.

"Why didn't you just give him the keys?" he said sarcastically as he drained the pasta into my sink.

"Very funny. Do you want a glass of Chianti?"

"Already poured one for myself. Harry and I have been in here praying that guy didn't do something terrible to all of us. I couldn't wait to hear the door close! Harry kept saying 'Good night! Good night!'"

"So that's why he's in his cage?"

"Yes! Even Harry had the good sense to worry!"

I poured myself a glass and looked at the kitchen table. It was simply but beautifully set for dinner with a cut baguette, wrapped in linen and placed in a sweetgrass basket from Charleston. Crystal goblets reflected the light of the candles borrowed from my living-room mantel; a glistening salad of butter lettuce and tomatoes, grated Parmesan and olive oil, tiny dishes of coarse salt and freshly ground pepper all waited at attention; and my silver pitcher was frosted from the ice water it held.

How could I not value Kevin's opinion? This was what he did. He went to great lengths to be sure everything was as lovely as it could be. So did I, most of the time, but the difference was that he did it with some innate joy as opposed to my joyless sense of duty.

That was me. If he had not set this glorious table I probably would have jumped down Kevin's throat and told him he was wrong about the man I had interviewed and I would have just ignored Kevin's instincts. Whether it was my family, my waning volunteer career, or a new tenant, I had to be right, have the last word. My way or no way. Maybe this was one of the rules that needed to be broken, one of the things I needed to change. In a rare instance of détente, I conceded the point and decided to let Kevin have his way.

"Okay. You and Harry win. I give up. What do y'all think I should do?"

The tiniest of victorious smiles crossed his face as he plated our dinner.

"Give me his check," he said. "You know me. I'm not usually so suspicious about people, but something about him—no, *everything* about him—was inappropriate. I'll have my friend in human resources run a background check on him."

"Fine. Fine."

Kevin looked down his nose at me with raised eyebrows, challenging my sincerity.

"No! I said *fine* and I meant it! Now let's eat."

Chapter Three

THE CANDIDATES

I put a crisp five-dollar bill in the envelope and sponge-sealed it. Did twelve-year-old boys eat ice cream in the dead of winter? My sons would have eaten ice cream at three in the morning any time of the year. Oh, who knows? The little varmint next door would probably spend it on a ball of crack, I thought. In the next moment, I had an ever-so-fleeting pang of guilt when the mental image I had of *said varmint* included freckles on his little nose and braces on his teeth. Well, it was enough that I had recognized his good deed, and if I did truly contribute to a drug habit it would not have been my intention. Or problem.

I had bigger fish to fry, as Mother liked to say.

I had scheduled an interview with a lady from Ohio or Pennsylvania at eleven and then another young woman was to stop by at four. Both had references and both sounded very nice on the phone. The lady from Ohio (or was it Pennsylvania?)—Jean, I think— was a client of my hairdresser. The other gal was the friend of Irene Waddlesnotte's niece—a most unfortunate family name. Originally from Alabama, I thought she had said. I'll admit that my anxiety was growing. I wanted a tenant in that apartment and the money in my account.

It was ten-thirty. The *New York Times* crossword puzzle was completed (there was nothing quite so uplifting as a Monday puzzle), Harry was fed, the house was clean, the fireplace was crackling with another log of imitation wood, and I was dressed for the day. Even though I wasn't necessarily going anywhere, I made it my habit to shower and dress nicely each day. I mean, maybe Charles's home-wrecking vamp, Judith, might get hit by a truck or a taxi and I could be called on to identify her mangled body. What a cheery thought! I decided to write a note and make tea.

Dear Robby,
This is just a little note to say how much I appreciate that you shoveled my steps and sprinkled salt on my snowy sidewalk. This winter has been particularly harsh and it is so kind of you to think of your neighbors. Your mother must be very proud to have such a fine young man as her son most definitely is. Please accept this small token of my gratitude and treat yourself to an ice cream cone!
Cordially,
Miriam Elizabeth Swanson

I put the kettle on to boil and placed cups and saucers on a tray with spoons, napkins, and a plate for some cookies. I spooned two heaping teaspoons of loose Irish Breakfast tea leaves in my favorite teapot. I used milk in my tea, but what if my visitor had a preference for honey and lemon? Well, guess what? I didn't have any lemons, so that was just too bad for her. And honey? Too messy. The only reason I was serving tea was to have the time to grill her about her life and past. I had taken Kevin's paranoia to heart and my intention was to find out everything I could before I signed a lease with anyone.

By the time the doorbell rang, I realized I had worked myself into an unpleasant state of crankiness. As you know, I deeply resented having to rely on paying strangers under my own roof in order to afford my home. The other, and perhaps more shameful, part was that my world had become so small that I hoped my new tenant would also be a friend. If my tenants were my friends, then I wouldn't have to hate their presence as much.

I buzzed her in, went to my front door, and opened it.

"I'm Miriam Swanson," I said, extending my hand. "Won't you come in?" She was attractive in a coarse kind of way. Overprocessed hair worn in a style too long for her age, too much décolleté exposed for daytime . . .

"Thank you." We shook hands. "I'm Jean Waring."

Nails obviously fake . . .

"It's very nice to meet you, Jean. May I take your coat?"

Cashmere? Who bought *that* for her?

"Thank you."

She handed it to me and stood with her back to the fireplace. I folded it neatly and placed it on the arm of my sofa.

"Gosh! It's so cold outside! Isn't this weather unusual? I can't recall winter being quite so nasty and cold."

I nodded and said, "Won't you sit down?" I indicated the wingback chair next to the fireplace for her and I would sit opposite her in the club chair. "Would you like a cup of tea?"

"Oh, yes! That would be lovely!"

"Yes, it is unusually cold this year." I poured a cup for her. "Milk?" I poured another cup for myself and added milk.

"Oh, no. Just plain tea is fine. Anything hot . . ."

I put a cookie on the side of her saucer and handed it to her. "Anything with caffeine, I always say. Keeps me going! So, now, tell me about yourself. Where are you from?"

"I agree. Thank you! Well, I'm from Pennsylvania. Near Philadelphia."

"And what brings you to New York?"

"A fresh start. I work in the banking industry and I just decided that since I'm single—"

"You've never married?" I didn't believe that for a minute.

"Oh, well, yes, but a million years ago. I got married right after high school and had a baby six months later, if you know what I mean."

"Oh!" I thought I might have kept that detail to myself.

"But that didn't last long."

"Young marriages usually don't."

"Yes. Anyway, I went to college, got an MBA, and my mom helped me take care of my daughter, who is now all grown."

I drained my cup and reached over to pick up the teapot. "More?"

"Yes, thank you." She held her cup out and I refilled it.

"And you never married again?"

"No, I didn't. I had a long-term boyfriend. You know, married. I always thought he would leave his wife, but he never did. He broke my heart."

My hands started to shake. The floodgates swung open and panic swarmed my brain. She was exactly the kind of woman who had ruined my family. Right here in my living room! What made them tick, this breed of woman who thought it was perfectly fine to sleep with another woman's husband, steal his affection, and destroy a family? My cup rattled against the saucer, but I managed to place it on the tray. Even though I became completely unglued in the space of less than a minute, I wanted to know how she justified her life.

"And, so tell me, Jean . . ."

I couldn't find the words to ask the questions. I could feel my throat constricting and I could hear my heart pounding in my ears as my blood pressure rose. I knew my face was red and suddenly I began to perspire.

"Are you all right, Mrs. Swanson? Can I get you a glass of water? Call someone?"

"No, I'm fine. Thank you. I'm just getting over a nasty flu—fierce! I'm sorry. Now you were telling me about your *friend*?" I pulled a tissue from my pocket and blotted my face, composing myself.

"It was the same old story. I was young and pretty, he was married and bored with his fat wife. Every time I asked about her he always rolled his eyes and said she was just the most predictable, boring, and unsexy woman in the world."

Had not my own mother called *me* dull?

"Right. So, you just thought, Oh, what the heck? Or what?"

"Are you kidding? I never thought that. God in heaven, I can't believe I'm actually telling you all this!"

"No! Please tell me! I'm always so curious how these things get started, you know? Please, continue . . ."

Bathsheba looked around the living room and continued her sordid tale.

"Well, it's hard to remember, it was so long ago. But he pursued me. I wasn't interested in him *like that,* but he was smart and funny. Even though he was fourteen years older than I was, I got so used to being around him all day, the age difference disappeared. He was just Mark. You know what I mean?"

"Yes, I think I do." Harry came hopping out from the kitchen, whistled, and arched his wings. The Banking Slut nearly jumped out of her jacket. "This is Harry. Harry likes to be a part of things."

Harry continued to stare at her and wagged his red tail feathers. Even Harry knew an easy mark when he saw one.

"Oh! Well, he sure is a good-looking bird. What kind?"

"Thanks. Harry's an African gray. So what happened?"

"The usual thing. Wife found out. I got fired. He said he was sorry and gave me a bunch of cash so I could start over again in another city."

"Charles is a horse's ass!" Harry said.

"Did your bird just say, 'Charles is a horse's ass'?"

"Yes."

"Oh. Who's Charles?"

"Charles was the love of my life until a gal like you came along . . . and well, you know the rest of the story. But I suppose things worked out better for her than they have for you."

"What is *that* supposed to mean?"

I couldn't believe this tramp would dare to take umbrage with my words, but I answered her anyway.

"Just that she and Charles have two children and a nanny and scads of money and that they are seen all over New York together having a wonderful time."

"Jeez. If I were in your shoes, I'd move. Who needs it?"

I imagine she thought she had evened the score.

"Excuse me for just a moment. I'm going to put Harry back in his cage."

I wasn't angry. If anything, I felt a little sad. She had been duped and I wondered if there had been others that Charles had duped. How many women were there like her who had been taken past their childbearing years with no promise of a future?

I remembered then that Judith had once sent me a message. It said she didn't want to take Charles away from his family, she just wanted to share him. What was Charles? A summerhouse in the Hamptons?

I gave Harry a piece of cucumber and went back to the living room. She was standing and had on her coat, which she was buttoning.

"I'm assuming we won't be neighbors?" she said.

"I'm sorry. You seem like a very nice woman but I just couldn't . . ."

"I understand," she said. "I'm sorry, too."

I let her out and from behind my curtains I watched her walk down the street all the way to the corner. She didn't want to live with someone who would always be judging her and I didn't want a reminder of Judith in my home. At least she understood that. She was the kind of woman who would be better off in a high-rise apartment building with the degree of anonymity it offered.

I looked in the other direction and saw Kevin just barreling down the block, carrying a sack that I guessed was his lunch.

"Hi! What's the rush?"

"Thank God you're home! Come inside. You're not going to believe what I have to tell you!"

"What on earth?"

We all but jumped through the door and into my apartment.

"Want to split a chef salad?"

"Sure. I'll get plates."

"Okay. Here's the skinny. You know that nice man you interviewed yesterday?"

"Yeah. I was just going to call him. Why? What?"

"Miriam? He's a registered sex offender."

"Stop! No way! How did you find out so fast?"

"My friend in HR? She dates a detective. He looked him up for her. He even double-checked it. Miriam, we almost had a perv living with us! She ran to me as soon as there was no doubt."

"Merciful mother!" My heart was racing again. This was too much for one day.

"Miriam? He has a *criminal* record!"

"No! He seemed so nice!"

"Nice? Nice? Miriam Swanson! Didn't I tell you he gave me the willies?" Kevin opened my refrigerator and stared inside.

"Yes. You surely did. Thank the good Lord and all His angels and saints that your radar works, Kevin. What do you need, hon?"

"Salad dressing. They forgot to put it in the bag."

"Here," I said, and scooted him aside. "Blue cheese okay?"

"Perfect."

I dumped the chef salad into a bowl, spooned in some salad dressing, and started tossing it all around. Then I ground some pepper over it and gave it a sprinkle of salt. Kevin handed me two plates and I mounded the salad in the center.

"Voilà," I said. "And thanks for saving our lives."

"Voilà, indeed. You're welcome. So call the guy today and tell him no thanks so that he can start forgetting where we live."

"No kidding. Right after lunch."

"Want to know what's even more bizarre?"

"Go on . . ."

"That he was a friend of Mr. O'Hara."

"Oh! I hadn't even thought of that! Well, it just goes to show you."

"That you never know about people, right? Let's sit at the dining-room table. A change of venue. Do you think O'Hara was a deviate?"

"Heavens! Absolutely not! I mean, he subscribed to *National Geographic,* for goodness sake."

"Right. Harmless. Hmmph. *National Geographic.* When I was a young lad—"

"Kevin, you're not going to tell me stories about gaping at photographs of topless Aborigines, are you?"

Dead silence. I giggled.

"Well, he's dead," Kevin said. "It doesn't matter."

"And, I'm sure it's not true. Are you home for the day?"

"No, but you could twist my arm. Don't you have another candidate this afternoon? Oh! I forgot to ask. How was that woman this morning?"

"Unsuitable."

"You're not sharing, Miriam. Come on, honey, let's have it."

I told Kevin the details of Jean's interview and he shook his head. "I'm definitely sticking around for the afternoon. I want to meet this gal from Birmingham. What's her name?"

"Liz. Liz Harper. Works in admissions at Hunter College."

"That can't pay much. Does she come from money?"

"I think not. Turns out she's the daughter or niece of a friend of mine."

"And we care, why?"

"Exactly. I mean, does she think I'm running a day-care center for adult children? I raised my kids, thank you."

"Well, maybe she'll be okay."

"We'll find out at four."

By three forty-five that afternoon I had made the dreaded phone call to the pervert and lied very nicely that my niece was going to be using the apartment. Kevin was upstairs painting and blasting an old recording of *La Bohème*. The doorbell rang. She was early, which I took as a good omen. I flipped on the gas burner to heat the kettle for tea and buzzed her in.

Kevin was bounding down the steps as she was coming in and I was opening the front door to my apartment. We nearly collided head-on in what would surely have been an auspicious beginning to our relationship.

"Oh, golly! Sorry! Hi! I'm Liz Harper."

"Yes, you are!" Kevin said, grinning like a cat. "Didn't mean to scare you half to death."

"My goodness! Won't you come in? I'm Miriam Swanson. I think my tiny vestibule is violating your personal space."

"Oh! No bother at all! Thanks!"

"May I take your coat?"

"Thanks." She pulled off her gloves, stuffed them in her pockets, and handed her coat to me in kind of a wound-up wad. Perhaps she thought I was going to stuff it in a cubby.

"I'll get the tea going," I said.

Kevin was enthralled with her. I could tell by his solicitous remarks.

"Don't you just love living in the city? I knew someone from Birmingham once; they say it's such a beautiful place! Did anyone ever tell you that you look like Cameron Diaz? You're thirty-one? Nooooo! Impossible. I would have guessed you weren't a day over twenty-five. I should be twenty-five and know what I know now . . ."

I heard her say, "And I'm just thinking how wonderful it would be if I *did* know what you know!"

They burst into a fit of laughter and I felt a twinge of annoyance. I was actually a little jealous and it surprised me. In the next breath, I asked myself what was I thinking to be bothered by Kevin's easy rapport with a girl young enough to be my daughter? But only technically. It was ridiculous of me and I got over it.

I hung her coat in the closet, checking the label. It was a classic, single-breasted black merino-wool tuxedo coat made by Searle. Sensible. Investment dressing. Not covered in cat hair. After all, my Harry was not fond of cats. Her hand-crocheted scarf was at least ten feet long, which I imagined she needed because her neck rose from her shoulders like a swan's.

I fixed the tea and carried the tray to the living room, where they were chatting away like magpies.

"Tea, anyone?"

"Oh! What a great idea! Thank you!" Liz said, smiling.

"Why don't I pour, Miriam?" Kevin said. "You sit right there like the regal creature that you are."

Attention! My ego was healed.

"We've just been talking about Liz and her work at Hunter College . . ."

"And I said that I like my other jobs just one whole heckuva lot better."

"And what are your other jobs?

"Bartending and nannying. I like kids."

Bartending?

"And where do you tend bar?"

"Oh, I work for several caterers and we work private parties and benefits . . ."

I wondered if she had ever worked at the museum. I'll admit that I liked her appearance and her taste. She was tall and blond, not with classical good looks, but rather angelic in an angular way. She was dressed in moderately expensive clothes, a sweater set and a wool skirt. And pearls. She wore pearls. How bad could she be?

We chatted on for a while, and after Kevin and I were satisfied that she wasn't dangerous, that she could afford the rent, and that she lived rather quietly, we led her upstairs to see the space.

"Oh, my . . . ! Y'all! This is so freaking beautiful! It looks like something from a magazine! I love these colors! It's so . . . I don't know . . . cool!"

Freaking?

"I'll have it all finished by the weekend," he said. "Except the closets."

"Oh, who cares about some dumb old closets? I can do them myself!"

Kevin was shooting me his best see-I-told-you-so look and I just shook my head.

"Kevin? Why don't you get your eyebrows off the ceiling and let's let Liz have a few moments here alone?"

"For what?"

"You know . . . to see herself in the space?"

"Please. She's seeing just fine. No props needed for this one."

Liz was pacing off the floor in the bedroom, squealing with delight every thirty seconds.

"Y'all! My bedroom furniture will fit perfectly! And my towels match the tile!"

"Wonderful!" Kevin said.

Her exuberance was contagious. I have to say I hadn't felt so optimistic in a long while, but that same exuberance was a little much.

"So what do you think, Kevin?" I whispered to him. "Don't you think she's maybe a little gauche for us?"

"Let her have the place, Miriam. She's not

gauche. She's, I don't know, young and full of life!"

Then Liz appeared at my side and made the impassioned speech that sealed the deal.

"Mrs. Swanson? I know you could have any tenant that you want. Anyone. But this apartment is the absolute maximum dream I could ever have. If you'll just give me a chance I'd like to prove to you that I can be the ideal tenant. Really. Seriously. I mean it, y'all. I just . . . I mean, I don't know what else to say . . ."

Oh, pass the Kleenex, I thought. From the moment I saw Kevin's delight I knew that I was going to let her move in.

Chapter Four

Mizz Liz

Dear Mrs. Waddlesnotte,
Many thanks for recommending Liz Harper as a possible tenant. I have met with her and found her to be a perfectly lovely young woman who will no doubt contribute much joy to my town house. Mr. Dolan and I look forward to her arrival with enthusiasm and we only have your excellent judgment to thank. What would the world be if we did not help each other? All best wishes to you!
Cordially,
Miriam Elizabeth Swanson

The February misery of blasting cold wind was preceded by the snowiest, coldest, iciest January on record in many years. It didn't seem to matter how many logs I burned, the house was drafty and chilled. But I had a new tenant coming and that was a great relief. Finally, finally, February and Liz Harper arrived.

It was around ten o'clock in the morning when Liz and all her worldly possessions pulled up in front of the house. I was surprised at how compact the rental truck was. She wasn't even using a moving company. Were friends helping her? And who were her friends? Would she entertain a lot? Good heavens! I certainly hoped not.

I went out to the front steps to greet her.

"Good morning! Situation in hand?" Of course I had no intention of doing anything more than saying hello.

"Hi, Mrs. Swanson! Yeah. I just need the keys. Cold, huh?"

"Cold is a fact of life in the big city, hon. No matter the season." I reached in my pocket and handed the keys to her. "Make an extra set. You know, in case your purse gets snatched. I mean, that kind of thing usually never happens in this neighborhood, but it does happen."

Liz smiled and said, "I'll do that, but don't worry. I always keep my keys in my pocket. My purse has my driver's license in it and that would lead them to a home address in Birmingham. Can you imagine? Too far for thieves to go to torment my mother!"

Kevin was coming down the steps and threw in, "Or tramps and gypsies!" He did a five-second Cher impersonation and we rolled our eyes and moaned.

"Going to work?" I asked him.

"Nope, just around the corner for the newspaper. Miriam's a worrywart. You ladies need anything?"

"Advice on how to lay out my furniture?" Liz said.

"Soon as I return, sunshine!"

"If you need me, let me know," I said and closed my door. Sunshine, indeed. Sure, go help her lay out her furniture.

Harry was in the kitchen imitating the doorbell. Somehow Harry had escaped meeting Liz, but I would make a point of introducing them over the next few days. After all, Liz had to sort through boxes of dishes and everything to organize her new home. I didn't want to seem meddlesome.

I made myself a cup of hot tea and tried to imagine how many trucks it would take to move all of my possessions. For years I had collected china, crystal, a tonnage of sterling silver, and all sorts of things. Then, with the decline of Mother's good sense, I came into a considerable amount of family memorabilia. I was the keeper of all the old photographs, my father's christening gown, my grandmother's tea service, and so on. My apartment looked like a retail store. It was jammed to the rafters with goodies and curiosities.

I had the family's portraits and a few beautiful landscapes of the Lowcountry. Many of my museum friends collected contemporary art. I wouldn't hang angst art in my basement. It's all that modern business that looks like the artist was furious or miserable or both when he slapped his paint on a canvas. No. I liked tradition. I walked on rugs that had been in our family since the Revolution, and that would be the BIG Revolution, not the industrial, the women's, or the sexual. My embroidered linens were the handiwork relics of aunts and cousins from a time when women took pride in the creation of such things. And my sets of silver flatware were more weighted and intricate than anything available on the market today. I treasured all these things not just for what they were but for what they represented—gracious living. History. And yes, they were all testimony to the ashes of my privileged background.

Like everyone, I was subject to mood changes, and on another day I might tell myself that I had too much junk and needed a yard sale in the worst way. That was because I hated to polish silver, to starch linens, and to dust everything that needed dusting. Maybe I would give some things to my sons. Someday. When they remembered how to be nice to their mother.

I peeked out of the window and watched Liz's movers struggle under the weight of her king-size mattress. It was curious that a single girl in the city would want such a large bed when every square inch of living space came at such a premium. Maybe she liked to toss and turn. It was a little sad that everything that Liz owned was in one orange and white U-Haul. If I ever moved I'd need a convoy of eighteen-wheelers. I laughed at the thought of them roaring down a highway to somewhere.

But, as you know, I had no intention of ever moving. Where? Florida? Never. Where then? Nowhere. I was leaving horizontally in a permanent, breathless recline.

People came and went, bringing in boxes and pieces of furniture. The racket overhead was almost intolerable. Kevin must have been up there with her by then.

I said, "Harry? Do you hear all that noise? Shhh! Right? Can you say 'shhh'?"

Angel that he was, Harry said, "Shhh!" And then gave a wolf whistle. Maybe he *had* already sneaked a peak at Miss Liz.

"Let's call Miss Josie, shall we?"

Harry gave me a look and I dialed Mother's number. She had changed her recording on her answering machine.

We mean this in the nicest possible way. If you are selling something, there is no point in leaving a message because your call will not be returned. We are not kidding. Have a nice day and please wait for the tone. Thank you.

Well, it was considerably better than the other one, but it was still somehow impolite.

"Mother? Hi, it's Miriam. Just wanted to chat. Call me when you have a moment, okay?"

I hung up and looked at the phone, feeling lonely for her company. A visit to Sullivans Island was long overdue. The Land of Mango Sunsets. I craved it.

How mysterious and dreamy the Lowcountry was in the winter! For as hot and sultry as it was in the summer, the wet rolling fogs of January and February covered the islands in thick mist so dense you could imagine ghosts slipping in and out of it, whispering their histories in your ear.

When I was a young girl, we would have family gatherings at our Sullivans Island beach home all summer long, but it was the winter ones I loved most. The house was uninsulated and sometimes it was so cold indoors you could see your breath. I couldn't recall ever being bothered by the cold then, but I remembered the older people complaining and someone would always say, well then, why don't you put on a sweater? In those days you didn't demand the perfect temperature, you ate leftovers—another incarnation of yesterday's dinner and indication that the world was a perfectly wonderful place. After an early supper of maybe black-eyed peas over rice and a thick slice of baked ham, fried with canned pineapple, my grandmother would take the binoculars and go out on the back porch that faced the marsh. She would sit in her favorite ancient wicker rocking chair to watch the birds and the sunset. In retrospect, I imagine what she had been truly seeking was a little well-earned peace and quiet. She could have had it, that is, until I showed up. I would crawl all over her and beg for a story.

"Let's settle down, sweetheart," she would say.

Once I stopped wiggling, my grandmother would tuck me in against her side with an old afghan to block the chilly air of the evening. I would snuggle and relive the same tales her mother had told her long ago. Her voice was so soothing and musical, and most of all, the stories she told were fantastic.

I would close my eyes and be transported to the Isle of Palms as it was hundreds of years ago. Native American women from the Seewee tribe were cooking venison over an open fire or whole fish on bamboo skewers. I could almost hear their babies gurgling and laughing, hanging from tree limbs, tightly and lovingly laced in their deerskin cradle boards. The women would suspend them from a branch while they performed whatever chore was at hand—gathering berries or firewood.

My grandmother would get to the part of the story where she talked about the ingenious opening in the bottom of the cradle boards that allowed the baby's natural business to drop to the ground without the baby being soiled. I would dissolve in a fit of snickers and she would narrow her eyes at me in mock horror that made me giggle even more. Like most children of my day, I thought talking about babies swinging from trees and watering the ground was very naughty business.

In later years, my mother had told the same stories and others to my sons—stories of black bears lumbering through the shallow waters looking for fish, of the shining eyes of wild jaguars that would eat you alive, and of drunken pirates, their crazed gunfights and buried treasure. Those tales gave the boys nightmares. But then she would tell of the adventures of soldiers and their bravery and of Edgar Allan Poe, who wrote "The Gold Bug" when he was stationed at Fort Moultrie. Those yarns gave the boys imaginary games to play for hours on end.

In the summers, my sons would run shirtless and free all over the island, climbing the forts and picking wild blackberries. They would arrive home filthy, knees skinned, faces freckled and sunburned. I would swear to this day that the light of their exuberant smiles actually brightened all the rooms. Of course, I would march them straight to a good scrub. After baths, I would make thick tomato sandwiches slathered with my mother's homemade mayonnaise because it was just too hot to eat anything else. They would swing together in the same old Pawleys Island hammock that had hung on our porch forever until the lightning bugs came out and then they would run around to catch them.

Those were magical days when we were all together, our eyes so filled with one another. Every wonder of nature was right before us and history was never more alive. And we were happy. I missed the days when my sons were little boys and they looked up to me. And I longed to take my grandchildren to Sullivans Island to tell them the stories, but Dan and Nan had no interest or time to fly across country for something so frivolous. Or they claimed to be impossibly busy and booked up.

But that wasn't the truth. We all knew it.

Oh, I had been a very foolish woman to tell my boys they had to choose between their father and me. They had never really declared a choice but had drifted away from both of us, never understanding why I had drawn a line in the sand in the first place. I thought they should come to my defense and try to talk some sense into their father's head. Could they have saved my marriage? Now I think not, but at that time I resented that they would not try. I was so deeply and pathetically desperate then to hold everything in place, for our lives to return to their orbit, and for Judith to disappear. Along with the two illegitimate children of hers that my husband had fathered.

I never should have let the duplicity and the immoral philandering of any man, even their father, come between us. But it had. I couldn't stop it. I harangued them mercilessly to tell their father how wrong he was, that I was a wonderful spouse and how could he do this to us? Once the cat and the kitties of Charles's other family were out of the bag, there was no stopping the bad news. Charles simply moved out and I was left alone with my town house and very little cash.

You know how you always hope that when life gives you a great challenge you'll be noble and wise and do the right thing? That you'll conduct yourself in ways that won't embarrass anyone? That you won't be an emotional albatross? Well, I was flat-out robbed of the opportunities to be noble or to be a raving lunatic.

Charlie, my oldest, was already in medical school, studying twenty-seven hours a day, and Dan was in California married to Nan. The only good thing about my behavior then was that at least I had maintained enough dignity to wallow in the privacy of my bedroom. But I cried enough tears to refill Lake Superior, which is what I thought I was.

Charlie had helped the most. He was the one who found the contractor to convert the town house into apartments. I turned my space into a small three-bedroom apartment in case the boys ever came back for a visit. It was a useless conciliatory act but my way of demonstrating contrition. Soon after, Charlie moved himself to Harlem and immersed himself in his studies, which he had to do if he was going to be a pediatric surgeon someday. Did I say that he thought I disapproved of his live-in girlfriend? Well, it wasn't because she was Jamaican. Really. It wasn't. It was because she had the worst personality I had ever encountered. Yes, she was studying to be a pediatrician, so obviously she wasn't a dummy. It was just that every time we had lunch or dinner I felt like I was going to fall asleep in my plate. I wasn't the only boring woman on the earth, you know. And okay. To be perfectly honest? I did think there were too many cultural differences for me to ever be comfortable with her. I knew I owed Charlie a phone call. Admittedly, I was avoiding him because the last time we spoke it had not gone well.

I had invited him to dinner on the spur of the moment and he said, "Is this invitation for me alone?"

That was all he had to say and I knew we were heading down a dark path.

"Well, Charlie, sometimes I just like to get caught up with my son and discuss family matters."

"Matters not intended for outsiders, right?"

"Yes. Is that so terrible?"

"Mom? Priscilla and I have been living together for two years. Get used to it. She's family."

"These days playing house seems to be acceptable to the world, according to your father, at least."

"Playing house? Hmmph."

"Oh?" That's nice. Thanks for the compliment.

"Anyway, Priscilla and I have plans for dinner tonight. Maybe some other time."

"Well, dear? If you'd rather eat jerk chicken, that doesn't make you a jerk."

It did not result in a chuckle and a promise of another date. He hung up on me.

There you have the picture of my failure with Charlie and as a stand-up comedian, his general attitude of frosty nonchalance, and a sketch of the geographic location of my other son, about whom there just isn't much to say. It seemed like the world always worked against our relationships and any return to affection.

I knew it was well within my skills to exert some effort toward breaking down the walls between the boys and me. But I was too proud and so very hurt. When I thought about calling them, I would preconclude that it was too late. The damage was done.

When thoughts of my loneliness skidded to the forefront of my disappointment, that was when I missed my mother the most. I didn't want her to tell me where I had gone wrong, though. No. I wanted her to tell me that I had been right. But she would never say I was. I would go to the end of my days trying to please my mother and never somehow hit the mark. The root of the problem was my own stubbornness. I knew it and I hated myself for it. She told me I had unrealistic expectations of everyone. I disagreed. It seemed to me that I never asked for more than I gave.

I dialed her number again. This time she answered.

"Mother?"

"Hello, Miriam. I was just going to call you back. I have been one very busy bee today. Law! It is so gorgeous here! Not a cloud in the sky!"

"Well, that's wonderful! It's still dreary as the tomb here."

"I know. I saw your weather report on some morning show while I was having my morning tea. You know, you should really come—"

"And that's one reason I'm calling, actually. I want to try and get out of here for a few days."

"Come tomorrow!"

"Oh, sure! I just wanted to know if you're going to be around for the next few weeks."

"Unless I drop dead, I'll be right here."

My mother wasn't even close to dropping dead. With all the vitamins she took and all the organic food she ate? She was guaranteed to rival any celebrity from the Old Testament.

"Okay, I'll start looking for a good airfare. So, what's keeping you so busy?"

"Saving the planet."

"Somebody's got to."

"Well, I got involved in a project to make disposable, biodegradable plates and so forth from potato starch. You just throw them in the compost heap and in six months they're fertilizer."

"Well. How about that?"

"Don't be Miss Blasé Big City with me, Miriam Elizabeth Swanson."

"Sorry. I still have problems envisioning you eating from paper plates—"

"Potato starch . . ."

"Whatever. Anyway, here's news. I have a new tenant. A gal from Birmingham. Liz Harper. Very nice."

"Lawsamercy, Miriam! What are you doing up there in Yankee land—running an ashram for wayward southerners? You've got that Kevin fellow from Atlanta and now . . ."

I smiled at Miss Josie's joke and in the next

breath realized that my mother was in excellent humor nearly all the time. In fact, I couldn't recall the last time she had been in a foul mood. When I was a child she spent every bit of energy she had to spare giving me lessons in polite behavior and in the art of appearing happy.

"How do you do it, Miss Josie?"

"What's that, darlin'?"

"Stay so upbeat."

"Me?" She paused for a moment. "Is this a serious question?"

"Dead serious. Only because I've been on such a downer lately . . ."

"Is this about Charles?"

"No." Yes.

"Judith?"

"No." Yes.

"The boys?"

"Not really. I'm just a little melancholy, you know? I think all this dismal weather is at the bottom of it and I just miss . . . Oh, I don't know what I miss."

"Hmmph. Child? You've got yourself a case of SAD."

"You're telling me?"

"No, sweetheart—I mean, seasonal affective disorder."

"Oh. That. Probably so."

"Well, let's start by changing all the light-bulbs in your house to full-spectrum light-bulbs. They'll suppress your brain's secretion of melatonin."

"Wait. I have to get something to write with." I rummaged through the kitchen drawer and found a ballpoint pen that actually worked after tossing aside four that refused to coop-erate. "Hang on. Okay. Gosh, I have to clean out this drawer. Okay, full what?"

"Spectrum. You need me to come orga-nize you. And get yourself outdoors for a walk every day. There was a study that showed an hour's walk during the winter in sunlight was as effective as two and a half hours un-der bright artificial lights."

"An hour? Forget it! Besides, I'd break my neck on all the ice!"

"Then call Delta or Continental, come see your mother, and I'll take you for a walk on the Sullivans Island beach every day! And, you're probably not feeding yourself correctly either . . ."

"But I am wearing a sweater."

Silence from the south.

"That was a joke, Mother."

"Of course it was. I knew that. Old as the hills, but a joke nonetheless."

I sighed hard. I wasn't that humorless, was I? "I'll book a flight, buy the lightbulbs, and I'll call you back."

"Good. The sooner the better. I'll get you all straightened out—"

"Bye, Mother. Thanks, okay?"

We hung up and I thought it pleased her to think that I needed her. The fact of the matter was that I did need her. I hadn't felt so unloved and misunderstood in quite a while. What was the matter with me?

I watched a documentary on dolphins that bored me into a stupor. I changed the sheets on my bed, sponge-wiped the bathroom counters, and changed the towels. The sounds of my washer and dryer made me feel slightly better. Finally, it was cocktail time, and before I could pour a measure of the Famous Grouse into a tumbler, my doorbell rang. I opened the door and there stood Kevin with a telltale sack of Chinese take-out food.

"Want to indulge in a little Who Flung Dung?"

"Got hot-and-sour?"

"You know it, Petal Puss."

"Come right in." I stood aside, and Kevin all but ran past me to the kitchen.

"I'm freezing," he said. "It must be twenty thousand degrees below zero out there. Brrrr!" He dropped the bag on the kitchen table and took off his gloves, hat, neck scarf, and coat. Next, he turned on the gas of one of my cooktop burners and warmed his hands, rubbing them together. "I couldn't ask them to deliver? I had to go fetch it myself?"

"Starving?" I unpacked the food and opened the foil container of egg rolls. "Here." I handed him one on a paper napkin. "Regain your strength."

"You know me. I spent all afternoon upstairs with Daisy Mae and she didn't even throw me a cracker! I wait until my blood sugar drops to nothing because I'm too OCD to quit styling, so I wind up tearing down Third Avenue like a convulsing maniac . . ."

I put two plates and bowls on the table with flatware. "Oh! She probably doesn't have a thing to eat either. Should we invite . . ."

"Ha! Our Liz has a date! Don't worry about this one, honey. She's an operator. She went out already."

I opened a bottle of red wine and poured out two glasses, offering one to Kevin.

"What's her stuff like?"

"You wouldn't live with that junk for five minutes."

"Really? Well, she's young." We clinked to yet another new conspiracy and sat down to serve ourselves a hasty meal. "Tell me everything."

"Strictly gross dregs of yard sales and what germy trash people leave on the curb."

"Please! Are you kidding?"

"Nope. God, this lo mein is to die—"

"Oh! You got beef with broccoli! I adore it, you know . . ."

"Petal, that's why I got it!"

"And to think I was going to have a grilled cheese sandwich with a scotch."

We dove into dinner and the wine and spent the next hour or so discussing the merits and taste level of Liz Harper's furnishings from her coffee mugs to her mangy stuffed animals.

"There's not a stuffed dog, cat, monkey, or bear left on Coney Island," Kevin said. "Or at Six Flags."

"You're terrible," I said with a giggle, pouring out the last of the wine.

"Wait till you see! You'll see!"

"Should I open another bottle? I have some kind of Sterling Pinot Noir."

"No. Thanks. I'll just have a vodka, if you have any. I have to work tomorrow—we're changing windows on the Fifth Avenue side."

If Kevin thought a vodka was easier on his head than a glass of wine, I wasn't about to argue. I poured him a good shot over some ice cubes and the overhead noises started.

Thump! Thump! Thump!

"What in the world?" Kevin said, and looked up at the ceiling.

"It sounds like someone is . . . like they're, you know . . ."

Thump! Thump! Thump!

"When's the last time anyone had sex in this house?" Kevin said drily.

Thump! Thump! Thump!

"Well, I can't speak for you . . ." The banging, pardon the expression, was getting louder and picking up speed.

"Puh! Lease!"

Ka-thump! Ka-thump! Ka-thump!

My neck and face got hot and even Kevin's face was red and flushed.

Ohmagod! Ohmagod! Ohmagod! Came the voices from upstairs.

"I'm opening a window," I said, pulling up the one over the sink. "It's hot as fury in here!"

"You said it, Petal!" Kevin opened the back door to the garden and stepped out for a moment, no doubt for a reprieve from the sheer embarrassment of the occasion.

Kathumpkathumpkathumpkathump!

I opened the front door and stepped out into my foyer for a moment. The thumping continued in earnest. I thought, God in heaven! I wish they'd wind it up for the sake of the rest of us! But they did not. The Love Boat continued to rock and roll. Finally, it became quiet. When my own pulse returned to normal, I went back inside and closed my door.

Kevin was in the kitchen reading his fortune cookie as though nothing had happened at all. He had generously freshened his vodka and I poured a large one for myself. Scotch? Vodka? Who cared?

"It says, *Much excitement just landed in your life.* Hmmph, Confucius doesn't know, pardon me, crap. If I smoked, I'd offer you a cigarette."

"I'd smoke it, too." We touched the edges

of our glasses for the second time that evening and took a long sip. "Good grief, Kevin. What are we going to do?"

"Get her a rug to muffle the music?" Then he looked around. We realized at the same moment that Harry was missing. "Harry!"

"Where's my baby? *Harry? Harry?*" No response. I began to panic.

"He wouldn't go out in the courtyard, would he?"

"Oh, Lord, Kevin! I don't know! *Harry?* You check there and I'll check the rest of the house."

A thorough search revealed nothing. My pulse raced again. On the verge of tears, I opened the front door of the apartment remembering that I had opened it earlier, only to see Harry on the steps, hopping down from the second floor. Following him was a familiar face.

It was Agnes Willis's husband. Liz was carrying on with Agnes Willis's husband, Truman.

I scooped up Harry and bolted through my door, closing it as quickly and discreetly as I could. I didn't think Truman had seen me. My most fervent hope was that he had not. Kevin

appeared in the living room. His face was relieved to see me holding Harry.

"You found him! Where was the bad boy?
Harry? You had us scared to death!"

"Yes." My heart was pounding like a jack-
hammer.

"What's the matter, Miriam?"

"Oh, Kevin. You *don't* want to know. I've
got to get out of here."

"Miriam! What in the world? Come sit!
You're shaking all over!"

"What if I told you that Liz was involved in
an illicit affair with the husband of a friend of
mine?"

Kevin was slack-jawed and bug-eyed.

"I'm putting the famous gray on his swing
and pouring the Famous Grouse for us. This
occasion calls for strong spirits."

Kevin took Harry from me and I continued
to shake. My hands got cold and then my
neck got hot and I began to perspire. I had
leased my apartment to a lying tramp. I had
to think this through. I had carefully avoided
a perv because of Kevin's instincts and an
admitted *other woman* only because she
had come clean with me. But, what about
Liz?

Kevin put the tumbler in my shaking hands and I took a drink, feeling its warmth all the way down my throat.

"Well? Who is the hooligan?" Kevin said.

"Kevin. You know I cannot reveal his name. My indiscretion added to his would be too much for me to bear. In any case, *that's* not the real problem."

"You'll tell me when you're ready, Petal. Just calm down and tell me what you're thinking."

I took another long sip. Kevin dropped some ice cubes in my glass and covered them with another measure of scotch.

"Infidelity makes me crazy, Kevin. I can't live with it! I simply can't! I'm thinking that this is a complete disaster and that I don't want to be a party to this girl bringing home married men and carrying on with them in my house. It would be like a rerun of Charles and Judith night after night! I couldn't stand it!"

"I understand why you're upset. So am I. I was so sure about her, too," Kevin said. "She didn't seem like she would resort to that kind of behavior. She's pretty enough to find single men."

"Kevin? I have to think about this, but right now, I want her out of here. I just want her out. Out of my house!"

Kevin squatted down next to me and took my free hand in his.

"Listen to me, Miriam. Let's not jump the gun. Maybe she didn't even know he was married. Maybe she did a onetime stupid thing, I mean, we all make mistakes." Then, in almost a whisper, he said, "And, Petal? Face it. You need the rent."

It was true. I did. My bottom lip quivered, my eyes filled with tears, and I drained my glass. "Let me ask you something, Kevin? Is the whole world filled with this sort of fooling around? Isn't anyone faithful?"

"You know the answer to that. Of course there are plenty of faithful couples. I think what we have here is Daisy Mae from the backwoods of Alabama who did a foolish thing and probably doesn't even know it."

"Maybe."

"I think you should try to put it out of your mind for a while, pretend it never happened. Denial can be useful sometimes. And let's see where things go. You can't throw her out in the snow like 'The Little Match Girl.'"

"You're right, of course. Oh, Kevin! This is too much. I think I need to get out of here, go to Sullivans Island. Maybe the salt air will clear my head."

"I think that's an excellent idea."

Chapter Five

PHONIES

Dear Mrs. Willis,
My, how time flies! It seems like only yesterday that I had the occasion to see you at the museum when we discussed the beautiful floral display in the lobby. I have a special love of flowers, and if I had ever worked in a professional capacity it certainly would have been in the paradise of delphinium and lilacs! In any case, because we obviously share an appreciation of all things beautiful, it is my pleasure to invite you to Bill Blass's fall trunk show, which will be

held on the second Tuesday of March at noon. The details are on the enclosed invitation. All the ladies love Mr. Blass, don't they? I certainly do! Please let me know if you are able to join me. If you cannot, I would greatly appreciate having the enclosed ticket returned. Many thanks.

Cordially,
Miriam Elizabeth Swanson

I was organizing my clothes for my South Carolina trip, and despite what I knew about her husband, Truman, I wrote a note to Agnes Willis inviting her to see the Blass collection. Subtlety had not worked on the prissy old bitty, so I sent the ticket straight to her in a flowery message. Flowery message? Ah me, sometimes I just crack myself up even if others fail to value my humor. Too bad I wouldn't be able to afford a button of Blass.

Speaking of fashion, Kevin was helping me with my wardrobe, which was futility personified, as there was no *wardrobe* required on Sullivans Island. It was casual in the extreme, unless we ventured across the causeway and downtown to the Holy City. But, truth be told, once night set in, I was never anxious to leave the island. Who knew what magic might come to us once the stars came out? Mother and I might find ourselves twinkling and young in the smitten eyes of an old salt and a retired jillionaire (guess who gets which one?) who would spout poetry and feed us a seafood stew made from their catch of that very day. Everything was possible after sunset when the mists rolled in.

"Why are you packing these dreadful things?" Kevin held my old sneakers aloft in their Ziploc bags as though they were petite dead skunks.

"Oyster roast. Those are my oyster-roast shoes."

"Dear Petal . . . you'll never snag a man in these nasties."

"I'm not looking to snag a man. Nor am I looking to ruin a good pair of shoes with oyster liquor! You don't understand . . ."

"Enlighten me."

He dropped the bags on the carpet and crossed his arms, waiting. I started to giggle knowing that my description of an authentic oyster roast would strike Kevin as vile.

"Well, in the old days when I was Miriam the Younger, you would have a gathering of people in their worst clothes, standing around a smoldering, smoky pit, partially covered with a piece of sheet metal. On top of the metal would be a pile of oysters wrapped in soaking-wet burlap sacks. When the oysters begin to steam open they would be scooped onto your table with a shovel. The table is usually a piece of plywood or an old door on two sawhorses with a garbage can on the side."

"Stop. This sounds perfectly disgusting."

"It gets worse. Then, wearing a workman's glove, you pry them open with an oyster knife."

"Wait! I'm getting a vision! Martha Stewart is arriving in a police helicopter to stop the madness!"

"She probably should. Anyway, you use the same muddy knife to scoop the slimy devils out and into your mouth. The oyster liquor drenches your shoes, little by little."

"Hence the Ziplocs."

"Correct. Then you chase it with a soda cracker and take a swig of beer or something."

"Miriam, darling, I just cannot see you doing this. Sorry."

"Well, nowadays they bring in someone who steams them and delivers them to your table. It's become pretty antiseptic, I'm afraid.

As bohemian as the old days sound, I still hate all this gentrification."

"I agree. It's suspect. Are you sure you want to take these pants?"

He referred to my flannel-lined jeans that had seen better days.

"Yeah, it gets damp at night. I like to walk the beach. Anyway, I've been going to oyster roasts all my life. If they didn't taste so fabulous, I wouldn't go."

"Still sounds horrible."

"Right? But it's not. Listen, some bubbas use the hood of their pickup truck as the grill! They put it back on the truck the next day."

"Shut! Up! Do you actually *know* people who do that?"

"Of course not. And if I did, do you think I would tell you?"

"Well, it's just going to be Harry and me while you're gone. Right, buddy?"

Harry had waddled into the bedroom.

"And that harlot on the second floor. Do you know what Liz did yesterday?"

At the mention of her name, Harry whistled and we shushed him.

"Please! There's no telling!"

"She took my catalogs from Victoria's Secret, the Walker's Warehouse, and a number of other places."

"That's a little strange." Kevin picked up a red wool turtleneck sweater and stuffed it inside a weathered denim barn coat that was lined in red plaid. "What do you think?"

"Let's pack it. So, I marched myself upstairs, and what do you think she answered the door wearing?"

"Her altogether?"

"Just about . . . I said, 'Listen, Liz? Do you know that tampering with the mail is a federal offense? And, why don't I wait right here while you go put on some pants?'"

Kevin laughed. "So what did our little pole dancer say?"

"She did not know it was a federal offense and she did not put on her pants."

"Well, JMJ, with a little crucifix over the M!"

"You can say that again. But here's the bad part. She said, 'But I didn't think you would be interested in lingerie or exercise clothes.' She was right, of course, and I thought, Well, that's another cause of my trouble, isn't it? It made me plenty mad with her and with myself."

"Well, honey, you and I have talked about

this. Realizing these things is good. It's healthy. The question is: What-do-you-plan-to-do-about-it?"

"Oh, Lordy. Well, I think I'm going to lose a little weight. Or attempt to anyway. I have actually been thinking about belly dancing or kickboxing and I can't decide. Either one might put me in the hospital."

Kevin sat down on my bed, grinning and shaking his head. "Petal? Petal? Why don't we start with something kinder and gentler, like walking?"

"It's terrible outside. Ice everywhere? I could break my leg! Or something else!"

"Like a nail! I'm going to buy you a tread-mill . . ."

"Be serious. I don't have room in here for another toothpick."

"They make one that folds down and slides under your bed."

"I despise treadmills!"

"Well, Miriam? Precious? Mother used to always say, pride knoweth no pain."

"Oh, hell's bells." I let a tiny expletive slip. "Buy the treadmill and I'll pay you back."

A few days later I was at thirty thousand feet, en route to Sullivans Island. Although I was landing in Charleston, I never thought of it that way. The island was my destination, as was my mother's side.

All it took was a trip to the island to remind me that my boys were not close to me, but I still had blessings. Kevin was so dear and generous to offer to take care of Harry. And to help me pack. And to buy me an instrument of torture that, when used properly—the exercise guru Tony Little himself guaranteed it—would tighten up my, excuse me, buns and lower my cholesterol at the same time. Well, we would see about that part. And I had not heard from Agnes Willis nor had I breathed a word to anyone about her husband, Truman, banging the brains out of Liz Harper, pardon me again, Resident Ho. He had been there the night before I left—at least I assumed it was him as the bouncing and thumping had a familiar ring. I had turned up a CD of Pavarotti singing *Tosca,* filled the tub with bubbles and my ears with cotton. It was only partially successful.

The plane began its descent. We circled to land as though the pilot couldn't spot the airport's landing strip. Why they always did that I could not conceive, but I can tell you this—the circling reminded me to have my anxiety attack. I white-knuckled the ends of the arm-

rests, squeezed my eyes closed, and begged
God to let me live. Once we landed and the
door opened, I regained normal breathing and
my composure. I picked up my bag on the Jetway and went in search of a taxi.

And though it was the dead of winter, it
was probably fifty degrees outside and the
sky was as blue and clear as it could be. It
felt like a July heat wave compared to the
gray-skied and bitter New York I had left behind.

The polite but thankfully not chatty driver
of the clanking taxi van played gospel music
and sang along in low tones, tapping the
steering wheel in time with the rim of his wedding band. I relaxed a little more. We drove
along Route 526 East, which was especially
beautiful. Here and there were lovely patches
of marsh and short docks rooted in glistening
water. Natural creeks cut the marsh grass in
serpentines from the Wando and Cooper rivers. Pelicans swooped down on unsuspect-
ing brim and drum, gobbling them up for
snacks. Birds of prey circled, their keen eyes
zeroing in on rabbits and squirrels, which all
went about their innocent daily business in
the thicket unaware that death was on the
way.

The small patches of remaining forest surrounded yet another housing development that seemed to have popped up overnight like Jack's beanstalk. Rows upon rows of nearly identical slapdash houses were ugly and cold-looking. There were no trees above six feet to be seen and the minimal shrubs of boxwood and azalea were uniform. There was no shade where children could play, no charm in the development's layout, and no neighbors who would have known one another for more than a year. Some developer was getting filthy rich, poor people were getting cardboard houses with mortgages they couldn't afford, and the Lowcountry was being raped between the eyes. This was one topic on which Mother and I always agreed. Developers had all the conscience of a hungry predator.

As we rounded the corner at the Piggly Wiggly and Royall Hardware, I began to relax. I had not visited Sullivans Island in almost a year, and filled with anticipation, I welcomed the fact that I could leave my worries behind for a few days.

When the cab stopped in the driveway on Raven Drive, I could hardly believe my eyes. What had Mother done? The whole front yard that had been home to flower beds was now fenced in behind a wall of bamboo. Did I hear chickens? Was that a nanny goat?

I paid the driver, dropped my suitcase at the base of the steps, and went to have a look. There was my mother, Josephine, with a hoe in her hand, hacking away at the earth. I gasped so hard you could have knocked me over with the flick of a finger. Hearing the car pull away, she turned and spotted me.

"Well, hello, hello! It's my big-city girl! Welcome back to the Island!"

As you know, in our family's opinion, all others held no merit.

"Mother!"

We hugged and then hugged again.

"Come, come. I have lunch waiting for us!"

"Mother? What in the world are you doing? The yard? Are you becoming a farmer?"

Mother threw back her head and laughed with a sound so young I could hardly believe she was twenty-something years older than I was. She grabbed my roll-on bag as though it was empty, while I, ever the pitiful weakling, struggled under the weight of my duffel bag, hoisting the straps to my shoulder.

"Well," she said, "it's kind of an experiment to see . . ."

"What?" We climbed the steps to the porch. "If the gentrification police can lock you up in the pokey for running an unauthorized e-i-e-i-o? Doesn't the town have ordinances prohibiting, um, *goats*?"

Mother laughed again. "No, they actually don't. And she's pretty special. Cecelia is a Nigerian dwarf."

"Oh. I see."

"Let's get you inside and I'll tell you all about it over lunch."

"Okay. Good. I'm famished. The porch looks good."

"Thanks. I re-covered the cushions on all the chairs." She ascended the steps with no visible effort, sailed through the house and up to the second floor, never pausing for a breath, and dropped my bag at the foot of my old iron bed. "I'll see you downstairs."

I listened to my mother's feet padding down the long hall to the steps. She had her own clipped and energetic rhythm. There was something so reassuring about the sound that I almost choked up with tears. Her fading footsteps used to be calming and now their sound was an emotional trigger? What was the matter with me? Maybe it was the same for everyone, I told myself. You came home, middle-aged, a marital discard, and therefore a social liability, and your widowed mother—albeit a hippie who would absolutely mortify you in most circles—is waiting for you. Okra soup is simmering for your lunch and the fragrance makes your heart swell. In that moment, you find yourself wanting to re-live your childhood, to be young, innocent, and free of guilt.

In your old bedroom is the quilt, the same one your grandmother and her friends made just for you when you were a little girl . . . all that predictability in coming home, that there was a time when you could depend on the fact that you were wanted, missed, wel-comed, and really loved by someone who knew you and loved you despite your flaws.

Was I still? Yes. I was.

I sat on the bed for a moment and ran my fingers over the little squares of floral, striped, and checked cotton. If I was possessed by things like fountain pens and thank-you notes, how obsessed were my presumably female ancestors and their friends who executed these miniature stitches, each of them placed at perfect intervals? How many dresses, blouses, and kitchen curtains had they saved, cut in small squares and triangles, hemmed, and laid out in a star pattern to create this quietly magnificent work of art? How many people had worked on it? Two? Six? Ten? Were they all friends? Were quilts sprung from a sense of friendship or boredom or necessity?

These days women got together to drink wine and invest money—not that I had a problem with that. Women should absolutely have their own money and wine is a good thing. But what did they really achieve? There *was* something sacred about a quilt that a bulging bank account and getting looped could not rival.

I hung my few clothes in the closet, checked my face in the bathroom mirror, and then stopped dead. Maybe it was the bright blue light of the Carolina midday, but I noticed for the first time that the corners of my mouth seemed to be frozen in a permanent frown. Something had to be done about that.

Over soup and a crusty loaf of bread that she swore she had baked herself, I listened to my mother rattle on about the news on Sullivans Island. There was a gentleman who was teaching her to fish with a net. She pointed through the glass sliding door to a corner of the porch.

"See that?"

"No."

"Look again. It's hanging from the nail."

"What in the world?"

"I'm crocheting my own net! Even got the little sinker weights worked in it. Isn't that something?"

"Mother? Why are you doing this? I mean, it's not like you can't afford to go to Simmons Seafood and buy whatever you want . . ."

She laughed again and then turned to fix her eyes on me. "Miriam? That's not the point! You may think this is crazy talk but I'll tell you the whole story, if you'd like to hear it."

"Okay. By the way, this soup is delicious."

"Thank you. Listen; remember that 9/11 fiasco?"

"Who doesn't? It happened just down the street from me."

"Right. More soup?"

"Sure. Just half a bowl."

She got up to serve us another portion. "Well, it had an impact on me. A powerful one. I just got to thinking that if all the big cities of the world got blasted to smithereens, the odds are they wouldn't be blowing up this place. Or at least it would take a while to discover it. And, if radiation didn't kill me, I wanted to figure out how to live without the Piggly Wiggly. I decided that I would surely live longer if I kept a garden and ate organic vegetables and chickens fed without grain-laced pesticides and—" She stopped and looked at me again. "You think I've gone batty, don't you?"

"Not exactly. This is so good, Mother."

"Good. Everything in the soup was grown in my yard or a friend's yard. Well, what then?"

I wasn't sure of what to say. She looked like Farmer Brown's wife in her jeans and flannel shirt. And she hadn't colored her long hair in a year or more. It was ponytailed and wrapped in a knot on the back of her head, held up with two sticks—not the garden variety, thank heaven. Her once perfectly manicured fingers were now short and plain but buffed to a beautiful pink patina. She almost glowed with satisfaction and good health. But didn't she miss her Chanel suits?

"What are you thinking, Miriam?"

"I'm sort of thinking that putting up tomatoes and all this stuff you're into would be hard to execute efficiently in a pair of pumps."

She smiled from some deep inner place and shook her head in a way that meant she was resigned to the understanding that I might never understand *her*.

"You're right. But why would I try? And how do you like this?"

She kicked off her clog, held out her bare foot in my direction, and lo and behold, my mother was wearing a toe ring. Indeed, I thought. She had clearly lost all interest in the genteel outside world.

"Very nice, Mother." I was horrified.

"I think it makes a statement for a gal my age, don't you?"

Just then there was a rap of knuckles on the sliding-glass door and I looked up to see a man standing there with a string of fish. Mother got up to let him in.

"Harrison! Come on in!"

"Miss Josie? How are ya, darlin'? I brought you some fish."

He looked like a medium-size Ernest Hemingway, tanned and weathered by the sun, deeply creased forehead and blazing blue eyes that sparkled from across the room as he caught sight of me. He was dressed like a bum and I suspected his fingernails were dirty more often than clean. And he smelled like he had been rolling around in the marsh.

"I'm well, thank you! Can I offer you a bowl of soup?"

"No, thanks. Just ate."

"Miriam? This is my friend Harrison Ford."

"I'm the other one, ma'am. The good-looking one. Not that wimpy actor."

"Hello," I said, and squinted at him, wondering what he was smiling about. Maybe he thought he was funny. I estimated his age to be in the zone of mine. Or a year or two older.

"Harrison, this is Miriam, my daughter."

He nodded slightly, turned away, and said to Mother, "Want me to put these boys in the freezer?"

Was he ignoring me, then? My neck got hot. Well, go right ahead, Swamp Thing.

"Heavens, no! Let's eat them tonight. Why don't you join us for dinner?"

"Only if you let me fix 'em . . ."

"You come back around six o'clock and I'll have the grill going. How's that?"

"Sounds fine." He slid the door to the left and turned back to me. "Nice meeting you."

"Yes, it was nice to meet you, too."

A *whoosh* and a *thwack* followed as the

heavy door rolled into its frame and he was gone down the steps in an instant.

"He's a sweetheart," Mother said. "Brings me fish all the time."

"What's his story?"

"I met him at Wally's."

"Excuse me? What?" Wally's Bar was the island establishment for beer, arm wrestling, and more beer. Everyone went there at some point or another, but if you read the police blotter report in the *Moultrie News* or the *Island Eye News,* you couldn't help but notice that most disturbances on the island were somehow traceable to Wally's. "What in the world were you doing in there?"

"Drinking a beer with some friends of mine and listening to a little country music. I love the banjo, you know. Thinking I might learn to play it."

"Country music? Banjo? Are you serious?" I cleared my throat in disapproval. Country music was like nails across a blackboard for me. I would have preferred rap.

"Oh, Miriam. Honestly. Sometimes you're such a prig."

"I am not."

Mother picked up our dishes and began

cleaning up. "I love you. You're my only child. Trust me. You're a prig."

I snatched the sponge, rinsed it out, squeezed it, and began wiping down the countertop.

"Thanks a lot," I said.

"Miriam? Look at you! You're at the *beach* and what are you wearing? A silk blouse all tidy and tucked into your wool skirt, stockings, for God's sake, little heels with Pilgrim buckles, and pearls! Girl! We have to loosen you up! You need some fun in your life."

"Kevin says the same thing, but the last time I let *Fun* in the front door, it was wearing a thong and cavorting with the husband of one of my friends!"

"Your new tenant?"

"You don't want to know."

"Honey, I always want to know. Don't throw those vegetables away. I compost, you know. What's her name? This hussy."

I drained the broth and scraped the vegetables into a large can by the sink. I could feel my pulse picking up speed. "Liz Harper, lately of Birmingham. So you want to hear the story?"

"I said I did, didn't I?"

"Well, she seemed like just what the doctor ordered, you know, to add a little life to my otherwise dreary existence. At least Kevin seemed to think she was perfect. I had my doubts." Just thinking about it caused me to be short of breath.

"Why? You missed a spot."

"Where?"

"Right there." Mother pointed to a large smear that I had not seen.

"I hate black cooktops. And granite. Can't see a bloody thing unless you lean into the light . . . Anyway, I thought it was suspicious that she worked at a college in a minor position and was able to afford to live on the East Side."

"Where? Are you all right?"

"I'm perfectly fine."

"Okay. What does she do?"

"Hunter College. Something in admissions, I think. So, then she tells us that she bartends for a caterer and does some nanny work. I mean, who does that sort of work?"

"Plenty of extremely respectable people, Miss Priss."

"Whatever. Anyhow, the next thing I know, she's got Truman Willis upstairs in the sack with her, going wild. *Ka-thump, ka-thump* all night long!"

"You could *hear* them?"

"Yes. Kevin says I should not go crazy and throw her out."

"He's probably right."

"He says she probably didn't know Truman was married."

"He could very well be right about that, too. But you could *hear* them?"

"Yes. Disgusting. I mean, here I am trying with all I've got to get Agnes, his wife, to appoint me the chair of the decorations committee for the museum's spring benefit. Let me tell you, since Charles ran off with that concubine of his, it has not been very easy for me to maintain my social standing."

Mother started to laugh and I looked at her like she was certifiably insane. Funny thing, she was looking at me the same way.

"What?" I said. "Tell me what you see funny about this?"

"Oh, Miriam. Sit down. Let your mother give you some advice."

"Thanks, but I don't need any advice. I mean, aren't you the one who taught me right from wrong?"

"Yes. I was. Would you like a cup of tea? It's a little chilly in here."

"Sure." It wasn't chilly at all.

She removed two oversize mugs from the cabinet and put the kettle on to boil. I couldn't imagine what she could tell me that would change the way I felt about Liz and her shenanigans. Or about my life.

"Do you remember how insanely busy I was when your father was alive?"

"Sure."

"I was always chairing a gala or worrying about a raffle prize or trying to sell space in an ad journal. Remember?"

"I surely do. You're the one who taught me the value of volunteerism."

"Yes, and it is terribly important. But I never depended on my volunteer work to influence or improve or secure my social standing in any way."

"That's not exactly what I meant."

"Yes, it is. It is *exactly* what you are expecting! An able-bodied person has a responsibility to give back to their community. That's just good citizenship. But it was your daddy's money that gave me a highfalutin social life and I knew it from day one. Let me ask you something. Do you really think that Agnes Willis is your friend?"

"Of course she is! We've been friends for years!" I knew in my heart that my friendship with Agnes was *finito,* but I wasn't prepared to admit it.

The teakettle roared like a freight train and startled me.

Mother smiled and lifted it to pour. "This thing's enough to scare the liver out of you. It should have come with a warning, don't you think?"

"Probably." I took the mug from her and said thanks.

"Anyway, you don't have to answer me. Just ask yourself this. If you had the flu, would she bring you soup or call you to see how you were? That's what friends do."

I stared at my mug of tea and then buried my face in the steam, taking a long sip. "What's the point, Mother?"

"The point is that social pecking order in that world is nonsense—the way women bicker over napkin folds and a centerpiece is just ridiculous. But! It is noble, even personally fulfilling, to do good works. It is *good* to give away assets to help others. It is. But that's not all there is to life, Miriam."

"It has been the framework of my life for so many years, I don't know what I would do without it. It's what Charles loved about me— I mean, that volunteering gave us a marvelous life beyond his work and raising the boys."

"Charles is a shallow bastard, Miriam, pardon me. If you ran the biggest charity ball in New York, do you think it would bring him back to you?"

"No."

"If you were twenty years younger and skinny as could be, do you think that would bring him back?"

"No." I felt nauseated. "Why are we talking about this? I don't like to talk about this. You know that."

"Because you need to put this disappointment behind you, for once and for all."

"I have."

"No, darling girl, Mother begs to differ. Here's what I see. I see my wonderful, beautiful daughter, very unhappy, clutching at straws, trying to hang on to a life that isn't worth the effort."

"Mother? Charles and my boys and my volunteer life are all I have. Charles and my boys are gone. My volunteer career is going nowhere. What am I supposed to do?"

"Get another life."

"Easy for you to say. My bills are paid by the rent I receive, a large portion of which is coming from a home-wrecking tramp, like the one who decimated my life. I came here, Mother, to you and to this island to try and figure out what to do."

I just stared at the counter and didn't say a word. Soon the lecture would end. I could go to my old room, crawl in bed, and have a nap.

"Look, this gal Liz? Don't use your passion all up worrying about her. Life is so precious, Miriam. You have to realize that this battle cannot be won. Don't waste any more time, honey. That's all."

Chapter Six

What's That Smell?

Kevin had called me the minute he saw Agnes Willis's envelope in the mail and read it to me. "Listen to this," he said.

**"Dear Mrs. Swanson,
Thank you so very much for your kind invitation to attend the Bill Blass fall show. Unfortunately, I will be hiking in Spain at that time, so I am returning the ticket as you requested. On another note, the gala committee would like to include you on the invitations committee and it is my most sincere hope that you will accept.**

Your beautiful handwriting will be such an asset!

> **With kindest regards,**
> **Agnes Willis"**

So! Despite the fact that *she knew* I was salivating to be on the decorations committee, she was throwing me in the invitations dungeon. Hiking in Spain, indeed. Maybe she would twist an ankle. Not enough to put her in a wheelchair, but enough to ruin her day. The invitations committee. I was so mad I wanted to spit, which is just a figure of speech. Ladies do not spit unless they are in the wine country and do not wish to be sauced before noon.

Invitations. If I had been a teenage girl I would have screamed my head off and then left terrible comments about Agnes Willis at myspace.com. Or facebook, whatever that was. If I had been a teenage boy I would have punched holes in all the Sheetrock walls of my bedroom. My only alternative was to take a shower. Swamp Thing was going to arrive within the hour, and heaven forbid, I shouldn't please my mother by making an effort to pass for an authentic Geechee Girl, a Daughter of the Dunes.

I combed out my wet hair, watching myself in the huge mirror that lined the wall behind the basin. My hair was getting longer. It was already well past my chin, skimming the collar of the old but still serviceable terry-cloth bathrobe I found in the closet. Maybe being satisfied in terry cloth was a little pitiful. Basically, it made me look lumpy. I wasn't lumpy. I decided to let it drop to the floor around my ankles in a puddle in an act of defiance buoyed by false confidence. I had not looked at myself naked in quite some time.

I was not the prettiest sight in town, to be sure.

Embarrassed and feeling slightly panicked, I wondered if my figure was salvageable. I decided to assess it by region. My upper arms were sort of droopy but I knew they could be substantially improved with weight training. I had done it before; I could do it again. My stomach was not exactly taut. Was I too old for Pilates? What if I had a massive stroke while I was doing crunches? It would be a very stupid way to die. I looked at my breasts and inhaled to make them lift. They seemed reasonable, I thought, and in the next second it seemed absurd to refer to my breasts as reasonable. I mean, what did unreasonable ones look like? Are they argumentative pendulous melons?

My thighs? Well, what can we say about anyone's thighs? The only probable reason they weren't completely cottage cheese was that I did a fair amount of walking. But I definitely didn't walk enough to lose any weight.

While I blew my hair dry I thought about Agnes Willis. She was as skinny as a supermodel. It was unnatural. She probably purged. Maybe she dined on laxatives. Maybe she took Truman's wallet up to a plastic surgeon on Park Avenue and Eighty-sixth Street and got herself liposuctioned twice a year. God knows, her face was over-Botoxed and stretched like a drum. At that moment, I hated her guts.

I looked at my war chest of cosmetics and realized that given the location and situation, Mother was right. They were inappropriate.

I had planned to set my hair in some Velcros to get that Park Avenue Patty helmet going and then said, "Oh, to hell with that" to the thin air, and tossed the whole bag of them in the wastebasket, along with my bomb-shelter-size can of hair spray. Au naturel was the Island standard? They would get au naturel!

I put some moisturizer on my face and a dab of pale pink gloss on my lips and looked in the mirror. Staring back at me was an anthropologist straight from the bush.

What to wear? I looked through the clothes I had brought and decided to wear a cotton turtleneck that someone had left in the bottom drawer along with a pair of jeans that were one size smaller than mine. Then I shrouded myself in my own dependable oversize cable-knit cardigan that was at least ten years old. I slipped on my old loafers and took one last look in the mirror. Perfume? Nah. To hell with that, too. Jungle Woman did not concern herself with such trivia. If Charles could have seen me he might not have recognized me. Kevin would have roared. But, I looked younger somehow. I took this new persona downstairs, where Harrison Ford and my mother were preparing dinner. And I wondered for a moment about the nature of their friendship. It certainly seemed to me that she had more of a social life than I did, and that was truly not right.

"Hi!" I said. "What can I do to help?"

To say they stopped dead in their tracks would be an exaggeration, but I saw the glint of satisfaction in my mother's eye and amusement in Mr. Ford's. It was obvious I had successfully dressed to please.

"You can help us drink this delicious bottle of scuppernong wine," Harrison said, and handed me a goblet. "Here! Cheers!"

"Thanks," I said. It was cloyingly sweet, much sweeter than wine I was accustomed to, but I sipped it, not wanting to be rude. "It's very nice."

"Harrison and his friend Butch made it!"

"Really?" Why was I not surprised? There was a screw cap to the bottle and the label was handwritten. But I didn't realize they grew grapes around Sullivans Island. "There's a vineyard on the island?"

"No, out on Wadmalaw," he said. "Land's cheaper."

His words were true enough. Although Wadmalaw was being gentrified and developed like every other stitch of coastline in the country, its interior farming environs were probably much cheaper than Sullivans Island and Kiawah, which were two of the most fashionable sandbars in America.

"Right," I said. "I remember going out there when I was a kid and buying vegetables. The dirt was very dark and cool."

"Were you barefoot?" he asked, as though he could not envision such a thing.

"Of course! I had my flip-flop days, you know." I narrowed my eyes at him and realized he was thoroughly amused. "Did you light the grill, Mother?"

"No. I forgot. Why don't you and Harrison do that for me?"

"Sure thing," he said, and refilled my glass.

"Ah, Wadmalaw! It's positively thriving with all the small farms out there that grow vegetables for the gourmet market. Somebody's growing those fat little pygmy carrots for Thomas Keller's kitchens," Mother said. "I adore them! Until this year, I haven't had much luck with them, but now I have a cold frame of them coming along." She smiled and looked at me. "They are loaded with vitamins and antioxidants. Yummy little devils."

Mother continued to ramble about the merits of carrots and Harrison slid the door open for me to step out to the porch. The sun was hanging low and the color of, well you know, mangoes. Light streamed through the remaining wisps of cirrus clouds. The horizon held broad strokes of royal purple streaked with red and rose quartz and the sky was fast becoming lapis. Venus was there, and for a moment, I felt an urge to make a wish. All at once I was filled with wishes—that Charles would regret what he had done, that my boys would come back to me, that my life was happier, that I had someone to love—on and on my wishes went, one after another. I knew Harrison and I were supposed to be going down to the grill, but the sight was so powerful and my heart was so melancholy. Neither one of us moved. I suspected he was having similar thoughts. Finally, when the sun slipped away, we sighed and went down the steps.

"Some sky, don't you think?"

"Well, Mr. Ford, when day becomes night around here, it's no joke."

"You're right, Mrs. Swanson. Every event of nature seems to be packed with drama."

"Mrs. Swanson?" The formality sounded too stiff.

"Didn't you just call me Mr. Ford?"

"I guess I did, didn't I?" I flipped the light switch on the post of the pergola that housed our grill, refrigerator, and ice maker and we were instantly washed in warm yellow light.

Harrison threw back the hood of the grill

with a clang. "Didn't anybody ever give you a nickname?"

"No. Well, when I was young, my girlfriends called me Mira or Mizzy."

Nodding and congenial, he reached in the cabinet, removing a brush and a small bottle of oil, perfectly at home, as though he had rummaged Mother's cabinets a thousand times before. He probably had, and I wasn't sure how I felt about this stranger being so familiar with my mother's possessions. I was glad she had a friend, to be sure, and I supposed I was just being protective of her.

As he neatly painted the grill with oil, I watched him from the side. Sun damage and crow's-feet aside, he was actually quite handsome in profile. But he was dangerously short, so short that I could look him in the eye. But then, I was five seven. So maybe he was five eight or nine. But five eight wasn't short. Charles had been six four. He was probably still six four. Five eight or nine was normal or even tall in many cultures. I snapped out of the height of my fog realizing that Harrison was talking to me. Height? Ah well, my humor is truly lame, but we already know that.

"What? I'm sorry."

"I said, Mira?" he said. "Doesn't suit you at all. What's your full name?"

"Miriam Elizabeth."

"I can't see you as Mira. Nope."

"Right? A couple of my sandbox enemies tried to call me Mitzi and I broke their crayons."

"I would have recycled them. You are definitely not a Mitzi."

"What is *that* supposed to mean?" Why *didn't* he think I could have been called something lighthearted like Mitzi? No, he thought I was a lesbian storm trooper or something.

"Well, Mitzi is, I don't know, red-haired and freckled, a tomboy? Flouncing around? Ditzy? You're too feminine to be a Mitzi."

"Oh. How about you?"

"Nope. I've always been Harrison."

"I have a bird named Harry."

"I rest my case. Nicknames are not for everyone. But you should be Mellie—a little bit of Miriam and some Elizabeth. M and Ellie."

"Whatever you say . . ."

It was a banal conversation, ridiculous actually. Who cared about nicknames? But that wasn't the point. He was flirting with me. A man was flirting with me. At least it seemed so. I realized then that age difference aside, it might be important for me to understand the real nature of his relationship with Mother. Nah, they couldn't be . . .

The grill was fired up and warming. "I guess we should get some more wine," he said. "Think of all the sober adults out there . . ."

"Right," I said, and we were caught in the whirlpool of each other's eyes. I thought, Well, this is just too stupid for words, but I wasn't going to be the first one to move away. The elixir of scuppernong grapes had emboldened me, and besides, I was a little bit fixated on what appeared to be double dimples in his cheeks. Or maybe it was the fading twilight, but I decided that Harrison was definitely not a character from *The Old Man and the Sea*. Who was this man anyway?

"Right," I said, repeating myself, and cleared my throat. "It's turning into a beautiful evening, isn't it?"

"Yes, ma'am, Miss Mellie, it is."

Mellie. Okay. I could live with that.

We sat down to expertly grilled fish, just drizzled with olive oil and lemon juice and generously sprinkled with chopped parsley. Mother had prepared tomatoes and onions into a sauce and spooned them over a nest of steaming rice. Of course, she had grown the tomatoes.

"I still can't give up white rice," she said. "Brown rice is healthier, but my family's been eating white rice for a thousand years and I'm not fooling around with tradition!"

"Well said, Miss Josie," Harrison said.

I cleared my throat and said, "So, Harrison? Tell me about yourself. Is there a Mrs. Ford?"

"There was but she left me, oh, I guess it was a dozen years ago. Ran off with my favorite golfing buddy."

"Good grief! That's awful!"

"Yeah, it was. But you can get over anything in time, I think. Said I worked too much and I probably did."

"She was a fool," Mother said. "And so was Miriam's husband, Charles."

"You mean Mellie," Harrison said. "I gave her a new name."

"Oh? Well, why not? Mellie. I love it!"

I could feel my heat rising and knew that my estrogen shortage was probably obvious.

"Charles was indulging in the classic midlife crisis and I let him go have his adventure. We had some good years, though, and he gave me two gorgeous, sweet grown sons. Do you have children?" I gritted my teeth as my lie about my sweet sons and the good years slipped between them. "By the way, the fish is unbelievable."

"More?" Mother said, and moved to serve another portion to me before I could respond.

"Thanks. Yep. One daughter. Louisa. She works in Costa Rica, teaching English and health. She's married to a great guy. No children, though. I don't quite understand that, but having children is their business."

"It's a different world out there today than when I was a young woman," Mother said. "I'm not so sure I'd have the courage to raise children in all this insanity. More rice, Harrison? *Mellie?*"

"Thanks, yes. Miss Josie? You are absolutely right. The world is a crazy place."

We continued eating until nearly everything was gone. Harrison, after some prodding, talked about his recycling work—apparently he and Mother were the reigning royalty of the Lowcountry movement not only to conserve and reuse but also to raise awareness of how easy it was to incorporate these practices into daily life.

"If each person just did one thing, think what a difference that could make," Mother said.

"You're preaching to the choir, Miss Josie. Why don't I clear the table and then squire you ladies down to the beach for a little walk to shake it all down. It's so bright we can probably see cabdrivers in Lisbon."

We put all the dishes in the sink, covered them with hot suds, laughing about the numbers of eyeglasses, toothbrushes, and sneakers they had gathered in the past year. Their projects were mildly interesting if not actually remarkable. Even to a dedicated skeptic like me.

The cleanup was fast and Harrison poured out some of a second bottle of wine. We had not had enough wine to be tipsy, but just enough to feel relaxed and happy. We bundled up in jackets and gloves and rode over to Station Eighteen in Harrison's Mercury Mountaineer. He opened the sunroof and I began to let my mind drift as I took in the natural beauty above me.

When we parked, Harrison helped Mother down from her seat and then held out a hand for me. I could feel his strength as he held my elbow and knew that he would never have let either of us fall. It had been forever since I had felt the grip of any man besides Kevin, who was a dear, to be sure, but he did not elicit the same response from my nervous system as Harrison. I blushed again, hoped he could not see it in the dark and wondered what was going on with me. Was I having an episode of "Any Port in a Storm"?

The night was crystal clear and there were countless stars overhead, sparkling and multiplying as our eyes adjusted to the darkness. It was chilly but invigorating to be in the salty night breeze. We moved through the white dunes, pristine even in the dead of night, and began walking east. The tide was low but sliding in quickly enough to be the perfect background music—rising with a muffled roar and receding in whispers. The phosphorus ocean sparkled and in the reflection of its dazzle we found our voices again.

"Tell me more about you," I said in what I considered to be a rather bold move.

"Me?" Harrison said. "Well, I spent twenty years in investment banking and did all right."

"He made a killing," Mother said. "Don't let him fool you."

"Mother!" Sometimes my mother's mouth was a loose cannon.

"That's okay. Anyway, when my wife told me she preferred my best friend's bed to mine, I threw my golf clubs in the Ashepoo River and took up fishing. Fishing is good for the soul. Gives you time to think."

"I imagine so," I said.

"So after I settled here and as time went on I started finding out about mercury levels in the water, hence *in the seafood*. Then it was chemical runoff from parking lots into the water supply and *into the seafood*. We're basically poisoning ourselves. Then I guess it was just *waste* that was bugging me—you know, we are such a wasteful society—all the landfills and so on. Anyway, those were the beginning thoughts that made me want to change my life and to help clean up and preserve the world around me. Just quit wasting stuff, you know?"

He and Mother seemed to share in this wacky concept of living green, but more important, living without the commercial trappings of the world over the causeway.

"So, you don't watch television?" I said, teasing a little. "No *Desperate Housewives*?"

"No, of course I watch television. Just not

for hours on end, that's all. And needless to say, I'm not interested in desperate housewives, or desperate anybody, for that matter."

"Understood. Me either." I wondered if I came off as desperate. "Well, do you use electricity?"

"Yes, of course. Of course I do. But very little. In fact, I've been kicking around a small windmill test project for the island."

"Harrison is absolutely brilliant, Miriam. Lots of people have generators that run on fossil fuel but Harrison wants to use the wind. Think about it. How much wind do we get in a hurricane? A lot. Or even when it's coming in from the east? We've been using solar panels for years, but windmills are so beautiful and peaceful. I wouldn't mind seeing them in the landscape."

Was there a twinkle in Mother's eye? Was *she* his . . . no way!

"Well, to date, we're not getting very far," Harrison said. "We need to come up with a turbine that can produce power at a steady average wind speed. So far, no luck."

"Meaning?" I said. My throat tightened at the actual possibility of Mother and Harrison together.

"I'm putting my energy into other things—like opening a flex fuel station in Mount Pleasant so we can pump E-85 fuel. And photovoltaic systems."

"Photo what?"

"Solar cells."

"Ah. Right. What was I thinking? I thought you were a nice retired banker just catching a few fish now and then," I said.

I could see him smiling in the dark.

"Banking was another life. I like this one better. It might actually do some good."

I thought about what he said and decided Mother was right—he was an interesting man. And he may have been flirting a little with me, but I was sure then it was unintentional and meaningless. Obviously, I had misread his signals. He was Mother's friend and I was pretty sure more. My heart sank from my own vanity. But honestly, I was very glad that Mother had someone in her life. Besides, could I truly envision this guy at a gala in New York? How about never?

Anyway, saving the planet was a good idea. It was surely a fact that most of the population did not live in sync with nature. At all. I had endured prolonged blackouts in New York and always worried about the people on life support. Worse, I worried about old people who lived on high floors of apartment buildings and how they would go out for groceries. Would they simply die of heart attacks trying to get home, climbing forty flights of steps? It was a dark subject to ponder.

I said, "Well, windmills are certainly more aesthetic than those horrible open transformer substations and those huge buzzing towers that we always suspected gave people brain cancer."

I turned around to see that I had walked ahead of Mother and Harrison. They had not heard a word I said. They were huddled together trying to light something. Maybe Harrison smoked. That's pretty nasty, I thought. But within seconds the sweet-smelling memories of an old rock concert reached me. My mother and Harrison were burning a special kind of weed. This was something I absolutely could not abide.

I felt sickened with disgust. My mother must have been absolutely crazy.

I waited until they caught up to me and then I looked at them both and said, "Have y'all gone mad? Y'all must be out of your cotton-picking minds. Gross!"

I started walking back to the house. I could hear them calling after me but I ignored them. I was too furious and too shocked and it was too late to fly back to New York. I would leave first thing in the morning but not until I had given her a piece of my mind. And him? Maybe I'd push him into the Ashepoo and let him look for his golf clubs. Didn't *anyone* lead a respectable life anymore?

Chapter Seven

MELLIE SLOWLY EMERGES

Dear Mrs. Willis,
Many thanks for your thoughtful as-
signment to the invitations committee.
I will serve with pleasure. At present I
am in residence on Sullivans Island in
South Carolina, but on my return, I will
be in touch.
Cordially,
Miriam Elizabeth Swanson

Old habits died hard. I began my day fulfilling
my obligations and that was that. It didn't
matter if I was in Timbuktu. But I have to say
that I was beginning to think my obsession

with writing all these thank-you notes was becoming slightly more than disingenuous. Besides, what I really wanted to say to Agnes Willis would never find its way into ink. Moreover, it was becoming clear that I had been taking my lead from others for about as long as I could stand it.

I was restless and couldn't sleep. Never mind that I was awakened at the crack of dawn by my mother's manly rooster crowing his head off loud enough to make his harem lay scrambled eggs. So I got up, packed, wrote my phony thank-you note to Agnes Willis, and walked down to the post office via the beach. It was a perfect morning. The damp air was chilled, but I welcomed the warmth of the rising sun on my back as I made my way toward the lighthouse.

Agnes Willis. Boy, she thought she had the world in the palm of her liver-spotted hand, didn't she? And why was it that women like her always seemed to come out on top? Maybe it was because their husbands had trained them to look the other way and because they all knew divorce was just too bloody expensive. I really needed to get over her. No, I realized that what I *really* needed to do was stop letting the whole freaking world contribute to my horrible inferiority complex I seemed to be carrying around in the chip embedded in my shoulder.

I looked around me at all the "dog people" people on the beach—they were actually frolicking, dogs and people! Out in full force, they were tossing things that their pets chased—Frisbees, sticks, and tennis balls. This was one of the things I loved about the tiny kingdom of Sullivans Island. The ruling town fathers and mothers passed a law allowing dogs on the beach only during very specific time slots. They loved passing laws, it seemed.

I imagine that in the years of my absence some big old black Labrador had licked the leg or snatched the egg-salad sandwich of some crazy rich Yankee who owned a house on the front beach worth millions. That northerner complains and the council agrees that it's not right; in fact, it's terrible. Let's be honest, since the south ceased growing cotton and our senators lost the support of the navy yard, tourism has been the cement that held the Charleston area's economy together. Crotch sniffing, jumping, untethered wet dogs running wild all over the beach just wouldn't do. The dog-owning local homegrown citi-

zens moaned and complained but the law
stuck.

What no one counted on was that a new
society would spring from the cause of ca-
nine discontent. The "dog people" came to
recognize, greet, and talk to one another.
They became friends and I heard several
marriages had come about as a result of the
Island's new mandate. Who knew? It was
clearly one of the details of Sullivans Island
living that only added to its magical reputation. It was charmed.

I walked past their gathering and over the
dunes to the post office thinking about Mother.
When she came home last night she did not
say a word to me and I did not come out of
my room to say a word to her. I was so flabbergasted. What if she had been caught?
What if she went to jail? If her arrest was written up in the papers in Charleston, surely
someone in New York would pass it along,
and inside of a city minute, my life would be
completely finished. And hers. And who was
this ridiculous man jeopardizing our lives over
a cheap thrill? It really was too much.

I bought a stamp from the machine,
slapped it on the envelope, and tossed it
through the out-of-town mail slot. Out-of-

town? It should have been labeled ANOTHER
WORLD. After all, Sullivans Island was not exactly a microcosm of the known planet. It
wasn't Charleston. It wasn't Manhattan. It
had no real claim to fame outside of Fort
Moultrie, which, all right, I'll admit was pivotal
in the American Revolution, the War of North-
ern Aggression, and every other war in our
history, and Edgar Allan Poe was stationed
there, and then there was the Pest House
and oh, shoot . . . in the time it had taken to
leave the beach, I had worked myself into a
snit and was not thinking straight. I removed
my cell phone from my pocket, dialed Kevin,
and started walking home.

"Miriam? Is that you? Is everything all
right?"

"Yes. No. Oh, Kevin, are you up yet?"

"Of course I am. I'm up, dressed, and just
fed Harry his breakfast. What's going on?
Are you ill?"

"No. Well, sick in my heart. Kevin, you
won't believe what happened last night."

"Spill it, Petal. Tell Uncle Sigmund everything. Nothing like a little morning drama to
get the blood moving."

"I caught my mother smoking pot."

"What?"

Kevin exploded with laughter. I joined in, only because he had the most contagious laugh in the world.

"Kevin! This is not funny! Stop!"

"You're right! It's not funny. It's hysterical! Puh-lease! You have to tell me the details! Was she using a bong?"

His laughter continued and mine did not. The idea that my mother, a heretofore dignified woman—former Junior League president for eons, a trustee of the Gibbes Art Museum for decades, on and on her involvement went with every traditional organization Charleston had that you can name—now the Queen of the Beach, might have stooped so low as to purchase a bong annoyed the devil out of me. I stopped and sat at a picnic table in front of Dunleavy's Pub, which still made the best burgers in the world.

"No. She was *not* using a bong, Kevin, and this is serious! I mean, what if my mother gets caught? What if it's all over the papers? I would be ruined! Ruined, do you hear me?"

He was silent.

"Are you there?"

"Yes, I'm here. Oh, Miriam, Miriam, Miriam. Listen to me. Smoking pot is stupid . . ."

"It also happens to be illegal, you know."

"I'm aware. So is taking catalogs from the hall that belong to a certain someone else. But Miriam, who died and put you in charge of the world?"

"Just what is that supposed to mean, Kevin?" I sighed deeply. Sometimes even my sweet Kevin could be exasperating.

"I mean, as I was saying before my dearest friend interrupted me, that smoking pot is stupid and illegal, but heavenly days, it really shouldn't be. Millions of people smoke marijuana, and if they're not selling it or in possession of massive quantities or giving it to little children, well, the world doesn't really care. Neither should you."

"Listen, Kevin, my position is precarious enough without my mother getting busted and ruining my life."

"Perhaps, but I'll bet you a thousand dollars that she won't get busted and you'll still have your self-righteous indignation to keep you warm at night."

Ouch. But my indignation, self-righteous or not, had nothing to do with the fact that my mother was using illegal drugs. They were separate issues.

"Not nice, darling."

"Sorry. But, Miriam, you are such a harsh

judge. Cut your mother some slack. How old is she?"

"If I told you, I'd have to kill you. But she's old enough to know better, that's for sure."

"So, what do you propose to do about it? Send her to the Betty?"

"Very funny. No. I'm going to have a talk with her and then I'm coming home. I actually called to tell you I was coming home early."

"Well, you know I would love it if you did, but I think you should stay. When you talk to her, try not to do it from the saddle of a high horse, okay?"

"I haven't changed my ticket yet. It's nonrefundable. They'll probably charge me a fortune . . ."

"Blasted money hogs those airlines are. Can't even carry my moisturizer on board anymore. Calm down about this, Miriam. Seriously. You haven't been to visit your mother in ages, and if you stomp off in a huff it would hurt her feelings, I'm sure."

"And there's something else."

"You've been holding out on me! What?"

"There's a man."

"And . . ."

"His name is Harrison Ford."

"Shut! Up!"

"Different Harrison Ford."

"Oh. Okay. And . . ."

"And I thought he was flirting with me but he might be my mother's boyfriend. I can't figure it out."

"Any resemblance to the other one? Hmm?"

"Stop it! He's like my age practically."

I could hear Kevin gasp and could envision his fingers brought to his lips as if to say, Well, shut my mouth.

"Do you know how bizarre this is to me?"

"It's fascinating is what it is. You simply have to stay. That's all there is to it."

"Maybe."

"But report back every six hours. I'll tell you, Petal, you make my life up here in the frozen tundra seem frightfully boring. There's only old Harry to hear my prayers."

"I'll call you later."

I could hear his signature giggle as I closed the phone.

Maybe I was too serious.

I looked up from my bench to see the stream of luxury cars heading for the Ben Sawyer Bridge and another day of work off the island. BMWs and Benzes were rolling down Middle Street and waiting to turn. Jaguars, Lexus SUVs, Land Rovers, and custom pickup trucks were lined up to my right, zipper-merging with the others. I marveled at the spectacular surge in wealth they all represented. The occasional minivan and school bus passed and I was reassured of some normalcy for a moment. But when the Perrier truck pulled up to deliver to Dunleavy's, I got up to go home. The Sullivans Island of my youth had been gentrified beyond what my heart could endure. At least at that moment.

Then like a lightning bolt from the clear blue, it hit me. Strange and peculiar as my mother's existence here may have seemed to me, since she had retired here, she was one of the last remaining authentic islanders—minus the marijuana, of course. If people like her didn't live the way she did, Sullivans Island would dissolve into just another overpriced, mainstreamed, McMansioned piece of branded Americana. That same authenticity was why Sullivan's was thriving, as well as Station Twenty-two Restaurant and Atlanticville and all the other little restaurants and businesses that dotted both sides of Middle Street. It was probably the reason the *age-inappropriate-for-my-mother* Harrison Ford loved it there, and others I had yet to discover. They were all on a mission to preserve or find their true identity and shunned the outside world as unnecessary. Maybe they weren't wrong. Perhaps Harrison would benefit from a manicure and a younger girlfriend, but maybe he and Mother were onto something. Why else were the streets of this island jammed with cars each morning, evening, and night all year round if all those people weren't seeking some sliver of unmanufactured, unplastic-coated reality?

I reached Mother's yard. Her chickens were pecking the ground, Cecelia was eating some kind of greenery, and I was almost wondering why she didn't have a couple of ducks to round out the symphony. In a much-improved state of mind, I started up the back stairs and heard the sliding-glass door open. There stood Miss Josie at the top of the stairs with her hands on her hips. Her body language was clear.

"I see you've packed your things," she said in a humorless voice.

"Good morning, Mother. I was thinking of going home."

"Is there a reason?"

What was I supposed to say then? That

she was getting toasted and fooling around with a man more suited for me? I tried to find the words. "Look, Mother, last night I saw you—"

"You're not old enough to lecture your mother, missy."

"I wasn't planning to."

"Good. Do you want some breakfast?"

"That would be lovely." I arrived at the porch and kissed her cheek. "How did you sleep?"

"Well enough."

I went inside and made myself a cup of strong instant coffee, thinking it was probably in order instead of tea. Mother cracked some eggs into a bowl and stirred them around with a fork. There were three of us then—me, Mother, and Her Attitude.

"Would you like me to put the bread in the toaster?"

"If you wish," she said.

"Are you angry with me?"

"No, of course not. But I had hoped you'd stay more than one night, Miriam."

So that was it. Back to "Miriam," were we? Kevin was right. She was upset that I was leaving. "Well, then, I will. How long would you like to have me around?"

She stopped, pushed a few stray hairs back from her forehead and sighed. Then she looked at me with the strangest expression. "For the rest of my days?"

We smiled almost identically. All at once it was wonderful to be with her, even if she was a card-carrying loon.

"Well, I'll stay two more days but you have to make me a promise."

"What's that?"

"That you'll be discreet. I don't want to have to bail you out of jail."

She put her hand on my arm and told me not to worry. She fed me the most delicious scrambled eggs I had ever eaten. She told me she loved me, I told her that I loved her, and neither of us said a word about Harrison.

"So, what would you like to do today?" she said.

"Maybe have that long walk on the beach?"

"Sounds like a good idea. How about after two? The tide will be low then, and in the meanwhile, I have some things to get done."

"I can help you. If you would like, I mean."

The next thing I knew I was on the receiving end of instructions in the fine art of crocheting fishing nets with my fingers and a small stick. She left to do her errands and I was deep in thought, comparing and contrasting my life in New York with island living.

The differences were enormous. It certainly was pleasant to be in the winter morning air without a coat and gloves looking at the marsh. It practically shook with the bustle of its life. Gulls, ospreys, and pelicans were swooping and soaring all through the sky. Little wrens chirped from deep inside the fronds of Mother's tall palmetto trees, which curtsied in greeting with every gust of wind. Crows were everywhere.

Now, crows fascinated me, despite the fact that their incessant cawing was not exactly Chopin. People said that they were the most intelligent birds on the planet, but only because they didn't know my Harry. I would concede that crow habits did ring slightly human, except that, unlike people, they mate for life. They were a curious breed. Once, years ago, I had seen one standing guard in a treetop while his buddies fed on the ground. And I had seen the lazy things drop pecans in the road so that cars could crack them open. Around dusk, you would see them start to gather in groups on wires and rooftops. At some signal that surely eluded me, they would depart for their nightly roost. Hundreds, even thousands of them, would roost together in a field because their vast numbers protected them from the jaws and claws of owls and hawks.

To even think about this was one of the biggest differences between living in any large urban area and living on an island—that you noticed what was going on with birds and tides and all these other aspects of life that never crossed your mind in a city. I giggled to realize that just around the time the crows were taking off to roost, I was having my first evening cocktail. Whoop-dee-do. Me, Harry, and the Famous Grouse. Some bunch of birds we were.

I remembered then that I had not asked Kevin about Liz. Well, if she had been carrying on with Truman Willis again, he would have brought it up. Nonetheless, I made a note to check on her nonsense the next time we spoke.

I thought again about serving on the invitations committee and how unfair the world was. All I wanted was to do something that made *me* happy for once, and I couldn't even manage to wangle a desirable committee assignment. Maybe the universe was trying to tell me something.

I heard a car stop and looked up. It was Harrison. There I was with my hair twisted up into a clamp, no makeup, and my collection of haute couture was on vacation. I could feel my face turning scarlet.

"Well, good morning!" he called out.

"Good morning," I said politely. I stopped working on Mother's net and tied a big loop with string to mark the ending spot. "Mother's not here."

He was coming up the steps and didn't even pause at the news.

"Oh. Well, that's too bad."

Those fiery blue eyes of his were boring a hole through mine, and I was embarrassed for no good reason except that it seemed weird for Mother's boyfriend to be so familiar with me. I did not return his smile.

"I imagine she'll be back soon. Was she expecting you?"

"No. I was just gonna take a ride out to Awendaw and thought you gals might like to come along. I have a friend out there with a big farm, beautiful land—raises pheasant and quail. All organically fed, of course. I thought y'all might like some for your supper."

I hadn't had pheasant or quail in ages and my mouth started to water at the mere mention of them. Against my better judgment, I leaped at the opportunity.

"I'll leave her a note," I said. "I mean, if you don't mind my company without Mother's?"

"I think I can behave myself," he said. He narrowed his eyes and grinned.

"Very funny. I'll get my jacket."

"I'll just wait right here," he said.

I left him standing on the porch and hurried inside. I could feel my stomach flutter and the muscles in my arms cramped and relaxed. I tried to tighten my abdominal muscles as I passed the hall mirror and thought for a second that it made a significant difference, therefore I should do it all the time. Why was I so nervous? It was ridiculous. He was just a big flirt. All men flirted. They did it because they could get away with it and because they thought women reveled in their attention. Okay, I did, but I would have liked it much better if he wasn't my mother's boy toy.

**Mother, Gone for quail and pheas-
ant with Harrison. Back soon. xxoo
Miriam**

I taped the note to the kitchen counter, and as casually as I could manage, I catwalked to Mr. Natural's side. He took a deep breath and I followed him down the steps. He opened my door, I got in, and he closed it. As he walked around the front of his car I thought how nice it was to have a man see that I got into a car safely, or to open a door or hold a chair. I wondered if men in Ohio or Colorado engaged in these traditional kindnesses for the women in their lives. They probably did.

Driving out Highway 17, we talked easily about the day and his friend's farm, and no matter how I tried to steer the conversation in other directions, it eventually returned to me.

"Tell me again why you're living in New York," he said.

"Well, because it's where I've been for all of my adult life. I own a town house in the city, my son lives there, and you know how it is. You become a creature of habit. Besides, I love New York. I have my friends and my volunteer work. I can't imagine where else I could go."

"I understand. I can't imagine myself anywhere else either."

We were quiet for a minute, passing all the
stalls of the sweetgrass basket weavers on
the side of the road.

"Do you see your son often?"

"Oh, I guess once a month or so. He's doing his residency in pediatrics at Columbia
Presbyterian, so he's very busy."

"I see. Married?"

"No. But he has a pretty serious girlfriend
who's also a resident in pediatrics. My other
son is married and lives in California. He
does something with computers that, well,
when he describes it, I get a headache and
can't remember a word he said. He and his
wife have two little children who are very
sweet."

"I know that, but you don't look old enough
to be a grandmother!"

"Are you kidding? I was born old."

"That's what your mother says, too."

"About me or about herself?"

"About you, Mellie. You're way too serious."

Before I could defend myself, he made a
sharp right turn, and if there had not been a

console between us, I might have landed in his lap.

"Almost missed it!"

"Yes, well . . ."

We drove down a very bumpy dirt road and it was all I could do to hang on. The car objected with such a clamor of squeaks and bounces that it was too noisy to talk. Finally, we stopped at a wide gate and he hopped out to push the call button. *Born old? Too serious? Had my mother said these things? Did everyone think that of me? Did he?*

He got back in the car and the gate opened. We drove through slowly and continued for a mile or so down a live-oak-canopied dirt road toward a beautiful house at the end. It wasn't grand like Tara but more like a traditional Lowcountry house—clapboard, red tin roof, huge porches with fancy pickets, rockers and hammocks, brick foundation, dormer windows, and brick chimneys on both ends. If the house was beautiful, the landscaping was breathtaking. Moss streamed from blooming camellias and more live-oak trees. Large azaleas flanked the front steps. Asparagus ferns stood on either side of the front door in blue-and-white ceramic planters. I guessed the main house was probably six thousand square feet. There were other buildings, too—a barn, stables, kennels, and a caretaker's cottage. It was absolutely gorgeous and I was very glad that I had come along.

"Makes you want to start singing old Gullah spirituals, doesn't it?"

"Yeah." I shook my head in amazement. "This is spectacular."

"Yep, that just about sums it up for me, too. This place has been in *Charleston Magazine, Southern Living, Architectural Digest*—you name it. Come on; let's see if Manny is home."

"Manny?"

"Oh, right! I didn't tell you his name. Manny Sinkler. Old banking colleague of mine. He moved here about the same time I did, but as soon as the house was finished, his wife decided she preferred Charlotte. Manny says she's never even spent a night here."

"That's awful. Poor thing. Are they divorced?"

"Now that you ask, I can't seem to remember."

"Well, certain personal habits can take their toll on one's short-term memory."

"Ah. I see. So, that's it." He got out of the

car and came around to open my door. I stood up and he planted himself dangerously close to me. "Listen, if you and I are going to be friends, you're going to have to be slightly less judgmental."

"I don't want to see my mother get involved in a scandal, Harrison. It's that plain and simple."

"I understand."

But he didn't. He stared at me and I could feel by the weight of the air between us that he was annoyed. It was similar to asking people who smoke cigarettes not to blow their smoke in your direction. They would divert their exhale but they were poised to deliver a great speech defending their right to kill themselves and you in the process.

"Now, aren't we here for a reason?" I said.

The front door of the house opened and out stepped Manny Sinkler.

"Hey! Y'all come on in!"

It was the classic Lowcountry greeting and we hollered back, relieved to be spared an argument.

Hey! How're you?

At first glance, Manny seemed like a fellow from the cover of *Field & Stream*—who may or may not have earned his fortune on insider trading? I mean, how did people acquire these fortunes? I guessed his age to be around fifty or so, thinning hair on top, and a bit of gray distinguished his temples. Despite a small paunch, he was boyishly lanky like the perennial tennis or basketball player. He was wearing khakis, loafers with no socks, and a dark V-neck sweater over a white T-shirt. Not that it mattered to me, but he probably had a thousand girlfriends, all of them under forty. All of them experts in erotic delights of the *Kama Sutra,* with a healthy libido and a penchant to demonstrate. Oh, so what? I told myself. Your dancing days are probably over anyway.

We climbed the steps to the porch and Manny waited there to shake my hand, which I thought was very nice. He held the door open to the house and we stepped into the center hall, our eyes adjusting to the low light. On the right was a paneled study, furnished in red-and-gold chintz patterns and lots of framed photographs. On our left was what appeared to be a continuation of the study, as it was decorated in the same colors, but the walls were lined in bookshelves, crammed with old leather-bound volumes. Large club chairs, upholstered in ancient crackled black leather finished with brass nail heads, stood in a semicircle framing the fireplace. A beautiful old English walnut desk stood before the window. It was so inviting, I would not have even minded paying bills or doing taxes in such a lovely spot.

Manny and Harrison were chatting away about the various attributes of hunting dogs when Manny turned to me and asked something about how long was I visiting. I answered something inane like, well, I've been coming here all my life but I'm just down to visit Mother and I'm leaving in a couple of days because I have to get back to my very busy and very important committee assignments in New York. And my bird. Yes, Harry was waiting. Actually, I'm not sure what I said except that my response caused the edges of both men's lips to turn up in an irritating grin, which confirmed to them that I had, in fact, no life. I could feel my scalp break into some annoying moderately sized perspiration episode, and I dismissed it to an overload of testosterone in the air. Not a lack of estrogen.

"I see. Well, come on back in the kitchen," Manny said, "and let me get y'all something to drink."

"Oh, I'm fine," I said. "Well, maybe a glass of water?" Was I just the biggest idiot or what? At first I thought he meant something alcoholic and the fact that I never touched a drop during the day kept me convinced that I was in no danger of an addiction problem. Except after funerals.

"Sure," he said, and kept smiling.

I wanted to kick him in the shin, just a little.

I got over my aggressive thoughts when I saw the massive chef's kitchen slash dining room slash family room combined with the smells coming from the huge, gleaming copper kettles on his stove—the whole scene was beyond any kitchen I had ever seen, except on the Food Network. He reached in the refrigerator and pulled out a bottle of mineral water. May I just add that the said designer refrigerator had pale green beveled-glass doors and the visible contents were arranged like a gourmet deli?

"Harrison? You thirsty there, sir?"

"Sure. I'll get glasses."

This fellow Manny had to be a stockholder in Williams-Sonoma because every blessed pot, pan, knife, cutting board, display of glasses, and rack of plates in his kitchen looked like it came from a catalog spread.

"You cook?" I said. Another pearl of genius fell from my lips.

"Me? Oh, yeah. I love to cook. My repertoire has some limits, but I like to get in here and put stuff together."

A man who cooked was nature's greatest aphrodisiac.

"What's in the pot?" I took the glass of water and said thanks, catching Harrison's eye. He was still grinning and it was beginning to annoy me. But not much, really. It was just that I wasn't accustomed to manly grins and was unpracticed in deciphering them.

"Quail stew. I belong to a supper club at church and once a month we have a sort of potluck get-together. Want to try some? You can tell me if it needs salt or pepper."

"Sure! I mean, I'd be happy to help you." Good grief! Why did I sound like such a pompous ass? But Harrison saved the day.

"Yeah, Manny, put some in this bowl so Mellie and I can make sure it's not poison. You don't want to kill all the Methodists in Mount Pleasant, do you?"

"Heavens, no," he said good-naturedly.

I took one bite and thought, Well, I may never allow Manny to ravish me in the sack—that is to confess that the odds of my seduction were probably thin—but I was getting his recipe for quail stew. It needed pepper.

"So, why don't you come with me?" Manny said.

I looked up in surprise, wondering whom he meant and what he meant. I must have appeared to be lost in another world because he repeated himself.

"To dinner? At my church? You, me, and about one hundred good God-fearing folk?"

"Great idea," Harrison said. "I wanted to get Miss Josie out of the house—maybe take her to the movies tonight. It's all I can do to get her over the causeway and this would be a perfect excuse. That is, if Mellie wants to go with you?"

I thought about Mother always on the island, seldom going downtown, Harrison's sensitivity to recognize it, and then about how long it had been since I had a bona fide date, and took the plunge.

"Sure. Why not?"

What on earth would I wear?

Chapter Eight

IN THE DARK

I said good night to Manny with a bear hug that revealed certain attributes of his, and bumbling with embarrassment and excitement, I climbed the steps. He had smelled the wafting aroma of pot, too. We looked at each other, shook our heads, and he said, I'll call you tomorrow. I thanked him, said fine, that would be nice, and I scribbled down my cell number on an old receipt from my purse. I didn't know if this fool was going to go for a kiss or what, so I left him at the bottom of the steps on the turn of my heel. But there had been a definite connection, just as there had been with Harrison, and the thought crossed my mind again that I might have been a little bit depraved.

I tried to remember the last sexual episode I had and it had to have been three years, if you counted those including a partner. The first chance for anything in ages presented itself and I couldn't get out of there fast enough. When I was a girl, there was only Charles who made it to home plate, as the young people say. And that was after he plunked a two-carat diamond ring on my eighteen-year-old finger and set a date. To be truthful, I didn't ever think much of the whole mess. Sex, that is. It was hardly ever worth the shower. Hmm, I thought, *that* could be a clue to why Charles opted out of monogamy. Anyway, I knew that if Manny came back around when I was in town, eventually, a sexual opportunity would *arise* and I would have to decide.

"All right, children!" I said to Mother and Harrison. "The grown-up is home!"

They laughed, and stuffed shirt/blouse that I may have been, I laughed, too. I kissed my mother on the top of her head and gave Harrison a little punch in the arm. Wasn't I fast becoming Miss Mellie Lighthearted?

"I'm going to bed, you bad kids," I said. "It's a school night." And then I grabbed some paper and began my first journal since high school, when I filled pages upon volumes with skin problems, dreamy-boy crushes, and girl gossip. Now it would probably be collagen instead of acne, men instead of boys, and a pot-smoking mother—which I would perhaps mention in code in case my diaries were subpoenaed in the event of a bust.

Dear Diary,
You won't believe . . .

I couldn't sleep, and attired in that fetching terry-cloth robe, I decided to sneak down to the front porch and take my chances that the goat and chickens wouldn't wail with mocking laughter when they saw me. I had heard Harrison leave, so no problem there.

The moon was full, the night was clear, and I could hear the ocean in the distance on the other side of the island. I heard footsteps and looked up to see Mother taking the rocker next to me. She pulled her jacket around herself a little tighter to keep warm against the damp.

"We've got enough rocking chairs to open a chain of Cracker Barrels," she said with a smile.

"That we do," I said. We were quiet for a few minutes and then I said, "Look at the moon, Miss Josephine. That old man is grinning down at us."

Strange as it may seem, there was an elderly man's hook-nosed profile covering the surface of the moon, cutting us a sly look from his left eye and smiling some cosmic all-knowing smile.

"Hmmph," she said. "He looks like your father used to look when he would get away with a little murder."

"I still miss him, you know?" I said. "I can't help but wonder what he would think to see us now."

"I think about him all the time. He'd be thrilled to see you and horrified to see my farm here."

"You think so?"

"Yep. He would have hated this. But, so what? It's my house now. Sometimes I think I can see him right out of the corner of my eye when I turn quickly."

"Really?"

"Absolutely. It's like he's been standing

there watching me and I catch him. Or some-time when I dream about him, I can smell him. Even after I wake up, I can still smell him. He was a wonderful man. An acquisitive workaholic, yes, and he was too concerned with other people's opinions, and yes, he was highly judgmental and shallow about appear-ances and so forth—"

"Mother! That's terrible!"

"What?"

"Daddy's dead, for heaven's sake. You're not supposed to speak ill of the dead. You know that. It's in frightfully bad taste."

"Well, excuse me, Emily Post. I lived under his thumb for enough years to say what I think to my only child on my own porch in the middle of the night. It's not like I took out an ad in the *Charlotte Observer* thanking God for giving him a fatal heart attack!"

"Which you think would have been justi-fied?" I couldn't help but giggle, and when she heard me she chuckled, too.

"Listen, Little Miss Mellie. There's love and there's marriage, and after some time, they are usually two different things. We were married forever. When we were young and the pheromones were flying like mad, we were as passionately in love as any couple you will ever meet. But after so many years, you get over your girlish expectations and settle yourself into what you're willing to give each other. You honor your vows, to the greatest extent possible. And you learn to compromise."

"A business deal? You make it sound like a business deal. Like you got gypped. Do you think you got gypped?"

Mother gave a great laugh at that, and in the dim light I could see her shaking her head and smiling. "Heavens, no! Oh my! No, no. I never got gypped. I loved your daddy. But, honey? He was not an easy man to live with. Did I get to do everything I wanted with my life? Who does?" She looked away wistfully and repeated, "Who does?"

"What would you have done that you haven't?"

"I don't know . . ." After a long pause she said, "Well, you might think this is crazy but I definitely would have learned the tango or traveled more or maybe I would have studied astronomy."

"I can see you in a tango costume, Miss Josie. You would've been red-hot."

"Would've been . . . isn't that the awful part?"

We were quiet again. Heaven knew that I had certainly never done with my life what I had wanted to do. I had never even had the chance to think about it. And Mother's *would've been* comment was like a knife in my heart. So many years had passed for her, for both of us really, that there was a long list of things she would never do and a shorter list of things I would probably never do either. It was awful to admit certain dreams would never be realized.

"But I have you, Miriam Elizabeth. I'm oh so very grateful for that."

"Do you mean that?"

"Yes, I mean it with all my heart. I would hate to come to the end of my life all alone. And knowing you has made it so much richer."

The hour was growing late, but perhaps because my heart and my hormones had been given a stir, I wasn't sleepy. It seemed to me that Mother wasn't particularly fatigued either. We continued to rock as the thin clouds followed the moon across the sky. In a rare moment of unsolicited affection, I reached over and put my hand on top of hers. Even in the darkness, I noticed that her knuckles were enlarged. Her hand seemed awfully thin and felt cold to me. For the first time in years, I thought about the fact that in all likelihood she would precede me in death. I couldn't bear the thought of it. There were too many issues to settle, and besides, we hadn't done enough living together.

"Are you listening to me?" she said.

"I'm sorry. My mind wandered. What did I miss?"

"I said, how was your date with Harrison's friend? That Manny fellow. Was he nice?"

"Oh, well, it wasn't exactly a date. He belongs to a church out on Highway 17 North, and we brought a quail stew he made as part of a huge covered-dish dinner. Lots of people were there—probably a hundred? Anyway, we didn't talk much because we were pretty busy serving plates. I worked in the buffet line with him."

"Harrison brought me some. It was delicious. But this man took you out to dinner and put you to work? I'll tell you, this is some world!"

"Oh no, no. It wasn't like that. Manny's a really nice man—a great cook, for sure. Did y'all go to the movies?"

"No. Just for ice cream. And? Is there chemistry?"

"Mother? You drink a little wine and everyone seems more attractive, don't they?"

"I imagine so. Are you going to see him again?"

"He said he would call but who knows? Next visit, maybe." I sighed and said, "Oh, me! I almost hate to go back to New York tomorrow." I didn't tell her or ask her if she knew whether Manny might or might not still be married. I saw no reason for extreme disclosure.

"I thought you were staying another day . . ."

"Couldn't get the flight, but I'll be back. This is so pleasant. Gosh. There's something so bohemian about being outside at this hour, don't you think?"

"Bohemian? What on earth do you mean?"

"Well, you know . . . the world around us is asleep and we're out here stealing the night. I haven't been up this late in years!"

"You have a little courtyard, Miriam. Don't you ever go outside at night to look at the moon? Wish on the stars?"

"Are you kidding? Somebody might hop over the wall and get me!"

Even in the blue light of deep night, I could

see that Mother was incredulous. Her eyes were narrowed in such a way that she need not have said one word and she didn't. Her face said, Why are you living like a prisoner, Miriam? A paranoid. But I didn't feel like I was living like a prisoner. I was living the life, or the crumbs of the life, that Charles and I had built. Granted, the road I walked was pot-holed with sadness, but it was also rather satisfying at times. Besides, who didn't have sadness? And fears?

Then Mother dropped the bomb.

"Tell me about my grandsons, Miss Mellie. What's going on with them?"

I cleared my throat and thought for a min-ute. "Well, you know how it is. Charlie's busy learning to save mankind from disease. Dan and Nan have their lives with their little ones. God, I swear, California just seems like an-other country sometimes."

"Why don't you go and visit them? I mean, it's just a plane ride."

"What? Whose side are you on, Miss Jo-sephine? Aren't the children supposed to come to the mother? I mean, when my boys were little, did you ever spend Christmas in New York with us? Noooo. You insisted that we come to Charleston, remember?"

"What are you talking about? I never insisted on anything of the kind."

"You would always say, 'Oh, why don't we have Christmas together in our home? I just want to see my family together here one more time . . .' What was I supposed to say?"

"I don't know. But I was always glad you came. So was your father. It was so nice to have the delightful squeals of little boys on Christmas morning as they found their Santa. I used to make them mountains of silver-dollar pancakes. I can smell the warm maple syrup. Can't you?"

"Not quite. I mean, coming to Charleston was the kind of thing that couldn't please everyone. Anyway, I think children should have their holidays in their own homes. If I had it to do over again—"

"What possible difference would it make?"

I tried to think of the right words before I answered her and decided to just put my opinion out there on the table for her to hack to death.

"Look, Mother, this may sound a little crazy, but here it is. Maybe the more memories children have in their own home on holidays, the harder it is to break family ties later on, do you know what I mean?"

"Do you mean to say that when they look back in later years they don't see you as the matriarch? That they see me?"

"Yes, making it that much easier to walk away from me. And to not care."

"Hogwash. Being home with us at Christmas and Thanksgiving and Easter gave you a chance to be a child again. Did you think about that?"

"But I never wanted to be a child, Mother. You know that. I hated being a child."

"Miriam?"

"Yes?"

"That is the most pathetic explanation I have ever heard for why your children aren't as attentive as you would like them to be. Seriously. It's pathetic. And if you think children should celebrate holidays in their own homes, why don't you practice what you preach? Go to California."

"I'm not comfortable doing that."

"Why not?"

"They've never asked me to come."

"Oh, mol-asses! Since when do you need an invitation to visit your own children?"

"Well, Nan's a little stiff."

"Stiff? Holy moly, Miriam Elizabeth Swanson, if *you're* calling her stiff, she must be in rigor mortis!"

"Oh, thanks. Summers here were good, though. Maybe I could coax them to come here for a visit. Probably not." Was I really blaming Nan? And my mother?

"I'm having none of this," she said.

She was provoked. I had caused it but it was time to have my say. Gently. Politely.

"Don't be angry with me," I said, taking small steps into the quagmire.

"Angry? I'm not angry in the least. Like my grandmother used to say, that's all a lot of stuff and nonsense. Stuff and nonsense."

The Queen of Denial had spoken again. The princess sang the chorus.

"Well, it just seems bizarre that the life you chose for me is the one you ultimately threw away."

"What do you mean *chose for you*? You chose your own life."

All my old anger began to rise like the rolling boil of custard left on a high flame.

"Mother? You can't possibly believe what you are saying."

"I most assuredly do!"

I could feel my breath quickening and glanced at my wristwatch. The hour had passed to talk about these things—too late in the night and too late in the game to change them.

"Are you going to answer me?"

"No, ma'am, I'm not. It's almost morning."

"Miriam? I want an answer from you and I want it now. I have been listening to you whine and complain since the day Charles left, and I will not go to sleep having you believe I am the reason for your troubles. You, my dear daughter, are the cause of your own troubles. Not me."

That was a damn lie. In fact it was the most damnable lie to ever fall from her lips. But I wasn't going to have an argument with my mother at that hour over something I couldn't change. She could say whatever she wanted to say. I knew the truth.

"Well, everything is perspective; isn't it, Mother?"

"Yes, it is, and the way I see it, you could have changed your life a thousand times and you didn't do it."

"Change my life? And do what? Go become a surgeon? A mathematician? A rocket scientist? Aren't you the one who told me I would be a smart cookie to drop out of college to marry Charles?"

"Let's try to tell things as they were, all right? You were very anxious to marry Charles and be a grown woman with your own house. You couldn't wait to think of yourself as an adult . . ."

"Yes, but—"

"When you were nothing of the sort. And by your own admission, you didn't love to study. Your father said that forcing you to stay in college was just throwing good money after bad and—"

"He said that? He actually used *those* words?"

"Honey? He's been dead for a long time. I don't remember his exact words . . ."

"Excuse me, Mother, but aren't you the one who just said we should try to recount the past as it actually was?"

"Yes, I did. Okay. I apologize. Are you looking for a fight?"

"Absolutely not, but I think it's important for you to realize certain facts."

"Such as?"

"Such as, you had an enormous influence on me. I am your only child. You got married young? You pushed me into marrying young.

You did tons of volunteer work to secure your family's position? So did I when you pushed me. I joined every committee I could instead of going to NYU or something."

"I never told you not to finish your degree."

"Yeah, sure. You would have lectured me, saying that it took away from the time I should be spending with the boys and Charles. And you know what? I think you would have been jealous if I had gone on to get, God forbid, a degree in anything except home economics."

"That's absurd."

"No, it's not. I followed in your footsteps as closely as I could, and what did I get? Two apathetic sons who won't give me the right time of day. A husband who mortified me in front of every person I know. A gay man for a meaningful other and a tenant who's a whore. And no career. Nothing to fall back on except my back."

"But Kevin is a dear man."

"Don't be condescending, but yes, he is. Thank God for Kevin. But it's not much, is it?"

"I never had a career and I managed to stay happy, you know."

"But Daddy didn't deceive you the way

Charles did me. Daddy didn't have two other children on the other side of Charleston as Charles did. And Daddy didn't leave you nearly destitute as I was left."

"And it's all my responsibility? My fault? Tell me how that's so."

"Because I did every single thing that I thought you wanted me to do and it all blew up in my face."

"You need to get over it, Miriam. I never told you that your life had to be a Xerox copy of mine."

"Maybe not, but it was surely very strongly implied. Just as you've been implying for months now that my life in New York is meaningless. You see? Now that you've become a hippie, I should, too? Well, I'm not doing it, Mother."

"You know what, Miriam? Your anger is as misplaced now as my supposed bossiness may have been then. But I can't believe you would even think such a thing . . ."

You didn't know her then, when I was a younger woman. I did. She wasn't merely bossy; she was insistent. When I was on the threshold of marriage, she used every manipulative trick and maneuver she knew to mold me as her junior.

Darling, you have to have linen finger-tip towels for the guest powder room.

Who's going to iron them?

Hire someone. Miriam, watch. Here's how we make "Cinderella's Slipper." Isn't this a wonderful napkin fold?

Wonderful.

And this one's called the "Artichoke"! Perfect for a breadbasket!

I had to take lessons in flower arranging, learn to make a pound cake and biscuits from scratch, to do needlepoint and crewelwork, and perhaps most important, how to write a sincere thank-you note. I didn't believe she had malicious intent and all of these skills bore merit. But they were jammed down my throat like a religious fundamentalist doctrine and they gave me only a heightened sense of her, not of myself.

What if I had strung Charles along, finished college and gone on to study international finance or electrical engineering? I think she was afraid to let me live my own life. I might have become something or someone she didn't recognize and then what? Who would she be? Her tutorial took place while I was still malleable. I was always afraid that I wouldn't do as well as she had or that I wouldn't live up to her expectations. And she knew it.

It was all deep in the past, and oddly, she seemed not to care any longer. Maybe it was her advancing years. Maybe she thought her project with me had failed. Or perhaps there was another reason. Maybe she had mellowed or forgotten and just plainly did not understand my resentment.

That was all I could think about the next morning as the plane ascended high above the Lowcountry. I watched the blue-and-green shoreline and the curlicues of inlets and streams, tracing them with my fingertip against the window, missing them before they passed from my sight.

Soon we were suspended over fields upon fields of the thick white mounds of endless clouds. Soon I would be back on Sixty-first Street talking to Harry, having a cocktail with Kevin, telling him about Manny, who had not called, and hearing about Liz. Over the next few days I would organize my address lists for the invitations committee, paste a smile on my face, and deal with Agnes Willis. I thought I knew what was waiting for me. I could not have been more wrong.

Chapter Nine

THE BIG SPILL

Dear Mrs. Willis,
Enclosed please find my address list
for the spring gala invitations. I look
forward to participating on the com-
mittee and to seeing you again.
Cordially,
Miriam Elizabeth Swanson

The tone of my note to her was terse. So what? Let her figure that out, as if she cared anyway. At least I got it in the mail as soon as I got back to New York.

Returning to New York from the Eden that is the Lowcountry of South Carolina was always a considerable shock to the nervous system. The arrival hallways of LaGuardia Airport were too small for the masses of humanity who pushed their way through them. Your bags *did* look like everyone else's, and you were right to think that the woman who bumped against you in the taxi line might be an accomplice to the man who's trying to pick your pocketbook.

Knowing these things makes it a little easier to confidently maneuver the obstacle course that is life in the big city, but these are not the details you savor. So you put on your street face, hold your purse firmly under your arm, keep your eyes open, and try not to get in the taxi with the Stanland terrorist schizophrenic who's off his meds. The reorientation continues in a cab with no shock absorbers over the bridges, down the FDR Drive, and somehow, the unseen but irresistible lure of living in Manhattan sinks its hook squarely in your heart. It always took me by surprise.

Every minute of the day and night, lights are on, things are happening, people are dying, being born, being cured. Deals are being cut, careers are made and ruined, products are launched and discontinued, beauty is lauded in every sector, and people are falling in love. Tap shoes at Radio City and on Broadway are lifting the hearts of thousands of patrons with each performance. Over at Lincoln Center, ballet dancers are in flight, sopranos are hitting impossible notes, while the genius Rembrandt and Monet wait in their glory in the museums. There are rolling racks of clothes propelling across Thirty-eighth Street, dirty water dogs and pretzels are being consumed by the ton, and at night, in orchestra seats at Carnegie Hall, old men are sleeping off the wine they drank with dinner, completely missing the first act of a visiting symphony's interpretation of the work of Mahler or Stravinsky.

By the time you pay your cab fare and open the front door of your house, you feel rich, blessed, and somehow a little smarter than the rest of the population because you own a piece of the rock. And strangely, the place—any place—you left behind seems less appealing than it was the day before when you sang its glories. The Big Apple was my adrenaline and I was thrilled to be back.

In contrast to that, I had only been gone for a few days, but it felt like a week. I was relaxed and well rested, ready to take on Liz Harper and Agnes Willis. Harry was in his cage and got excited when he saw me come in.

"Hello, sweetheart!" I said to him, and looked inside the refrigerator to see if there were a few grapes for him. "I missed you!"

"Good morning!" he said.

I opened his door, he climbed to the top of his cage, and I fed him the fruit. As he stood, his head twitched this way and that as though he wanted to be sure it was me. Then he wagged his red-feathered tail and stretched his wings like an archangel.

"I'm glad to see you, too," I said.

"Charles is a horse's ass."

"You know it, bubba."

The mail from the past few days was neatly stacked on my kitchen counter and my message light was blinking, which I ignored. It was only three-thirty in the afternoon and already getting dark. I switched on every full-spectrum light in the house as I walked to my bedroom rolling my luggage, gearing myself up for the unpleasant task of unpacking. I was returning lighter, since I had left my sneakers under Mother's house and my flannel-lined baggy jeans in a heap on the floor of the closet along with my old cardigan.

As I put away my toilet articles, I caught a

glance of myself in the mirror. My hair was unkempt and my face was bare. I started to laugh, knowing this wild-girl look would never get any traction in the fully coiffed world to which I had returned.

After an application of cosmetic war paint and a quick toss of dirty clothes into the washer, I decided to go to the grocery store. I rebundled to face the elements, putting on my camel-colored coat with a wide brown leather belt. I stuffed my crazy hair in my favorite crocheted hat, trimmed with dyed brown fox, and wrapped my neck with a man's brown cashmere scarf that someone had left at my house. I put my cell and bank card in my pocket with my keys and left the house.

It was in the low thirties outside, windy and damp. Because I had foolishly worn a skirt with low-heeled pumps, the stiff breeze stung my legs every time I crossed a block. I took my rolling cart as I needed paper towels and other bulky and heavy things, and congratulated myself for thriftiness in saving a delivery fee, as though ten dollars more in my pocket would change my life. I was fighting my way up Third Avenue and caught a side view of myself in a shop window. I was slouching again and reminded myself that standing up straight took off years and pounds. Then I had a sudden urge to call my mother to take my mind off the fact that I was freezing. I pulled out my cell phone and dialed.

She answered right away.

"Mother?"

"Miriam? Is that you?"

"Yes. I, uh, just wanted to let you know that I got home all right."

"Well, praise the Lord! You sound out of breath. Where are you?"

"Walking up the street on the way to food-shop."

"Food-shop. What an odd term. How's the weather? It's beautiful here."

I noticed a handsome, well-dressed older man next to me at the corner of Sixty-fourth Street and knew instinctively he was eavesdropping on my conversation.

"It's beautiful here, too," I lied, and looked him in the face. "The sun's shining and the birds are singing—it's a gorgeous afternoon."

He smiled and shook his head. The light changed and we crossed the street along with ten or so others. I looked around a minute later and he was gone. But that was how it was in the city. You could make a connection in a split second, and in the next, the relationship was over, having served its purpose in letting you know you were not alone on the planet.

"Well, that's fine, sweetheart. It sure was good to see you."

"I loved being with you, too, Mother. Good for the soul. You know, someday, you're going to have to teach me how to cook."

She laughed a little and I could feel her cheerfulness actually lift me a little.

"Well, you'd better hurry up," she said. "I'm not going to last forever, you know."

"And, Mother, I'm sorry about the unpleasant words we had on the porch last night. It's just that sometimes I feel like my life has never been my own, you know?"

I could hear her sigh deeply and then she said, "Yes, but it is now, Mellie, and if it's not, you had better take control and grab all the happiness you can before it's too late."

I knew she was right and told her so. We talked a little more and then hung up, but not before I asked her to thank Harrison for introducing me to Manny Sinkler and to ask Harrison to tell Manny that I had enjoyed meeting him.

"Just ask him to pass it along to him, would you?"

"Sure."

"Manny was pleasant and I didn't get the chance to thank him for a nice evening."

"Yes, you did say that."

"He's got a gorgeous house, Mother. Really gorgeous."

"Aha! And could you see yourself living there? Hmm?"

"What? Me? Oh! Oh, no! Nothing like that. I was just thinking that if Harrison wanted to take you out there, you should go and see it. He's got a small fortune in copper pots."

She was quiet and I could almost hear her thinking that if I was unmotivated by romance, perhaps I was a gold digger.

"Or don't tell him anything," I said. "It doesn't really matter."

"We'll see. If my memory holds up, I'll pass along the message."

Sometimes Miss Josephine could be exasperating, too.

I was nosing around the butcher's department debating the merits of free-range chicken versus milk-fed veal versus organically raised lamb. I was in the mood for stew. Ever since I'd eaten Manny Sinkler's stew, it was all I could think about. Not the man but the food, which told me something about my state of mind. What had I been thinking anyway? He lived a thousand miles away, was still married to some degree, and, I reminded myself for the tenth time, he had not called, although it had only been twenty-four hours.

I decided on dark-meat chicken, thinking it was the closest thing to quail that I would find without spending a fortune on specialty fowl from some couture purveyor of exotic food. I also noted that what New Yorkers thought was rare and exotic—quail, wild turkey, pheasant, shrimp, crab, and on and on—flew or swam all over the Lowcountry and you could have all you could catch for the small cost of a hunting or fishing license. What a world, I thought.

I was anxious to get dinner started and opened my door, lugging the bulging cart behind me. It was a bit of a space problem to close the front door without dinging the walls, but I managed to get into my apartment with everything intact. I dropped my coat, hat, and gloves on the chair by the fireplace and then collapsed on the couch when I realized I had not seen that day's mail. I didn't feel like getting up and hanging my coat and unpacking my groceries, only to mess up the kitchen making a stew that might or might not turn out tasting like Manny's quail concoction. And what if Kevin was out? What if I had to eat it alone? Was I going to feed Liz? No, I was not going to feed Liz. Then it dawned on me that if I was missing the mail, it was probably in her apartment and I became irate at the thought of it. Maybe it would reappear in the hall as soon as she realized I was home. Patience, Mellie, I told myself, was a virtue.

It crossed my mind to call Manny and ask him how he seasoned his stew; then I decided against it. I would cook first and worry about the taste later. Meanwhile, I could hear Liz overhead clomping around in what sounded like size 16 army boots on a three-hundred-pound Marine. Surely she had some modicum of understanding about acoustics. I had thought about it, and the more I considered it, the more I was convinced I had leased the apartment to the wrong person. When the moment arrived I was going to set things straight between us.

I pushed myself up from the sofa and pulled the groceries into the kitchen, deciding to start dinner. Everything was put away and onions sizzled in a small amount of bacon fat I had combined with canola oil. My kitchen smelled good and I knew the aromas would work like a lasso on Kevin's neck the minute he stepped through the door. At least I hoped so. I dropped some chopped celery in the pot and was digging around for the bottle of dried bay leaf when I remembered I had used the last one in a soup several weeks ago. My choices then were to go back out in the cold, borrow some from Kevin when he got home, take the odd chance that Liz had some, although I suspected she had never heard of it, or do without it.

I turned off the stove, went up the stairs, and knocked on her door.

Liz opened it with my mail in her hands.

"What are you doing with my mail?" I said with no expression. My voice was annoyed and I didn't care.

"Oh! I just scooped it all up from the floor and brought it up here to sort and I was just about to bring it back to you when you knocked on the door . . ."

"Please do not touch my mail."

"Mrs. Swanson? Are you aggravated with me?"

"Do you have any bay leaf?"

"I was just trying to do you a favor. I wasn't

going to take your catalogs. What's bay leaf? Christmas candles?"

As I suspected, this nitwit did not even know what a bay leaf was.

"Holiday candles are indeed available with the scent of bay leaf, but I am looking for the real thing to flavor a stew I am making."

"Mrs. Swanson? You seem really aggravated."

She handed me the mail and I decided to reveal the source of my annoyance.

"Liz? May I come in for a moment?"

"Of course! Would you like some tea?"

"No, thank you. I can only stay for a few minutes."

I looked around her apartment and it looked more like a college coed's furnishings than an adult's. I mean, she had a mug rack and a box of pizza on the kitchen counter and a Lava lamp in the living room. Everything was tidy enough but Kevin had been correct as usual—all this stuff could've been bought at a yard sale or found on the curb. She sat on the sofa and it only seemed right that I sit as well, so I perched on the edge of a slip-covered armchair.

"Liz . . ."

"Gosh, Mrs. Swanson, what could I have

done?" She was getting upset, and her big blue eyes were becoming watery and red. She probably thought her check had bounced and that I was throwing her out.

"Look, Liz . . ." I started again, and then became very nervous. I mean, wasn't one of my problems that I thought I was in charge of the world?

"Yes, ma'am?"

"Um, you need a rug. Every time you walk across the floor in shoes it rattles the plates in my kitchen."

"A rug? That's it?"

"Actually, you need two rugs. One for the living room and something that particularly muffles sound for the bedroom. Maybe wall-to-wall. With extra padding."

She looked at me for a moment and then it dawned on her that I could hear every spring squeak and worse. She blushed and smiled sheepishly.

"Gosh, I'm sorry, Mrs. Swanson. How terrible for you! I wondered why you were playing your music so loud."

"Well, now you know." I was only partially relieved, but there was the other half of the story to tell. And I had a lump in my throat the size of a walnut. "Now, you are a young

woman and what you do is your business,
but I think you need to know that I *know* Truman Willis."

"Truman? How do you know Truman?"

"He's the *husband* of one of my close
friends."

There. It was said. Her eyes expanded so
wide that it seemed physically impossible
that someone without an ocular disorder
could perform such a feat without disaster.

"No! No way!"

"Yes. Way. He is married to Agnes Willis
and we volunteer at the museum together all
the time. I have known them for twenty years.
When Charles was my husband we sat together at all the benefits. Apparently, he has
no idea this is my house."

"Or he doesn't care. Ohmagawd! That
creep! Another married creep!"

"You didn't know?"

"No! How can men just lie like that? What's
the matter with them?"

"Honey, the divorce courts are filled with
them. Look what Charles did to me?"

"Same thing?"

"Worse. He had children with her."

"Jesus!"

"Taking the Lord's name in vain won't change the male species, you know."

"Sorry. It's just that—"

"Look, let me just say this and get it off my chest. I'm not thrilled to have a tenant who sleeps with married men under my own roof. That precise act is what brought me to the point of renting out the rooms that used to house my family." I stood and said, "I've got a chicken waiting for me that needs attention."

"I understand. It won't happen again. Sorry about the mail."

"Sorry about Truman," I said, and left. "In the future, just take yours and pile the rest of it on the table." She didn't know about Truman's marital status? My big fat fanny!

"No problem," she said, "and I'll see about rugs tomorrow."

I went down the stairs, leaving her alone with a cold pizza. Poor me, I thought as the hour became late and I ate alone with no knowledge of Kevin's whereabouts. "Poor all of us," I said out loud as I covered Harry's cage with a sheet.

"Good night," he said.

"Good night, sweetheart," I said, and wondered if she would continue to see Truman anyway. That would tell me a lot about her.

The morning came cold and clear and I rushed around gathering additional address lists from prior events. I was determined to do such a wonderful job on the invitations committee that everyone would surely notice. Maybe I would make a new friend. I mean, who knew? Anything was possible!

I walked over to Park Avenue, and for the life of me, I couldn't get an uptown cab. I walked over to Madison and found someone getting out of one, so I hopped in. Normally I would have taken the Madison Avenue bus, but I felt like treating myself to a private car.

"Fifth Avenue and Eighty-second, please," I said.

No response, which suited me fine. And inside of the proverbial *city minute* I wondered why I had thought a cab ride would be such a treat. This lunatic jerked the car this way and that and it was absolutely nauseating. I ate a mint.

Soon I was showing my volunteer ID to the security guard and taking the elevator down to the bowels of the museum and the volunteer room. When I opened the door it was madness inside. About forty women, many of whom I knew casually, were chatting, drinking coffee, and eating bagels or Danishes, carrying boxes from one side of the room to another, talking on cell phones and so on, and all of them were dressed like they were having lunch later on at La Grenouille.

Long folding tables were placed all around the room in a large horseshoe. Boxes of the invitations were on one table, the response cards and envelopes were on another table, and the directions were on a third. The Mount Fuji of outside envelopes were given by the box to individuals charged with the task of writing out perfectly spelled names and double-checked addresses. I was to be one of the chosen.

The rest of the volunteers walked in circles, from table to table, box to box, collecting and collating the inserts in appropriate little stacks to slip in the outside envelope. When they were sealed and stamped, another team of efficient women arranged them alphabetically by zip code in stacking baskets provided by the post office.

"Oh, Miriam! I'm so glad you're here! Why don't you sit by Diane over there?"

It was Laura Routentout, a young woman whom I privately called Rotten Tooth, as her bulimia resulted in frequent replacements to the caps of her teeth.

"Oh! Of course, Laura! How are you?"

"Fine! Good! You know . . . just hoping we don't have too many duplicates and too many errors. The usual. Can you stick around and help me take the bins to the post office?"

"Why, sure . . ." I said, and felt a tap on my shoulder.

"Darling, ladies don't schlep," said Agnes Willis, who popped up from nowhere. "We simply call the maintenance men to bring a flatbed dolly, roll them out to the loading docks, and the post office will pick up. Two phone calls and we're all set."

"Oh," Laura said, and turned scarlet.

Agnes smiled a prim little tight smile at me and said, "New girl," referring to Laura. "Her husband's firm endowed the Impressionist speaker's series for the museum."

"How wonderful," I said, smiling, and wished she would drop dead for constantly reaffirming my downward spiral.

We worked through the morning, gobbling down half of an overstuffed turkey sandwich and countless cups of coffee and tea, and we continued into the afternoon. By four o'clock I was nearly cross-eyed from the scrutiny it took to make sure I didn't make any errors. I felt like an eighteenth-century schoolgirl, painstakingly working with a quill and inkwell to avoid blots of ink or errors of any kind. Call me Elsie Dinsmore, the poor little wretch of my childhood reading. But we all consoled ourselves with the rewards of our efforts. Thousands of invitations were ready to mail.

Some of the women were picking up the sandwich trays, and Diane and I decided to take the coffee urns down to the kitchen to help out. We unplugged them and felt their sides—still warm but not dangerously hot.

"Let's go," I said.

Diane went in front of me, and as she opened the door, someone else pushed against it from the other side. It was Agnes Willis. Diane backed into me and regained her balance. But I was midstep, lost my footing, and went flying like something from an Abbott and Costello slapstick routine. The entire contents of my urn, the muddy coffee and the soggy nasty grinds, spread themselves in drips and clods over three huge bins of sealed, stamped, and hand-addressed envelopes.

The room became silent for the first time that day and then the gasping started.

Oh no! The invitations! What happened? Oh no!

With a quick glance from where I was lying across the center of the floor, I could see that more than half the invitations were completely ruined.

"Get up, Miriam."

I looked up to see Agnes Willis standing over me. I struggled to my knees. My stockings were ripped, my knees were bleeding, and my reading glasses were swung around, dangling down the center of my back. Needless to say, I was mortified right down to my DNA. Finally, Diane offered me her hand and I got up to my feet.

"You stupid clumsy sow," Agnes Willis hissed in my face. "Just get out."

The room inhaled a collective gasp and I knew they waited to see what I would say in response.

I looked at her squarely and so many things went through my mind. Yes, I was deeply embarrassed, but Agnes had broken the golden rule of the volunteer world and of the polite world at large—that you never humiliate anyone, especially someone less fortunate. I had her securely in my crosshairs.

"Agnes?"

I crooked my finger at her face and motioned for her to move closer so I could whisper my response. For a split second she hesitated, probably unsure that I might or might not deliver the well-deserved slap across her wizened face. Finally, she moved in and so did every other ear in the room.

"What?"

I looked her straight in the eyes and decided against whispering. "Your husband is screwing the ever-loving daylights out of my beautiful, blond *young* tenant."

"What! How?"

Large eyes seemed to be a popular phenomenon.

I removed my security ID from around my neck, held it between my two fingers, and let it drop to her feet. "How?" I said, threw my tote bag over my shoulder, and held the door open for myself. "With enthusiasm, Agnes. With great enthusiasm."

Chapter Ten

RUFFLED FEATHERS AND WORSE

Hot angry tears of bitterness drenched my cheeks. I couldn't make them stop. I ambled home from the museum in a state of disbelief, literally stumbling here and there on cracks in the sidewalk and accidentally bumping into people. The full force of the degradation, the terrible embarrassment I had just experienced, continued to send shock waves through me. I relived it over and over. I didn't know what to do at first—where to go, whom to call—I just wanted to run, run away and never see any of them again. The only place I had to run and hide was Sixty-first Street. There was no girlfriend to call, no husband

who would say there, there, it's all going to
be all right, that those women were a sorry
lot of pretentious eating disorders who
thought they were important because of their
husbands' careers and bank accounts. That
they were nothing, that I was someone worthy of consolation. And I had not heard from
Manny since my return, not that I would have
told him this story anyway.

It was so deeply disappointing that no one
had come to my aid besides Diane, who had
helped me up from the floor. But she had her
own agenda. She had probably moved to
help me get up because in that act, her hu-
manitarian stock would rise with some of the
others who thought Agnes Willis was the
epitome of every evil thing that encompassed
the reputation of the imperious society matron. Her kindness had nothing to do with any
loyalty to me. But, I thought, if my misstep
could serve as a catalyst to ignite a backlash
against the Agnes Willises of the world, it was
the only redemption in the entire debacle.

I went over it again. It was so hard to believe that not one woman there had taken a
moment to reassure me that it was just an
accident, that it could've happened to anyone, or was I all right. The bitter truth began

to sink in through my thick skull. That no one cared. It was a terrible sin that they considered themselves ladies when they showed so little compassion to the world. And none at all to me.

That one unfortunate moment, that one accidental flight across the room, had no doubt ended twenty years of hard work at no pay, with no recognition, no wooden plaque with VOLUNTEER OF THE YEAR engraved on a little brass plate, no anything but a legacy of horrible embarrassment. I would go down in infamy as the volunteer who ruined thousands of invitations and hours and hours of work. I knew I would certainly be the laughingstock of the year over so many dinner tables that night, and after that, the story would be retold all over Manhattan at every volunteer organization for years. No one would ever enjoy a cup of coffee or tea during an invitations committee meeting for the rest of recorded time. People would say, "You can thank Miriam Swanson for that." Botched paperwork would be referred to as "a Miriam."

I wandered more than walked the entire way down Fifth and then Madison avenues crying all alone. I passed so many people, hundreds, maybe thousands, and no one said, "Hey, lady, are you all right?" I cried for my embarrassment and with regret over the accident and for the revulsion it had un-leashed in Agnes Willis. What had she called me? A sow? How hateful! What a horrible woman she was.

But why had I told her about her husband? I must have been insane! Two wrongs were worse than one and I had stooped to her level. I regretted it.

I called Kevin's cell but he wasn't picking up. I left him two frantic messages. I didn't know what to do with myself. It was six. I had no appetite. When I finally got home, my apartment had never seemed so empty or so shabby. I knew that I had done a terrible thing to Agnes Willis. But she had done an even worse thing to me. I could never show my face at the museum again.

"It was a terrible day," I said to Harry, and put a cut-up tomato in the food dish.

He whistled, and I thought, Oh, Lord, there is nothing in my future but sadness.

Finally, Kevin returned my call. "Petal? *What* has happened? Are you all right?"

"No." I was sobbing then.

"I'll be there in a flash."

Minutes later, our front door opened and

he rapped his knuckles on my door, which I opened and then buried my face in a tissue.

He put his arm around my shoulder and led me to my favorite chair by the fireplace. I sat down with my elbows in my lap and the tears just streamed from my eyes. I knew I looked frightful.

"Good Lord, honey! Did someone die? What in the world?"

"Oh, Kevin, the most awful thing happened today . . ."

I told him about the accident, the terrible name that Agnes Willis called me, and the crash and burn of my volunteer career. He sat patiently on the end of a chair, listening to every single word.

"Well, first of all, they can replace the invitations tomorrow. It's the Met, for heaven's sake."

"I know, but all that hard work . . ."

"You're right, but it will give all those women something new to complain about. Good grief. This is some mess, Ollie. I'm pouring myself a vodka. Do you want something?" He looked back at me with an arched eyebrow and said, "Why am I even asking you this question?"

He slipped into the kitchen and returned

with two double, old-fashioned tumblers half filled with straight vodka over clinking ice.

"Lord, girl, look at your knees! They're all bloody!"

"I told you I fell! And I wasn't kidding! Oh, my word! I will *never* live this down!"

"I'll go get something to clean you up. In the bathroom?"

"Yes, in the cabinet. Or maybe under the sink. There's Bactine and Band-Aids." I took a sip of the cocktail, went into my room to pull off my ruined panty hose, tossed them in the wastebasket, and met him back in the living room.

"Here, wipe your widdle knees with this. So, you never told me. What did you say to her? Agnes, I mean."

"Oh, Lord. This is the very worst part of all of it. I told her that Truman was having an affair with Liz."

He was quiet for a moment and then he said, "Please don't tell me that. You did not."

"What?"

"In another arena I would have said, well, touché. But, Miriam, darling, I would not depend on Agnes Willis's hormone levels of self-control to keep that secret to herself. Nor would I trust anyone else who heard it. I

mean, the odds of it getting back to Truman . . ."

"It's too late now."

"Yes, it rather is. Well, perhaps you
should consider telling Liz so she knows
what's going on? You know? In case she
sees him?"

I cleaned up the scrapes and put three
Band-Aids on each knee.

"I'll have to think about that."

"Well, I think it's only fair."

"We'll see."

We were quiet for a moment. I had not
considered the impact this might have on Liz.
Kevin was right of course, but wasn't it enough
that I had told her that Truman was married?
I wanted the entire business to go away, disappear and never return. It was why the world
invented self-delusion.

"I *need* for chicken soup," I said. "Want to
go to Gardenia?"

Gardenia was our neighborhood café on
Madison, where you could get perfectly
poached eggs in the morning, a great grilled
cheese sandwich or a burger for lunch, and at
night, when the need arose, you knew they
were serving hot roast beef or turkey sand-

wiches, fabulous meat loaf and mashed potatoes, and always, homemade chicken soup.

"Sure. A little comfort food would do you
good. Go put on some trousers, wash your
face, and I'll walk over with you."

I changed, freshened my makeup, and in
minutes we were out the door, trying to cross
Park Avenue.

"Do you think this winter is ever going to
end?" I said as we hurried across the avenue
against the light, Kevin holding my elbow as I
was limping a little then.

"Whew! Made it! Do you mean the winter
or the winter of our discontent?"

"Either one." I stopped for a moment to
catch my breath. "That was one of the nicest
things about being on the island. The weather,
that is."

"Yes, you haven't given me the whole
download about this Harrison or Manny either."

"Kevin? Why don't we just make a list of all
my humiliations and advertise them on the
side of a building in Times Square?"

"You see? This is what happens. You go
away for a few days and suddenly I'm out of
step with what's happening with you."

"Not true. I'm freezing!" I shuddered, and although my knees were sore, I picked up our pace. Then Kevin had to work to keep up with me.

"Slow down, you wild thing! By the way, did you look under your bed?"

"Dust bunnies?"

"Treadmill. You owe me two hundred dollars."

"Oh, fine. Thanks, I think."

We hung our coats at the restaurant, got our table and menus, and although we knew what we had come here to eat, we looked over the specials anyway.

"They've got stuffed peppers tonight," I said with a heavy sigh.

"I can't eat peppers at night anymore. They give me heartburn."

"Since when did you develop such a delicate constitution?"

Kevin looked up from his menu with pursed lips, raised both eyebrows this time, and sighed. "Honestly, Petal, you're not the only fragile orchid in this jungle, you know."

The first piece of a smile in what felt like forever crept across my face.

We ordered two bowls of chicken soup

and hot herbal tea. When our waiter walked away I looked at Kevin.

"This has been a really, really crappy day, Kevin."

"I'd say so. I'm just so sorry you had to go through such an ordeal."

"I feel like I could start crying all over again and weep through the night."

"Miriam? Just stop it right now. Do not waste a single tear on this incident ever again. Seriously. I am much more concerned that Agnes Willis, in some insane jealous state, might hide in the bushes outside and throw battery acid on our Daisy Mae or some other crazy thing."

"Oh, please. Agnes Willis wouldn't dare do such a thing. She talks a big game in her school yard but she wouldn't cross over to a life of crime over Truman!"

"What do you mean?"

"Look, her pride may be hurt to have some-one else know about her husband running around, especially that it's me who knows. And especially that the others surely overheard what I said. But she knows Truman is unfaith-ful. I guarantee it. If she's in love with her hus-band, a woman always knows these things."

"But did you know about Charles?"

I was quiet then and thought about it for a moment.

"There were signs, lots of them, that I have to admit I chose to ignore. I knew that when I finally confronted him, it would blow up my world. And it did."

"Well, that's precisely what concerns me, Miriam. I don't want either one of them to take revenge on anyone besides themselves."

"Good grief, Kevin! Do you think I'm in danger?"

He looked around the restaurant, mostly populated with senior citizens at that hour, and then he looked back at me.

"I don't know, Miriam. I just can't answer that. But I hope not. Now, let's talk about something more pleasant. Tell me about Harrison."

"You're right. Well, this is the conundrum. When I met him, I wasn't impressed at all. But we had dinner—"

"Just the two of you?"

"No, Mother, Harrison, and me. Anyway, Harrison and I went downstairs to light the grill and I know I saw, I mean, there was, you know . . ."

"Interest?"

"Yes. I mean, he's completely inappropri-

ate for me because he's a little like Jungle
Jim or something, but he has this quality of, I
don't know, he's just this extremely thoughtful man. Not to mention, I decided he's definitely my mother's boyfriend, which is weird
in the extreme."

"I'll say. But being thoughtful is a greatly
undervalued asset in today's world."

"Truly. Anyway, next thing I know, he and
Mother are smoking you-know-what and I'm
shocked, and the next day he introduces me
to his friend Manny."

"Who's Manny?"

"A man."

"God, girl, there ought to be laws passed
against your jokes. Dreadful."

"Sorry. Anyway, I wind up at this church
dinner with Manny the Man dishing out quail
stew and thinking we might be, you know, a
possibility."

"So?"

"He has not called."

"Well, you *are* a thousand miles away."

"Right?"

"He's divorced, I assume?"

"Well, practically. His estranged wife lives
in Charlotte. He's been in Charleston for five
years."

"Sounds like somebody needs to do the paperwork."

"Exactly, but if he doesn't ever call me, then what do I care?"

"I'm thinking you do."

"Maybe a little. Maybe it's just pride."

Things were quiet for the rest of the week. I had not told Mother about my museum disaster because I knew she would say, see, I told you so, that it was a message from the Universal Spirit that it wasn't the best use of my time anyway. That one door closes so another can open. What door? The question was, how was I going to fill my days without my committee work? There was a time when I had served on committees at the library, a dance company, and two other museums. But over time I had reduced my responsibilities, thinking I would rather be meaningful in one institution than insignificant in many. Well, I guess that didn't go according to plan, did it?

I needed something to do, and walking around the apartment, I decided it was as good a moment as any to clean my closets. I would give all our old clothes to Goodwill or anyone willing to come and haul them away.

I started with the boys' bedrooms, thinking they would be the easiest. And they were not.

I did not know that emptying their closets would yield yet another burst of emotional confusion, regret, and guilt. It was a little like dealing with the bones of my own mother-hood.

First, I went to Charlie's room. He had taken a good many things with him when he moved into his apartment, but the amount of youthful possessions that he had left behind was considerable. At first, I felt that sorting his clothes was therapeutic. When I got orga-nized I always felt happier. It seemed like a good idea to stack his nicer shirts, pajamas, and so forth on the bed and ask him if there was anything he wanted to keep. But when I found his Little League baseball shirt and a sport coat that he must've worn when he was ten or twelve, I started breaking down.

Where was that precious little boy? How many ball games had I missed? How many afternoons had I left them with sitters so I could go to a meeting to plan a raffle, design a program journal, or listen to *the ladies* ar-gue over ticket prices and who was important enough to get this or that underwritten? So many it was impossible to count them. And those days I could have spent with my boys were gone forever.

But the mind games had been the culprit. Soon after the boys were born, Charles the Elder, the one who's the horse's ass, had embarked on a Chinese campaign of death by a thousand cuts. The little barbs of his running commentary were designed to make me feel inferior and worthless. The worse it got, the more I struggled to make myself interesting to him. In his warped mind, it wasn't enough to be the mother of our two boys. He knew women who had power and fully loaded résumés of elite education, national distinctions, and global experience. And he told me about them. Night after night. Instead of suspecting it was the beginning of his wandering, I signed up for and volunteered for every single job I could find. Not at the boys' schools—that would have been too pedestrian. No, my volunteer work was squarely rooted in the world-class arena of the arts in New York. Complex and all-consuming. But because he rarely matched my efforts with substantial financial support, I had never risen to any position of importance.

I saw then the miserable truth of all those years. A wasted life. In the process of trying to be someone Charles would admire and respect, I had walked away from my greatest joy, my children. And I did it over and over again until he left me anyway. I must have been insane.

Just as Mother had said, even if now I was twenty years younger, twenty pounds lighter, and I would add that if I held three doctorates in the most fascinating fields of study in the universe, and throw in a Nobel Prize, Charles still would not want me. The greater question was, Why did I ever so desperately want a man who made me feel like dirt to the point that I sacrificed a minute of time with my children? I swore to myself that if God ever granted me a chance to repair my own heart and to be a worthy mother, I would grab it.

My thoughts must have traveled the ethers because I was deep in those exact thoughts when the phone rang. It was my son Charlie.

"I can't believe it's you!" I said.

"Why's that? Are you okay? You're not crying, are you?"

"No! No!" I lied, and sniffed. "There's a lot of dust in this house! Allergies, you know."

"Oh. Right."

"Well, you won't believe this, but I was just cleaning out the closets in your room and it occurred to me that you might like to see all these things I found before I call Goodwill. I was just going to call *you*!"

"I don't want anything, Mom. You can just dump it all."

"Oh, come on. There are swim-team trophies and ribbons, yearbooks—all sorts of mementos you might like to have for your own children someday. Don't you think?"

"Use your own judgment, Mom. You know more about that kind of thing than I ever would."

"I just ran across pictures of you on a Halloween. I guess you were about ten? Dan was dressed up like Spider-Man and you were—"

"Frankenstein?"

"Yep! Frankenstein."

"I remember that year, too." He was quiet for a moment and then said, "I don't know where Dad was, but I remember it was cold and raining. You took us out around the block, like you always did. You made us wear big down jackets and you held this giant doorman's umbrella over us . . ."

"And all I wanted . . ."

"Was a *Fifth Avenue* candy bar! God! Do you remember how you used to send us out to get a *Fifth Avenue*? Those were the days, weren't they?"

Was I actually hearing a sentimental chord echo from the depths of my son's previously frozen chest cavity? I grabbed the straw.

"Yes. They were wonderful days, Charlie. I miss them a lot. Especially now, today, going through all your things. There are just so many memories."

"Yeah." He paused and added, "You gave us a good childhood, Mom."

"Thanks, sweetheart." I did? "I know I screwed up lots of things, but I did my best."

"All parents do. Or at least they think they do."

"Yes. But if I had it to do all over again, I would have done a lot of things differently."

There was yet another awkward silence for a few seconds and then he cleared his throat.

"It doesn't matter anymore, Mom. So don't torture yourself."

"Well, you're very sweet to say that, Charlie."

"Actually, I called to tell you something, Mom."

I was holding his New York Yankee sweatshirt from ages ago and had no idea then that years later I would remember that detail.

"What's that?"

"Well, Priscilla and I have decided to make it official."

"Do you mean, get married?"

"Yes. We're getting married and I wanted you to be the first to know."

"Well, Charlie? Are you sure? I mean, marriage is forever, you know. Or it's supposed to be forever."

"I know that." I heard a trace of annoyance in his voice and realized it was time to treat him like an adult.

But here it was. My son was going to marry a woman for whom I felt no affection and a decision had to be made right then and there. Here was my second chance. Either I was going to fully support him and hopefully regain some spot in his life that had a future. Or I could be my usual chilly, distant, noncommittal self on the whole thing and see where things went. But that would have given him one more piece of ammunition to justify distancing himself from me.

I needed Charlie and some symbol of love in my life so desperately that I leaped to support him. Maybe that wasn't exactly altruistic, but there it was. This was the moment the second phase of my parenting arrived. Besides, and I'd admit it to everyone, my heart couldn't stand any more loss. We would sail or sink together on the same ship.

I took a deep breath.

"Well, then, congratulations! Charlie? I know you will be a great husband, son. And Priscilla will be a good wife. A great wife. I am thrilled. Have you told your father?" Good job, I told myself. The first step is always the most wobbly.

"Thanks! Really, Mom. I thought you would go nuts or something."

"Why? Oh, Charlie! Honestly! Sweetheart! You're a grown man! If you don't know what and who you want in your life, who would I be to tell you?"

"I guess so."

"Priscilla is a perfectly lovely and brilliant woman and I think—no, I am certain that y'all are a great match! Seriously. I do . . ."

"Thank you, Mom. Really. Thanks."

"You're welcome!"

"Um, you do realize that if we have children they will be of mixed race."

"I think I do know that. That is your business, Charlie. Not mine. I will love any child you have. Count on it."

An unbelieving silence followed from his end of the phone. "Really?"

"Yes, really. Charlie, just lately I have come to realize certain things. One is that I have lost too much over pride. I am not going to lose you. Or your family. So there you have it. Now, why don't we make a dinner date to celebrate? Did you give her a ring?"

"Not yet. But I suppose I should, right?"

It was the first time in six years that my son had sought my advice. By taking the high ground, I was gaining a little territory. I knew Charlie and we both placed great store in the truth. He knew I was laying the facts right on the line.

"Oh, yes, I think absolutely, you must give her a ring. Why don't I go through my jewelry box and see what I can find that might help? Then we can go down to Corey Friedman on Forty-seventh Street and see what he can put together for you?"

There was an audible gulp from his end.

"Corey Friedman?"

"I. Friedman, son. I wouldn't trust anyone else with my grandmother's diamond."

"Your grandmother's? Your grandmother, my great-grandmother's diamond?"

"Why not? It's not like something from Elizabeth Taylor's jewelry box, but it's quite nice. A smidgen over a carat, I think."

"Mom, you realize this is like a one-eighty from your former position on this."

"Not really, sweetheart. I've been useless to you for too long. Look. These have been some difficult years. I was just so unsure of every-thing myself that no matter what I said, it always came out wrong. Really. That's the truth."

He was quiet for a minute and then he said, "I believe you."

"Thanks. I want to put the past where it belongs from now on." More silence followed and I said, "Listen! Go call your father and tell him and then call your brother . . ."

"I'm gonna ask him to be my best man, even though I never hear from him . . ."

"Who does? That's a good idea. We have to do something to pull this family together— you and me, I mean."

"Why not?"

"Anyway, ask Priscilla for a free date for dinner and then call me back."

"Okay. Okay! I'll do that right now."

"And, Charlie?"

"Yeah?"

"I love you, Charlie. Please. Tell Priscilla that I want to love her, too."

We hung up. I stood there and I felt a glow as if I was feeling real happiness for the first time in so long, I couldn't remember the last occasion. My little boy was all grown up and getting married. My eyes welled with tears and I went to my bathroom for a tissue. I looked in the mirror. Although I wasn't thrilled with the wrinkles and lines I saw, I smiled for a change and felt a little bit proud. And relieved.

We had not found the resolution to everything in one phone call, but I certainly had managed to remove a chunk of the wall between us. And maybe everything I said to him wasn't quite true, but over time I would make it true. I would learn to love Priscilla and I would give her the biggest welcome into my heart that I could manage.

Gee, that old saying about catching more flies with honey than vinegar appeared to be legitimate.

Then the noises above me started. First, there was a loud thud, like someone falling, and then I heard Liz scream *no!* Next it sounded like a small piece of furniture was knocked over and then Liz screamed *stop!* My heart started racing and I broke into a sweat because I knew *exactly* what was happening. Truman Willis was there and he was assaulting Liz.

I ran for the phone and called Kevin. Thankfully he picked up on the first ring because I was already almost hyperventilating.

"*Where* are you?"

"What's wrong?" he said, sensing the panic in my voice. When I told him, he said, "Miriam! Listen to me! Do *not* go up there! Call 911! It might *not* be Truman. It could be an intruder! I'll be home in two minutes!"

"Okay! Please hurry!"

We hung up and I dialed 911.

"There's a man in my house beating up my tenant upstairs! Please hurry!"

I gave them my address, my name, and hung up to begin pacing the floor. It seemed like an eternity before anyone came to the rescue. Kevin got home first. I was watching through my peephole and saw him going up the stairs, two steps at a time. I went out into the hall and saw him up there standing in front of the door. Suddenly things got very quiet.

"Liz? Are you all right?" I saw him banging on the door and calling out. "Liz? We called the police and they'll be here any minute! Liz? Answer me! Liz?"

I hurried up the stairs right behind him but he shooed me away before I could reach him.

"Go open the front door and wait for the police," he said.

"No! This is my house!"

"Don't be a fool, Miriam! There's no point in both of us getting hurt! Now go!"

I did as he said and thankfully I could see the blue lights spinning from the patrol car outside. I opened the door as quickly as I could and stood aside. Two cautious-looking police officers stepped in, looked at me, and said, "We got a call about a domestic disturbance?"

"Second floor," I said. "Please! Hurry!"

But it was quiet and whatever was going on up there had ended in a dead silence that frightened me more than Liz's screaming and the sounds of furniture being thrown around. Shaking from head to toe, I crept up the stairs and heard one of the officers talking into his two-way radio.

"Yeah, two ambulances. We've got an apparent heart-attack victim with a low pulse and a young woman who's pretty banged up."

Heart attack? Oh dear, heavenly Father!

Truman? I looked through the open door. Truman Willis was unconscious on the floor. His complexion was gray, like the color of wet cement. He looked dead. I rushed inside Liz's bedroom. Through the open door I could see that she was lying on the floor of her bathroom, a puddle of blood under her head.

"Oh my God," I said. "Oh my God."

Kevin was standing next to me. "Oh, no!" He knelt, and just as he was reaching out to feel her pulse, one of the officers put his hand on Kevin's shoulder with a firm jerk.

"Don't touch her," an officer said. "I have to ask you two to leave. This is a crime scene."

"She's my . . . my niece," I said, lying through my teeth. She bore no family resemblance. "And this is my house. I'm not going anywhere."

There were some suspicious looks between the cops, but given the assessment that Truman's life was in more serious danger, they ignored me. The emergency medical team arrived in minutes and immediately lifted Truman onto the stretcher, starting an IV.

"His pulse is very weak. Pressure's eighty over twenty. We gotta get this guy outta here . . ."

They were asking Truman questions but he gave no response. He was unconscious. The police asked me if I knew him. I said that I did and hurried downstairs to retrieve Agnes's number. I gave the number to one of the police officers.

"Friend of yours?" the officer asked, referring to Truman.

"Sort of."

"Do you want to make the call?"

"Absolutely not."

With a crisp understanding that this old coot Truman Willis had the dreadful luck to nearly succumb in his young lover's apartment, he stepped outside to make the call himself. He had probably done that sort of thing hundreds of times.

"This is all my fault," I said to Kevin. "Oh God. All my fault."

"Miriam, Miriam." Kevin was very upset and I didn't blame him for being furious with me. He had predicted that something like this could happen.

"This is so terrible! What have I done?"

"It could have been worse. Much worse. I'll lock up the house and meet you at Lenox Hill."

It probably wasn't the most sensitive thing

to say but I blurted it out anyway. "You know, Agnes will definitely be there."

He looked at me with a white-hot fury I would never forget. Maybe it was because he blamed me for Liz's condition or was appalled that my cowardice toward Agnes Willis would be worthy of mention at a moment like this.

"Good. I've been dying to meet her."

"What if she starts screaming at me?"

Kevin got in close to my face and whispered, "Then scream back, Miriam."

Minutes later, I crawled in the back of the ambulance with Liz, who by then was bandaged and on an IV. She was still unconscious.

I had never been in an ambulance before. I had never been the cause of this kind of mayhem either. This terrible assault had happened to Liz because of my anger toward Agnes. Liz's face had a deep gash. She would need a plastic surgeon. She had lost several teeth. She would need an oral surgeon. Her jaw was very swollen and I suspected that Truman had socked her. Because of her uneven breathing, they were concerned that a broken rib had punctured a lung. She would be black-and-blue all over for weeks. How would she go to work? She couldn't. Obviously. Did she have medical insurance? I doubted it. I would cover her bills even if I had to mortgage the house. I had to make this right. Oh, dear God in heaven, what had I done?

Chapter Eleven

AUNTIE AND UNCLE TO THE RESCUE

The waiting area in the emergency room was the same as all the others I had ever seen. Depressing. Faded walls, chipped floor tiles, rows of rickety plastic chairs. Racks of plastic pockets on the walls held the requisite brochures explaining flu shots, HIV, pregnancy, and all the assorted joys of living. I was fidgeting, scanning through one called "What to Ask Your Doctor" that outlined patient rights and how to feel empowered during your hospital stay. Empowered? How empowered were any of us when a man who made love to you three times a week could beat you to a bloody pulp and give himself a heart attack in the process? It was horrible.

I took a seat, got up again, and looked around at the others. The police officers were talking to the admissions nurse. To my left, a woman had a crying baby in her arms, whimpering and pulling away from her. Looked like an ear infection to me. A young man was vomiting in a cardboard box—probably flu, I thought, and kept my distance. There was an ancient man with a heavily bandaged foot and an elderly woman who was beautifully dressed, quietly weeping and blowing her nose. There had to have been a dozen people in various stages of distress, but that was a slow night for New York. All I could think was that I wanted to go to Liz and be with her. But they told me no. They said they had to evaluate her before anyone could see her. The doctor would come out and speak with me when the assessment was complete. Besides, there wasn't room. It was very overcrowded. I didn't doubt that but I wanted to be involved in any decision they would make about her care. I would make sure that I was included.

The doors swung open and Kevin appeared. He rushed in, breathless but all business.

"Miriam? What did they say?"

"Nothing. They just took her in behind those doors over there. They'll let me know when they're done with whatever it is they do."

"Does she have health insurance?"

"Couldn't ask. She's unconscious. But I wouldn't be surprised if she didn't. I'll tell you what, though."

"What's that?"

"She's got a pretty ugly gash across her cheek. Do we know a plastic surgeon?"

"Who would sew her up for nothing?"

"I guess so."

"I'd have to think about that. Oh God, this is some mess, Miriam."

"All I can do, Kevin, is think about how I caused this. I feel so horrible. I would do *anything* to roll back time."

"Miriam? Regret won't do anyone any good at this point. We have to think about how we are going to help Liz. That's our priority. Later on there will be plenty of time for self-recrimination."

I heard what he said but my eyes were

fixed on the door of the entrance. Agnes Willis had arrived. She spotted me and headed straight in my direction. Her jaw was clenched and she was wild with anger.

"This is your fault, Miriam Swanson! If my husband dies, you'll only have yourself to blame!"

I gasped. She was loud enough to get the attention of the police officers, who like any well-trained members of New York's finest, knew how to keep their eyes on everything at the same time.

"This is *not* my fault, Agnes Willis! Was it my responsibility to see that Truman Willis kept his pants on?"

She moved closer and began poking me in the chest with her finger. "This. Is. Your. Fault. Do you hear me? And I will sue you for your last dime if anything happens to my Truman . . ."

Kevin grabbed her hand and held it close to him.

"Mrs. Willis? Keep your hands to yourself, please?"

"*You* don't tell *me* what to do, you—you ridiculous little man!"

Kevin raised his chin to her and I thought in that flash of a second that he might slap her. I pushed her away from him, a little harder than I intended, and she stumbled slightly.

"Don't you *dare* call him that! Just who do you think you are?"

A police officer stepped over and said, "Is there a problem here?"

"Keep her away from me," I said. "I've had enough of her nastiness and viciousness to last ten lifetimes."

"Vicious? Me? Well, maybe occasionally, but at least I'm *somebody* in this town! You're *nobody*, Miriam Swanson, and everyone knows it."

A week ago I would've opened a vein and drowned in a river of my own blood and tears. At that moment I thought that what she said was downright hilarious and completely ridiculous. My fury dissolved and I started to laugh.

"Really? Really? Oh my God! What a joke! Hey! I have an idea! After you go see that philandering thug of yours, why don't you take your ugly face and your drooping flat ass right on down to hell, Agnes. If you're the benchmark for *something,* I would *so much prefer* to be *nothing*!" Mellie the Mouth had found her legs.

"What? How dare you speak to me this way?" She raised her hand and the police officer caught it in midair.

"What's the matter with you, lady?" he said. "I wouldn't be hitting anyone if I were you." The officer sized up the she-devil and said, "You know, the man we brought in is in big trouble." He checked his notes. "I'm assuming he's your husband, um, Truman Willis?"

"What do you mean?" Agnes said. "And you may call me *Mrs. Willis,* if you please."

"If I please? Okay. Well, *Mrs. Willis,* when that beautiful young woman in there regains consciousness, she may decide to press charges against your husband for aggravated assault or attempted murder. You'd better get a lawyer. *Mrs. Willis.*"

Agnes stepped back from me with a scowl on her face that was so ugly it was the stuff of nightmares. I had not ever entertained the thought that Agnes could be so downright unattractive. The officer pulled up his pants by his belt and walked back to his partner, who stood against the admissions desk shaking his head.

"And a little anger management therapy wouldn't hurt," I said. "For both of you."

Agnes was glaring at me.

My heart was pounding, I was breathing rapidly, and my ears were ringing from what I was sure was a surge of blood pressure.

Kevin applauded, and then one by one, every single person in the waiting room joined in. Red-faced and lockjawed, a shocked Agnes Willis sniffed loudly and turned on her heel. After a few minutes of conversation and then showing identification, she successfully pushed her weight around with the admissions people enough and disappeared through the swinging door.

When she was completely out of sight, Kevin said, "You could have won an Academy Award for that, Petal. You were *marvelous*."

"She's really horrible, isn't she?"

"Yes, and that neck of hers could use a good moisturizer."

The elderly but dignified woman tugged at the sleeve of my overcoat and I turned to her.

"Yes, ma'am?"

"Wasn't that Agnes Willis?"

"Yes, ma'am."

"I knew her mother. She was a bitch, too."

"I don't doubt that for a moment," Kevin said.

An hour passed and then another. Kevin and I talked about Agnes and Truman and how she had become the evil thing she was.

"I can't believe you were ever friends with Agnes Willis."

"I wasn't. Whatever kind of relationship we had was based on my ability to deliver something her project of the moment needed. When Charles closed his wallet I went on her marked-down rack."

"Bizarre."

"I used to think that being a member of her inner circle would be the most wonderful thing in the world," I said.

"Well, Petal, to the outside observer, the glamour is very seductive."

"Yes, but it's an unreal world. Do you know what I mean?"

"Inauthentic?"

"Exactly. I mean, think about this. Let's put aside the fact that every single nonprofit organization in this town serves some very good purpose, because they do."

"Agreed."

"And that they could not function without volunteers. The private donations of those same volunteers adds up to a substantial amount of money. So, they need the help and they need the money just to stay alive."

"No, you're absolutely right. We're not pooping on the actual value of volunteers here."

"Not in a million years," I said. "But with the really big bigwigs, here's how it goes in their private lives. The husband earns tons of money—millions—he travels, and even when he's in town, he's never home. The wife hires a nanny to raise the kids."

"Nanny is seen as a status symbol."

"Not exactly. They are a necessity because how mundane would the mother become if she raised her own children?"

"Ow. That's some statement."

"Oh, it's much worse. The mother now has way, way too much time on her hands, because she has to be available to serve as Mrs. Gotbucks. How she *can* spend that time is limited to the following: shopping, working out, having an affair, or volunteering for some worthy cause that will make her marriage more interesting. And she's lonely."

"Forget her lonely libido for the moment. Let me extrapolate here. The higher the visibility of the organization, the more likely the wife is to keep her husband in line and not in his secretary's bloomers because he's obliged to support the cause and to show up for the fetes she organizes."

"Right! And the importance of her position is reflected by her assignments. It's not just the money she wheedles out of her husband's *personal* bank account, it's the money and in-kind services from his firm, their contacts—"

"It's about power."

"That is *precisely* what it is about—not for all of them, but gals like Agnes Willis? That's all she's got."

"It ain't much."

"You can say that again because look at her. She's cranky for a lot of reasons, not the least of which is because she's starving herself to death, and no matter how much plastic surgery she gets, she's still going to be the age she is. She's angry because she doesn't understand why she's not satisfied with her life."

"Petal? Sounds a little bit like someone I know and love."

"Yeah, but you know what?"

"What?"

"I'm getting over it. I don't miss her company one bit."

"Well, hallelujah! But in that whole bowl of mixed nuts, weren't there some other gals that were *really* your friends?"

"Oh, sure! There were plenty! But you drift apart, you know? This one moves to Florida. Or they decide to volunteer for something else and you become irrelevant in each other's lives. So-and-so gets divorced and moves home to Nebraska with the kids. New York is such a transient place."

"But, come on, Petal, not all of them. I mean, I always thought it was odd that someone as fun and smart as you didn't have more girlfriends."

"Honey, there is no greater social pariah than a single woman. Inviting a divorced woman to your dinner party is just like bringing home a naked leper. At least to the other women in shaky marriages. Eventually I just became a loner, I guess."

"Well, you have me."

"Yep, and you I love. But, boy, I would give everything I own to turn back *this* clock. I am so worried."

"Me, too. I know you would. So would I."

We waited, reading every inch of a tabloid newspaper left on a chair by someone. Each time we inquired we were told that Liz was being treated and we would just have to wait. They were sorry but there was no news. Finally, I heard my name called.

"Mrs. Swanson?"

It was a nurse from the examining rooms calling me from the forbidden doorway.

"Yes?" I hurried over to her. Kevin was at my heels.

"Are you Liz Harper's next of kin?"

"Yes, I am." This lying business was going to catch up with me someday.

"Mm-hmm. Follow me, please. The doctor would like to speak with you. We are going to admit Ms. Harper, and as you can guess there are a few forms to fill out."

"No problem. Is she conscious yet? Do we know the extent of her injuries? I mean, I watch *ER* all the time and . . . what?"

The nurse, whose name tag read *Chantell Williams, RN,* was grinning and shaking her head. She was a large woman, to say the least, a kind of cool grandmother with dreadlocks and good humor.

"Did you say *ER*? Mercy, I wish real life was as easy as television. Follow me." She directed us to a doctor, who appeared to be younger than my boys.

"Hello, I'm Dr. Miller. I understand you are related to Ms. Harper?"

"Yes, I'm Miriam Swanson, her aunt, and this is our close friend Mr. Dolan."

"Well, let me tell you. Ms. Harper is a very lucky young lady. Her injuries could have been a lot worse."

Dr. Miller explained that Liz had a concussion but should be awake shortly. X-rays revealed that she had two broken ribs, indeed her lung had been punctured, and she had a cracked collarbone. He proceeded to explain that the slash on her cheek was quite deep but they had closed the wound.

"We stitched it up. But if I were her, I'd see a plastic surgeon," Dr. Miller said.

Kevin and I thanked him and breathed a sigh of relief, although neither one of us truly felt relief. Only the first hurdle had been cleared. I went with the nurse to complete the paperwork.

Nurse Williams and I sat at a desk in a little cubicle. I gave her Liz's full name, our home address, and her cell-phone number. That was all I could tell her. When it got to the question of medical insurance, allergies, and so on, I had to admit that I had no earthly idea about those things.

"I thought you said you were her aunt."

"Yes, but she only recently came into my life. She's my sister's child and we were never close." For a moment I closed my eyes and put my hand to my chest for emphasis and sighed. My acting seemed to be a natural talent.

"Uh-huh. You gonna call your sister?"

"Unfortunately she passed away last year."

"And her father?"

"Gone off with some woman. Haven't seen him in years."

"Uh-huh. Ms. Harper is single?"

"Yes. Can I see her?"

I knew Chantell Williams, RN, knew I was making up the details and I knew also that she did not really care. She just wanted her paperwork filled out.

"She's being moved right now to room 238. Wait a few minutes and then you can go up and see how she's doing."

"How *is* she doing?"

"She looks like she got hit by a truck. But she'll be fine and I'm not sure I can say the same for you. You need to calm down, honey."

"I could use ten milligrams of something."

"And I could, too. All right, Mrs. Swanson, that's all for now." She closed her folder and stood to leave.

"Um, may I ask a question?" I said.

"Of course."

"What happened to Truman Willis?"

"You his kin, too?" She cocked her head to one side, indicating I had to claim to be related for her to reveal anything to me.

"Uh, yes, distant cousin, but yes."

"I'm gonna tell you this, but if you say you heard it from me, I'm gonna find you."

"Me? Speak out of school? Everyone says I am the soul of discretion."

"Okay. I can't say much but I will tell you this. That wife of his is just about the meanest woman I have ever seen in all my life. Meeeeean! Whoo! Jesus, she gave me the chills. No lie. Chills up and down my whole body."

"But Truman?"

"He's gonna be fine. Your cousin, you say?" She arched her eyebrows.

"Yes."

"Uh-huh. Mrs. Swanson?"

"Yes?"

"Don't take up poker, okay?"

We smiled knowingly at each other and I went to find Kevin.

"She's on the second floor," I said. "Let's get some magazines for her and some soft candy or something."

We picked up some mints and reading material in the lobby gift shop and took the short elevator ride. We found her semiprivate room, and thankfully the second bed was empty. There was a curtain pulled around her, and when I peeked in, my heart sank all over again.

She was in one of those wrinkled hospital gowns. Her top lip was very swollen and her face was already turning to the color of plums. A large bandage covered the other side of her face, and in addition to her IV, she wore a heart monitor. The steady *bleep bleep bleep* was reassuring but unnerving at the same time.

I started to shake uncontrollably and Kevin took my elbow.

"Sit down," he said. "Sit right here."

"What have I done, Kevin? What have I done?"

"Get over your guilt, Miriam. It's not going to do any of us any good."

"I feel so terrible about this. Nothing like

this has ever happened in my entire life. I mean, who would have thought that telling one piece of gossip would lead to this?"

"Truly. But people are crazy, you know."

"We'll need to find her an oral surgeon."

"Yes, and someone very good to look at that gash. God, Liz is such a beautiful woman. This is just so wrong. I hope she presses charges against that bastard. I'd love to read about this in Liz Smith's column."

He had not said that she was no longer beautiful or that it was, in fact, my fault. And he was right; what happened to Liz was so very wrong. Whose fault it was didn't matter then. We were both deeply upset.

I knew enough about cuts and gashes to know that she needed somebody besides a resident to do the job. All I could think about was making her whole again as fast as possible. When Liz woke up, I wanted to be able to assure her that the disaster was under control.

"I'm calling Charlie."

"Your son?"

"Yep. I'll be right back. I'm calling *my boy*." I went outside, took out my cell, and dialed his number. I choked up from the emotion I felt for calling Charlie *my boy*. How long had

it been since I had used such a proprietary
term to describe him? Too long. That and
many other things were going to change.

He answered right away.

"Charlie?" My voice quivered.

"Mom? What's wrong? I left a message at
the house about dinner. Is next Thursday
okay with you?"

It was highly unusual for me to call him at
such a late hour and he probably thought I
had burned down the house.

"Of course. But listen, my new tenant, Liz
Harper, was viciously attacked tonight and
I'm at Lenox Hill with her. She needs a plastic surgeon, son. She's a gorgeous girl and
she has a terrible deep gash right down her
cheek. And she lost some teeth, and oh God,
it's a mess. It's just a mess."

"I'm just finishing here. Why don't I hop on
the subway? I can be there in say, fifteen?"

"Thanks, sweetheart." I put the phone back
in my coat pocket and went back inside to
Kevin. "I wish he wouldn't take the subway.
It's full of lunatics."

"Oh, Miriam. You're such a worrier."

"I know. Well, there's other news I haven't
had a moment to tell you."

"Let's have it."

"Charlie and Priscilla are getting married."

"No! Seriously?"

"Yes. They are getting married."

"She's Jamaican, right?"

I nodded.

"You're cool with this?"

Kevin knew all the reasons I had serious reservations about Priscilla. He looked at me long and hard. I could almost see the wheels of his mind turning as he thought that he would be obliged to adopt my position on the union for the sake of our friendship.

I inhaled and exhaled deeply and sat up straight in the chair. "Totally cool and copacetic. It's the twenty-first century, for heaven's sake."

"Absolutely! Well then, congratulations!" Brightening then, despite the dire circumstances, Kevin gave me a kiss on the cheek. "I mean, are we going to have steel drums and curried goat? Rum punch?"

"Whatever Priscilla and Charlie want, I guess? Curried goat? They eat that?"

"Yeah, it's quite good, actually."

"Uck." My gag reflex kicked in. "But really. I had a serious conversation with him this evening—before all hell broke loose."

"About your relationship?"

"Or lack of . . . I'm going to make a concerted effort to get closer to him. And her. He's the only family I have here, you know?"

"And I'm chopped liver?"

"Oh, come on. You know what I mean. I love you from head to toe and you know it."

"So what brought on this change of heart?"

"It was classic. I was cleaning out his room, and going through all his childhood toys, pictures, favorite things, and so on made me realize how much I miss being in his life. It's a good thing, don't you think?"

"Absolutely, Miriam. Ah, dear Miriam! The soft heart of a mother doesn't make you matronly or an old crone, you know. I mean, Jackie O had children and she was chic until her last breath. We'll have to get you big sunglasses."

"First thing tomorrow."

Simultaneously, we looked at Liz. She seemed so young to me.

"This is so unfair," I said.

"And unnecessary," Kevin said. He pulled a guest chair over to Liz's bed from the other side of the room. "I can only hope that lecherous creep, Truman Willis, is writhing in pain."

I looked up to see Charlie standing in the doorway. Kevin stood, they shook hands, and then my son gave me a hug.

"I got here as fast as I could, Mom. I don't think I've heard that kind of distress in your voice ever. Are you okay?"

It was obvious then, and perhaps for the first time, that my Charlie was a grown man, and seeing him in that light, I was overcome with such emotions that I didn't know what to say. It was a combination of *where did the years go?* And *this entire disaster can be laid at my feet.* And *please tell me everything's going to be all right.*

I managed to whisper, "I'm just so glad you're here."

I must have seemed dramatic to him because he looked to Kevin for an explanation.

"Your mother feels responsible for this and she is being very hard on herself."

"What happened? Jeez, poor kid. What's she got?"

Kevin went down the litany of her ailments, and when he was finished, Charlie seemed unshaken.

"Look, Mom, I did a rotation with Gerald Imber. He's a world-class plastic surgeon. I mean, I don't want to disturb the dressing on her wound to have a look, but I'm not worried. Imber will make her look like a movie star. He loves me. I'll call him in the morning."

"Even I've heard of him," I said.

"He's fabulous," Kevin said. "I want him to do my upper eyes."

Charlie looked at Kevin as though he had just dropped from the moon.

"When the time comes, of course."

"Right. And her teeth? I know about twenty guys who can give her a better smile than Paula Zahn. All the rest of the stuff? Bed rest and painkillers. She'll be fine in two weeks. Guaranteed."

"Heaven knows, I hope you're right," I said.

"You have to have faith in your doctor, Mom."

"Well, there may be an issue of money . . ." I said.

"Don't worry," Charlie said, "all these guys take credit cards."

"Send the bills to our Mr. Willis," Kevin said. "If he doesn't expire."

"Then we could send them to Agnes," I said, "which might be fun. Or I guess we would have to sue his estate."

"Don't sweat that," Charlie said. "No doctor worth his license is going to let a girl like this walk around with no teeth and a big scar. That's crazy. We'll work it out." He looked at his watch. "I gotta be at the hospital in six hours. I'd better get moving."

I got up and walked him to the door. I was so filled with pride that my little boy, now a grown man, could walk into a room and, in a matter of minutes, calm his mother's worst fears. My eyes were watery and I knew I had no powder or lipstick on—I probably looked like I was a thousand years old. And I was tired, so very tired.

"Thank you, Charlie. Thank you for coming. Really."

He looked at me like he was seeing me for the first time. He put his arms around me and pulled me into a big bear hug. "Aw, Mom? Come on now. Look, I want you to call me whenever you are worried about anything, not just medical stuff, okay?"

"Okay." I could hardly believe my ears. "I will. Be careful going home and give my best to Priscilla, okay?"

"Ha! You're turning into a regular sport, Mom. You really are."

He actually kissed my cheek. I watched

him walk down the hall. I would be diligent about my relationship with Charlie from here on out. I knew I couldn't regain the lost time I could have spent with him, but I would do all I could to help his marriage get off on the right foot, to get to know Priscilla, and to be a good mother-in-law. Well, I would try. The mother-in-law thing was sure to present a challenge.

Next on my list would be Danny and Nan. I would fly to California to see them with lots of little treats for my grandchildren. We would go to the zoo and take lots of pictures. I would buy them souvenirs and send Dan and Nan off to dinner someplace wonderful—my treat. I would babysit, make cookies, and spoil the kids rotten . . . I had a lot of making up to do, but at least I was making a plan.

But my first order of business was to get Liz on the road to repair.

"Miriam? Miriam?" Kevin said. "I think she's waking up! Hurry!"

I rushed to Liz's bedside. As promised, her eyes were fluttering and she was licking her swollen lips.

"Where am I?"

"We're right here, Liz. Kevin and I. Don't try to get up . . ."

"I'm gonna get a nurse," Kevin said. "I'll be right back."

I told her what had happened to her and to Truman. I told her all that I knew about her injuries and what the expected recovery time was. She was weak and her voice was barely above a whisper.

"It's going to be all right, Liz," I said. "If it's the last thing I ever do, I'm going to make sure that everything is all right."

"Well, look who's rejoined the land of the living!" The nurse had arrived with Kevin in her wake. "How are you feeling, Ms. Harper?"

"Awful. Everything hurts."

"Can we give her something for pain?" I said.

"I can, but *we* can't." Nurse Ratchet gave me the hairy eyeball from one end to the other. "Who are you?"

"I'm her aunt, Miriam Swanson."

"Let me guess," she said, deadpan, looking at Kevin with his round tortoiseshell eyeglasses and polished head. "You're the uncle?"

"Why are you people so suspicious of everyone?" I said.

"Because you wouldn't believe what goes

on around here," Nurse F. Hades said. (The
F stood for *from*.) "Okay, will the *family* excuse us? I have to check my patient's vi-
tals . . ."

Kevin and I stepped out into the hall. He
was miffed.

"Can you believe that old battle-ax in
there? *Be* in charge! See if *I* care!"

"I agree. Crass. Just crass. But on the
other hand, she probably knows the truth
about how Liz landed here. This is not a
country club, you know. And what Truman
did is criminal. For all she knows, we could
be lawyers. Or from the *National Enquirer*.
Who knows?"

"You're right, of course. Petal? I can't *wait*
to get our Liz out of here."

"I'm with you on that! But I can't wait for
her to be better."

"I'm exhausted."

"Me, too, but I'm going to sit with her tonight. Why don't you tell her good night and
check on Harry for me. Call me and let me
know the house is okay and all that."

"Deal."

The nurse came out and said, "Visiting
hours ended a long time ago. That girl needs
rest."

"And I intend to see that she gets it. I'd like an ice pack, please, so I can try to reduce her swelling."

"Hmmph," she said, and then her body language changed. She had concluded that I might not have been her aunt but I wasn't a threat to hospital security. "Good idea, actually. I'll have an orderly bring one when I get a chance. Can't imagine why she doesn't have one already."

"That's why it's important to have your *family* around in times of need," Kevin said, and pursed his lips into a tight square as only royalty could.

She actually giggled, pointed her finger at him, and walked away with a wink.

"Petal? Did that beast actually wink at me?"

"She thinks you're slick."

"Well, she's right."

Kevin sat close to Liz and held her free hand.

"Liz," he said. "Miriam and I don't want you to worry about a single thing. We are going to get you the best plastic surgeon and oral surgeon in New York. And believe me, we won't rest until you are as right as rain. If these bitches don't give you your pain medication on time, you just call me, okay? In fact, if I can do anything, you call me. My only regret is that I didn't get to mop up the floor with your, ahem, gentleman caller."

Kevin rolled his eyebrows and Liz responded with a lopsided smile.

"Thanks," she said, slurring a little.

He got up, kissed the top of her head, and waved at us.

"Call me if you need anything," he mouthed, holding his thumb and little finger beside his head like a cell phone.

"Okay," I mouthed back.

Liz was already drifting off to sleep by the time I closed her door and settled into the chair next to her. Worn out as my body was, my mind was racing. What a week it had been!

I wondered what my mother would have said about this horrible business with Liz and Truman and what she would have had to say about Agnes Willis's behavior. More than likely, plenty. Miss Josie would have said that Liz had probably been fully informed that she was playing with fire. But she would never have entertained the idea that Liz had gotten what she deserved from

Truman. She might have said that perhaps her father had been cruel to her and that may have been the reason Liz would be so willing to sleep with a man that much older than she was. But in any and all cases, a man should never raise his hand to a woman. She would have said that Truman Willis was not a gentleman to be sure and that Agnes, in her private moments, had to be terribly unhappy and embittered.

I could see my mother in my mind's eye as I told her the story over a cup of hot tea at her kitchen counter. That was what I wanted then—to be with my mother. To tell her this entire story because she would care about it. It was too late to call her then but I would surely have told her the whole story by tomorrow night.

Right in front of my eyes, life was changing. I had already determined that I was going to take Liz under my wing, and Charlie, Priscilla, Danny, Nan, and their two. I marveled at the sense of peace it gave me and how quickly it had all come about. In the time it took for the sun to rise and fall only once, I had begun to gather real purpose back into my life. Even the creaking rusted hinges on the door to my heart were open just enough to look at love again. Okay, maybe with one eye, but it was slightly less jaundiced than before.

Chapter Twelve

MOTHER HEN

Kevin and I brought Liz home from the hospital two days later and put her in Charlie's old room. She didn't even object. Between her collapsed lung, the pain meds that made her woozy, and her sling, traveling up and down the stairs to the second floor held little appeal. Besides that, the thought of her taking a tumble down the steps and breaking her neck scared Kevin and me out of our wits. We all agreed that being my houseguest was a better choice than being a prisoner upstairs. I intended to see that she ate well, rested, and recuperated as she should.

Liz looked worse than she had in the hospital because her bruises had taken on every color found in nature. But at least the swelling was reduced. And true to his word, Charlie had booked appointments for her to see Dr. Imber and a wonderful oral surgeon named Gordon Ferguson.

She told us that the day after the incident the police visited her hospital room and asked her if she wanted to press charges against Truman Willis.

"I just said, no, I don't. What good would come of it? Enough damage had been done. I just need to get better. Who cares about him anyway?"

Later on Kevin said to me, "Don't you think it's odd that Liz is so serene? I mean, if somebody waled on me like Truman Willis did on Liz, I'd at least be *furious!*"

"It's odd and it makes me wonder just what in the world her life was like before we knew her. She could take a beating like that and practically cower as though she deserved it? That curtain doesn't hang quite straight, does it?"

"No. It's peculiar."

We thought it was absolutely terrible that neither Truman nor Agnes had inquired if they could help with Liz's medical bills, especially when they surely knew in the days that followed that the charges against Truman had been dropped. I mean, Liz could have thrown a hand grenade in their lives but she had decided against it. Shouldn't that have scored some points with someone?

Kevin said he was not surprised about the silence or lack of gratitude from the Willis camp. His lone encounter with Agnes at the hospital had been revolting to him. And he thought Truman Willis was the scum of the earth. Kevin said there was no word strong enough to aptly define the Willis arrogance and he was one hundred percent correct about that. I think Kevin sort of looked at Liz like a little sister and he was just smoldering with anger that someone could do such a thing to her.

I said to Liz, "You know, honey, Truman Willis has more than enough money to pay the bills, especially the plastic surgery and for your teeth. A lawyer's letter to him is all we need. You are certainly within your rights to threaten a civil suit."

"Yeah, but then every time I touched my face or took a bite, I would remember that I had to sue the money out of him. I prefer to remember my stupidity instead."

"Your stupidity? What about mine? It was my big mouth that put this train wreck in motion!"

I had told Liz the whole truth of my relationship with Agnes, how our so-called friendship and most other friendships had fallen apart on the departure of my husband. Then of course, there was the calamitous coffee-urn story.

"I'm sorry, Mrs. Swanson, about what happened to you, but I would have loved to see the look on her face when you told her about Truman. You're probably the first person who gave her any, pardon me, crap in a million years."

"Darlin'? At this point, I think you can call me Miriam."

I apologized to Liz over and over but I desperately wanted her to understand that I never meant to hurt anyone except Agnes, and even that was wrong. Never again would I seek to inflict pain in anyone's life. Apparently, there was a little Buddha germinating in my soul.

"Miriam? Gosh, it sounds so funny to call you that. But, Miriam? Honestly, if I had been in your position, I sure might have said the *same thing*. I mean, at that moment you couldn't have thought something like this would happen."

"Not in a million years. Still. I did a terrible thing to Agnes Willis that caused an undeserved tragedy to happen to you."

"Yeah, but she definitely deserved some comeuppance," Liz said. "What a, pardon me, bitch she is."

Liz still cussed but excused herself when she did. I took that as a sign of personal growth.

"You're telling me? You would not believe how many times she embarrassed me just for the sport of it. Anyway, for someone who has a history of great self-control, I surely did lose my composure in a big way."

"Well, we all learned something here, right? When I look like a girl again, I'm gonna sign up at match.com or something and start looking for guys my own age."

"Good! And find an old poop for me while you're at it."

"You know, Miriam, that's not a bad idea."

"Oh, please! Actually," and I whispered for no reason, "I've met someone who might be fun to be with."

"You did? Tell me about him. Does Kevin know?"

"Honey, Kevin knows when I pluck an eyebrow."

Liz was propped up against four pillows, positioned in a way that allowed her to sleep without disturbing her shoulder. I sat on the opposite bed and told her all about meeting Harrison and Manny. I even confided that I had a flutter in my heart for Harrison but why it was impossible to pursue it. But that Manny was interesting, a great cook, and more than your basic southern man with beautiful manners. I hoped that something would develop with him but that depended greatly on how much time I was able to spend in South Carolina.

"Don't settle for a consolation prize, Miriam. Are you positive that Harrison is your mama's sweetie?"

"Trust me. You should see the way she looks at him. But Manny's not a consolation prize. He's a catch, too."

And of course, there was Charles and Priscilla's approaching wedding. Liz and I had a funny discussion of visions of goats turning on spits and steel-drum music.

"Where's it gonna be?"

"You know what? I hardly have a single

detail but I'm having dinner with them on Thursday and I'll know a lot more after that."

Talking to Liz in that way and in that situation was like talking to a daughter I had never had, and I enjoyed it so much. In fact, I enjoyed it so very much that it surprised me how nostalgic I became and I wanted her to know who I really was. Soon I was telling her about my mother and Sullivans Island and what it had been like to grow up there, how I had brought my sons there as little boys and how they had always loved it. And as I described the almost mystical aura of the island to her, naturally it became clearer to me how much I cherished Sullivans Island. Liz listened to my rambling with a child's innocence. I could see in her eyes that she, like everyone else, was enchanted by the romantic idea of an island with a mango sun.

"It must've been wonderful. I would love to go there someday—meet your mother and all. I'll bet she's great."

Here was an opportunity for me to do something to make up for the hell I had brought to her.

"Then we'll do it. I'll take you there."

"Really?"

"Yep, as soon as you've got teeth and the stitches are out of your face."

"Seriously?"

"Shoot! Sure! Why not? I'll find us some cheap tickets and we'll go!"

"That would be so nice to feel the sun, wouldn't it?"

Liz's eyes were drooping and I knew it was time for her to nap.

"Yes, it *will* be nice. Why don't you rest now and I'll wake you up when it's lunchtime."

She nodded and I left her to sleep.

We were taking all the right steps to set the world right again. Kevin would drop by every evening with different cosmetic samples to cover her bruises and scarves to use for a sling, and he even brought her two wonderful running suits that were soft enough to sleep in.

Between the incident and her return home, I had gone up to Liz's apartment and restored some order. I knew the complete disarray and the sight of her blood on the bathroom floor would be traumatic for her, so I cleaned up, tried to set things back in their place, and ran a dust cloth over the furniture.

When you considered everything, Liz was

doing fine. There didn't seem to be any psy-chological damage other than embarrass-ment and I kept thinking that was so strange. But when we talked about it again, Kevin said perhaps she was the kind of woman who just held things inside. The college had given her a leave of absence and said she could return as soon as she felt well enough. But her sal-ary was going to be interrupted, which posed a rent problem if she convalesced for more than a few weeks. Liz fretted over that, but I could not have cared less. In fact, I liked hav-ing her around and so did Harry.

Kevin and I said it so often that Harry had taken to saying "How are you feeling?" He might have been a bird but he was smart enough to know something important had changed his habitat. In the past I would have been a complete wreck over something like this, but for some reason I was less anxious having Liz in residence. And Harry? He was whistling all day long.

Thursday's dinner date with Charlie and Priscilla rolled around faster than I thought it would. I had all sorts of wardrobe problems, which Liz helped me resolve. I didn't want to look frumpy or prissy and that meant ninety percent of what I owned was not going to deliver an image of a cool, hip, open-minded, but loving future mother-in-law. Kevin brought me a heavy gold charm bracelet to wear for good luck.

"It's youthful and all the rage this season," he said. "Save the box so I can return it."

It was not a gift.

"Absolutely. Gosh, I had one of these a million years ago. It was silver. I wonder whatever happened to it?" In my youth, each charm represented something special to you and they were collected over the years and soldered on the links one by one. Now you bought them by theme. This one represented *Gone with the Wind.*

"It's probably in a shoe box with your high school report cards. Honestly, one of these days we have to clean the basement. Isn't that tiny Scarlett adorable?"

"Yes. You're right, of course."

As you might imagine, before I left the house, Kevin and Liz gave me all manner of advice.

"Try to find out as much as you can about her family," Kevin said. "That will tell you a lot. Diseases, education, religious affiliations, you know . . . the gene pool?"

He was right, not that it mattered.

"Find out what she likes to do in her spare time, then you can figure out future birthday and Christmas presents." Practical advice from Liz.

"The main thing I want to know," I said, "is that she is one hundred percent in love with Charlie. And that she's not as boring as I always thought she was."

I had chosen an Italian restaurant on the Upper East Side of the city that was very good but not pretentious, which was to say I could afford to take the check. I had debated bringing Kevin along and then decided it would be best if it was just the three of us. Having Kevin there would change the group dynamic and I really wanted to know as much as I could about my future daughter-in-law. Most important, I wanted to charm her into liking me. Maybe the charm bracelet would help.

I waited for Charlie and Priscilla to arrive. They were late but only by twenty minutes. I was sipping a cocktail to calm my nerves and wishing the dinner was over with. The champagne I ordered was chilling in an ice bucket next to the table.

A few more minutes passed and I started getting annoyed that I was being made to wait so long. Then a minute later, when I was just about to call Charlie to see if he was dead in a ditch, the headwaiter appeared at my table, to seat Priscilla and Charlie. Charlie gave me a tiny kiss before sitting down. With that little kiss, all the edges of my annoyance evaporated.

"Sorry we're a little late," he said. "Traffic's terrible."

"Well, that's how it is," I said, in a way that I hoped conveyed that it wasn't a big deal to be half an hour late. "But y'all should try to get to the church on time on your big day, right? How are you, dear? Priscilla?"

"It would be a terrible thing to be late to our own wedding," she said, adding, "It's nice to see you again, Mrs. Swanson."

"We're not having a church wedding, Mom," Charlie said.

"Oh! Well, that's just fine!" It was not fine, but was I there to object to anything? "Shall we have a glass of champagne to celebrate the happy news?"

I looked around to the captain and he hurried over to pour. When we each had a glass, I raised mine to offer a toast.

"To your happiness, Charlie and Priscilla!

And, Priscilla? Welcome to my family, fractured and peculiar as we are. Cheers!"

To my total surprise, they laughed, thinking I had made a joke. Given my track record in comedy, I laughed with them. Never mind that I offered a truth she would learn soon enough.

"Thanks, Mom!"

"Thank you, Mrs. Swanson."

Mother McCree, she was so serious. I thought, How will I endure a lifetime of this?

"Priscilla? You've told your family, I assume? And they're pleased, I hope?"

"Oh, yes, ma'am. They are thrilled."

"Thank heavens for that! I can't wait to meet them. So tell me, Charlie, have you spoken to your father? What did he say?"

"Dad? You know him. Dad is so bizarre. Basically he said congratulations, that he and Judith would attend, but that he was completely uninterested in contributing to the expenses."

"Oh, goodness. Well, that wasn't very nice. Did you ask him for a lot of money or something?"

"No, I didn't ask dear old Dad for a dime. I guess he just wanted to have his intentions understood up front."

"Oh. Well, that's your father for you." I turned to Priscilla. "Normally I don't use profanity, Priscilla, but I think you should know that my ex-husband, Charlie's father? He's a horse's ass. And tighter than a mole's ear."

"Yes, ma'am. That's exactly what I've been given to understand and it appears to be true."

I looked at her and smiled, thinking there was hope for our relationship after all. She smiled back and we established a bond roughly the size of a garden pea, but a bond nonetheless.

"And your brother? You've spoken to him?"

"Well, I left him two messages. Who knows with him? Maybe he's in Hawaii? Why would he tell us anything? I'll catch up with him at some point."

"Priscilla? Dan, my other son, lets months pass with no word. He's a computer whiz, which means his people skills are almost non-existent. But he's a very nice nerd. Really."

"I'm sure," she said, and smiled wide. "That's how those guys are."

"I'm the one with all the personality," Charlie said.

Charlie was delighted by our pleasant conversation, and as the dinner went on, more champagne and then wine was consumed. Tight-lipped Priscilla became more talkative. I made a mental note to be generous with the alcohol when I was in her company.

"Priscilla? Why don't you call me Miriam? Mrs. Swanson sounds like a name that belongs on my mother-in-law's headstone."

"All right. Miriam it is. And I should know this but I'm embarrassed to admit that I don't. Tell me. Has your mother-in-law passed?"

"Yes, she has, and let me tell you this— she couldn't go fast enough!"

"Mom! That's terrible."

"So was she!" I said.

Priscilla and I got the girlie giggles. I liked the sound of her laughter. I finally had a small inkling that we might do just fine together.

"Well, kids? I don't have nearly the resources as the old tightwad I divorced," I said, throwing propriety to the wind, "but I would love to help with your wedding. In fact, I'd be honored. So why don't y'all tell me what your plans are so far?"

They looked at each other, breathing a collective sigh of relief, and the details came rolling out. As distanced as we had been from one another, my willingness to begin anew and their natural excitement was healing old wounds.

"I have a friend who owns a loft in Tribeca that he rents out for parties," Charlie said. "He said we could have it for almost nothing."

"And my uncle back home is a minister. He wants to fly up and perform the ceremony," Priscilla said.

"Oh! How lovely," I said. "Is he a particular denomination?"

"He's a Rasta," Charlie said with a perfectly straight face.

I had such an adrenaline rush at the thought of Rastafarians marrying into my family that I nearly fell from my chair. I could see the pictures in their wedding album racing through my head. Not that I had anything against Rastafarians, and in fact, I liked Bob Marley's music quite a lot. It was just a tremor I felt, not a full-blown earthquake.

"Seriously?" I said as calmly as I could.

"Your son is a terrible liar, you know. My uncle David is a devout Baptist," Priscilla said, and gave Charlie an affectionate slap on his arm. "Stop! You bad dog."

"Her whole family raises ugli fruit and they

sell them along the roadside from the back of their trucks," Charlie said.

"Stop!" Priscilla said. "Miriam, what am I to do with this man?"

"Just promise me you'll love him," I said.

"I don't want to live one day without him," she said.

"That's good enough for me," I said. "So tell me. How many people are you thinking of inviting and how big is the loft?"

We went through the decisions they had made thus far and what they wanted for their wedding sounded like fun. They wanted a traditional band to play during dinner but reggae music for cocktails. The ceremony would be performed on a skirted riser and then we would retreat for cocktails to another area of the loft. While we would enjoy drinks made of mangoes and yes, ugli fruit, some laced with rum and others nonalcoholic, and other Jamaican traditional food, the room would be transformed to a dining room with a dance floor. The dinner itself would be a buffet of Jamaican and American specialties. And their guest list was small, only fifty to sixty people, which, I knew all too well, would grow to one hundred before it was all over with.

"Well, it sounds like it might get a little expensive," I said. "Have you done a budget? Because you have to figure in invitations, postage, decorations, Priscilla's gown . . . never mind the caterer and rentals and all that stuff."

"Mom? I told Priscilla that you'd been doing events all my life and we were kind of hoping you would help us figure this out."

"And I don't have a mother to help me," Priscilla said.

Suddenly everyone in my world was a motherless child.

I reached over and put my hand on top of hers.

"Don't you worry about a thing, Priscilla. It would be such a pleasure to help."

"How's that girl, your tenant? Liz, right? How's she doing?"

"Much better. She's seeing Dr. Imber on Friday afternoon and the oral surgeon on Monday."

"She looks like a nice girl and—"

"Charlie told me about her," Priscilla said, interrupting. "What a terrible thing! And how awful for you, too!"

That was how dinner went. You would have thought there had never been an awkward moment or an unkind word between us, that Priscilla had grown up next door, and my ex-husband, Charles, was a jerk, oh yes, but that in the bigger scheme of the world, who had ever cared about that?

When I arrived at home, I peeked in on Liz. She was sound asleep, so I quietly closed her door. I put my precious Harry in his cage and covered it. Then, after I changed my clothes, I went around, checking all the doors and windows, and slipped out into my court-yard for a moment. I had not picked up the twigs and other debris in some time and it was too early to think about doing that any-way. It was still winter and we would probably get another blast of snow before the season was all over.

Long ago, maybe ten years or so, I used to come out here with a book to read or with my scissors to cut herbs to season my fami-ly's dinner or to entertain friends with a cock-tail or a glass of wine before we all went to the theater or somewhere for a bite.

But now my garden was in a sorry state of neglect just like every other part of my life had been. It had always been so formal, with miniature boxwoods and topiaries, azaleas, and roses trained to crawl up the stone walls.

I wondered how it would look with a thousand pink-and-ivory tulips growing everywhere like they were native to the space. I could almost see white hyacinths everywhere to sweeten the air. I wondered what a new pathway would add, one that led to a cozy bench and a tiny fountain with water that trickled like music. More possibilities for change were right before me.

I pulled my bathrobe around me and looked up at the cold dark sky and around to other town houses and high-rise buildings. Lights were being turned off for the night, one by one. People were closing up their homes and going to bed, recharging minds and bodies for the challenges that lay ahead the next day. Suddenly I felt a part of things again. We were having a wedding and the dreaded dinner with my prospective daughter-in-law had gone very well. Exceedingly well, in fact. Charlie and Priscilla had not yet decided on a date, but if they married in the spring as they thought they might, perhaps it would give me time to bring my garden back into shape. I could invite their guests here for a postrehearsal get-together of some kind. It would be too late for bulbs that had not been planted, but I could bring in annuals for color and make it welcoming. I could put in bulbs the next October, and I would. I would have to ask Charlie what he thought about having a rehearsal dinner here. And Priscilla. Now I would have to ask her opinion, too. It didn't bother me in the least. In fact, I looked forward to it because women shared an unspoken understanding about the importance of certain things. She had said she had no mother to go to, had she not? I wondered if her mother was dead or alive and made a note to ask Charlie so I could better understand what role I might play.

I called Charlie in the morning and invited him to come have a look at the diamond for Priscilla's ring. He said he would be there at noon.

Twelve-fifteen the doorbell rang and he was there. Liz was watching an old movie in the guest room and was dressed in her sweatsuit. I was warming up some split pea soup from the deli—Charlie's favorite—and checked my hair in the mirror before I opened the door.

"Come in! Come in! It's freezing out there!"

"Yeah, it's still as cold as the devil!"

"Give me your coat, sweetheart, and go

say hello to Liz. I'll have lunch on the table in a few minutes."

"Sure. Liz?" Charlie called out to her. "How are you?"

"How are you?" Harry repeated.

I looked at Harry and stroked his feathers.

"Miriam is happy," I said. Then I repeated it, "Miriam is happy."

Harry cocked his head to one side and looked at me, paying attention to what I had just said. For him, they were old words strung together in a new way. I took Liz a tray and said to Charlie, "Soup's on."

"Thanks, Miriam. This looks delicious."

"Good, hon. Call me if you need anything."

Over lunch I took my grandmother's diamond ring from my pocket and put it in front of Charlie on the table.

"What do you think?"

"Oh, Mom! This is awesome! Priscilla is going to be thrilled! Now why do you think we should change this? I think it's great just like it is."

It was a platinum Art Deco setting with the single round stone raised up on a little mound that was set with tiny diamond chips and filigree all around its sides. The mounting added importance to the stone and its effect was feminine and lovely, albeit old-fashioned.

"You do? Oh, Charlie! I'm so glad you like it!"

"Like it? It's fantastic! Mom, Priscilla's family doesn't have two nickels to rub together. She's the first one in her family to go beyond a basic college education. I mean, they're very nice—her father runs a bed-and-breakfast and her brother runs a little grocery store. But trust me, nobody's got a diamond like this."

"That's fine, son. I'm thrilled that I can do this. So tell me. What happened to her mother?"

He was quiet for a moment and then he said, "Well, they told Priscilla that she drowned, but I think her father caught her fooling around and took her fishing. Know what I mean?"

"Priscilla told you this?"

"No, but she's implied it. The family line is that she drowned, but her friends claim otherwise."

"Have you met him? The father, I mean?" What? Dear God! My pulse began to race.

"Yes, he's a wonderful man, Mom. He's not like a murderer or something."

"Well, if her father pushed his wife off a boat, he damn sure is a murderer!"

"Mom. Be cool. I don't want this to change your opinion. Maybe she slipped. Look, they live in a remote little fishing village outside of Kingston with no Coast Guard or anything . . ."

I took a very deep breath. He didn't want the fact that a possible murderer would be having cocktails in my rehabilitated garden bother me?

"Let's just tell ourselves that she slipped, then, okay? Or got caught in an undertow? But in any case, never go fishing with him, do you hear me?"

Charlie started laughing. "God, Mom. When did you get so gullible?"

I realized then that he had been pulling my chain. Again.

"Was this a fishing trip with her Rasta uncle?"

"Got it."

"You know what, Charlie? Your humor is decidedly worse than mine. So what happened to her mother?"

"She just disappeared and that's the truth. Priscilla was about five."

"Well, that's awful. Never found her?"

"Not a trace. This soup is great. Got any more?"

"Sure." I got up to refill his bowl. "Makes you wonder, doesn't it?"

"About what?"

"People disappearing. There are thousands of people who just disappear every year. I mean, I think most of them probably fall off a bridge or move to another town and assume another identity, but all of them just can't forget to tell their families that they're leaving, right?"

"Who knows? Alien abductions?"

"Whatever. Just promise me you'll take the ring to Corey to appraise it and clean it before you give it to Priscilla, okay? He'll make sure the stones are in there tight and all that."

"Sure."

After we were finished and Charlie had his coat on to leave, I put the ring in a little velvet box and back in Charlie's hands.

"Thanks, Mom. This is incredibly generous of you, you know, and I just want to say . . ."

"That you love me?"

"You know I do."

He left and I thought that I would give him the world if I could.

Chapter Thirteen

The Migration Begins

I was on the treadmill, thinking that walking to nowhere was a little bit stupid but that it did give me a chance to muse. Earlier that morning, Liz had put herself in a cab and gone to her appointment with the plastic surgeon. I was glad that she felt well enough to go on her own, but I encouraged her to leave her things in my apartment, as the surgery she was facing would mean more painkillers and recovery time. Meanwhile, I was walking to nowhere hoping to speed up my metabolism, shed a few lbs, and gain slimmer thighs.

I suppose I would have to admit that my

reluctance to branch outside my tiny circle of people in my life had been passed on to Dan, my other son. Sometimes it seemed like he had all but disowned us. If I didn't receive regular Mother's Day cards and birthday cards, I would've thought it was true. But now that we had a wedding on the horizon, he was going to have to talk to me. Someone had to reopen the lines of communication and apparently the only way that would happen was if *I* picked up the phone and used it. Waiting for him to call was as bad as waiting for a soufflé to rise, not that I had ever had any luck with soufflés. So I resolved that I would call him as soon as my thirty minutes on the dang fool contraption had elapsed. As always, Miss Josie was right. It was up to me to keep my family together.

I still owed Kevin the two hundred dollars for the idiotic machine and reminded myself to write him a check. Gosh, there was so much to do. I still had not called Mother to tell her about all the craziness of the past week or so, nor had I discussed with her the fact that Charlie and Priscilla had decided to tie the knot. I wondered if Charlie had called her and then decided I would have heard from

Mother if he had. I checked my watch. I still had eleven minutes left.

I would call Miss Josie myself, give her all the news, and ask ever so cleverly if she had seen or heard anything about Manny. How could I pose the question? *So, how's Harrison? How's his stupid friend who never called me?* No, that wouldn't do. How about *Gosh, I sure had a great time when I was last down there with that guy, what's his name?* That was better to be sure. I had a lot to learn about playing it cool. I glanced at my wristwatch again. Six minutes of torture left to go.

I had promised Liz to take her to Sullivans Island, and if I wanted the advance discount price on the airline tickets, I was going to have to plan it. Obviously, I needed to discuss that with Mother, too. I added that to the phone-call agenda.

Maybe the treadmill wasn't so bad after all. I was getting my thoughts organized and making a plan for the day, and even I had to admit, I felt better about the world when I got off the ridiculous thing and took a shower. You know, I felt a little virtuous or something? Oh, who cared? Then, like there was someone else inside my head, that little voice I struggled to ignore said, *You'll care when this wedding happens and you have to face Charles and Judith.* I broke a sweat born of terror. *Dear Lord, please take fifteen pounds of fat from my body and I'll never ask for another thing. Thank You, Lord, amen. P.S. If You are so inclined, please throw in tone for my upper arms.*

Intellectually, I knew better. There just wasn't much of a point in having a panic attack over Charles and Judith. She was young and gorgeous with a body not to be believed and I wasn't and never would be. I told myself for the umpteenth time to simply get over it. I would enlist Kevin's help in finding a beautiful dress that flattered my protrusions and lumps somehow and I would be so gracious that I would outshine her anyhow.

Clearly, that was a dewdrop of fantasy.

How did I think that I could really outshine Judith? Not happening. This sidebar needed a lot of thought and planning for me to be even marginally triumphant. Time was up for the dreaded exercise routine of the day and I decided that adding another ten minutes to it might be a good idea. Maybe fifteen because the wedding would come and go and my backside would still be of terrifying proportions.

After showering and dressing for the day, I steeled myself and called Dan's cell.

"Hi, Mom." His voice was as flat as a pancake.

"Come on, Dan! Can't we start with *how are you?* I haven't talked to you since the earth cooled its core!" (More humor wasted on offspring.)

"How are you?"

Would you like sausage or bacon with that short stack?

I kept my voice light, sprinkled with good nature that he appeared to have no interest in whatsoever.

"Well, I'm fine! Fine! There's lots of news around here, you know. And how are you and your family?"

"Good. What's up?"

Sometimes his lack of personality and affection just completely irked the devil out of me.

"Have you spoken to your brother?"

"He called a couple of times but I've been really busy."

"Oh, well, are you sure everything's okay with you? I mean, is there something you want to tell me?"

"No, I told you. We're fine. What's going on?"

"Well, your brother is getting married, for one thing."

"To that black woman?"

I bristled.

"That is an unacceptable remark, Dan. Your brother is marrying Priscilla, who happens to be Jamaican and is a very beautiful woman, Dan."

"I'm sure she is. When's the wedding?"

"Right after Easter, and that's why I'm calling. When you speak to him I imagine Charlie will ask you to be in the wedding party, so I wanted to know if you and Nan and the kids would like to stay with me?"

Silence.

"I didn't ask you for a kidney, son. I'm inviting you and the children to stay with me. I would love to see them and you and Nan. It's been such a long time."

"I'll have to ask Nan. I'll call you back."

"Sure. That's fine. Okay, then . . . we'll talk later? Give my love to everyone, will you?"

We hung up and I was reminded of the details of his annoyance with me. Every Christmas since we all but stopped speaking, I sent him a check for the family so that they could buy what they wanted. I did the same thing on birthdays. So I wasn't completely negligent. But checks probably seemed impersonal or cold. That, however, wasn't the worst of it. I had never been to visit them since they had named their son Independence Maybank Swanson. He was nicknamed Indy May, and if that didn't give the poor child gender issues, I didn't know what would. Their daughter, now seven years old, was named Mary Freedom Swanson. When all the schoolchildren nicknamed her M.F. and snickered to her face and behind her back, I told them both it was wrong for parents to give their little children a name that could be construed to mean something so very vulgar.

Dan told me to mind my own business, Nan wept for days, and we had barely spoken since.

M.F. and Indy May Swanson were seven and four, and I hoped to heaven they could forgive their parents someday. Maybe if I could send them plane tickets it would soften their hearts, I thought. Buy their forgiveness? Why not? Just because I didn't approve of the names they gave their children did not mean I did not care about them at all. I had stood my ground long enough to significantly damage what small relationship we had, and it was time to let it go. I mean, what if I dropped dead? Would they tell their children, *Well, sweeties, the reason you never knew your grandmother is that she didn't like your names*. How completely horrible would that be? No, if they had any more children they could name him or her Garbage Dump Mc-Gee Finnegan Swanson, call him/her GDMF, and I would not utter one single word about it. Not one word. Sometimes it just wasn't worth it to be right.

Where did I think I was going to find all the money to do the things I wanted to do for Charlie and Priscilla's wedding? And to fly Liz to Sullivans Island? Or to fly Dan and his family to New York? It surely wasn't under my mattress. I looked all around me and thought, Well, what *about* that apartment sale? I would discuss it with Kevin, who was a marvel at all retail ventures.

I mean, did I really need three silver coffee services? One was more than I cared to polish. Did I need four sterling-silver sets of flatware for twelve in different patterns and one for twenty-four? Ten sets of mother-of-pearl-handled silver flatware for fish and another six sets for dessert? Twenty silver trays, bowls, and fruit baskets? Thirty-six silver goblets? Fifty toast racks? Sixty-five sterling saltcellars with little spoons? That crazy collection of my grandfather's German beer steins and all those risqué Meissen figurines of topless fräuleins eating fruit and playing lutes under trees in Vienna? An inventory was most definitely in order.

So was a call to Miss Josie. I dialed her number and she answered.

"Miriam? What's new, dear?"

"How much time do you have?"

I gave her the full download on the state of my world, and when my report ended, she had a few things to say.

"Unload all that stuff that you don't need anyway, come home, and bring Liz."

"Are you sure? About bringing Liz, I mean?"

"Honey, that child needs an old lady's wisdom. Big-time. And as for you, missy, Manny's been asking after you like an old hound dog looking for his master. He's plain pitiful."

I found that to be surprising, but maybe he said it to amuse or compliment Mother. Men were capable of that kind of behavior.

"Then he should pick up the blessed phone and call me once in a while. And P.S., you're not an old lady."

"Yes, I am, and men are stupid. You know that."

"So are women."

"And you really like Priscilla?"

"Very much."

"Give them a coffee service for a wedding gift."

"Fabulous idea!"

"Say it's from me."

"Okay. You gave it to me in the first place. I'll give them flatware from me."

"Sounds good. But you had better save a coffee service and some flatware for Dan and Nan or you'll never hear the end of it."

A few minutes later we hung up. So Manny was asking about me, was he? Good. That was promising, even if he didn't mean it.

I looked over the coffee services and decided to give the two less elaborate ones to my children and I would keep the third until after the wedding. There was a lovely man over on Second Avenue who polished silver and made it look like it belonged in a museum. I wrapped two of the silver services in newspaper and put them in grocery bags, threw on a coat, and hailed a cab. I would bring the trays and flatware to him on a second trip.

"Oh, these are beauties," Mr. Lefko said as I unpacked each piece and placed them on his counter. "I can make them sing!"

"Wonderful! I'll be right back with the trays and some flatware."

I took a cab home, packed the other things, dropped them off, and decided to walk home. The air was brisk but it felt good against my face. For some inexplicable reason I was in excellent spirits. I pulled out my cell and called Kevin.

"Do you have plans for dinner?"

"No, why? Is my best girl inviting me over?"

"Yes, I am. In the mood for, I don't know, roasted chicken with mashed potatoes? Steamed carrots?"

"My mouth is watering, Petal. I'll be home at six-thirty and I'll help you."

"Sounds perfect."

I picked up what I needed for our dinner, and when I arrived at home, Liz was there in my kitchen filling a glass with water.

"Dr. Imber wants to do the surgery Tuesday morning," she said.

"Good. Just so you know, I'm paying your bills and you can pay me back."

"Oh, Miriam! How can you?"

"With my AmEx card? I get points. You can pay me back ten dollars a week for the rest of your life. Are you ready for that?"

"Are you kidding?" She threw her good arm around me and squeezed. "How can I thank you? I can't wait to have this all over with. On Tuesday, I'll have a mouth full of temps, but Dr. Imber said that was okay with him."

"Well, good then. Because as soon as you have your stitches out, we're heading south to visit Miss Josie."

"Do you really mean it?"

"Yes. Prepare yourself to fall in love with a sandbar."

That night, the three of us had dinner, and although I had cut Liz's chicken in the tiniest pieces, she still had difficulty chewing.

"My jaw still hurts so badly," she said. "And I'm so sick of this sling."

Kevin, who was usually so ready with quips for every occasion, became somber.

"I just hate this entire business," he said. "It makes me so angry."

"How do you think I feel?" Liz said.

"How do you feel?" I asked.

Liz looked at her plate for a few moments and then said, "It just amazes me how some people get away with this kind of insane violent behavior and go on with their lives completely unfazed."

This girl had definitely experienced some kind of abuse. I was sure of it. Kevin gave me a nod of agreement.

"Guiltless," I said. "I can see Agnes and Truman now eating heart-healthy Dover sole and monkfish at Le Bernardin and pretending nothing ever happened, except for his heart attack, which I'm sure they blame on me. And Liz."

"I just hope to God there's a hell," Liz said in a quiet voice, gently chewing a mouthful of mashed potatoes.

We smiled at her, and Kevin said, "Daisy Mae? Sometimes you are so adorable and you don't even know it."

Monday, Liz saw Gordon Ferguson and came home smiling.

"I really think I'm going to be okay," she said. "Eventually. See?"

I inspected the inside of her mouth and agreed with her, although I'll admit privately that looking inside Liz's damaged mouth res-

urrected and nearly jet-propelled the undi-
gested remains of my morning's breakfast.

The next day Gerald Imber worked his
magic and came out into the waiting room to
speak to me. My hands shook as I handed
my credit card to the gal behind the desk,
thinking it would be twenty thousand dollars
or more. But Dr. Imber's bill was only for the
anesthesiologist.

"Ms. Harper's in recovery and did just fine."

"Thank heaven. How many stitches did
she need?" I asked.

"About a zillion, but they're mostly internal
and the others are very tiny," he said. "The
good news is there's no apparent nerve damage and in a couple of months she'll be able
to cover it completely with makeup. Just make
sure she doesn't go out without a heavy dose
of sunscreen on her face."

"Right. I'll make sure to tell her. Um, Dr.
Imber?"

"Yes?"

"There's no charge here for your surgery?"

"Mrs. Swanson? Your son Charlie is one of
the finest young doctors I've ever known. He
worked like a dog for me. This one's on the
house."

"Oh! That is so incredibly kind of you! How can I thank you?"

"Little kiss right here," he said. His eyes twinkled as he pointed to his cheek.

I delivered a very polite smooch and thought the world wasn't such a terrible place, after all.

Once I got her home, Liz slept all afternoon as the anesthesia made its way out of her system. That evening, Kevin and I shared a bowl of spaghetti Bolognese in my kitchen, waiting for her to wake up. Harry was on top of his cage, playing on a new jungle gym I had just bought him.

"She's been through a terrible ordeal, hasn't she?" he said. "I wish I knew a nice single guy I could introduce her to, but in my world? Well, there just aren't many."

"Well, she's going to want to be all healed before she goes back on the prowl, don't you think? Do you want some Parmesan?"

"Of course to both." Kevin poured another glass of Chianti for both of us.

"Isn't it funny that she hasn't said anything about her family? I mean, she didn't call her mother or anyone, at least not that I'm aware of. Did she say anything to you about calling her folks?"

"Not a word. It is strange."

"I wanted to talk to you about something else, Kevin."

"Please! You sound so serious! Are you raising the rent?"

I laughed and said, "No, how could I do that? No, no. I want to raise some cash to help Charlie and Priscilla with their wedding expenses. And heaven knows, Liz needed help with her bills. I put Ferguson's bill and Imber's anesthesiologist's bill on my AmEx card. Points, right?"

"Well, that's using the old bean. How was Imber's bill? Through the roof?"

"How about zero?"

"You're kidding, right?"

"No. He did it for Charlie as a favor. And he's just about the nicest man I ever met to boot."

"Wow. That is unbelievable in this day and age. But how is Liz ever going to repay you?"

"I don't even care if she does, Kevin. If she can, Liz can pay me back whenever. I don't care. But I will have to pay the AmEx bill, which is why I have to sell some things."

"Understood. But Charles not helping the kids? I don't get it. Really. I just don't."

"Charles is a horse's ass," Harry said.

"God, I love that bird," Kevin said.

"Me, too. Anyway, Charles is so disgusting to me sometimes. Charlie merely called him to announce his biggest news of his entire life and Scrooge just jumped all over him and told him not to dare ask for a nickel. So I'm not asking him either. Give him the opportunity to yell and scream at me? I think not."

"Good grief. You're right. Don't call the bum. Too demoralizing. I agree. What is the matter with that man?"

"A lot. Charles has lots of issues. But why he's so stingy? I don't know."

"It just doesn't make any sense that you wouldn't want to help your son get married. You know, honeymoon expenses or something?"

"Let's not dwell on him and his peculiarities. Anyway, the only way I know to raise some cash is to sell some silver and so forth. I was hoping you might help me figure this out?"

"What? The Old Curiosity Shop is finally deaccessioning?"

"Yes. It's about time, right? I've got boxes of silver stuffed under the bed, in the back of closets . . . Let's just say that in my younger days I had a little thing for silver? And then my mother gave me all of hers, which was a lot, and well, all totaled, it's an embarrassing amount of tarnish. But I'm glad I hung on to it because now I can use it for something worthwhile."

"Petal? You always surprise me with your resourcefulness. I would be thrilled to help you. This Saturday I'm free. Why don't we dig it all out, photograph it, and I'll get an appraiser to establish approximate values. Have you thought about whether you want to auction it or just sell it straight out or what?"

"Well, I was thinking about a house sale like they have in the suburbs? You know? Garage sale but indoors?"

Harry imitated the doorbell sound five times in a row.

Kevin looked at me like he was certain my brain was a small wad of low-fat Swiss cheese.

"What?" I said.

"Petal Puss? Not happening. Even Harry knows it's a bad idea. Let Uncle Kevin handle this for you. I've got so much attitude, I'll have people thinking they're getting bargain prices on Queen Betty the Second's treasures. Seriously."

He was right, of course.

That Saturday, Liz had removed her bandage because she had to clean the wound and apply a special ointment every four hours. It was hard to look at because it was angry and red and the stitches were unsightly, too. But we could see the line of the scar wasn't nearly as bad as it could have been and that was a blessing to be sure.

"It's going to look much better when the stitches are out," I said.

"I hope so!" she said.

"I still wish I could have wrung his neck," Kevin said. "So, ladies? Let's get this show on the road."

Liz and I helped Kevin as he photographed each piece of silver I was willing to relinquish, including a separate picture of the hallmarks. Next, we cataloged the beer steins, and when we got to the Meissen, the nymphets caused no end of wisecracks.

"Charles loved these hideous things. There's just no accounting for taste, is there?" I said.

"Why are all their bosoms round like little tennis balls?" Liz said. "Do you think they really were that perky?"

"Perky bosoms. I love it. Me? I like the britches on this fellow," Kevin said.

It felt so good to be letting these things go. What had once seemed extremely necessary to a refined life now felt like nothing more than clutter and pretentious excess. I kept a few things—two trays, a breadbasket, candlesticks, one set of flatware, a pair of Chinese export vases, and some things I thought the boys' wives might enjoy—but the rest of it held no meaning for me.

With Kevin's small digital camera and the wonders of technology, he was able to print the pictures out on four-by-six-inch glossy stock. He arranged them all in a leather photograph album, and to my surprise, it all looked absolutely professional.

"I can't believe you did this in one afternoon, Kevin. This looks so amazing, I can't believe these gorgeous objects are all mine."

"It's incredible," Liz said.

"Yes, it is incredible, if I say so myself." He laughed. "Monday I will give this to my friend and he will tell us where we can get the best prices."

"Who's that?"

"Thomas Britt. The interior designer."

"Why do I know that name?"

"Maybe because he's all over *Architectural Digest* and he's basically the king of good taste in the entire country?"

"Oh. That's fine with me, but why would we take it to a designer and not somebody like a retail dealer?" I asked.

"Well, we could, but first of all, interior designers frequently accessorize their client's homes. The wives of these new-money Wall Street hedge-fund types don't want to have shiny new silver in their dining rooms. They want furnishings with a provenance."

"You're not going to tell anybody that she's been forced to sell her grandmother's tea service, are you?" Liz said.

"Actually, I'm keeping that," I said.

"Yeah, okay, but seriously, Kevin. I mean, my God, between Charles and the coffee thing, hasn't Miriam suffered enough embarrassment in this town?"

I started to laugh because as the old Miriam died and Mellie continued to emerge, everything was bathed in a new light.

"Why would I care one whit? It's very liberating. Anyway, I wouldn't be the first wife who sold her silver, would I? To be honest, I can't even afford the polish! So how ridiculous is that?"

"Listen, no one says who owned it. It's offered anonymously. The quality of the collection will speak for itself. And it may not all go in one swoop. So let's just see what happens."

"That sounds like a plan to me," I said, feeling like a sack of rocks had been lifted from my shoulders.

That night, Kevin went to the theater with some friends and Liz moved back upstairs after thanking me a thousand times for all I had done for her. I couldn't remember feeling so good about myself in years. The tragedy had brought us close together, if not exactly like mother and daughter then like aunt and niece. I felt so grateful to be able to help her, and not just financially. I had to say, she had been more stoic than a lot of other beautiful young women might have been. That made me think yet again that she had probably come from a life of some other kind of suffering. She had never spoken about it. I would not ask.

"Miriam's happy," Harry said from his perch.

I burst out laughing and said, "Yes! Miriam's happy!"

I called Charlie because in all the hullabaloo, I had not had the chance to tell him about Gerald Imber's gift.

"He was just amazing, Charlie. Seriously. You did the nicest and most charitable thing by calling in that favor. I mean, with a little concealer, Liz is going to be beautiful again."

"Well, I'm glad it worked out. Hey, are you going to be home tomorrow night?"

"Where else would I be?"

"I'm going to give Priscilla the ring at dinner . . ."

"You are? Oh! How exciting!"

"Right? And I think it might be nice to come over and let you see it on her finger, you know, so she can say thanks and all? What do you think?"

"Oh! I would love that! Did you take it to Corey?"

"Yeah, and you should see this thing—it's like a headlight now! And you know what?"

"What?"

"He said it's worth like nine or ten thousand dollars."

"Mother McCree! Give it back!"

Silence.

"I'm just *kidding,* Charlie."

"I knew that."

"Don't lie to your mother. What time will y'all be here?"

"You're right. You had me for a moment. How's nine?"

"Sounds just fine."

The next evening I had a fire crackling in the fireplace, and a nice bottle of champagne on ice. I bought a small wedding cake with white icing and a silver spun-sugar bow on top and placed it on my best crystal cake plate. I decorated my silver cake knife with thin pink and white satin ribbon streamers. I was ready for a happy occasion.

They rang the doorbell and I couldn't open it fast enough. Priscilla was radiant. Charlie had never been so handsome or animated. We oohed and aahed over the ring, and hugged over and over. Priscilla sliced the cake, Charlie opened the champagne, and they toasted me. *They toasted me.*

Priscilla choked up, and with her voice cracking with emotion, she said, "Miriam? I just don't know what to say. I love your wonderful son, I love this exquisite ring, and I know I'm going to love you, too. I already do.

I'm going to be a good wife, and I promise, I'm going to be a good daughter-in-law, too."

"And a good doctor," Charlie said.

I wanted to weep. I looked at them, so in love, so happy, sitting close to each other on my old sofa, Charlie's arm around her shoulder, squeezing her arm with pride, the fire burning . . . everything I could want for my son was right in front of me. An exotic, beautiful, brilliant woman who promised us her love and fidelity. I wanted to freeze the moment and hold it forever. Screw Charles Swanson, I thought. We didn't need him in our lives anymore. And, by the way, it was permissible for Mellie to cuss from time to time.

Chapter Fourteen

WITHOUT A STITCH

While Liz paid a visit to Dr. Imber to have her stitches removed, I drafted three budgets for Charlie and Priscilla's wedding, each of them based on seventy-five guests. The most expensive included the predictable— serious invitations, two bars with premium liquors and wines, Irish-linen tablecloths with damask overlays, ballroom chairs, rented trees laced with tiny white lights, velvet pipe and drape to disguise service areas, important floral designs and standing candelabra for either side of the riser, modest centerpieces for the tables with votive candles everywhere, and a rented parquet dance floor.

I included an eight-piece band for dancing and a four-piece reggae ensemble for cocktails. The menu depended on what caterer they chose, but I threw in a round number. A photographer would take formal portraits of the wedding and candid shots during the reception. He would produce leather-bound albums for the bride and groom and smaller ones for the families.

The second option was to print the invitations on someone's computer on nice paper and bring all the expenditures down a notch or two. Or three. For example, dinner could be served all buffet style. The third option was a down-home Jamaican-themed party with handwritten invitations, punch bowls, draped picnic tables with centerpieces in conch shells, palms on the riser for the ceremony, and whatever Kevin would beg, borrow, and steal from the display department at Bergdorf's. The guests could cook their own goat on skewers in a fondue pot. Oh, come on, that was funny, wasn't it? A little? Anyway, I was leaning toward the third, as it sounded like the most fun to me.

In any and all scenarios, the wedding cake would be filled with rum-soaked fruit, as this was an important tradition to Priscilla. When

I compared the possibilities, the differences in the costs were dramatic.

I called Charlie to discuss it.

"Hi! How are you?"

"Fine. How are you?"

I was still so surprised by our newly reestablished comfort with each other and I was ever so grateful to have it.

"Great! Listen, I put together a couple of different budgets for this wedding reception and I know you have to go over all the details with Priscilla, but I was just wondering if you had some range of money in mind. You know, that you could afford to spend and still have a nice honeymoon?"

I told him what I thought the differences were between the options I had come up with, and he said, "Go for it, Mom. Do it Miriam Swanson style. I'll ask Priscilla, but I know she has always secretly dreamed of some kind of an elegant affair. It's bad enough that we're using a loft instead of the Waldorf, right? But we've got the money, we just don't have the expertise to organize this. At least I *think* we've got enough money."

I assumed that meant that Priscilla handled their finances, but I said nothing.

"Got it. Well, and I'm going to help you

wherever I can. You know, I should really take Kevin down there to see the loft with me. He's the über-fantasy design guy in this whole town. I know he would have some great ideas."

"Well, here. Call this guy."

He gave me the name and number of his loft-owner friend and I made an appointment for that evening. If Kevin was free, we would give it the once-over.

"I don't know why I let you drag me into these things, Petal," Kevin said, and we bumped and barreled our way downtown in a cab at six o'clock.

"Oh, come on. You just need a glass of wine and you'll be fine. Tough day?"

"Please! I had this whole outrageous spring thing planned around *Alice in Wonderland*. I commissioned life-size papier-mâché white rabbits and Cheshire cats from a fabulous artist in Belgium. They came in so monstrous-looking that they're sure to give every child in the city a psychotic episode. I swear. Head-line: KINDERGARTEN SUICIDES. They look like they could eat you alive. In one bite. All those pointed teeth and red-rimmed, evil eyes . . ."

"Well, that surely won't do. What's your fallback position?"

"Switch to Buckingham Palace and do something royal. Tea with the queen instead of Alice. I have things I can use. Oceans of pearls and so forth. But it's so annoying. And I hate repeating themes."

"Well, look, we'll stay in this place for ten minutes and then I'll take you out for dinner at some cool place in Tribeca. How about Odeon? I haven't been there in ages."

Kevin looked over at me and smiled. I knew he loved Odeon.

"I can't do this without you, Kevin, and you know it."

"That's why I'm here, Miriam. That's why I'm here."

We walked around the loft with Charlie's friend and Kevin jotted notes in his Moleskine. He paced the length and width of the large space, inspected the kitchen and the bathroom, and asked how many amps of power were available.

"Do you mind if I bring in chandeliers? I have my own electrician," he said.

"I don't know about that."

"He's union, from Bergdorf Goodman. I've known him for years."

"I'm kind of funny about another electrician working with my wiring."

"And I'm kind of funny about another electrician working with my Venetian chandeliers. How about if I gave your guy a couple of hundred bucks to be here just in case my man has questions about breakers and so forth?"

"That sounds fair. Sure. That's good. I'll give you his number."

After a cocktail and over steaks and eggs in a booth at Odeon, I finally said, "So what do you think about the loft?"

"Only for you, Miriam. What do I think? I'll get my guys in there and we will transform that dank, dismal hellhole of the most depressing warehouse I have ever seen in the entire world into Cinderella's palace. Priscilla is going to feel like a fairy princess, like every girl should on her wedding day. The good news is there's lots of room for a huge dance floor. So don't worry about it. Now, tell me about Liz and when are y'all heading south? It's just me and Harry again, right?"

"Oh, Kevin, you're the best friend I have ever had."

"That's okay. You're mine, too. But at some point, I want to go to Sullivans Island. And by the way, I gave the scrapbook of pirates to Tom Britt. Waiting to hear. But I have to tell you this."

"What?"

"Mr. Britt was seriously impressed with the book. He said he hadn't seen silver like yours in ages. I mean, Miriam, I think you're sitting on a huge chunk of change."

"Well, that's good, because with everything that's going on, I'm going to need it."

I found the airline tickets for Liz and me at the right price and naturally I asked her again if she still wanted to go.

"Miriam—gosh, I still feel so funny to call you that—anyway, I would love to get out of here for a few days. I've got cabin fever, you know?"

"I imagine that you do! Well, the sunshine will do us both a lot of good."

So I bought the tickets, and a week later, Liz and I were on an airplane to Charleston. Her arm was still in a sling, so I helped her with her luggage, which we gate-checked. As the plane circled over the rivers of Charleston, Liz couldn't stop staring through her window. The view was, as usual, absolutely spectacular, beyond anything you could capture in a photograph.

"I can't believe how *blue* the sky is and how *all* those little waterways just weave in and out of everywhere. The whole landscape looks like it was designed by Leonardo da Vinci or somebody!"

"Bigger."

"Michelangelo?"

"No, hon, the hand of God sculpted this."

Liz was quiet for a moment and then she said, "You don't talk about religion much, Miriam."

"What is there to say? You want proof? Look outside the window. And wait until you see the sunset."

"Papaya?"

"Close enough."

"You know, when I was a little girl I went to church every Sunday and to Bible study and all that. But I'll bet you I haven't been in a church, except for a wedding or something, in ten years."

"How come?"

"Because, well, with all the ugly things that happened to me growing up, I just had a hard time believing there was a God out there who loved me."

"Such as?"

"Such as, I don't know. We can talk about it sometime, I guess. But right now I'm just wanting to think about happier things."

So Liz had her demons bottled up and didn't

feel like giving them a forum. I certainly re-
spected that. She hadn't been that lucky since
she'd met me, so I could only imagine what
was in her past. Still, she had an optimistic
streak in her, some stamina to survive. She
didn't want to dwell on the past and I sure
could have taken a lesson from her on that
topic, as I had done way more than my share
of wallowing.

Liz continued staring at the Lowcountry as
we circled, mesmerized by the vast and vi-
brant panorama. I white-knuckled the arm-
rest during the descent and smiled as though
nothing were wrong when she looked back in
my direction.

"We're here," I said as brightly as I could
manage, although I had just endured my
classic out-of-body experience with the landing.

We got our bags and were on our way in
minutes. I thought to myself that it surely was
a good thing that not many people knew how
easy it was to fly in and out of Charleston or
we'd be overrun with tourists.

Liz had the same visceral reactions on the
drive to Sullivans Island as I always did. Glistening water, short docks dropped along the
water's edge on tilted pilings, while small

boats bobbed alongside them, the high-tide marks in the marsh grass, erosion lines in mud banks home to the white-and-gray craggy oyster beds, birds everywhere—only the coldest heart could have remain unmoved.

"Miriam, this is so beautiful you could just cry."

"And, guess what? There's no more land like this," I said. "Well, maybe some here and there, but, boy, it sure is disappearing fast."

"That's a *major* mortal sin," Liz said.

"You're telling me? My mother and her friend Harrison are all involved in every environmental movement they have going on around here. You won't believe this. Her latest thing is collecting Stonyfield yogurt containers and sending them off to this company called Recycline, which makes toothbrushes out of the containers."

"You're lying."

"Honey, you can't make stuff like this up. Something like fifty million pounds of used toothbrushes are tossed out every year."

"Gross!"

"Seriously, right? Last time I was here she was making biodegradable plates and bowls out of potato starch."

"Man, I can't wait to meet them."

"They're pretty wild."

When the taxi pulled up to our Sullivans Island home, it was nearly dark.

"We'll catch the sunset tomorrow," I said.

I heard the sliding-glass door open and looked up to see my mother at the top of the steps. Perhaps it was the light, but just in the few short weeks since I had seen her, it seemed to me that she was considerably thinner.

"Welcome!" she called out. "You must be Liz!"

She may have lost some weight, but she had given up no spirit. Her voice was just as young and full of energy as it had ever been.

"You girls hurry up now! Miriam? Let's show Liz to the guest room."

I gave my mother a kiss on her cheek. She gave Liz a hug and took her bag right from her hand.

"I'll show you the goat and the chickens later," I said, and winked at Liz.

"Laugh all you want, missy, but they serve a purpose!" My mother turned her attention to Liz. "Look at you, sweetheart! You've just had the bug-eyed devil of a time, haven't you? Well, no matter. You're here now and the salt air will have you doing cartwheels in no time! How's that shoulder?"

"Collarbone, actually. And it's a lot better, but it's still hard to blow out my hair."

"Six weeks to heal? I think that's what they say, right? And we don't worry about our hair at the beach."

"Yeah, well, this is week three and my collarbone feels about half better, so I guess that's about right."

Mother went back downstairs and I helped Liz unpack.

"I didn't bring much," she said.

"Don't need much," I said. "And if you do, we have stores. It feels like the middle of nowhere, but there's a Gap just three miles from here."

"There's a Gap three miles from *everywhere*."

"Truly. I'll see you downstairs in a few minutes."

In my bathroom I was washing the airport/airplane/airport film of unknown bacteria and germs from my face and hands. I heard a car pull up and then another. I looked down through my bedroom window to see Harrison and Manny. Harrison had flowers, probably for Mother. Manny had flowers. Manny the

Man had flowers for *me*? Well, that was pretty sweet.

I ran my fingers through my hair, pulled off my sweater set, threw on a white T-shirt, an oversize blue chambray shirt, those tight jeans of unknown origin from my last visit that my sweet mother had laundered, and my loafers. Here's a news flash: the jeans were looser. *All praise the mighty treadmill!*

I swiped a pink-tinted gloss across my lips and applied some mascara. No blush was necessary, as Mother Nature stepped in to help with a power surge and my cheeks were as rosy as could be. Look out. The lusty Daughter of the Dunes was back in town. I couldn't get downstairs fast enough.

"Well, look who's here!" I said.

They were all gathered around the island in the kitchen, getting to know Liz.

"Hey, girl! Welcome home!" Harrison said, and opened his arms for a hug.

I was so happy to see him that I thought, Oh, what the heck, and I hugged him in a sisterly way.

"What about me?" Manny said. "I brought you flowers!"

"So you did! Thank you!"

I hugged him, too, unexpectedly close, and

he looked at me with a look of intent. Although I hadn't seen it in eons, I knew exactly what that kind of expression meant. I returned his look with the boldest one I could muster. In other words, if you had to put the pheromones flying around between us in big sacks, it would have taken a couple of musclemen to carry them down to the edge of the marsh to release them back into the wild. It was utterly ridiculous and even trashy to entertain lusty thoughts about him, because I really had only marginal feelings for him in any other area, except for the fact that he could cook.

"So, you're looking pretty good, Mr. Sinkler. What's happening around here?"

Before Manny could answer, Harrison did.

"We are all invited to an oyster roast down at Woody and Elizabeth Wood's house," Harrison said.

"Oh! Sounds fabulous! I haven't had oysters all year," I said. "Liz? Do you eat oysters?"

"As fast as I can get them in my mouth, which might be a little bit of a problem with this sling. Yikes! What a nuisance this thing is!"

"Ma'am," Harrison said, "you are in the company of two of the south's finest oyster

shuckers and it would be an honor to shuck
for you."

Honestly. Harrison was so adorable, even
if he was shacking up with my mother. Why
couldn't Manny be that quick on the uptake?

"It's going down to the forties tonight,"
Mother said, "so we'd better wear a jacket
and some gloves."

Harrison took charge again. "Liz? You
come with Miss Josie and me. And Mellie?
You go with Manly."

"Manly," Manny said. "Do you know how
many *variations on the theme* I have endured
in my life? Get your coat on and let's get going before they eat them all!"

A few minutes later we were bundled
against the night air, I had on my oyster-roast
sneakers, and we were on our way down the
island.

"So, how have you been?" Manny asked.
"Harrison told me about Liz's attack. That
must have been pretty scary."

"It was unbelievable. Especially since I
knew the man who attacked her."

"No kidding. Wow. That's intense. But she
looks okay, except for that scar, but you can
hardly see it. But that sling must be a drag.

At least her arm's not broken. Who was the guy?"

"Husband of an old friend of mine who was seeing Liz on the side."

"Oops!"

He actually snickered, as though it were humorous.

"Yeah, big oops! The wife found out, went crazy with him, he whaled on Liz and gave himself a heart attack in the middle of it. He didn't die, though, which was sort of a pity. The skunk. What a night!"

"Truth? The guy had a heart attack?"

Even in the darkness of the car, Manny turned white. Odd, I thought. "Truth. So what else is new around here?"

"Jeez. Sullivans Island pales next to the Naked City. Gas went down ten cents a gallon. There's no smoking allowed on the island anymore. Spring's coming. But you sure look good. Did you cut your hair or something?"

"Yes. Just had it shaped up a little. But thanks! You look good, too."

I had not cut my hair. I had lost a small amount of weight, and evidently, it showed. My inner slut reminded me that all it took was a small compliment and my next thought was about what he would be like in the sack. I knew he was thinking about it, too. Fortunately, for the sake of propriety, we arrived at the party before we could make a run for a No Tell motel.

There had to have been a hundred people at the Woods' house, and everyone was in fine spirits, slapping one another on the back and telling stories. We said hello to Woody and Elizabeth and thanked them for having us. Their daughter, Caroline, had on the cutest hat and I could have taken it right off her head. Woody immediately led Harrison off to the side to tell him about his latest fishing tournament and a new boat he was considering.

Elizabeth said, "Come on! Let's get y'all a place at the table and a pile of oysters! They're from right around Bluffton."

"Fabulous!" Manny said.

Everyone knew Bluffton oysters were the Lowcountry's version of Russia's beluga caviar—plump, tender, and just the right combination of sweet and saline. They didn't need cocktail sauce or lemon juice. Just a freezing beer or a glass of cold sauvignon blanc to wash them down and you'd think you'd died and gone to heaven. If you liked oysters, that is.

Their yard was strung with lights and huge sheets of plywood on sawhorses. People were standing all around them, shucking and eating as fast as they could. We were doing our part, too, all of us opening them for Liz. Harrison reappeared a few minutes later.

"That Woody is a great guy," he said. "He and his friends Mike and Linda Rumph do this for their friends once a year, and I think that's pretty nice. Don't you?"

"Yes, it is," Liz said, tossing her blond hair away from her face. "What a perfect night."

"If Kevin could see this, he would pass out cold on the ground," I said, and we laughed.

"No, he'd be wearing Burberry from head to toe and he'd be fussing about getting his gloves dirty," Liz said.

"That was an extremely accurate insight, Liz!"

Sometimes she wasn't as dumb as I thought.

I had eaten all I could and decided to walk down to Woody and Elizabeth's dock to look across the water.

The night was beautiful and clear, and

from the edge of the Woods' property you could see the softly lit silhouette of the new bridge that connected Mount Pleasant to Charleston. I stood there at the rail for a few minutes and then I heard footsteps. Someone else was coming. It was Manny. He had followed me. A good sign. He came down the ramp to the floating dock and stood beside me. I knew he was there to stir the estrogen pot.

"Some gorgeous night, huh?" he said.

Look, I never tried to promote this man to anyone as Shakespeare's replacement, did I?

"Yes. It's perfect. The temperature, the damp air."

As sure as I knew anything, I knew that this was a seminal moment, not just in my renewal as a woman of this Island, but in who I was and who I hoped to ever become. I had never slept with a man unless I had some desire for a relationship with him. Did I want a relationship with this man and was I going to sleep with him before I knew the answer to that question? No and maybe.

He was going to kiss me and how was I going to handle that? With surprise? Welcome? Passion? No. My lips were, for the first time in my entire life, going to speak for my libido. So as he lowered his mouth to mine I thought to myself about him, you damn fool, you have no idea who you are kissing. You have no idea who I am. I am not angry. And, I am not sold on you.

But he sure could kiss, bubba, and that's not worth nothing. So I'll admit, I let it continue for a few minutes, and sure enough, my temperature rose. But my temperature rose if a store clerk disagreed with me over a coupon expiration date or if I saw a television ad regarding something emotional that had no chance of happening to me. I was desperately lonely and I knew it. No one had kissed me in so long. And so I kissed him back and didn't much care where it might lead, thinking he didn't seem dangerous and so why shouldn't I have some intimacy in my life? Why shouldn't I have arms around me that seemed like they cared, even if it was only for the moment? I hated that thought and pushed it away as fast as I could because this was no time to grow a conscience.

Rats. Couldn't help it. Kissing him seemed cheap. But here came the denial. Why should I be any different from everyone else? Hadn't life become tawdry and tasteless in every sector—just look at anything on television, as though that was some moral guide for living. The world applauded, rewarded, and idolized cheap, easy, and fast.

So let's be perfectly carnal here. This little make-out session we were having felt pretty darn good and I felt the telltale twinge gaining strength. I wasn't going to be happy until this entire episode ended on a mattress with torn-apart sweaty sheets. I might not have been twenty years old, but at that moment, that fact didn't mean diddly-squat. I was satisfied with my rationalization.

"Let's go," he said.

"Okay," I said.

"I have a crazy idea," he said.

"You must if you're taking me out of here on an impulse like this," I said, and laughed.

"We'll see y'all later," I said to Liz and Mother as I passed them on Manny's arm.

They exchanged knowing looks and waved.

Manny opened the passenger door of his SUV and I hopped in. He went around to his side, opened the door, and all but leaped in, too. We were just a couple of postpeak track stars still going for the gold.

He started the engine and we rolled along up the island toward Breech Inlet. On the radio, James Taylor was singing a song I loved from his early career, and between the oysters and the little wine I had consumed, I was feeling pretty mellow.

"Where are we going?"

"You'll see."

Manny turned right on Station Twenty-six and then left on Bayonne. He parked along the side of the road, turned off the engine, got out, and came back with a small cooler. He reached in and pulled out a bottle of tequila, opened it and took a swig, and then bit into a wedge of lime that he had presliced and brought in a plastic bag. There was no end to his talents.

"Here," he said, handing me the bottle and a fresh wedge of lime. It appeared that I was to have my own wedge. It could not have been for sanitary purposes. It must have been a decorous touch from Manny the Gourmand.

Not quite understanding if he thought this was the elixir of love or if I was taking step one on the road to hell, I took a large sip. Unaccustomed as I was to tequila, my throat ignited the whole way to my navel. I bit into the lime. The flames subsided.

"Do this often, do you? Is this a new style of seduction?"

He took another sip, bit his lime, and laughed. "No, no."

"Then what in your wildest imagination would make you think that sitting on the side . . ."

He handed the bottle back to me and I took another swallow and chomped the lime.

"You swig like a man," he said.

"Oh, shut up." I handed the bottle back to him. "As I was saying, why would I want to spend the evening on the side of the road drinking tequila from a bottle?"

"I have this fantasy," he said.

Holy moly, I thought. The last time someone said that to me I wound up in a nurse's uniform.

"Okay," I said, and drank two giant gulps, "let's hear it."

"I want to make love on the beach."

Was that all?

"Isn't it kind of chilly?'

"I've got a double sleeping bag and some other stuff in the back . . . back there."

He motioned to the rear of the SUV and I thought, Holy crap. If I tell him no, this relationship is over before it gets started. If I tell him yes . . . what? I had never had sex on the beach either and had always thought it might have been romantic, like something out of *The Days of Wine and Roses.* Or whatever that movie was where they are rolling around the edge of the surf. Maybe it was *From Here to Eternity*? Deborah Kerr and Burt Lancaster? In any case, it was still winter and I wasn't going near the water under any circumstances, but another swallow or two or three of tequila could fortify me for at least a little fooling around.

"So, let me get this straight. We went to one church dinner, you never called me, then we went to this oyster roast for all of an hour, and now you want to *do it*? On the beach? Just like that?"

"Yeah. Shoot! We're grown-ups. Why should teenagers get to do all the fun and crazy stuff?"

At this point, my judgment was just a little fuzzy.

"Right!" I said, thinking his words sounded perfectly logical. "We're not dead yet!"

So we stumbled down to the beach, arm in arm. Manny carried a huge tote bag and I had the half-empty bottle and the baggie of limes tucked under my arm. The beach was very dark and windy. I could hardly see where we were walking. The tide was coming in, so he picked a place in the soft white sand above the waterline.

"This feels very wicked," I said.

I stood there while he unfolded and un-zipped the biggest sleeping bag I had ever seen. From there on in, I was one giant head case of confusion. I couldn't decide how to proceed. Should I get undressed in the night air and just stand there like a naked freezing idiot until he gave me some come-hither sign or the secret handshake? Did he intend to undress me? Maybe, I should just kick off my smelly shoes and leave them in the sand and see what happened? I took a bold first step. I undid the toggles on my Talbot's pea coat, put my gloves in my pocket.

"You next," I said. I unscrewed the cap of the tequila bottle and threw a healthy mea-sure down my throat.

He laughed and took the bottle from me.

"You know what I think?" Manny said.

"Darlin'? There just ain't no telling what you're thinking, so tell me." I was definitely feeling the effects of the alcohol.

"I think let's take off our shoes and coats, crawl in this big old cocoon, and just see what happens."

Good thing he mentioned the shoes because my veterans of a zillion oyster roasts and fish fries would most assuredly have left an unpleasant calling card.

"Perfect!"

And so we did. With the removal of each other's clothing—piece by piece, I might add—we would fling the garments outside the sleeping bag, farther and farther away, as far as we could throw. We giggled, knowing that retrieving our things would be more reason to stay warm and snuggled together in the down-filled, wind- and waterproofed L.L. Bean sack of debauchery.

"Are you sure you want to do this?" I said.

"Well, we're here and we're already naked, so we may as well . . ."

It was a pragmatic plan from this non-Romeo I had next to me. Besides, it was a little late in the game to change course.

When things got going, I was surprised by his aggressiveness. It was as though he had to catch a train. In the short history of my experience in these matters, slow and steady wins the day, but he was so manic that I was having a hard time concentrating on what you're supposed to be concentrating on at a time like that. His crazy gymnastics were causing the sleeping bag to creep toward either the water or the dunes and it was turning all around. I couldn't see a thing, as I was pretty well buried under a down flap and pinned by a fighter pilot continuously landing on an aircraft carrier. It was the craziest sex I had ever had or heard of, and I thought, well, you know, it might not be what you'd hope for with the love of your life, but Manny Sinkler was not the love of my life. And, as insane as it was, it was insane fun. Then his aria arrived on the crest of high tide. It was as though a deep grunt came from some operatic animal inside of him and we were completely drenched from head to toe. I started laughing and tried to escape from being dragged out to sea, but Manny was not cooperating.

"Come on, Manny! Get off of me! We're gonna drown if we don't get out of this thing and I'm freezing."

"Was it good for you?"

He was kidding, right? Somebody please tell me he was kidding.

"Come on! Move!"

"Is there any more tequila?"

"Focus, Manny, focus! Brrrr! Did you bring a towel by any chance? Where's the tote bag?"

I finally made it to my feet and spotted the tote bag. There was no towel in it, only, of all

the things in the world, two rolled-up sombreros. It was so blasted dark, I couldn't see
a stitch of our clothes anywhere.

"Manny Sinkler? Have you gone mad?
What in the world are the sombreros for?"

"Well, it was part of my fantasy. I wanted to
get drunk on tequila, make love on the beach,
and then dance naked in the moonlight . . ."

"In sombreros?"

"Yeah. You think I'm nuts, right?"

I really deserved better than this wack-job
excuse for a lover, I thought. But then the
new Miriam, the Mellie in me, took the other
side of the argument under consideration.
We had come that far, fulfilling two-thirds of
his crazy dream, so why not go the distance?
I handed him a sombrero and put the other
one on my head.

"I will do this for you, Manny, for one minute only. But then you have to help me find
my clothes before I get pneumonia. Deal?"

He placed his sombrero on his head and
said, "Deal."

We danced a waltz, sort of, and then,
because everything was beyond ridiculous,
we broke into the Mexican hat dance—
crossed arms, extended heels, and the
whole choreography to the best of our

abilities—stopping only when the flash-lights hit our faces. There, on top of the dunes, holding an armful of our clothes and two very strong flashlights, stood two un-amused police officers of approximately twenty-five years of age.

They walked toward us and at least I had the presence of mind to cover myself with the hat. I thought I would die. I wished I would die. I did not die.

Officer Number One said, "Well, we'd ask you two for some identification but we're as-suming you're not in possession of your wal-let at this time?"

"No, uh . . ."

Officer Two then said, "Have you been drinking any alcohol tonight, sir?"

"Uh, a little tequila."

Officer One then said, "Tequila? Ralph? I think what we got ourselves here is a theme party."

Officer Two (Ralph) said, "Is that what this is, sir?"

Manny and I looked at each other. I was no longer drunk enough to not feel complete and total mortification down to the last stringy hair on my sandy wet head.

"Sort of. Yes. I apologize, Officer. You see,

I'm in love with this lady, and ever since my wife died . . . well, this is the first happiness I've known in so many years . . ."

Manny was an impressive liar.

They looked at each other, and Officer One said, "Ah, hell. Here. Take your clothes, get dressed, and get on out of here. No real harm done."

Officer Two said, "I had to give you a parking ticket, sir. You parked by a fire hydrant."

"Thank you, Officer," Manny said. "Thank you."

The mood in the car on the ride home with Manny was one that would be difficult for a dignified and refined person to understand. The southern lady in me was furious that he would put me in that position in the first place. The hellcat I longed to become on my Mellie days wanted to laugh uproariously that we had gotten off scot-free. And I wondered what else Manny had in his fantasy folder. The mother in me could only imagine what those poor young officers, younger than my own sons, had thought seeing two old codgers in their birthday suits. So on the ride home, we exchanged very few words, just half smiles of chagrin and relief, and simply said good night.

When I sneaked up the stairs, I found Miss

Josie and Liz bundled up in blankets in the old wicker rockers on the back porch. They gasped when they saw how completely disheveled I was. I knew I looked like a wreck.

"Well, would you look at what the cat dragged in," Mother said. "What in the name of great jumping Jehoshaphat's mother-in-law happened to you?"

"Mother? Liz? I fell off a dock. I'll see y'all in the morning."

And I had worried about my mother smoking pot, fretted that she might sully my reputation if she got arrested for it. Can you imagine how my moonlight escapade with Manny Sinkler would have looked plastered all over the newspapers in New York? What would Charles have said? Agnes Willis? To tell you the truth? I laughed myself to sleep. I couldn't wait to tell Kevin. Or maybe I would just keep this one to myself.

Chapter Fifteen

LIZ'S BIZ

Over the next few days, Liz and Mother were developing a serious bond. Like a mad scientist, Mother was mixing all sorts of creams to hasten the healing of Liz's scar.

"All right," Mother said, handing her the first of two small jars. "I want you to apply this every four hours with clean hands. And don't go out in the sun without this sunscreen over it."

I loved that Mother told Liz to make sure her hands were clean and that Liz didn't mind. She simply did as she was told with a huge smile on her face. Miss Josie had been right. Liz needed mothering—and apparently grandmothering, too.

"This smells good enough to eat!" Liz said. "What's in it?"

"Oh, all sorts of good things like vitamin E and C and a little eye of newt."

They laughed like white witches in cahoots. Just as you might imagine, Mother's vegetable juicer was working overtime. The carrot-apple-celery combination was a reward chaser for the consumption of a tall glass of kale, beet, and parsley. You cannot appreciate the full impact of a bout of blastro intestinitis until you've gagged on kale juice.

Anyway, Liz and Mother had hybridized into two organic peas in a pod.

Manny surfaced the day after our wild night in an attempt to restore some normalcy to our relationship, or whatever you might call the scandalous thing was that we had. We walked over to Dunleavy's for a drink and tried to talk about what had happened on the beach. He attempted to apologize and couldn't keep a straight face. I tried to give him a hard time and couldn't keep a straight face either. We had nearly been arrested for acting out Manny's completely juvenile sexual psychodrama, and the only good that came from our conversation about it was that he finally admitted it *was* juvenile.

I said, "You know? All I want in this life is a reasonable man who's self-supporting, who's nice to me, funny, you know, likes straight sex—not role-playing modeled on a kinky Berlin nightclub from pre–World War Two . . . Shouldn't be too much to ask for, should it? I mean, you *do* engage in normal sex from time to time, don't you?"

"On occasion," he said, trying again to be serious. "I'll do better next time. But I must say, you are a good sport."

"Thanks, you big dope."

He leaned across the table and whispered, "Ever play naked Twister?"

I leaned toward him and we were nose to nose. "Yeah, every Thursday after my bridge club. What's the *matter* with you? I thought you were a banker!"

"*Was* a banker."

"Well, since you obviously have too much time on your hands, do you want to be my date for something?"

"Sure. You name it."

"Okay. I already suspect I'll have to take an oath to have sex with you on an outside window ledge of the ninety-eighth floor of the Empire State Building, but if I do, will you take me to my son's wedding?"

"Ninety-eighth?"

"Ninety-ninth?"

"I accept!" We shook hands to seal the deal.

However you chose to describe what Manny and I had going so far, I had to say it was devilishly good fun. But I would like to add that the thought of a serious future with him could provoke an outburst of shingles. And in all sincerity, I was not going to crawl out of a window onto a ledge to get it on with this crazy man.

Although he swore that he had not told Harrison or anyone the sombrero story, something in the pit of my gut told me otherwise. The camaraderie between Manny and Harrison was not quite as harmonious as it had been my last visit home. Harrison was a little cooler toward Manny, and every time Harrison came through the door, he looked at me differently. He wasn't smirking exactly and he wasn't criticizing either. Maybe he was storing my suspected secret wild side away for future reference. Go ahead, I thought.

It was late morning on a warm sunny day in the middle of the week. Liz had gone fishing with Mother and Harrison, and I was home alone, lying in the hammock, reading Proust in French. Okay, that was a lie to see if you're paying attention. I was, as you might guess, struggling with part of the Wednesday crossword puzzle in the *New York Times*. When, for the ninetieth time I could not remember a four-letter word for a three-toed sloth, I decided to surrender the masochistic exercise in frustration to the garbage can and call Kevin to make sure Harry was still alive and that all was well.

"You busy?" I asked, knowing he was probably at work.

That was one of the many annoyances about cell phones. No matter where you were, you felt obliged to answer them. I could be getting a mammogram or trying on swimsuits and a tiny rush of panic would set in if I couldn't hop quickly enough to check my caller ID. Kevin was a big boy. If he wanted my call to go to voice mail, it would.

"Well, of *course* I'm busy, but I have *such* a juicy bit of fat for you that I'd put Karl Lagerfeld himself on hold to talk to you. Let me just close my door. Hold on."

I braced myself for something oozing shock.

"Okay? Are you ready?" he said.

"Please! I can't breathe!"

"Well, Agnes Willis has resigned as chair from the museum's benefit committee."

"No! No kidding? Why?"

"Well, the inside skinny I heard through Manuela in alterations who was fitting a gown for one of Agnes's friends who was running her mouth to her girlfriend—I guess she was shopping with her—was that the chairman of the board of trustees heard what Agnes had said to you during that *most* unfortunate incident with the coffee urn. They said that he called a meeting with Agnes and said that the museum could not afford to have their volunteers treated with *such* disrespect and that it was terribly damaging for the museum's image."

"I can't believe it."

"Believe it. So apparently Agnes like went all menopausal on him and stomped out."

"Well, holy hopping moly, if you live long enough you see everything, don't you?"

"So that's vindication numero uno."

"What? There's more?"

"Oh, yes, Petal Puss. Then Manuela told

Christiana, who also works in alterations, and P.S., brought me a divine coffee cake just this morning, that Truman Willis bought Agnes about a million dollars' worth of clothes, that they were going on safari and then to India, and that they've put their co-op on the market. I guess you ran the old crone out of town. How do you like them apples?"

"Goodness! Wait until I tell Liz!"

"New York will be much safer without them."

"And *nicer.* Gosh. I can hardly believe it. Usually my enemies *flourish.* This is one of the few times I've ever seen this happen! Justice, I mean."

"And here's the best news of all, sweetheart."

"What?"

"I found the perfect dress for you to wear to the wedding."

"Really? You are too much! What's it like?"

"Navy, silk chiffon. Cap sleeves, off the shoulders, flattering to the upper arms? Fitted waist and a thousand yards of skirt. Tea length. It's divine. And it's an Arnold Scassi. On sale, seventy off. It was in the back of a hold rack from the Cruise Collection and I guess they just missed it. I snatched it. With my discount, they'll have to pay me to take it home!"

"What size?"

"Ten, I think, but it doesn't matter. We'll make it fit."

"I'm a solid twelve."

"We will make it fit if I have to take it to the Scassi cutting room myself."

"You realize I'd die without you, don't you? Kevin, how can I thank you?"

"Lower my rent. I want to go to Paris on vacation and I don't have enough cash to stay at the Ritz for the week."

"Couldn't I just give you a lung instead?"

"I'm just fooling with you. So, you haven't told me a thing about what's doing down there. How's that Manny fellow and your mother and Harrison? And how does the magical isle agree with our Liz?"

"It would take me hours to tell you all that's going on around here. Mostly Manny and I have been laughing ourselves silly. You know all those discussions we had during the snowstorms about me having more fun? Well, I'm doing just that."

"Well, praise the Lord!"

"I know. Liz and my mother are joined at

the hip. Mom's on a mission to heal Liz, body and soul. And Liz is devouring all the attention, poor thing. Harrison is well. He's just this great guy who's the glue between Miss Josie and the grave. I mean, I don't think my mother looks well, but Harrison keeps her going. Right now he's got her and Liz out in a fishing boat catching our dinner. Unless I go out with Manny."

"So? What's so hilarious and fun about this Manny?"

"He's just off-the-wall. I don't know. I mean, it's certainly nothing serious."

"Just good for the ego?"

"I guess." I was divulging no details. "And how's my Harry?"

"Well, he must miss you because he keeps saying 'Pretty Miriam! Pretty Miriam!'"

"Golly. Maybe I'll call you back tonight and you could put the phone up to his ear?"

"Good-bye, Petal! You're losing it!"

There was no doubt that it was a possibility.

I decided to go for a walk on the beach and pulled on a jacket, as it was getting chilly. I checked the tidal clock and the tide was going out. The beach would be wet and the sand softer than usual, but that was perfectly fine with me.

I backed the golf cart out of the garage and waved good-bye to Mother's goat. If I thought it was a sign of politeness to communicate my comings and goings to a goat, I actually might have been losing my mind. But I was so elated by the Agnes news that I would have kissed Cecelia if she had puckered up.

Riding the three short blocks over to the beach path, I realized sloth was my first problem, not goat communiqués. I should always walk whenever possible to zap my metabolism out of its coma. Why was I so lazy? The dress was a ten, which meant it was probably more like an eight, which meant that if I didn't get twenty pounds off my fat derriere, I was going to look like a muffin with my natural endowments popping over the top of my baking cup.

How would I ever lose that much weight? An ounce at a time, the little comedian in my brain said. Dieting depressed me.

The sun was climbing and felt wonderful on my back as I walked toward the lighthouse. My body didn't know that my brain hated to exercise, so if I just did it anyway, it would still work. I walked as brisk a pace as I could, wondering how much of this nonsense I needed to do to make a real difference. Probably more than I envisioned.

The wedding. It was going to happen, and as happy as I told myself I was for Charlie and Priscilla, I just simply dreaded facing Charles and Judith. I felt so dumpy and defeated every time I thought about them, laughing, watering their houseplants with Evian, and that even a rag from the back of her closet made her look like a movie star. The last picture I had seen of them in the newspaper was taken at a benefit for the City Opera. Even in the postage-stamp-size photograph—with the help of a magnifying glass—Kevin and I could see that she wore a lavish diamond necklace and diamond cluster earrings.

"Van Cleef," Kevin said.

"Aren't they just nauseating?"

They were smiling, her arm linked through his, and she sparkled from the neck up in a way only the holiday tree in Rockefeller Center could. Charles had *never* given me anything so extravagant. The most painful part of the picture to me was that she was so young and poised, looking not unlike Audrey

Hepburn in that fabulous black gown she wore in *Breakfast at Tiffany's,* and she was on the arm of the man who had sworn to love me forever.

And Kevin, God bless him, knew what I was up against and he wanted me to show them all. He had found the ideal dress, and if he could go out of his way to do something so very thoughtful for me, I would try my best to drop some ballast. Well, to be perfectly honest, I would wait and see if the dress fit. Then I could kill myself or not.

I thought about Mother and Liz then and wondered if there was something going on with Mother's health that she was keeping to herself. She was a sly fox, but it seemed like the bottles of wheat germ, fish oil, vitamins, and health products I couldn't identify in the kitchen cabinet were on the rise. And she *was* considerably thinner. I could tell by the way her clothes hung and her eyes appeared slightly sunken. I wondered when the last time was that she had a complete physical. I made a mental note to talk to her about it.

I stopped to look out over the harbor. Not more than twenty feet from where I stood, a school of porpoises were playing in the surf. They could see me watching them and I thought, conceivably irrationally, that they were all the more active because they had an audience. They swam like girls in an old Esther Williams movie, but wasn't that how nature was anyway? In a constant battle with itself to stay in sync? Sure. Add chat sessions with porpoises to my animal-kingdom friends and somebody please call a shrink.

I started walking home and eventually reached the spot that I was reasonably sure was the precise location where Manny and I had entertained the Sullivans Island police force. Maybe we should put a small plaque somewhere to commemorate the lunacy. Or not. Lordy, Lord. If I had told Kevin that story, he would have definitely howled.

When I got home, Mother was in the kitchen, emptying the dishwasher. Liz and Harrison had gone to the vegetable stand in Mount Pleasant to buy potatoes.

"I don't know why I can't get them to grow over here, but I just can't," she said. "How was your walk?"

"Great," I said. "I feel invigorated! Y'all catch anything?"

"Some blue mackerel. I'll tell you this. I'm getting so sick and tired of blue mackerel and seafood in general, I'm thinking I might just break my own rules and make some lasagna with sausage! And a Pepperidge Farm frozen garlic bread. Golly, I used to love those."

"Well then, let's call them and ask them to go buy it! Really! I mean, even monks break their fast once in a while. But did you have *fun* fishing at least?"

"Sure. It's always fun." She paused for a moment and then slapped the countertop. "You know what? You're right! Let's have lasagna."

She called Harrison's cell phone and gave him a grocery list. I could hear him laughing through the phone from across the room. He thought it was really hilarious when she asked for a bag of Oreos and a pint of Chunky Monkey.

"Well, we may as well go the whole way to hell, Harrison!"

As she hung up she looked at me and said again, "Did we have fun fishing? Sure. Then Liz and I went for a walk on the beach while Harrison cleaned up the boat. Let me tell you this. There's a lot about Liz Harper you don't know."

"Like what?"

"How about a cup of tea?"

"Sounds good."

Mother put the kettle on to boil and I brought mugs and spoons to the counter. When Miss Josie suggested tea out of the blue, a considerable block of time might follow the invitation, so I settled on a bar stool and told myself to get comfortable. When the tea was brewed and I had stirred a spoon of clover honey into my mug, Mother began to talk.

"Miss Mellie, this is not something that should be repeated to anyone without Liz's permission. We were talking about your childhood here and she said something like, boy, I'd give a lot if I could say I grew up like Mellie! Then here came the saga. I have to tell you that I was appalled and heartbroken at the same time. But what's really peculiar is that Liz told it all to me as though she was describing any old memory. Her tone of voice was devoid of any emotion, as though all these horrible things had all happened to someone else."

"Good heavens, Mother, what did she tell you?"

"Well, for starters, when Liz was just a little girl, her own father abused her."

"What do you mean *abused*? Do you mean he had actual sex with her?"

"No. He used to come into her bedroom at night and touch her inappropriately."

"That is completely disgusting. Didn't she tell her mother? Another adult?"

"Yes, but no one believed her. But she said she noticed that her mother began drinking and then drinking heavily and taking pills to calm her nerves, which to my mind meant her mother knew it was all true and did nothing about it. When Liz went crying to her grandmother she called Liz a liar and beat her with a belt."

"Oh, Mother. Oh, that poor child. I presume this was her father's mother, protecting her disgusting son?"

"Naturally. She lived with them on their little farm outside of Birmingham in the country. Old Granny probably thought that if her son got kicked out, she herself would have nowhere to go. So she accused Liz of doing all kinds of things and Liz's mother believed the grandmother. She would say things like Liz stole money from her purse or that Liz broke something that in fact her grandmother had broken. Or that she was sassy."

"What is the matter with people? This world is so filled with evil."

"Well, sometimes it sure looks like the devil

is winning, doesn't it? Anyway, eventually her grandmother died and her father left, but only after Liz's mother actually caught him coaxing Liz into an obscene act."

"How obscene?"

"I didn't ask for details, but it was obscene enough for Liz's mother to finally throw the Satan out and divorce him. After that, Liz's mother supported them by working double shifts at a grocery store. She eventually remarried when Liz was about eighteen."

"And he was a nice man, I hope?"

"No. He was not. Liz began attending some small local college and she still lived at home because there was no money for her to board in a dormitory. Very quickly into her mother's new marriage, this joker, his name is Ed, I think, he starts giving Liz the eye. Liz and her mother fought about it like two cats in a bag and it became clear that Liz had to leave."

"Why? After what she knew about her father, shouldn't her mother have believed her? Shouldn't Ed have left? Press some kind of charges? Get the creep locked up?"

"Of course he should have been locked up. He should have been shot! But Liz's mother didn't want to believe Liz's side of the story and, in fact, accused Liz of trying to come between her and Ed."

"I'm sorry. That's just crazy. If I were Liz I wouldn't have taken that."

"Well, Miriam, Liz knew that her mother's marriage was all her mother thought she had."

"Basically she chose this creep over her daughter?"

"Yes, you could put it that way. These are uneducated, simple people who don't have money and don't understand that they have other options. It happens every day."

"But not just with poor people, Mother. I mean, we both know abusive relationships happen everywhere. At every level of society. It's horrible."

"True enough. But Liz said she just looked at her mother's swollen ankles night after night and at how tired and worn out her mother was, and she couldn't stand it anymore. As long as she remained at home, she was a financial burden to her mother and a threat to her marriage. Liz had two options. To stay, which was intolerable. Or, Liz could leave Alabama, borrow money, complete her education somewhere else, and try not to look back."

"Good grief. If I were Liz I would hate my mother's guts! And my father's! And Ed's!"

"She probably does. But you have to understand that Liz probably felt some kind of guilt, too."

"For what?"

"Do you want a piece of pie?"

"No, thanks."

"Well, I'm going to have some. Because victims always feel guilty." She sliced a piece of an organic apple tart from Whole Foods and put it on a plate. "The perpetrator tells the victim something like, you know, if you tell, you'll be in big trouble, so it continues. How would a twelve-year-old know that it's a trap? Or even a teenager? And telling did her no good."

"No, I know you're right. That's some horrible predicament for a young girl. I mean, could *you* just bail out and not look back? I couldn't. Could you?"

"Heavens, no! But you have to imagine that her feelings about her mother are terribly conflicted and probably that warehouse of resentment is the source of how she found the strength to leave."

"Yeah. Sheer hate would have propelled me out of there! You know, she's never said a word about it. I'll be darned. So what in the world did she do?"

"She had a friend from school who had a widowed aunt in New York. In exchange for keeping her house clean and running errands, Liz was able to stay there and attend night school at SUNY Purchase and finish her degree. Then she moved to the city, and I think you know the rest."

"I had no idea. Boy, she's some tenacious fighter, isn't she? I wonder what happened to her stepfather and her mother? Does she speak to them? *I* sure wouldn't."

"Not a word. Her stepfather was and probably still is a horrible person, but he's all Liz's mother has. In other ways Liz understands that Ed is reasonably good to her mother—doesn't drink or gamble or anything like that. And he brings home a paycheck."

"Oh. Let's just lower our expectations one more time. Coming in on the heels of a pedophile father, he just tried to take sexual advantage of his stepdaughter and ruin her mental health for the rest of her life, that's all."

"And we think we have problems."

"We have no problems. None at all. I mean,

this sure explains why she was fooling around with a man so much older than her."

"Miriam Elizabeth? I gave up practicing psychology without a license a long time ago and suggest you do the same. Now, would you like some of this pie or not? Or a little lunch?"

"Are you serious? Who could eat after a story like that?"

"You have to eat to keep up your strength for the rest of the day." Mother got up and inspected the contents of the refrigerator. "There's a little soup here and enough chicken for a sandwich to split. More tea?"

"Sure. Okay. Whatever makes you happy, Mother, is fine with me. Poor Liz!" I turned up the gas under the kettle and got some more tea from the cabinet. "So can I ask you something?"

"Of course! Do want mayonnaise?"

"Just a little. When's the last time you had a physical? You're looking a little thin to me and a little drawn."

Mother started to laugh.

"What's so funny?"

"I had a physical six months ago and you don't have to worry about me! The reason I'm losing weight is going to make you laugh. Do you want toast?"

"Plain bread is fine. What?"

"Harrison and I are taking tango lessons! Remember the last time you were here and we talked about the things we wanted to do that we had not? And I said—"

"That you wanted to take tango lessons! Fabulous! Do you love it?"

"I adore it! Harrison is the most wonderful partner—you'd never believe how light he is on his feet! Now, put this soup in the microwave for me."

"In a perfectly green world you wouldn't use a microwave, you know."

"If it was solar-powered, I would."

"I want to see you tango with Harrison. I mean, I have to see this."

"You will at the wedding! I can hardly wait!"

She put my half of the sandwich on a salad plate in front of me.

"Thanks. So did I tell you that Manny is coming to be my date and that I asked Dan and Nan to stay with me with the children?"

"Manny said he would come to New York?"

"Sure, why wouldn't he?"

"I don't know. Seems like a big step, but what do I know about the dating world? What about Kevin?"

Was she saying she was not dating Harrison or that she was in a committed relationship with him and just didn't get dating around?

"He'll be Liz's date. Don't you think?"

"I guess." The microwave chimed. "Stir that thing, sweetheart, and give it another minute. Seems like you should warn him, though. Now tell me about Dan and Nan."

"Dan? Talking to him is like talking to a robot. Apparently he and Nan are still miffed with me."

"About the children's names?"

"Yes."

The microwave pinged again and I carefully removed the hot bowl of soup. It smelled wonderful. I ladled it into two mugs and put them on the counter with our plates.

"*Bon appétit!* Well, for once I agree with you. This needs salt." She reached for the shaker, sprinkled her soup liberally, and continued. "If you want to change your own name to something stupid, that's your business. But to hang a name on a child that is going to give them endless taunting? Isn't it hard enough to be a child today?"

"Well, they're supposed to call me back and they haven't so far. Who knows? Maybe little M.F. and Indy May will place the calls themselves. Goodness. I can't stop thinking about Liz. That poor girl."

"It's the most heinous sin of all. To rob a child of their innocence. To steal their trust? Absolutely unforgivable."

"Well, I won't say a word. I'll let her bring it up."

A few minutes later, the sliding door opened and Liz stepped through. She brought the blue light of late afternoon with her, streaming through the clouds and across the porch like prisms. Harrison stepped in behind her with three bags of groceries in each arm, and testosterone filled the air. I noticed the sounds of birds singing and the rustle of Mother's palmettos.

While Mother had revealed Liz's terrible truths over our simple lunch, my mind had been in that dark and frightening place of suspended reality. Now that they were home, Harrison and Liz, the real world, the lovely world, began to turn again. It was only Mother and I who truly belonged to each other, but it was clear that Liz's survival depended on our support. Somehow, as much as Harrison seemed to give Mother's life structure and joy, just being in any part of his orbit gave me a kind of reassurance that I never knew I needed so badly. I was very far away from admitting I had any feelings for Harrison other than platonic ones because to say it would have broken my mother's heart. It wasn't unusual for older men to take a shine to a younger woman, so why was it any different for a woman to have her eye on a younger man?

Before dinner that evening, with a glass of wine in hand, Liz, Harrison, Mother, and I stood on our porch and watched yet another magnificent sunset. As usual, Mother Nature did not disappoint us and began working her magic with a red-and-orange spell.

I told them about my phone call with Kevin and said, "So, what do you think about Agnes and Truman? Isn't that something?"

"Hopefully, they'll move to the back half of Madagascar," Harrison said.

"How utterly stupid people are to each other!" Mother said.

Harrison remarked that it would be so nice if Liz had a nice fellow to run around with, and that if she would like, he could beat the bushes.

Liz smiled and said, "Well, that would be a first!"

"Having someone beat the bushes for you?" he asked.

"Nope. Having a nice fellow to run around with."

Mother said, "You know, Liz. I see no reason why you have to rush back to New York so quickly. Why don't you stay for a while?"

Liz looked at me and I said, "Well? Until you lose that sling, your ribs quit hurting, and you have your lung capacity restored, there is no better place I could think of to convalesce than on our sacred little Island under the watchful eyes of Miss Josie and her barnyard friends."

"Why are you in such a hurry to go back?" Harrison said.

I didn't answer them right away, but I had my reasons. I had a wedding to plan for my new daughter-in-law and my "born again" son. I had my friend, Kevin, to whom I owed a great debt. And last, I had that blasted town house that wasn't worth a tenth of the trouble it caused, and I saw it then for the first time, as clearly as a D-flawless diamond. That town house was no better than Marley's chains.

"I've got a few things to do," I said, "but I'll be back. Very soon."

I caught the glint of pleasure in Harrison's eye and he looked away that same instant. He didn't need to say a word to me, but I knew from the slope of his shoulders and the way they straightened up. I knew from the deep breath he took and the time it took him to exhale. He was pleased. Maybe he wanted the three of us to be his island harem, the thought of which made me grin, too. I was completely bewitched.

Chapter Sixteen

SEX, LIES, AND PENICILLIN

Three absolutely wonderful things happened the next day. Dan called to say that he and his family would love to stay with me during the weekend of Priscilla and Charlie's wedding. He actually said *love to stay.* He and Nan must have had some heart-to-heart discussion and decided the rift between us had gone on far too long. I was thrilled by the news. My whole family would be together and I would make certain they would have a marvelous time. I would take lots of pictures, maybe on a ferry ride to the Statue of Liberty, and I would bake something chocolate just so my grandchildren could lick the bowl.

"Oh, Dan! This makes me so very happy! You just don't know . . ."

"Well, good, then. We're looking forward to it." He said, "Are you sure you have room for all of us?"

Even though his words sounded wooden, I could detect an undercurrent of happy anticipation. A mother knows her son's heart, doesn't she? Doesn't every grown man want to sleep in his old bed, feel like a kid again, and have his mother wait on him hand and foot?

"Absolutely," I said. "You and Nan can stay in your bedroom and the kids can sleep in Charlie's old room."

"I spoke to Charlie. I'm going to be his best man, Mary's going to be the flower girl, and Penn's going to be the ring bearer."

Apparently they had adjusted the children's names, and they sounded so normal I wanted to congratulate him, but I kept my big mouth shut.

"Well, that's just about the nicest news I've had in years!"

Of course, Dan's family staying with me meant that Mother would have to stay elsewhere, but as soon as I hung up the phone, Liz immediately offered her apartment.

Mother accepted. I would find a nearby hotel for Manny and Harrison. There were so many luxurious but reasonably priced boutique hotels springing up like weeds all over Manhattan that I knew it wouldn't be a problem to find one. I hoped.

Right before noon, Kevin called. He was completely breathless and I thought something tragic had happened.

"What? What?" I said.

"Honey chile, baby girl? You just won the lottery! Tom Britt offered you three times as much as I thought he would and I said yes! Of course I was very cool about it. Apparently we haven't been following the silver market very closely!"

"Of course you were cool. What did he say?"

"He said, 'I'll take the whole lot!' *You got the picture?* He's a great guy. You'd love him."

"Oh, Kevin! That is fabulous news! And how's my sweet Harry?"

"Well, I just taught him to say 'jackpot'! He's a smart bird, you know."

"Yes, I know. But why? Because you taught him a new word?"

"No, actually. Last night I caught him chewing on the arm of your chintz chair by the fireplace."

"What? That's my favorite chair!"

"And don't think he doesn't know it either. So I said, 'Harry, if you don't stop that right now you're going night-night.' On my mother's grave, he looked right at me and said, 'So what?'"

"Well, how do you like that? The little devil. Tell him his mother is coming home tomorrow, so he had better straighten up."

Finally, right before Mother, Liz, and I were about to walk over to High Thyme for lunch, Manny called.

"When are you headed back north?"

"Tomorrow, I think. Unless the sky falls. Why?"

"I wanted to make dinner for us tonight. Just us. You free?"

"Sure. What can I bring?"

"Whipped cream?"

"You're a little weird, you know."

"Yeah. But you have to admit, I'm fun. I'll pick you up at six."

We hung up and Liz was standing there, ready to walk out the door.

"What's weird about him?" she said.

"A lot, I think. Where's Miss Josie?"

"She just brought in the eggs and she went to wash her hands. Those eggs really are better than the ones you buy at the store, aren't they?"

"It's because she gives them some special enriched organic feed. At least I think that's the reason."

"Well, I'll tell you this. If I had two good arms, I wouldn't mind helping her milk that nanny goat of hers. You know, get her up on that milking stand and sing her a little song? But you couldn't pay me any amount of money to gather eggs. No, ma'am. Chickens are as mean as snakes."

"How do you know that?"

"Because I grew up on a chicken farm—not a chicken farm that makes you rich. One that barely keeps you fed. And we had goats."

"Really? Good heavens! I didn't know that!"

"Oh, Miriam, someday I'll tell you all about it. But that's why I understand your mother so well. She's growing all this stuff to see if she can live off the land if they drop a bomb. And keeping a goat is interesting. But we grew a lot of the same stuff because we had to put food on the table."

"Interesting?"

"Yeah. They have personalities."

"If you say so." I looked at my wristwatch. Mother had been upstairs for what seemed to be a very long time. "Criminy! She sure is taking her time, isn't she?" I went to the base of the stairs and called out. "Mother? Let's go, Miss Josie!"

"Coming!"

I waited there for her, and when she appeared, I watched her come down each step, holding the rail for support. Something was not right.

"Are you feeling well, Mother?"

"I'm feeling exactly like I'm supposed to be feeling. Just a little tired today, that's all."

"Then let's take the golf cart. Come on, Liz."

All through lunch Mother wasn't herself. She didn't seem feverish but she seemed exhausted and distracted and just picked at her food. Liz and I did most of the talking. You could guess that the windfall of the silver sale, the wedding plans, and the history of my hot-and-cold relationship with Dan and his family dominated most of the conversation. Mother must have said at least three times how pleased she was that Dan and I were reconciled and that she couldn't wait to meet Priscilla. As off-kilter as Mother seemed to be that day, I thought it was so good that she had something to look forward to. As people aged, it was important for them to have plans and events lined up. It seemed to keep them more optimistic, especially if they knew they were needed in the lives of others. It was true even for me. As I continued crawling out of my post-Charles-departure slash museum-fiasco funk, I had to admit that I felt more alive and truly useful than I had in years.

"Can I box that up for you?" the waitress said to Mother when she saw that her chicken Caesar salad was barely touched.

"No, thanks. That's okay," Mother said.

"Y'all want to look at the dessert menus?"

"No, thanks," I said. "We'll just take the check when you have a moment."

"I need a nap," Mother said, on the ride home.

"I think I could use a nap myself," Liz said. "Maybe it's the salt air, but I've never slept so much or so well in my whole life!"

"Or maybe it's a combination of salt air and severe bodily damage?"

"Right. I knew there was a reason I felt like

somebody beat the crap out of me, pardon me."

"Yes, because somebody did. I'm sure Kevin still thinks you should've pressed charges."

"Only for the fun of reading about it in the paper. Truman Willis is not exactly a menace to all of society."

"Just to his paramours. You're right. He wouldn't do well in jail. I can just see him looking around for the gentlemen's squash courts at Rikers Island and trying to find a partner."

Even Mother smiled at that remark. Maybe I should stick to dry humor.

I pulled the golf cart into its parking spot. Mother and Liz went inside the house through the garage entrance, but I went outside to have a look at Mother's barnyard.

Cecelia, Mother's Nigerian dwarf nanny goat, wandered over to the edge of the fence where I stood. Looking at her face and eyes was a little bizarre. Her eyes were too far apart. Her ears stuck out and up so much that I wondered if they caught rainwater and if that was bothersome for her. Cecelia was the patron saint of music. But if you asked me, the sounds that came out of her name-sake's mouth were not terribly liturgical.

I could understand why people had dogs, cats, and birds. In my life, I had given shelter to them all. You could even add gerbils, guinea pigs, turtles, and fish to the list. The desire to possess goats or chickens had never crossed my mind for a nanosecond.

"You'd better watch yourself. If my soon-to-be daughter-in-law, Priscilla, doesn't like you, Miss Cece, you could wind up turning on a spit."

I was actually talking to a goat who did little to impress me with her personality or intelligence. Yes, I talked to my Harry, but there was a difference. He answered me. And I would have sworn on a stack of Bibles that he knew exactly what he was saying.

I continued to watch the chickens pecking around inside their run. They didn't seem to be very nice to one another. Cecelia moseyed over to her shed and feeder of grain. Yes, I enjoyed the eggs and the yogurt that came from these animals, but raising them did not hold one iota of interest for me. Wasn't it enough that I had ceased using hair spray and Velcro rollers? That my cosmetic applications were reduced from Spackle to a little mascara and lip gloss?

When the horrible day arrived that my mother died, I knew this place would come to me. What would I do with Cecelia and all her feathered friends? I could not see myself milking a goat or putting my hand under a chicken's backside for the mere reward of an egg. It made me laugh just to think of it. No. Bomb or no bomb, I'd take my chances that the grocery stores would stay in business.

I heard a car coming and turned to see Harrison Ford pulling up in the driveway, and my heartbeat trilled. He was growing on me. That was for sure.

"How're you?" he said, and closed the door gently.

Just as an aside, I liked the fact that he did not slam doors. There was enough noise in the world.

"Well, I'm just fine! Out here talking to Cecelia . . . you know, having a conversation with a goat. One-way, I might add. What's new with you?"

"I'm here to collect Miss Josie and take her to our regularly scheduled tango lesson. Did she tell you about that?"

"Yes, and I think it's great. But you know, I

think she may have forgotten because she told me she needed a nap and I think she might be in bed."

"Not feeling sprightly?"

"She's very tired today, for some reason. Would you like some tea or a cup of coffee?"

"No, I'm all set, thanks. Well, she has her good days and her not-so-good days."

We pushed the sliding-glass door open and the house was as still as a tomb.

"Why don't I just slip up to her room and see if she's awake?"

He nodded. I went upstairs as quietly as I could, peeked in Mother's bedroom, and there she was, snoring gently. I pulled a blanket up and over her shoulders and closed her door without a sound. I quietly opened Liz's door and she was sleeping, too, propped up on pillows. Poor thing. I still felt so guilty about her injuries and I imagined I always would.

When I got downstairs I found Harrison on the porch, staring out across the marsh.

"Look! There's an osprey."

"Where? Oh! I see him now!"

"Incredible, right? Just magnificent. DDT almost killed them all, you know. But now they're back."

"Yes, they certainly are. But back to the subject at hand, there will be no fandango or tango lesson for Miss Josie this afternoon, I'm afraid. She's snoozing."

"Oh. Well, then will you come to stand in for her? It's only an hour."

"Oh, Harrison, I can't tango. Or at least I haven't since I took ballroom-dancing lessons when I was a child."

"Ten years ago or so . . . oh, come on. I've only had one lesson, so I'm still in the walking-and-let-the-music-fill-your-soul stage."

He gestured so dramatically with a fake Spanish accent that his invitation was irresistible.

"Does anyone ever say no to you?"

I left a note on the kitchen counter. *Gone to tango with Harrison. Back at five.*

Fifteen minutes later we were in a dance studio in Mount Pleasant. It was classic—ballet barres along the mirrored walls, dust motes in the air, and a lone instructor, a small man with black slick-backed hair who waited on a piano bench, reading the newspaper. The veneer of the upright piano was chipped and abused. I suspected it probably had not been tuned in years. But the instructor stood as we entered and smiled.

"I am Manuel," he said, and extended his hand. His accent was beautifully and authentically Spanish.

"This is my friend Mellie," Harrison said. "She's pinch-hitting for her mother today."

"It is a pleasure," he said. "Shall we begin?"

This fellow wasn't wasting any time. He started the music on a small boom box.

"Now. Please stand straight, close your eyes, and let the music fill your soul."

"I thought you did that last week," I mumbled.

"Ms. Mellie? We do not talk while we tango."

"Sorry."

"Now. Listen to the music. Hear the beats. ONE two THREE four. The first and third beats carry the weight of the rhythm of the dance."

He was right. They did.

"Now, as you feel the beats, I want you to put your weight on the balls of your feet and walk to the music, like a great tiger from the jungle. Walk slowly, just toward me."

I tried very hard not to snicker and walked with my partner, Tony the Tiger, toward Manuel. You may call me Sheena.

"Very good! Very good!"

The next thing I knew we were walking around the perimeter of the entire room like two big cats. Then we walked backward to the music. Meow. Suddenly, Manuel turned off the music and became solemn.

"Now we will learn the embrace! Mr. Harrison is the leader, and you, Ms. Mellie, are the follower."

"I'm not so sure that's an equitable arrangement." I pouted and Manuel smiled.

"It is the essence of the dance, Ms. Mellie. You will see. Now stand together, facing each other."

Something happened to me when Harrison pulled me toward him by the small of my back. I felt a flutter in the pit of my stomach. There was no denying it was, well, an urge. An urge about the size of the custom house in downtown Charleston.

"Don't be nervous," Manuel said. "Now we will walk in the embrace with our heads turned slightly to the side. Ms. Mellie to the right and Mr. Harrison to the left. I will play for you the famous 'Libertango.' Are we ready?"

For the next forty-five minutes or so, Harrison and I danced some very rudimentary version of the Argentine tango and it was about the sexiest forty-five minutes of my life. We even learned a few variations on a two-step pattern that made it look like we actually knew what we were doing. I was addicted.

"You two are naturals," Manuel said. "You should dance together all the time."

Oh, ha-ha, that's not possible, no, we're not, but thanks anyway.

When Harrison dropped me off back on the Island, I was still dazed.

"That was amazing, Harrison, thanks."

Do you see how nonchalant I was about what had actually transpired? I mean, what the devil was I supposed to say? That being next to him created a flammable situation?

"Well, your mother is determined to tango at your son's wedding, so by golly, we're going to tango."

"Heck, I might even tango myself! That was great fun."

"Old Manuel is from Buenos Aires, where the tango began. He's something, isn't he?"

"He sure is. He sure is."

Harrison and I were stuck in each other's eyes once more. It made me very uncomfortable to think that again and again, intense feelings for my own mother's boyfriend were cropping up. What was the matter with me?

I said, "Well, listen, thanks again."

"You're leaving tomorrow, right?"

"Yes. I have to."

"When are you coming back?"

"As fast as I can," I said, and realized how that sounded to him.

He smiled from ear to ear, and said, "Okay, well, travel safe and hurry back."

My face must have been bloodred when I came back in the house. Liz was making a peanut-butter sandwich. She was alone in the kitchen.

"So how was your tango session?"

"Amazing. I'm going to make Kevin take lessons with me when I get back to New York."

"I saw you and Harrison out there staring at each other. What are you messing around with Manny for?"

"What are you talking about? Harrison is the meaningful other of my dear mother."

"No, he isn't. They're just friends. Harrison lost his mother when he was just a kid. Then his wife dumped him. But good. Then his daughter moved to Costa Rica, and he says they have a good relationship and all, but do you or anybody else ever hear any news about her?"

"No. But I know my mother is supersweet on Harrison. I can see it in her eyes."

"Whatever. I'm just telling you what I think. Harrison's heart has been shot full of more holes than a slice of Swiss cheese, but I'll bet you two months' rent that he's way in love with you."

"Girl? You've been watching too many soaps."

"Probably. Or maybe not!"

"Manny is picking me up at six. I have to get cleaned up."

"Uh-huh."

"What's that supposed to mean?"

"Something's not kosher with Manny. That's all."

"Liz? Do you know something that I don't?"

"Nope. Absolutely not or I would tell you. It's just that I've known enough creeps in my life."

I showered, put on a little makeup for the occasion, and decided to wear gray slacks and a black cashmere turtleneck sweater. Instead of loafers, I wore a pair of black suede mules with a low heel. I glanced in the mirror and decided I looked too dull. Thinking Mother might have something to liven up my outfit, I went down the hall and knocked on her door.

"Come in!" she said. "I'm just reading."

In the corner of her room, near the sliding-glass door to her mall balcony, she was sitting in her club chair and ottoman covered in the palest shade of yellow velvet, piped in the same green of Granny Smith apples. The light from her floor lamp combined with the fading light of the afternoon illuminated her face. She had never looked lovelier than she did at that moment.

"Hey, Miss Josie! How are you feeling?"

"Fine, fine. Don't you look nice? Going out?"

"Yes. Manny the Man said he wanted to make dinner for me. I won't be out late. Anyway, do you have a scarf or something I can borrow to do something exciting for this boring outfit of mine?"

"Sure. Look in the middle drawer. There's a red paisley scarf in there that might look nice. But just take whatever you want."

"This one?" I held it up for her to see.

"Yes, that's the one. You know, I still have my mother's locket there in my jewelry box. Why don't you take it? I never wear it. It has my daddy's baby picture in it."

"Oh, Mother! Are you sure?"

I lifted the lid of the silver chest and there it was. It was beautiful, hand-engraved in Old English on one side with my grandmother's initials, and a tiny ruby chip was set in the other side.

"Well, try it on and let's see how it looks."

It slipped easily over my head and the round gold locket hung perfectly in the center of my chest. The perfection of its craftsmanship stood out against my black sweater.

"It's really sweet, isn't it?" I said, opening it to look at the faded tiny photograph of my grandfather. "How precious was he in that little cap?"

"My daddy was a darling man. You keep it, sweetheart. It's not worth a fortune but it has great sentimental value to me."

"I will treasure it, Mother. Thank you."

"How was your tango lesson? Did you let the music fill your soul?"

She giggled and I just shook my head.

"It was so much fun I couldn't believe it."

"Harrison's a gem, isn't he?"

"Probably one in a million . . ." I heard the door open downstairs and knew Manny was there. "I guess that's my *hot date*. I'll see you later."

He was in the kitchen talking to Liz.

"Something smells awfully good!" I said. "How're you?" I said to Manny, and gave him the tiniest of kisses on his cheek.

"Some*body* smells good," he said.

I said, "Thanks."

"Vegan chili," Liz said. "I found it in the freezer. You kids have fun tonight!"

On the ride to Manny's house, we were awkward with each other, conversation coming in bits and pieces. For some reason, I couldn't think of anything I wanted to talk to him about. All I could think about was the tango music, and yes, him. Harrison, that is.

When I told Manny about my dance lesson with Harrison, he said, "Well, I'll bet he wouldn't look as good in a sombrero as I do, right?"

I wanted to say, Harrison Ford wouldn't be caught dead in a sombrero, and if he was, it would be Halloween, and he's about a thousand times more appealing than you anyway.

But I didn't say that.

I thought I said, "Manny, no one looks quite like you in a sombrero."

But what he heard me say was "I'll bet you have the better kitchen."

"Kitchen? I definitely have the better kitchen. What's that got to do with a sombrero?"

You see, this is what happens at a certain stage in your life. You have to become vigilant so that your tongue and brain stay connected. Obviously I needed more than crossword puzzles to stay sharp.

"Oh, my goodness! How silly of me! I was just thinking what a fabulous kitchen you have, that's all."

"Oh, thanks. I'm pretty proud of it. Harrison's got a nice house, though. Ever been there?"

"No, as a matter of fact, I have not. Where is it?"

"Old village. On the water. He never really furnished it, though. I think he was so blown out by his wife dumping him that he can't think about stuff like curtains and rugs and all. But it's a great house. Lots of character."

"Like him."

"Yeah, like him."

I could sense some annoyance from Manny, as though he was a wee bit jealous of Harrison, which of course was completely a waste of energy. I decided some flattery was in order or else the evening was going to fall to pieces.

"So, Mr. Manly Man, what are we having for dinner? You're such a divine cook, I'm sure it's something heavenly."

This brightened him right up.

"Well? I've got rack of lamb all ready to pop in the oven, little red potatoes roasted with garlic and rosemary, and a pear-and-endive salad with Roquefort crumbles."

"No dessert?"

"Yep. I made a cake this morning."

"Chocolate?"

"Is there any other kind?"

"Can't you drive faster?"

The predictable happened. We drank a great bottle of red wine, we ate like starving animals, and then we peeled and shed and dropped articles of clothing and jewelry until we reached his bedroom, whereupon we had sex in his bed like crazy teenagers. Well, he had sex like a crazy teenager, I got pushed and pulled around the bed, wound up sweaty and upside down, thinking at first he might have had more fun without me. But after a few minutes I decided, what did I know? I was not any kind of an expert on the machinations of physical passions, and anyway, it was wonderful to be wanted. But then I thought, shoot, I had read enough magazines in my life to recall that there were ways I could coax Manny along to include me in the action. To be blunt, he didn't exactly send me to that place where you became one with the cosmos in a state of exquisite joy and relinquished all earthly desire, except to repeat the act as soon as humanly possible. No, he didn't, but it was better than nothing. I reassured myself that all I had to do was redirect some of his enthusiasm.

He got up to go to the bathroom and I noticed that in addition to the disorder all around me, my locket was missing from the bedside table where I had put it. Thinking it had slipped in between the bed and the bedside table, I reached down, and sure enough it was there. But my hand hit something plastic and round, like a pill bottle. I pulled it up to see what I had found. It was a bottle of penicillin, prescribed for Helen Sinkler. Wasn't his estranged wife named Helen? Yes, she was. And the prescription was only two weeks old.

Chapter Seventeen

DENIAL

I said nothing to Manny about finding the bottle of his supposed ex-wife's pills. In fact, I put them back where they were and let the evening continue as though I didn't smell a nine-hundred-pound skunk. Later on, back at the island, I didn't tell Mother or Liz about it either. We sat on the porch enjoying the crisp air, feeling the first stirrings of spring, and I said I wished I could stay longer.

"I've got to get Priscilla and Charlie's invitations in the mail . . ."

"Are they going to be regular or decaf?" Liz said, and we all whooped it up. Yes, I could laugh about it, too, because at that point, I was finally liberated.

"Don't even imagine it! But I've got to firm up things with the flowers, and oh goodness, there are a thousand details . . ."

By the time Manny drove me to the airport the next morning, I had regrouped my emotions and neatly compartmentalized the pill discovery, telling myself the facts would reveal themselves eventually. I told him I couldn't wait to see him at the wedding and that was the truth. It was hard to believe it was just a few weeks away. He said he was excited, too, that he hadn't been to New York in ages, and he wanted to take me to some crazy little restaurant that he loved. We talked about the Jamaican menu and could he tango and did he want to stay with me or did he prefer a hotel? We decided that because my estranged son and his family would be there, it was probably best for him to stay with Harrison, and I should not worry, he would find them a place.

The thing that nearly convinced me that I should entirely forget my concern about the bottle of pills was that he made an unsolicited grandiloquent speech about how he was so honored to be included in a family event of this importance. He said he knew how much it meant to all of us. And that he had been such a desperately lonely man for so long. To top it all off, he told me he was crazy about me and kissed me good-bye in public without the slightest trace of self-consciousness.

I did not know what to do except wave good-bye to him, thank him for the ride, and tell him I was crazy about him, too.

Hours later, and after a long episode of lying to myself, I turned the key in my door. Harry was there on the coffee table and whistled to see me.

"Charles is a horse's ass," he said.

"He's not the only one," I said. "There's a whole population of them out in the world." He climbed on my fingers and I stroked his feathers. "Mellie loves Harry. Let's unpack and get you a treat."

I spent the afternoon doing laundry, watering plants, going through tons of mail, the bulk of which I threw away. Charlie and Priscilla's invitations had arrived and that was a great relief.

Finally, when I was satisfied that my house was back in order, I opened the package from the printer and took a deep breath. There I sat, alone at my kitchen table, holding my older son's wedding invitation in my hands, running my fingers over the words and thinking how significant that very moment was. If my Charles, Charlie's father, had not been such an egomaniacal sociopath, he might have been there with me to share the rush of joyous emotion I felt. I would have said, look Charles, look at this. Remember ours? Remember how we fretted over the wording? I saved one, you know. And he might have said, well, go get it and let's compare it to our son's. It might not have been a landmark moment, but it would have been another tiny stone to stack on the others that made the huge mountain of memories that are shared over a lifetime. I was not about to allow myself to become sentimental over being alone then. Charles was the one who was missing out. But truthfully, I felt the smallest of pangs, having to remind myself yet again that life had changed and perhaps it was better this way.

I had yet to receive Charlie and Priscilla's mailing list and added that to the to-do list I had started. I made another note to pick up the silver coffee services and flatware for my sons, to ask Kevin to bring home boxes and tissue to wrap them, and to drop off my silver tea service to be polished as well. My living room was a little ragged-looking with so much silver and all the other items gone, but I thought I would just ask Kevin what he thought. My eye probably needed to adjust to a leaner amount of accessories. Maybe with a little rearranging and moving things around, I could make it look fresh again.

Then there was the matter of the garden cleanup for my soiree the night before the wedding. I planned to handwrite those invitations, and all at once I panicked at the thought of inviting Charles and Judith. I had not even considered that I would have to see them except at the wedding. Was I cosmopolitan and sophisticated enough to handle having her in my home? To my knowledge, she had never been here. Well, I would take a poll with Kevin on that one. And obviously, I would ask Charlie.

I came to the sane but uncomfortable conclusion that it would look odd to exclude them from the evening. Maybe they would have the decency to decline. Or they could host a Sunday brunch without Mother and me and we all could avoid a whole lot of unnecessary awkwardness. Oh, sure. Perhaps I would magically sprout the brass appendages to call Charles himself and inquire what he thought was appropriate. There was a piece of me that giggled over putting Charles and Judith in the hot seat, but the other part of me knew you couldn't upset people who had no conscience to begin with. In any case, I hoped to have an intimate dinner party for Charlie and Priscilla and that it would be warm enough for our guests to spill out into the garden.

While all these happy plans and details danced across my mind, Helen Sinkler's pill bottle continued to rattle around the back of my brain. As I understood it, Manny and Helen had been separated for years and there was nothing more between them. I seemed to recall that someone said that she never even spent one night in that gorgeous house.

Then why were her pills there? And next to the bed? No! I would have no part of second-guessing Manny after such a wonderful and intimate visit.

Then I thought, Oh, so what if she had perhaps spent one stupid night there? Maybe Manny wasn't even in town at the time. Maybe she was house-sitting. I mean, let's be serious here. Would he be carrying on with me like a wild animal if he was still sexually involved with his wife? Of course not! How low-down would that be? No, it simply couldn't be true. After all, our first date had been a church supper!

The truth was that I really didn't want to know the truth.

Manny may not have been the greatest lover, but he was presentable and made me feel good about myself. He was extremely nice, and most of all, he was reasonably smart and fun. I'll admit that on the plane ride home I had entertained the thought that if Helen was still somewhat in the picture, maybe I could make him forget about her. If I pursued it carefully, something serious might develop between us. Because of him, I no longer saw myself going through the rest of my life alone. Manny had shown me a new vista and that alone was a priceless gift. Perhaps most important, he had made me know I was still plenty desirable.

I knew, or at least I hoped, that Charles and Judith would be shocked to see me on the arm of someone like Manny Sinkler. Manny was about Charles's age, more handsome than Charles by a landslide, and Manny was, if anything, much more successful. From everything I had seen, Manny Sinkler was worth many millions. It would make Charles twitch.

Manny and I still had not discussed why his marriage fell apart, but I guessed it was for the same reasons that many successful men lose their wives—because their career is their mistress, the one they love the most. Their office is their true home. Their wives, children, their academic and community accomplishments, all the second and third houses, the expensive cars and vacations, were all lumped into a psychological trophy case behind thick glass in another realm that only rarely included the husband.

Manny was retired and he was probably poised to find a true partner who appreciated all he had accomplished in his career. Not someone who could remind him of every mistake he had made in the last twenty-something years and that he really was not a god. I could actually see myself in Manny's life permanently. With a little work and some luck, we could be great together. I adored every detail of his house, the property, and the fact that it was just minutes from my mother's house. And a commitment to Manny would protect me from further thoughts of Harrison. Harrison was too dangerous.

While I was waiting for Kevin to come home, I took a chance that I might reach Charlie and called him. He answered.

"Hi, sweetheart! I just wanted to let you know that I'm back from Sullivans Island and your invitations came in. Charlie, they are just simply regal."

"Regal, huh? Well, that's sure to thrill Priscilla. In fact, I'm walking around with our guest list in my back pocket. Want me to drop it off later?"

"That would be so great because we have to get them in the mail *tout de suite*!"

"Well, we've already e-mailed everyone anyway—"

"E-mailing wedding invitations? Gadzooks! What's this world coming to?"

"Mom. Did you really just say *gadzooks*?"

"It's an undervalued, nonoffensive expletive. Sort of. My father or grandfather used to say it. I think it came from a comic book."

I giggled and I could hear his surprise at my giggle in his voice.

"Like *egad*? And *golly gee willikers*?"

"Exactly! Well, anyway, there are a few

things we need to talk about to get your wedding boat afloat."

"Such as?"

"Well, I am assuming that Priscilla's family will be arriving on Friday."

"Probably. I mean, I'll check, but I think so."

"Your grandmother and her man friend are getting here Wednesday, and Dan and his clan are flying in Thursday."

"What? Miss Josie has a man?"

"It's hard to say exactly what their relationship is all about, but I just assume . . . anyway, he's a great guy and that's her business. Now, are y'all having a rehearsal? And what about a dinner afterward?"

"No, we didn't plan anything because the loft is booked Friday night."

"Well, my thought was that I would like to invite all our out-of-town guests for a buffet supper. If you would like me to, that is. And if we do that, you know, there's no reason why you can't have a little impromptu rehearsal right here, say, an hour earlier. Everyone can stay for a bite and a cocktail or two? What do you think?"

"Mom? That is a truly excellent idea! Priscilla and I were just talking about this last night. Our apartment is way too small and we don't live in the greatest neighborhood, you know. But don't spend too much money, okay? I mean, I can help with this, too, and I'd like to do that."

"Well, I'll tell you what. You take care of the wine and liquor and I'll take care of the food and help. How does that sound?"

"That sounds like a deal."

"I have one more question."

"Sure."

"What do we do about your father and Judith? Should we invite them Friday night? And what if he has a guest list for Saturday?"

Silence. Then Charlie said, "I wouldn't be upset if you didn't include them in anything, but Priscilla's family might think it was strange."

I told him about my brunch idea and he burst out laughing.

"Are you kidding me? Dad has already declared his position on this. He wouldn't bring us a bag of sausage biscuits from Burger King!"

"Well, it appears that I am going to have to be the grown-up here. I'll call him and see what he says."

"Good luck!"

"Very funny! I'll see you later! Oh, and Priscilla has hired a caterer, made the arrangements for a cake and the music, right?"

"All done. Her aunt is bringing the cake from Jamaica."

"Better check with the airlines. They are so particular these days. She might be better off to ship it and ice it here."

"Good thought."

"Okay, Kevin's got the decorations covered and he's ordering rentals. My job is flowers and the photographer. So don't worry about centerpieces and flowers for the bar and so forth. You just take care of Priscilla's bouquet, boutonnieres, and flowers for the wedding party, okay?"

"Whew! We should've eloped!"

"And deny me the opportunity to see you get married? No, son. It's worth every penny."

Soon I heard the outside door open and knew that Kevin was home. He rapped his knuckles against my door and then rang the bell for good measure.

"Hey! Welcome back! How was your trip?"

"You wouldn't believe!"

"Let me just take all this stuff upstairs,

change into something else, and I'll be right back."

Shortly after, we were having a glass of wine and I was retelling the past few days, except for the naked parts.

"They're all calling me Mellie, Kevin. A crazy combo of Miriam and Elizabeth. What do you think about that? Can I be Mellie?"

"Mellie? Hmm. You know? Of course you can! I think Mellie sounds young and fun and that you can store Miriam away for your old age. Mellie. I like it. But you're still Petal Puss to me."

"Thanks, sweetheart."

I told him about Liz and Mother and elaborated on how they had taken such a shine to each other.

"Liz is already a thousand percent better," I said. "Mother couldn't be happier than when she has someone to cluck over . . ."

"And how *are* the chickens?"

"Vile, as you would expect. But I'm actually a little concerned about Mother."

"Why is that?"

"Well, she's moving slower and sleeping a lot during the day. It's just not like her."

"Well, excuse me, but don't we have a doctor in the family? Almost two? When she's here for the wedding, have Charlie look at her."

"Why didn't I think of that? You're brilliant, of course!"

Then, I described the rapturous dance lesson I took with Harrison, begged him to take a few tango lessons with me, and he agreed immediately.

"I adore the tango! Oh, great heavens! The dress! It's got tango written all over it! I can't believe I forgot to bring it down to you. Don't move!"

Minutes later, Kevin unzipped the garment bag and pulled out the dress of my dreams. It was beyond perfect for a wedding, a dance, or to wear as you ascended to heaven through the clouds. It was the *Dancing in the Dark* dress in navy blue.

"Kevin? You have done it again! Boy, do you have the eye!"

"Go try it on!"

I grabbed it and ran to my bedroom. Okay, here's the bad news. I couldn't zip it up past my waist.

"And the verdict?" he said at the bedroom door.

"I'm going to commit suicide."

"No, you are not."

I opened the door and showed him the back of the dress.

"Okay, not so terrible. You are not allowed to eat anything but lettuce, steamed veggies, chicken, and fish until after the wedding. No food at night. And you are getting on that blasted treadmill for one hour in the morning and another hour in the afternoon."

"I hate that plan. I despise exercise and you know it."

"Tough noogies. You have three and a half weeks and all you need is ten pounds at a maximum. You can do it, girl. I'll help. I'm taking all the cookies, scotch, and vodka upstairs with me tonight. You are to drink water until it comes out of your ears."

"That's too strict, Kevin. I'm not that disciplined."

"I'll give you drugs to sleep. I've got a bunch of over-the-counter things. You'll go to bed early at nine with a little help from my friends. It will work, Miss Mellie Petal Puss Swanson. Guaranteed."

"I'll try."

"Don't despair. It looks gorgeous on you even unzipped!"

"Can we start this regime from hell tomorrow?"

"Yes. Now hang that sensational baby up, I'll pour you another glass of wine, and tell me everything else that I missed."

When he was brought completely up-to-date, one question still loomed heavily in the air.

"So, are you actually going to call Charles?"

"Why not? He doesn't scare me anymore. What's he going to do? Bite me?"

"You're right, of course. But I would call him at the office so you don't have to deal with that nasty viper of his should she answer the phone at home."

"Excellent thought. I'll call the cad first thing in the morning. So now can we talk about the garden and how we're going to make this living room look like it should? I think I've taken the shabby-chic thing one step too far."

"It does look a little drab, but you know, Petal, you can cure a thousand problems with fresh flowers and good lighting. Let me think about it overnight."

The doorbell rang, and as Kevin left, Charlie arrived with his list.

"Come in! Come in!"

"Hi, Mom!" He gave me a hug and handed

me the papers. "Can't stay. I have to be back at the hospital at five-thirty in the morning."

"Not even for a cup of coffee? Darling? Why are you working so hard?"

"You wouldn't believe how many sick people there are in New York. Seriously! But I sure appreciate this and so does Priscilla. Thanks, Mom."

"I'm honored, Charlie."

We looked at each other then and I knew we were mother and son again. I was positive of it. Before I could weep all over him, he was gone.

The morning brought bright sunshine, and that combined with two cups of strong tea with skim milk, a glass of hot lemon water for a diuretic boost, and the actual breezing through a late-week *New York Times* puzzle fortified me to call Charles. Kevin and Charlie's opinions were sufficient to make me see that I simply had to extend the invitations.

Probably because he heard from me so rarely, he may have thought there had been a death in the family and took the call right away.

"Charles Swanson."

Not "hello, this is Charles," or "Miriam, is

something wrong?" Or even just "hi, Miriam."
I mean, he knew it was me because his dim-
witted secretary had surely told him. Didn't
the intergalactic class of money warriors have
their calls screened?

"Hi, Charles, it's Miriam."

"I knew that."

"Of course you did," I said sweetly. My little
dig at his pomposity went unrecognized and
unrewarded. "So, how are you?"

"Busy. What's up?"

Did he inquire about my health or my life?

"Well, we have a family wedding, you
know. Your son's getting married the weekend after Easter?"

"I'm aware."

Wasn't he a sweetheart?

"Come on, Charles. Be nice. There are
details I thought you might like to know about
so that you and Judith could make some decisions."

"Such as?"

"Such as, would you like to invite anyone
to the wedding ceremony and reception?
Such as, I'm giving a rehearsal dinner on Fri-
day night at my house and would you and
Judith like to come? That's *such as*,
Charles."

There was a brief silence from his end followed by a long pithy sigh.

"Sorry, Miriam. I've just been under terrible stress. You are very kind to consider us and I will go over it with Judith and call you back."

I didn't jump for the fish like a trained seal, but I did take it. After all, he was the one with terrible manners and a nasty disposition, not me. And he did sound terrible. Gee. Too bad.

I got on with my program and spent most of the day refilling my favorite fountain pen. My handwriting wasn't comparable to professional calligraphy, but it wasn't bad at all. Charlie and Priscilla's invitations were almost all addressed and ready to mail, except those I had set aside for Charles.

Because of Charlie and Priscilla's ages, my divorce and Charles's remarriage, and because Priscilla's mother was presumed deceased, we had omitted all parents' names from the invitations. As much as I still loved traditional everything, even I had to admit that if the whole family was included, the invitations would've looked like a corporate organizational chart. As it was, they were simple and elegant.

It occurred to me that I had been home a

couple of days and had not heard from Manny. Liz had phoned to say that she was staying on the Island with Mother until the wedding, that Dr. George Durst, the island's finest family practitioner, was seeing to her wounds, and was that okay with me? And that a dentist friend of his was going to complete her dental work for a huge savings. I said of course it was, and knew that half the reason was because she was crazy about my mother, who probably wasn't feeling tip-top herself. If I knew Liz, that sling was gone and she was milking Cecelia.

When another week passed and it was getting to the point of absurdity that I hadn't heard a peep from Manny, Charles finally called me back.

"Miriam? It's me. Do you have a fax machine?" he said.

I laughed. "Why on God's green earth would I have a fax machine?"

"Right. Why would you? Well, do you have an e-mail address?"

"What do you think, Charles? That I spend my lonely nights in chat rooms? No, I do not have e-mail."

"Well, all right, then. I'll messenger the list over to you. When you have calculated a per-

person cost, let me know and I will reimburse you."

"Why? Are you inviting a thousand people?"

"No. Sixteen. And I can expense it."

"Oh! Well, thank you. What about Friday night?"

"I will try to be there. I'm not sure about Judith. She has some conflict."

What? Guilt? Was Judith uncomfortable to face me?

"Oh, well, that's fine. Okay, then, thanks."

As Kevin commanded, I got on the treadmill, but I set it up in front of the television and watched *The View* in the morning and *Oprah* in the afternoon. Each day those two hours flew by. Kevin and I took six tango lessons and we were getting pretty darn proficient. And, we found a great pair of shoes for me and dyed them to match the dress of my dreams.

The good news was that I was almost eleven pounds thinner, and because Kevin insisted that I take a pill to sleep every night, and that I used whitening strips on my teeth, my face looked remarkably younger. Or more rested. Or something. But better for sure.

I bought case after case of bottled water

and drank so much of it I thought I might start growing gills. When I wasn't mesmerized by the television while I hiked and hiked to nowhere, I had time to think about other things.

Such as Judith.

I decided she wasn't coming Friday night because she didn't want to play second fiddle, and that was fine with me. As it was, I would have to hire a team of psychics with sage smudge sticks to smoke out my rooms to get rid of Charles's icky karma. I wondered what Judith was wearing to the wedding. Probably something wildly expensive that made her look like she was barely twenty. I knew she was almost thirty-five and I wondered how she was dealing with it. Hopefully, not well. If there was one thing a middle-aged woman knew that a younger woman did not, it was that you could trade on your looks for only so long. All the plastic surgery and personal trainers you could endure would only make you look good for your age. And while exercise might prolong your life and actually improve the quality of your health, eventually the Grim Reaper would nail you. Judith was still young enough to believe she was bulletproof. I was old enough finally to understand that quality of life went beyond good health, that one should consider other things such as integrity, kindness, and how one would like to be remembered.

I had to confess, Manny's not calling was making me suspicious and irritable. It was early evening on the Wednesday before Easter and just a little over a week before Dan, Nan, and all the others were to arrive. My excitement was building but my annoyance with Manny was, too.

True to his nature and as proof of our long friendship, Kevin was working very hard to help me pull things into shape.

I had picked up the silver coffee services, sets of flatware, gift wrapped them and had mine polished as well. Mine looked extraordinary on the sideboard of my dining room. In Charlie's old room where the children would sleep were baskets of small gifts for my grandchildren—coloring books, crayons, and so on. All the old clothes had been hauled away, new linens bought and laundered and waiting on the beds.

The museums of my boy's childhoods were pared down and spruced up to look welcoming for Dan's family so they would not feel like they were intruding. Even the bathroom got a little face-lift with new towels, and a complete disposal and replacement of old toiletries.

Kevin decided my lumpy chairs and faded sofa could be remedied by restuffing the cushions, and he was right. It made all the difference in the world. We gently vacuumed the curtains, rebunched the panels, stuffing them inside their lining with plastic dry-cleaner bags that no one could see, and then we readjusted their tiebacks. It made them look almost new. He polished the brass fire-place tools and the small brass fender, and the effect was amazing. The living room was beginning to sparkle. We threw out all my old magazines and stacked the coffee table with art history books and a long-ignored crystal bowl filled with handblown replicas of various kinds of fruit that had been stored away for years.

And my garden? Now there was the serious challenge. I scrubbed each windowpane of the leaded-glass doors and Kevin removed the storm doors and took them to the basement. I raked and carried out bags of old leaves and garden debris. Who needed a treadmill? The sanitation workers deserved and would receive a generous tip from me. That was for sure.

"I know just what this needs," he said. "I'll be back in an hour and a half."

Kevin brought home a small fountain to hang on the back wall that looked like it had just been dug up from some ancient Roman ruin and smuggled out of the country. While investigating where to put the electrical work, he discovered a line for one that had been in the exact same spot probably fifty years ago. The next day, my electrician came and tested it for safety and assured us there was no need to replace anything.

"They don't make anything now like they used to," he said, and hooked up the whole kit and caboodle in less than an hour.

Moments later we flipped a switch and the lion's head graciously poured water from his mouth into a pool that recirculated it and brought it back to his precious little head.

"Thank you so much!" I said, and thanked him again with a check. "Amazing."

"We need a koi pond," Kevin said.

"Don't get carried away," I said, and giggled.

Later that afternoon, Kevin and a friend of his from the store carried in two small Charleston benches and placed them on either side of the fountain. They looked like they had been there forever.

"Where in the world did you find them?" I said.

"Flea market. I was just walking by and spotted them. Get this. Twenty bucks each! It would have cost more to rent a truck to deliver them, but my friend has a small van and he was free and so . . ."

They were inexpensive because of their age and weathered condition. But old and weathered was exactly what I wanted, and I was thrilled.

"They are absolutely perfect, Kevin."

"I know, right? Those benches were just waiting to come live in your garden, Petal. I swear they were."

Later on, he and his friend rolled in two enormous faux-cement planters, and placed them in the flower beds on the outside edges of the benches. They were filled with huge forsythia that with any luck at all would pop into bloom in a week. From my door to the fountain they poured bag after bag of fresh pea gravel, until the curved pathway looked right. Once I had trimmed up the boxwoods and azaleas and wiped down the table and chairs, I was stunned at the difference.

"I wish we had taken before-and-after pictures, Miss Mellie, I could have sold a story to the *Times*."

"I'm exhausted," I said.

"Me too. So you go shower up. I'll go do the same. Then let's have a well-earned and celebratory cocktail in the garden with you wearing the dress. What do you say?"

"I say, I'm so sick of steamed broccoli and bland fish I could scream. And if that dress doesn't fit me . . ."

"It will. Now go!"

I showered and put on fresh makeup. Then I crossed my fingers, put on the foundation garments I intended to wear, and slipped the dress over my head. I zipped it up with ease and looked in my full-length mirror. I looked so good I hardly recognized myself. Well, not really, but the dumpy Miriam was gone forever and cool Mellie was alive and well. I slipped on the pumps and thought I was looking pretty fine.

Kevin rang the bell and I raced to the door.

"What do you think?" I said, and took a spin around.

He slapped his hands on either side of his face and his jaw dropped. "Oh, dear mother of God and all the angels and saints in heaven! You look ravishing! Divine!"

"Not too bad, right?"

"Not too bad? How's smashing! Oh, Petal, I'm calling John Barrett first thing in the morning. He's got to do your hair and makeup himself. This is too amazing. Oh! I can't wait to see the look on your stupid husband's face!"

In Kevin's eyes, John Barrett was the king of hair in Manhattan.

Because he hates to miss a thing, Harry had hopped out from the kitchen to see what the commotion was all about. He listened to Kevin refer to Charles, and, well, genius bird that he is, you know what he had to say without even hearing Charles's name. We repeated Harry's favorite Charles mantra with him and laughed like justice, revenge, and a pony under the Christmas tree had all arrived.

"Let's drink martinis!" I said. "You forgot to confiscate the gin and there's vermouth in the cabinet, too. I'm going to hang this dress back in its bag."

"Probably a good idea. But let me have one more look."

I gave the skirt one more spin around, and he said, "It was so worth the pain and suffering, now, wasn't it?"

"Yes, yes, yes. But ugh!"

I changed clothes and rejoined him in the kitchen, where he was just pouring out our drinks.

"So, tell me. Have you heard from Manny?"

"No. And I don't know why, but I have a sneaking suspicion he's going to bail out."

"Have you called him?"

"Honey, ladies, even ladies named Petal Puss Mellie, do not call gentlemen."

Chapter Eighteen

I Do, He Won't, and She Does

Wednesday before the wedding, I was in the kitchen writing out place cards when Manny finally called. In a halting voice, he said some things had changed in his world and he would not be able to come to New York after all. Just like that. But I had suspected the call was coming and I was ready. Or as Manny himself would've said, I was loaded for bear.

I said, "Well, darlin'? Are you sick in the hospital?"

"No," he said. "In the head, maybe. But no, I'm not in a hospital."

"Well, then, whatever could be the matter? Because I have never heard of a gentleman breaking a date with the mother of the groom four days before the ceremony unless they were in ICU on life support."

Scarlett O'Hara herself, live in the flesh, could not have delivered the line with more aplomb.

"Mellie, I'm afraid I haven't been completely honest with you."

"Manny, don't worry about it. Just tell me what's happened. We're friends, aren't we?"

In the bug world, the female black widow spider weaves her web, catches a male, mates, and then devours him. Now we know why.

"Well, it's like this. You know Helen and I have been separated for many years."

"Yes. I know. I'm divorced too, you know."

"Well, Helen and I never actually got around to finalizing the divorce because frankly, well, she didn't want to. Now she has threatened to do some pretty drastic things if I don't give our marriage another chance."

Was he implying that she would commit suicide?

"Then you simply must give it another chance! What choice do you have?" I actually believed him then.

"And that's the thing. I wouldn't want her . . . my conscience can't take it, Mellie."

"And neither could mine. Listen, don't sweat it. We're still friends."

"Do you promise? I am just so sorry."

"Of course! Thanks for being so honest with me, Manny. That means a lot."

We hung up and I stared up at the ceiling as though there was something written up there that would make me not want to break down and cry from the anger I was feeling. I was nearly hyperventilating in a matter of minutes. It wasn't from the anger I was feeling toward him. It was much deeper than that.

I had known his divorce wasn't final. I had found evidence of Helen's presence in his bedroom. I had told myself that maybe I could lure him away from her if in fact he was still interested in her. I had even gone so far as to envision myself spending the rest of my life with him. I had rationalized continuing and growing and consummating the relationship with him eighty ways to hell and back. And here's the ugliness and where evil was lurking all the while.

I was no better than Judith.

I was no better than the whore who had

succeeded in stealing my husband. Never mind my grand scheme to make Charles jealous and fill him with regret that he had chosen Judith over me—the great show I had so carefully orchestrated to play out at the wedding had gone up in flames. Tango lessons and a great dress? A diet and white teeth? Who really cared about that? That was just some trivial matter of my own badly and irreparably bruised ego.

This news from Manny pointed to something much more severe—a terrible and tragic flaw in my own character. When I saw so vividly that the thing I hated most about Judith was present in myself, I was filled with nausea and violent self-loathing. I did not know if there was a thing in the world I could do to make myself feel better except to forgive Judith and to ask her to forgive me for judging her so harshly. Could I do that? I did not know if I could.

What I did do was keep myself busy, and given the amount of remaining details to be sewn up, keeping my mind occupied with other matters was effortless. And Mother, Harrison, and Liz were arriving that night.

Priscilla's aunt had indeed shipped the cake, and I had safely tucked it away in Liz's refrigerator because, as you might imagine, hers was nearly empty. I had asked Liz's permission and she had no problem with me entering her apartment while she was away. And knowing that Mother would be sleeping there, I gave it a good dusting and wiped down the bathroom and kitchen on Wednesday afternoon.

Kevin knocked on the door at seven that night.

"The troops here yet?"

"No, they land at seven-thirty. I've got a roasted chicken, mashed potatoes, string beans, and a tomato pie waiting. And a fruit pie. Apple. You'll join us won't you?"

"Sure. What's the matter? I can see you're upset."

"Want a glass of vino?"

"Oh, no. What's happened?"

He came in, closed the door, followed me to the kitchen, where I poured him a glass and refilled mine.

"Manny called. He's not coming."

"So *that's* the cause of the crease between your eyebrows. Well, okay. Who cares? That means more tangos for me!"

"Who cares? How's this? He's not sick. He's getting back together with his wife, who he actually, well, he *sort of* implied-said she'd kill herself if he didn't take her back."

"Holy crap, Petal. That's heavy. Did she hear about you or something?"

"Not unless she talked to the Sullivans Island Police Department."

"What?"

"Oh, it's just a ridiculous story that I'll tell you sometime. Listen, Kevin, here's why I'm so upset about this . . ."

After I told Kevin what I was thinking and feeling and how I was no better than Judith, he strongly disagreed.

"You know what? You're wrong and that's all there is to it. This guy led you to believe he was available, so you believed him. Even his friend and your mother approved, didn't they?"

"Yes."

"You find a bottle of her pills. Okay, that might arouse some suspicion, but it was proof of nothing. I mean, you might wonder why she was taking them to begin with and could you catch something, but we can talk about that later."

"Very funny."

"Whatever. So you indulged in some daydreams about a future with him? Big hairy deal! I would've slept with him just for kitchen rights, the way you described it! And they were *daydreams*. You didn't set up housekeeping with him, take his money, have children outside of marriage like a movie star, like that pig whore slut Judith."

"But I would have, Kevin, and that's the point. I was ready to push Helen out of his life and move right in."

"I disagree. This is a very different situation."

"How is that?"

"Because you got fooled by a liar, Petal. Plain and simple."

"No. I feel terrible about myself."

"Oh, suck it up, Mellie. I'll bet you a thousand dollars that when you find out the truth, and you will, the truth isn't exactly what he told you. You're the victim here, honey. And I have a feeling in my gut that this guy is a practiced liar."

"I don't know. You want to know the worst part? I didn't even really love the guy."

"Oh, so what? Two adults were playing with each other. Look. It happens every day."

"You're right."

"Quit pouting, go wash your face, and put

on something nice. The South Carolina contingent is going to be here any minute. We've busted our fannies for weeks to make this a wonderful time and I wouldn't let some horse's ass named Manny ruin a minute of it."

"Manny is a horse's ass," said Harry, who was listening intently.

"Don't forget Charles," I said to Harry, and laughed for the first time all day. "He's still one, too!"

Even Kevin laughed. "God, I love that bird."

I fixed my face, changed into a red cashmere V-neck sweater and gray Capri pants. I thought I didn't look like I had been languishing in the throes of deep misery all day long. I spritzed myself all over with my favorite cologne.

The doorbell rang and I glanced around my living room before I answered the door. Everything looked perfectly beautiful. I had put together a lush arrangement of flowers on the mantel over the fireplace and a long and low arrangement of flowers combined with fruit on the dining-room table.

"Hello! Hello!" I said, and gave my mother, Liz, and then Harrison a hug.

"How are y'all? I'll take your suitcases upstairs," Kevin said, and shook hands with Harrison.

"Let me help you," Harrison said. "You must be Kevin. You look really good, Mellie. What'd ya do?"

"Nuuuthin' . . ."

Nothing? How about cut my hair, waxed my eyebrows, got highlights, lowlights, whiter teeth, exercised like a maniac, lost a billion pounds . . . weren't men incredible?

They disappeared up the steps.

"Lord! You got so skinny!" Liz said, in all innocence. "You been sick?"

"Yeah, sick of being a plump matron," I said. "Besides, you forget I have a date with the enemy this Saturday." Honestly, some-times Liz had a brain like a sieve.

"Well, she's gonna turn puce and paisley when she sees you, honey," Mother said. "I haven't seen you look this good in years."

"Thanks, but too bad I don't care anymore. So how was your flight?"

"Fine, fine," Mother said. "Your house looks beautiful! What have you done?"

"Just got rid of a bunch of stuff. And, Liz? No sling?"

"Nope! That nice doctor said my lung is fine, my ribs are still a little bit tender, collarbone is fine, and look . . ." She pushed her hair away from the side of her face and the scar that had given all of us nightmares had all but disappeared. "Y'all can hardly see it, right?"

"It's a miracle," I said.

"It's my aloe cream," Mother said. "Works like a charm."

I kept thinking that my mother looked terrible. She was thinner and more drawn than I had ever seen her. But her spirits were so good that I didn't want to mention it. We made small talk about all the wedding plans until the men returned and dinner was on the table. Finally, we got around to the subject of Manny.

"Are you cool with him not coming?" Liz said.

"Oh, definitely," I said. "His wife must be some kind of a really wacky gal to threaten to kill herself if he didn't take her back. At least that's what Manny led me to think. Can I serve y'all some tomato pie?"

Harrison, Mother, and Liz exchanged looks and I knew right then, without a shred of doubt, that Kevin had been right. I didn't quite have all the facts. I just calmly continued the story as I knew it and hoped somebody would gather up the strength to come clean.

"I mean, who knows? Maybe she ran around on him or something and couldn't live with her guilt. Anyway, the whole thing is too much drama for me. The Willis family cured me of theatrics forever!"

"Me too," Liz said. "Gosh, Mellie, this is so, so good. I haven't had tomato pie in ages."

"Thanks. I always like to eat comfort food when I get off a plane."

"I taught her how to cook," Mother said. "She learned everything she knows from me."

Everyone had a laugh at that. Kevin asked if there were any family photos of me milking a goat and another round of snickers ensued.

"Well, Miss Josie?" Liz said quietly. "You might have taught her a lot of things, but you didn't teach her how to smell a rat."

The table fell silent. I glanced over at Kevin, whose eyebrows were somewhere in the range of the chandelier and still rising toward the ceiling.

"Meaning what, Miss Alabama?" Kevin said in a flat voice, the kind that demanded a response.

Liz blushed deeply and looked to Harrison and Mother for support.

"Mellie gave me the goods on Truman Willis. Shouldn't we tell her what we know about Mr. Sink So Low?"

Harrison, ever the Honest Abe, cleared his throat and put down his fork.

"Okay. Mellie? I'm gonna tell you what I found out about my so-called friend Manny."

"I'm ready," I said.

"Remember I told you that we had worked together in Charlotte?"

"Yes."

"Well, he was in the commercial side of the business and I was in the corporate side."

"In English?" Liz said.

"We didn't have a whole lot of contact with each other. And he came on board just around the time I decided to chuck it all. I'd see him around and he was pleasant, but we didn't really have any business dealings. I thought I knew him well enough to support you to, you know, go out with him if you felt like it. I mean, there was no reason I knew of to discourage you from seeing him."

"We all liked him," Mother said. "He surely seemed fine to me."

"So let's cut to the chase here, y'all. The suspense is killing me," I said.

"He sucks," Liz said. "Pardon me."

"That would be the finale," Kevin said, in the droll voice he used when he was getting annoyed. "We're still looking for Acts Two and Three."

"Well, Liz is actually right about that, but here's how we found out. A few nights ago, I finally convinced my good friends here, Liz and Miss Josie, to go over the causeway after dark for dinner on Shem Creek. I had to do some heavy pitching, but they finally relented."

"We went to Shem Creek Bar and Grill," Mother said. "I had those little crab cakes they make that are so good."

"And I had stuffed flounder," Liz said.

"Puhleeze!" Kevin said.

"Patience, my man, we're almost there," Harrison said. "So, I got up to use the men's room and who do I see in the corner booth?"

"Manny and who? Helen?" Kevin asked.

"Bingo. Anyway, he's loving up on her in a way that I don't think is appropriate to be doing in public and she's all over him, too. So I go over to them and say, 'Oh! Hello.' Then I say, 'Manny? Could I ask you to step outside with me for a moment?' He says sure and excuses himself. We go out on the porch and

I said something like, 'Just what's going on here? I thought you and Helen were all done.'"

"What did he say?" I asked.

"He hemmed and hawed around and finally it comes out that they're getting back together because he can't afford to divorce her."

"What?" I said, with slightly more volume and excitement in my voice than I would have liked. "He's as rich as cream! That's just some bull, y'all!"

"Here's kicker number one, Mellie. It's all Helen's money. I called an old buddy of mine the next morning who still works at the bank and asked him for the story on Manny Sinkler. Well, he laughed and laughed until I thought he was going to burst something and he finally calmed down and said it was about the biggest brouhaha he'd ever heard of in twenty years. Turns out Manny got fired for some *huge* impropriety that could have sent him to jail. He came to Charleston to sulk over his ruined reputation and career—because once you do the kind of thing he did, you don't work in banking anymore."

"What did he do?" Kevin said.

"There was very strong suspicion of insider trading, so the department head seized his computer, examined his hard drive, and guess what they found?"

"Evidence of insider trading?" I said.

"Nothing they could absolutely nail him on but enough to fire him. And, a drumroll, please, there were just a few too many visits to pornography Internet sites on the company computer. About sixty thousand, so the story goes . . ."

Kevin stood, rapped his hands on the edge of the table like he was playing bongos, and roared with laughter. I was completely and totally astonished. And horrified.

"What? Porn sites? The dog! Sixty thousand?" I said. "I can't believe *Manny* did that!"

"Manny is a horse's ass! So is Charles!" Came the call from the kitchen.

"Excuse me," Harrison said, "but what the hell was that? It sounded like your voice coming from the kitchen!"

"It's my very smart bird, Harry. I'll introduce you to him later."

"Did he actually say . . ."

"Yes, he did."

Harrison chuckled and shook his head in disbelief. "Unbelievable. Anyway, they threw his—and forgive me for agreeing with Harry—horse's ass out that very day and told him he'd better never show his face around any bank in the world or he'd spend the rest of his days in the pokey."

"Isn't that incredible? I can't believe Helen didn't put a bullet right through his brain!" Mother said.

Harrison said, "Helen's too dignified for a cold-blooded murder, but she banished him to Charleston until she could cool down. She runs the family's foundation—they made a huge fortune in textiles—and she thought eventually, when she got over the shame and embarrassment of what Manny had done, they could divide their time between Charlotte and Charleston. But she was more furious than she thought she'd be and so she made herself get busier so she didn't come to Charleston too often. Manny got lonelier and he started running around. So she got wind of it and threatened to divorce him, and I think she cut off his allowance and was threatening all kinds of legal action."

"He's lucky that's all she was cutting off," Liz said.

I wiggled my eyebrows at Kevin and he covered his mouth and snickered.

"So, apparently there was a recent show-down between them and Manny's sworn on a stack of Bibles to behave himself. He seriously doesn't want to be poor and doesn't know how to be poor. Evidently Helen really loves him, although I can't imagine why. This chicken is delicious, Mellie. Can I have some more?"

There wasn't anything to do except laugh and be shocked, retell bits of the story all through the rest of dinner and dessert, and then be stunned some more.

By the time the dishes were all done and everyone was ready to say good night, Harrison was dragging his feet getting out of my door and up to Kevin's apartment, where he was staying. In addition to everything else, Manny had never booked a hotel.

"What's on your mind?" I said.

"I'm just really happy to see you again, that's all. And I feel pretty stupid about the whole Manny affair . . ."

"Do you think we could refer to it another way? Like the Manny business?"

"Gotcha. Anyway, hopefully he's the last low-down, lying, perverted, 'scuse me, horse's ass you'll ever have to endure."

There were those eyes of his again, casting a net over me from head to toe. I finally found my voice.

"Wouldn't that be nice? I guess I'll see you tomorrow."

"Okay, then. Good night."

He leaned in and kissed my cheek. He smelled so good I wanted to lick him and felt that crazy fluttering thing traveling all through the southern climes. Let me assure you that in the entirety of all my days, I had never felt the urge to lick anyone. But Mellie was not Miriam, and Mellie, despite the recent hoodwinking, was determined to enjoy every minute possible of the rest of her life.

The next afternoon, my arms flew around Dan, Nan, Mary, and Penn as they came through my door. Clearly, everyone had decided to put their best foot forward because their arrival couldn't have been more joyous.

Oh, I've miss you so, son! And I missed you, too, Mom! It's so good to see you, Nan, you look just radiant! Guess why? Another baby? Yep, we're due in December. What marvelous news! Congratulations! And look at my gorgeous grandchildren! Look how you've grown! Do I smell chocolate cookies, Grandmomma? Yes! They're still warm and in

the kitchen just waiting for you! Now, don't be afraid of Harry, my bird. He's in his cage, but don't stick your finger in there. He's very shy until he gets to know you! Oh! I'm so happy you're all here!

I got everyone all settled in their rooms and put together a plate of sandwiches for them. Mother, Harrison, and Liz came down to join us and the stories went on and on. The noise grew to such a level that I suggested they all take a trip to a museum for a couple of hours. The rehearsal and dinner was just a day away and I needed to get things organized.

Liz said, "Why don't I take y'all over to St. Patrick's Cathedral and Rockefeller Center? I can show y'all the NBC studio where they film the *Today* show. How does that sound?"

"Cool!" little Penn said.

"Can we go to the American Girl doll store?" Mary asked.

"Well, that's up to your momma, honey . . ."

Harrison went with the crowd and Mother stayed behind with me, ostensibly to help, but I could see she didn't have the energy for such a long walk.

"Well, Miss Josie? I've got two hams to

bake," I said, "and ten pounds of potatoes to cook."

"Give me a potato peeler and a place to sit," she said.

"I cook them with the skins on. Gives them more flavor."

"Well, suit yourself, then. I'll go have a nap. Those children wear me out!"

"I'll come with you. The hams are in Liz's fridge."

I preheated my oven and followed Mother up the stairs, watching her moving so slowly, my heart heavy with concern over the effort it took for her to pull herself up each step, holding on so tightly to the rail. By the time we reached Liz's apartment, it occurred to me that she might prefer staying downstairs in Charlie's old room rather than deal with all these steps. Maybe the kids, if they were getting along with Liz well enough, wouldn't mind sleeping on Liz's pullout sofa. While I took the hams and balanced them on my hip, I asked her what she thought about that plan and she objected.

"It's because I keep moving that I keep moving, missy. Don't you know anything about old people?"

"It's your call, Miss Josie. And you're not

old. I'm just thinking about you, that's all. Get some rest and I'll let you know when the games begin again, okay?"

"Okay." She stopped and turned to face me, resting her hand on the door to Liz's bedroom. "I love you so much, sweetheart. You know that, don't you?"

"Of course I know that! I love you, too! You know that, too, don't you?"

She nodded, too weary for any more talking, and I left her. I left her and went downstairs and carefully put the glazed hams, scored and studded with cloves, in the oven to bake, knowing my mother's death was near. Not tomorrow, but soon. Don't ask me how I knew it, but if you did I would tell you that it was a Lowcountry thing. When you grow up on Sullivans Island, you know things. That's all. Her slowing down wasn't a sign of death, nor was a slow ascent of a flight of stairs. People could be forgetful, move more slowly, and take more deliberate steps as young as sixty and still live to be a hundred.

No, this was something particular in her eyes, not a light that was fading but as though her eyes were trying to memorize me, freeze-frame the moment, and tuck it away in the pocket of the gown she intended to wear into eternity. She would show my ancestors these pictures of her time spent in my family's life just like photographs of events of which she was especially proud or those that had given her something sublime that she had stolen away with her passing to share.

I didn't know if it was her heart or some blood disease, but something was prowling around, waiting for a chance to snatch my mother away, and I couldn't stand it. What was I going to do about it? What could I do? Here I was, still in this collapsing wreck of a house after all these stupid years, and for what? My chest felt heavy.

I put chunks and chunks of potatoes in salted water and turned the heat to high. I chopped celery and onions, mixed mayonnaise with mustard, and hard-boiled a dozen eggs.

I called Charlie. He and Priscilla would be at my house by seven. We were ordering in a Chinese feast from their favorite restaurant. He said he couldn't wait to see everyone, and their arrival couldn't happen fast enough for me either. Seeing them all together for this occasion would lift away the strictures of depressing thoughts about Mother and take them away in the wind. I was determined to appear upbeat, become upbeat, and remain upbeat.

A few hours later, the potato salad was assembled and safely tucked away in Liz's refrigerator with two dozen deviled eggs and two perfectly baked hams. The only thing I had to cook tomorrow was the tomato base for my red rice and, of course, I had to pick up the cakes and breads. Tomorrow? It was almost here. I had a thought about Charles. What if he really came alone tomorrow night? What would I wear? And next I asked myself a critical question. Why should I give a rat's ass about what Charles thought about me anyway? (Yes, I said *rat's ass.* I thought I told you that Mellie was given to potty mouth now and then.) Now, Harrison? That was another issue. Ah, well. Did I hear the mournful music of a thousand gypsy violins? Harrison Ford and Petal Puss Mellie would probably go down in chaste history as a monstrous bummer of unrequited love. However! And this is a pretty darn gargantuan *however,* what if Liz had been right that night on Sullivans Island when she announced that she thought Harrison had feelings for me? Well, time would tell, just as time had pulled the sheep's clothing from Manny Sinkler's spineless back.

Soon my house was filled with my family, and a buffet line of chicken chow mein, Peking duck, egg foo yong, wonton and hot-and-sour soup, a shrimp dish, and a double order of beef with broccoli was lined up all the way down my kitchen counter.

"I can't eat with chopsticks," Mary said, and Penn echoed her.

"Mellie? You got a couple of rubber bands in this house?" Harrison said.

"Sure," I said, and reached in the drawer. "Here."

"Come here, you little bandits! Uncle Harrison is going to show you how to use these things."

He squatted next to where they sat at the kitchen table, removed the paper wrapper from the chopsticks, rolled it up, and secured it between the two chopsticks with a rubber band, creating bamboo tweezers.

"Now watch!" He picked up a tiny piece of chicken and fed it to Mary and she giggled with delight.

"Want me to fix yours, too?" he said to Penn.

"Uh-huh," Penn said. "Please?"

Over the next two hours we ate and refilled our plates. Nan and Mother were huddled with Priscilla, listening to her stories about growing up in Jamaica. Every now and then I could see

Mother inject a comment that noted the simi-
larities between Priscilla's home and how it had
been on Sullivans Island. I could have sworn I
even heard Nan say that she would love a visit
to Sullivans Island and/or Jamaica, but maybe
I was hearing things. Liz was regaling Dan with
the details of how his wonderful brother, Charlie, had practically saved her life. And Charlie
was giving her the old "Ah shucks, ma'am,
'tweren't nothing!" routine. He should've been a
snake-oil salesman. On the side I asked Charlie what he thought about Mother. Was she ill?
Charlie agreed that she didn't look so healthy,
but without her records he couldn't say.

Kevin was everywhere at once, refilling
glasses with wine and beer and bringing Harrison and me details and snippets of everyone's conversations. Mostly we—Harrison
and I, that is—sat with my darling grandchildren and encouraged them to try some of the
spicier dishes.

"What a wonderful family you've got, Mellie. I'm jealous."

"Well, then, maybe we'll just have to adopt
you."

Chapter Nineteen

THE TANGLED TANGO

We engaged the services of two young women from the catering company for whom Liz occasionally worked. She liked and trusted both of them. I thought I'd take the gamble on her recommendation as a way of confirming my faith in her. But truth be told, I hadn't had a party in so long, I knew of no one else to call. They arrived at five, went to work with Liz like a team of pros, and set everything up, including moving Harry upstairs. You just couldn't trust Harry's mouth.

Priscilla's father, Joseph LeBreu, and her uncle, the Reverend David Small, who would conduct the ceremony, rang the bell thirty minutes before the appointed hour and declared themselves delighted to meet me, my family, that they were just a little parched, and could they imbibe something calming before the ladies arrived? Of course they could, I said, and Liz took them over to the bar, where I saw them pour generous measures of their favorite dark rum bought by Charlie especially for them. Their delight and appreciation of Charlie's thoughtful gesture would be mentioned again and again. Who could blame them for being nervous?

I put on my favorite little black dress, the heretofore sausage casing that now fit like a dream, fastened my pearl choker around my neck, and decided that if Harrison Ford didn't figure out how to say that he wanted me in his life someday because of all his baggage, then somebody else would. Granted, I was wearing city hair—meaning a round-brush blowout—but the occasion called for it. Island Girl would be back when it was appropriate. At the last minute, I decided to wear some deep rose lipstick and see how that went over with my advisory team of personal stylists. Kevin and Liz, that is.

I was so grateful for the mild weather. The temperature kept bouncing around the sixty-degree range, but my garden was comfortable because it was self-contained and protected from wind. The last two days of relative warmth coaxed the forsythia into opening enough so that we had lots of color. If we could direct the guests outside, I knew that body heat would warm it up, too, at least for the early part of the evening. I turned on the fountain, lit all the hurricanes, and it seemed to me that my home had never been this inviting or glamorous. It was going to be a marvelous night. I could feel it in my bones.

Priscilla arrived with her aunt and her best childhood friend, Allison, who was to serve as her maid of honor. Priscilla wore a beautiful dress of a creamy silk charmeuse with no jewelry, except for her engagement ring and a watch. I said hello to them and welcomed them as warmly as I could, given the tumult of emotions I was feeling. I mean, you don't have a wedding in your family every day, do you?

Priscilla seemed to glide through the rooms saying hello and thank you for one gift or another, and she was just as gracious and lovely as she could be. I was thinking then she probably missed her mother that night more than ever. That naughty little voice in my head, the one that had finally seen the light and converted to a kinder gentler spirit, saw it was a possible opportunity for me to do something more for her. *Let her feel some love!*

"Priscilla? Can I steal you away for a moment?"

"Of course!"

I took her back to my bedroom, closed the door, went to my jewelry box, and opened it. I took out a pair of drop pearl earrings that I had worn at my own wedding, carefully tended for years, and put them in her hand.

"I want you to have these," I said. "Every bride needs pearls and they will be beautiful on you."

She burst into tears, threw her arms around me, and then in a moment of uncharacteristic informality, she plopped down on the edge of my bed.

"Got the jitters?" I said.

She nodded and said, "Just a little."

I handed her a tissue, then another, and sat down beside her.

"Miss your mother, huh?"

"Oh, you just don't know. I'd give *anything* . . ."

"I know you would, sweetheart. That's why I asked. But you do have *me* . . . and your *aunt* . . . and *my* mother, sweet thing that she is. And your old friend came so far to be here . . . And you know, I believe your mother's always with you in spirit. Love lasts forever."

"I know. Not the same." She blew her nose.

I said, "Look. If you weren't thinking about your mother at a time like this, it wouldn't be normal. But you don't want to be the weeping bride, right? Where's your vanity? Don't you want your pictures to be flawless?"

She smiled then.

"And you know what? You only have one *mother* and I can't take her place, but why don't you try calling me mom. That is, if it doesn't make you vomit. It might make you feel a teensy bit better? What do you think?"

I'd finally succeeded in making a joke that someone thought was amusing. Priscilla really smiled. "What do I think? I think I love you . . . *Mom.* Thanks. Thank you so much."

"First, of many private gab sessions, I hope. And I love you, too. Now go out there with your new pearl earrings on and tell 'em all your *mom* gave them to you!"

She stood up, her hands shaking a little as she fastened the earrings, and said, "I'm gonna be fine. Charlie and I are gonna be fine."

"I know that." I smiled my most confident smile. "Now, take a deep breath and let's go practice getting married."

She strode out like a runway model on the way to a ball and I was pleased with myself to no end. My rusty maternal instincts were in the process of resurrection and rejuvenation.

I could even see myself taking a trip to California. I had a lot of making up to do with Dan and Nan, and I would do it. I hadn't felt so happy in . . . I could not remember when!

I scanned my living room and well, well, well. Who do you think was right in the middle of it, sporting a five o'clock shadow, downing a scotch on the rocks, and talking up a blue streak like he owned the place? Charles Swanson. There was no Judith in sight.

He turned to see me and his surprise was all over his face.

"Hello, Charles," I said, and offered my cheek for him to kiss, which he did after a moment's hesitation. "So glad you could join us."

"Miriam! You look absolutely incredible! I barely . . . I mean, it's shocking!"

"Call me Mellie, Charles. Miriam is in a closet waiting to die."

He had absolutely no idea what that meant. Even *I* thought it sounded a little psycho scary, but I was nervous and it just came out of my mouth. Just like that.

"I have to apologize for Judith . . ."

There was no apologizing for Judith.

"Charles. Do you think I'd have come if I were Judith? The wedding is one thing, but coming to the home she wrecked is quite another."

He harrumphed and I thought that he had some crust to harrumph at me.

"Well, frankly, she was a little insulted that our children were not asked to be in the wedding party."

"You can't be serious." His face was deadpan. "Oh, my! You *are* serious!"

"It's just that . . ." He was staring at the carpet.

"Hold the phone right there, Charles. First, you tell Charlie that you're not interested in helping . . . oh, you know what? We're not having this conversation tonight, okay? Or ever! She should consider herself lucky to be invited *at all. And you, too.*"

"Actually, I agree with you. I do. However, I

must say, *Mellie,* you do look like a million dollars. And I truly appreciate being included even though I didn't act . . . well, I didn't do . . ."

"Oh, put a sock in it, Charles. Who cares? Let's just make tonight and tomorrow wonderful for our son and his new wife."

Priscilla's aunt Diana Small overheard Charles's remarks and leaned in to me, whispering, "Did you have one of those extreme makeovers or something?"

"No, he's my ex-husband and we don't get together often. Um, ever."

"I see!" she said, and chuckled to herself.

In Harry's absence I added, "Basically, he's a horse's ass."

"I understand entirely!" Her eyes met mine and I had a friend forever.

The rehearsal and the dinner went off without a hitch. Dan had thoughtfully brought his camera and he and Nan took hundreds of pictures.

"It's digital," he said, showing me his camera, which looked like a regular camera to me. "I can e-mail the pictures to you or send them on a CD. Or you can look at them online and just print what you'd like to have."

"Oh, Dan, my sweet boy, your mother lives

in another century. I just got a cell phone this year! But I guess I'm going to have to give in and buy some kind of a computer gadget gizmo getup, huh?"

He laughed, realizing I'd probably try to buy a computer at a bakery or something. "Mom? Why don't I just get one for you, load it up, and have it shipped to you?"

"Oh, sweetheart, would you do that for me? I'd be more than happy to pay you for it."

"Please. It's what I do for a living. It's the least I can do for you, Mom. You've never asked me for a thing."

What? I hugged him, kissed his cheek, and sighed so deeply the curtains probably moved in every room in the house. In his mind, he seemed to believe I had *never asked for a thing*. He seemed completely unaware that I had expected him to square off against his father and come to my defense when we all found out about Charles and Judith. He didn't know about the aching, almost crippling disappointment I felt when he had not. *He didn't even know.*

The most ridiculous thing was that I could have been in his life a lot more often if I had not believed that my pain had chased him to

California. So much time lost . . . and for what? My pride.

The only real argument we had ever had was over his children's names. I wasn't going to mention their names or have a negative opinion about the new baby's name then or ever. No. His two precious children should be the headliners of my bragging and I should know his whole family much better than I did.

Then, perhaps because my brain was at long last emerging from too many winters of mothballs, I saw that Charlie probably had never understood my feelings either. But because he was more practical than Dan, he had helped me convert the town house. In addition, he had been around and Dan had not. It wasn't a child's place to get involved with his parents' marital problems. It was very wrong for me to have tried to use my sons as tools to make Charles love me when he did not and never would again. Even if my boys had succeeded in making Charles give up Judith, he would have stayed with me only from a sense of duty, and what self-respecting woman wanted that?

Charles was here tonight, for the first time since our divorce had become final, and what was really happening with him? I only knew that his compliments were of no interest to me. My strength was a pretty self-satisfying thing, or maybe I was just finally over Charles Swanson. It used to be that I was angered by the humiliation, by the loss of position and friends, but what should have really made me angry I had overlooked—that there was nothing wrong with me and that the man who had promised to love and cherish me should have tried harder to honor his vows. It was a question of honor and Charles didn't have a clue what honor meant.

Our family and friends milled all around the house and garden, looking up at the Manhattan skyline and sitting on the benches to chat. My grandchildren scampered all through the rooms, but Nan, who had dressed them beautifully, kept them in check. I was so proud of their manners when they would stop to engage in conversation with one of the adults. Best of all, throughout the evening I would look around to see Mother watching Harrison eyeballing Charles staring at me. Mother's glances at Harrison were full of amusement, but in no way proprietary or jealous, which was something of a relief. Harrison's looks toward Charles were a combination of curiosity and disgust. Well, *disgust* is probably too strong a word, but it was plain that Harrison didn't think much of Charles. He had known a thousand men like Charles in his day. If they all fell off a steep cliff, he probably thought civilization would be well served. And Charles? It was like he was seeing my whole act for the first time.

Convoluted as this may sound, my house had taken on a new personality, as if it seemed deliriously happy to be the stage for the occasion. Every corner of every room had that knowing "dowager" glow. Best of all, I was surrounded by a number of people who truly loved me and I was obviously very content with my life. *Screw you, baby.* Charles never saw what he had given up until that night. To be honest, we all know I wasn't the same girl he left.

At the first opportunity, I grabbed Kevin by the arm and whispered in his ear. "You fabulous man! I adore you and I just want you to know it."

"Charles is absolutely dying," he whispered back. "Sweet bliss."

"He's a dope. Please tell me what I ever saw in him anyway," I whispered back.

"Tell me. Who did the flowers? They're spectacular!" Priscilla said within earshot of Charles.

"Oh, you know I did. Wait until you see what I've got planned for you tomorrow!"

Charles suffered a little whiplash.

"You had to use some fancy New York caterer, I'll bet?" Diana Small asked, only for my benefit, knowing Charles's ears were all over the room like an agent from the IRS. "This is the sweetest, juiciest ham I have ever had in my life! And, honey, I can cook some ham now! You hear me? And those deviled eggs? Mmm, mmm!"

Charles shook his head.

"Oh, darlin'! Aren't you nice? I cooked! If a woman can't cook a little dinner for her family and friends, what's she worth?"

Judith couldn't boil water in the microwave and I knew it.

Anyway, as wildly successful as the evening was, by the time I got into bed, my legs were throbbing and I wondered how in the world I would survive tomorrow. Charles. I didn't want him back; I just wanted him to be sorry and to say it. He had not said it, but it was all over his face.

But the best reward was to come. My bedroom door opened and Mary and Penn crept in.

"Think she's sleeping?" Penn whispered.

"Dunno," Mary said.

I opened one eye and they jumped back. But then they started to giggle like young children do and it sounded like a delicate, even angelic wind chime.

"Wanna jump in your grandmomma's bed?"

"Yeah!"

I threw back the covers and they hopped in, hugging me with their cherubic tiny arms. The smell of baby shampoo and the innocence of their affection was an opiate like no other. Why had I ever denied myself this? But no more.

"Wanna hear a story about when your daddy was a youngster like y'all?"

"Yeah!"

"Well, when he was very little, even younger than you, we used to go to Sullivans Island down in South Carolina. And do you know what we called it?"

They shook their little heads.

"We called it the Land of Mango Sunsets."

"That's a silly name," Mary said. "Why'd you call it that?"

"Well now, if you adorable little varmints can stop squirming around and settle down, I'll tell you all about it."

They settled down almost immediately, Mary in the crook of my left arm and Penn in my right, with his thumb sheepishly traveling in and out of his mouth.

"It's a magical place where magical things, only good ones of course, but where magical and wondrous things happen every day . . ."

I told them all about the olden days and the histories of the Indians and pirates and how their daddy would run all over the island with his brother, their uncle Charlie, gathering blackberries and playing on the forts, and about the enormous mango-colored sun. My voice got softer, as it might when you were telling secrets. Now and then I would hesitate from exhaustion or while trying to decide what part of the stories to tell them next. I would feel a little tug and they would say, "More, Grandmomma, tell us more!" But soon the tugging became less frequent, then stopped, and wonder of wonders, we all fell fast asleep.

And what a night of sweet dreams it was!

In the morning, I got up very early for two reasons. One, I had to make pancakes and muffins, and two, I had to help Kevin decorate the loft and do all the flowers. The wedding ceremony was to begin at six. I had packed my dress and shoes and everything I needed the day before, so all I had to do was cook and run.

The children ate so many pancakes slathered with butter and drenched in syrup, I thought they might burst or have sugar episodes. Once Harrison, Mother, and Liz came downstairs, the muffins disappeared along with lots of hot tea and coffee with leftover ham on buttered toast. The kitchen looked like it had been under nuclear attack. I was loving the mess!

"Look at all this!"

Nan said she would clean it all up and I kissed her cheek.

"Oh!" I said. "Did you see that big package in your room?"

"Yes, is that for us?"

"Yes! Gosh, in all this excitement I forgot to tell you! It's a sterling-silver coffee service that once belonged to one of my grandmother's sisters. I know they're old-fashioned and everything, but I thought you might like to have something that belonged to the family. I can ship it to you if you can't carry it, so don't worry."

"Great heavens! Thank you! How amazing!"

"Nan? Let's settle something right now, okay? I need a name. You obviously don't like calling me Mrs. Swanson and I think it's too formal, too. You don't like calling me Miriam and frankly I don't like the name anymore either. Everyone seems to think these days that they should call me Mellie. Priscilla is calling me mom because she doesn't have one. And you can call me anything you want but you have to call me *something*."

"Can we rotate between mom and Mellie?"

"Golly, that's so California . . . just kidding! Of course you can! Now I have to run!"

I was in John Barrett's chair at eight forty-five. I looked in the mirror and he looked at me in the mirror and smiled.

"You're going to be the most exquisite creature at the entire affair, Mrs. Swanson."

"I'll settle for second place. There's the matter of the bride."

"Ah, the bride. Well, you are generous."

"But there *is* the ex-husband and the horrible woman he married."

"Then I'm pulling out the big guns! Trust me, she'll want to crawl under a rock."

"Perfect."

A woman did my nails while Mr. Barrett styled my hair, and then I spent a mere fifteen minutes in a makeup artist's chair, almost not believing the difference it made.

At the counter I took out my credit card and John Barrett shushed the girl who was ready to take it and charge me for the services.

"Mrs. Swanson. Take this lip liner, lipstick, and gloss. This powder and blush. Here's a light hair spray just in case. Do you have a comb?"

"Gosh! No! I forgot . . ."

"Here's a comb, too! It's all on the house. No tips, nothing! Just go! Kevin and I go way back. We all adore him!"

"I'll send you a piece of wedding cake! How can I thank you?"

"You're Kevin's family and best friend. Every now and then, it's nice just to do something for somebody, don't you agree?"

"Yes, I do!"

The elevator door opened; I stepped in and blew him a kiss as the doors closed. What a fabulous man!

I shouldn't have worried about getting a taxi because one pulled up to the curb as soon as I put up my arm. I had some good karma going then. The cab lurched forward and we bumped our way downtown to the loft. When I walked in, I could hardly believe my eyes. The hideous space that I thought would be so depressing had become a sultan's tent of thick ivory silk, hung with five chandeliers at different levels, ropes of the tiniest white lights, and multiple strands of pearls strung from the tops of the chandeliers to the edges of the walls and then down to the ground. Huge Asian carpets laid on the bias covered most of walking area except for the dance floor, which would be set up with the ballroom chairs for the ceremony. The false wall behind the long and wide riser was covered in curtains swagged with more fabric and a wide bough of fresh flowers of every shade of pink you could imagine. The little candles I had envisioned had become three-foot-tall, round, clear-glass containers filled with pearls on which rested thick ivory candle columns.

I spotted Kevin at the back of the room, giving directions to a couple of the guys, and went over to say hello. And to deliver a dramatic gasp for the benefit of his vision and efforts.

"Wow! Wow! Wow! How are you, genius?"

I gave him a kiss on the cheek. "This is some glamorous miracle you've performed here!"

"Mrs. Petal Puss! Look at you! What a transformation!"

"*Merci!* But seriously! This is breathtaking!"

"I overordered pearls for the store and I always have lights. Got the satin from a casket company, but don't tell the bride."

"You're terrible. Where can I hang my garment bag?"

"Closet over there and all your flowers are in water behind the pipe and drape over there. We got a thousand votives and fifteen containers—twelve bowls and three cylinders. If there's not enough greenery for the bowls, I can send one of the guys out."

"I've got my clippers and I'm going to work!"

Kevin had been there since very early in the morning with six visual-display directors we hired for the day who had worked with him for ages. They offered to shop the flower market for me, and the sweethearts picked up everything I needed because they had two vans. But I had to say over and over to Kevin that I could not believe what he had accomplished in that hideous place.

"Well then, make me an honorary uncle!"

"It would be an honor to claim you as a relative!"

We stopped for lunch, and over sandwiches and sodas we made a list of what remained to be done.

"If you need pearls for the tables, let me know," Kevin said. "Ahem, I'm kind of long on pearls?"

By four o'clock, I had completed what I thought were the most beautiful floral arrangements I had ever assembled and put them in place. The wedding party's flowers had been delivered and I opened the box, wanting to have a look at Priscilla's bouquet.

It struck me that these were the most important flowers of the entire day. I lifted her bouquet up and held it in my hands. I said a spontaneous prayer for them, hoping the flowers would somehow absorb it and send strength to Priscilla and Charlie for the days when they would need it. I knew it was a sentimental gesture that would probably never have meant anything to anyone except me. So what? I was feeling sentimental.

I was delighted to see that Charlie had ordered corsages for my mother, Liz, Nan, and Priscilla's aunt Diana, and he had also chosen one for me with navy ribbons. There was even a corsage for the evil one, Judith. And he had remembered to include a basket of rose petals for Mary. There were boutonnieres for Charlie, Dan, Charles, Penn, and even for Kevin and Harrison. My Charlie was a thoughtful man. With a heart like his, he would be a great doctor. That was for sure.

The caterers began to file in, the photographer arrived, and the band set up to do a sound check.

All I had to do then was freshen up, throw on my dress, and wait for the good times to roll. Before I went to the ladies' room to change, I caught Kevin.

"Kevin?" I didn't even know what to say. We stopped and looked around the whole room together and we both smiled as wide as we could. The only words that came out of my mouth were "Stunning. Amazing."

"The room? Well, I couldn't have my nephew Charlie get married in a slum, could I?"

"No, doll, I mean *you* are stunning and amazing. And so is the room. Obviously."

"Honestly? This one was a challenge. Now let's put on our party clothes and have ourselves a well-deserved adult beverage."

By five-thirty the whole wedding party was there, except Judith.

Wow! Look at this place! This is unbelievable! It's like a fantasyland! Mellie! The flowers! Kevin! How did you do this?

"It was nothing," Kevin said, and pretended to swoon.

I said, "So, Charles, where's Judas?"

"Did you say Judas?"

"No! Heavens! I said Judith!" That tongue-brain thing was having trouble again.

"Sorry. She didn't want to be in the wedding pictures with the family. What can I say?"

"Oh?" I paused for a moment then. "Perhaps that's best." Who wanted her anyway?

"You sure look great, though," he said.

"Oh, thanks. So do you."

Harrison was listening to Charles and covered his mouth with his hand. When Charles slinked away, Harrison said, "You do look gorgeous."

"You don't look so bad yourself," I said. "How's Mother?"

"She's rallying. She's really been looking forward to this."

"Well, I guess she must have been because she had her hair done and actually put on a pretty dress!"

We completed the family photographs on the riser and I almost had to push Harrison up the steps to join us. Liz and Kevin were included and there was no reason Harrison shouldn't be. He was Mother's escort, and considering the sultan's tent, all the palm trees and pearls, it wasn't a strictly by-the-books event anyway.

The photographer took other shots of Priscilla putting on her veil, of her aunt Diana standing beside Priscilla and her cake, which, by the way, was almost too beautiful to eat, but I also knew it wouldn't take much to overcome that obstacle. There was a picture taken of Mary looking up to Priscilla and of Penn looking up to Charlie. One of Charles shaking hands with Charlie. Then with Charlie and Dan.

I was wondering how many glasses of bubbly (or shots of whatever it was he drank these days) it would take for Charles to ask for a picture to be taken of us with the happy couple, when the musicians began to play chamber music and guests started to arrive. Waiters passed goblets of champagne, sparkling water, and white wine on silver

trays. The bar was open and anyone wanting something stronger was welcome to
step right up. In honor of our southern roots
and the momentous occasion, Harrison,
Mother, Kevin, Liz, and I all ordered mint
juleps, clinked our glasses, and began to
sip.

"Here's to Charlie and Priscilla," I said. "Be
happy always!" I could not help but indulge
myself in the thought that beyond my children's happiness, surely there was someone,
someone available and willing that is, for me
to love who would love me in return.

"Here's to marriage!" Kevin said. "The ultimate triumph of optimism over experience!"

"Here's to love," Mother said. "A well-
tended love can last forever!"

"Here's to love in general," Harrison said.
"The more everlasting, well-tended, optimistic, and happy? So much the better!"

"Well, here's to George!" Liz said.

"Who's George?" we all said at once.

"Dickel. Didn't George Dickel make bour-
bon?"

There was a communal groan.

"Well, Liz? Here's to you, sweetheart! Let's
hope the next wedding is yours, to some
magnificent man we all love!" Kevin said.

Kevin was so sweet to say that. We all wished Liz would find some happiness, a good husband who would give her children and some security.

"Here, here!" we all said, and toasted Liz.

"It would be a miracle, but I'll drink to miracles!" she said.

Priscilla was secluded with her family and her girlfriend. Charlie was in another room with Dan.

Then, in the midst of the arriving throng of Charlie and Priscilla's friends and Charles's friends or business associates or whoever they were, in stumbled Judith. Maybe it was her four-inch spike heels or maybe it was her pumps combined with a little prehydration. Whatever the case, she definitely stumbled around until she found Charles's arm. I had to say, though, her dress was gorgeous. It was a short, flesh-colored silk georgette tank dress with a long jacket. The front bodice and hem of the dress and the cuffs and borders of the jacket were all embroidered with tiny crystals and beads that shimmered each time she caught the light. She was thinner than I remembered and still had those two rock-hard oranges from the produce section of the A&P inserted in the front of her chest.

I was sure they had been a necessary investment for an unendowed lingerie model. Still.
That didn't mean they didn't look stupid.

At last, when it seemed that everyone was
there, the chamber group stopped for a few
minutes and started to play again. It was six
o'clock. Guests began to take their seats. We
executed the processional in a pretty traditional manner. First, Priscilla's uncle the Reverend David Small appeared center stage
and then Charlie and Dan. Harrison led
Mother up the aisle. She was smiling and
smiling. Kevin led Priscilla's aunt Diana to her
seat. Harrison did a return trip and led me to
my place. And finally, Charles led Judith to
theirs. The music rose slightly and the guests
turned to the back of the aisle. Priscilla's
friend Allison walked slowly to her place. Little Mary and Penn were next. Mary, ever the
older sister, yanked on the sleeve of his jacket
to slow his pace. She dropped her petals as
though she were a professional flower girl
and Penn made faces to anyone who would
look at him. I knew Nan was going to get to
him later, but I thought he was adorable and
punishment would have been undeserved. I
couldn't wait to spoil both of them rotten.

The music grew louder, we stood, and all

eyes were on Priscilla and her father, Joseph. She could not have been more enchanting. Her simple ivory satin gown flattered every inch of her beautiful figure and she was wearing the pearls I had given her. As she passed my seat she reached out and squeezed my hand. I couldn't help it. My eyes filled with tears.

The ceremony was over in minutes or so it seemed. But I have always had this theory that once two serious people agree to marry, all the rest is just a formality anyway. Still, there's nothing like a wedding.

As soon as everyone left the chairs, the waitstaff began moving them to the tables, lighting all the votives, and the reggae music began to play on the floor below the riser, while the band itself, as discreetly as possible, moved their instruments and so forth back into place. People gathered around the bar on one side of the room and Priscilla and Charlie on the other. Some of the staff began passing drinks again and simple hors d'oeuvres. The room had taken on its own vibe—one of romance, but most importantly, of love and happiness.

The waiters finally gave us the signal that dinner was ready to be served and the full orchestra began to play. There were at least

ten musicians and two singers and I wondered where Charlie and Priscilla had found
so much wonderful music. I would learn later
that most of the musicians were friends of
theirs and had agreed to play as a wedding
gift. And for as long as they had known them,
Priscilla and Charlie had seen that their
friends, and their friends' children especially,
had always received excellent health care. It
sure seemed like a fair trade to me.

We found our way to our tables. Some
were round, ours was a rectangle, and all of
them were beautiful.

Harrison was opposite me and next to Mother,
Aunt Diana, and then Kevin. To my right was
Uncle David and Liz and Joseph, Priscilla's father. We had arranged it that way so the older
members of the families would have a little time
together. Priscilla and Charlie were seated with
Dan, Nan, Mary, Penn, Allison, and another
close friend of theirs from the hospital.

The rest of the room held about eighty
people, and of course, Charles had his own
round table of twelve, just across the dance
floor from ours. We watched as Charlie and
Priscilla danced the first dance while we enjoyed a salad of mixed greens and conch frit-
ters that was delicious.

"What's the main course?" Mother asked.

"Roasted goat," I said.

"Great beard of Moses! Are you serious?" Mother said.

"It's a Jamaican specialty," Aunt Diana said.

"Well, I am sure glad Cecelia isn't here!" Liz said.

"Who's Cecelia?" Uncle David said.

"Miss Josie's pet goat," Harrison said.

"I think I'll ask the bride to dance," Joseph said, and stood to leave us.

We went down the line of who was to dance with whom, and just about the time the roasted goat was before us, the band mercifully played a tango. Mother looked at Harrison and they went right out to the dance floor and began slowly at first. Little by little, people left the floor and stood on the side to watch them. They were beautiful together and my mother seemed like a young girl. The photographer took plenty of pictures.

Kevin looked across to me.

"Want to join them?"

"Sure! Why not?"

Well, by now you know, knowing Kevin and me as you do, that we had prepared a routine that was a little more dramatic than the norm. We let Mother and Harrison have the inside perimeter of the floor and we began at the opposite end, taking the outside edges. Walking like big cats, the music filling us with sensual passion—such as it was between two people of our opposite persuasions—but never mind that. We were hot. The band got excited and extended the song. Every eye in the room was watching. Harrison and Kevin became competitive with each other, and in minutes I could see that Mother was beginning to tire. I had only the treadmill to thank for my endurance.

But then I saw Harrison leading Mother over to us and he said to Kevin, "I think our Miss Josephine needs to rest for a moment. Would you mind if I cut in, and could you escort her back to her seat?"

"It would be a pleasure, sir!"

As Mother left the dance floor on Kevin's arm, the band stopped playing and applauded her. Then, in what had to be the most thrilling moment of acclaim Mother had known in decades, every single guest stood and every waiter stopped what they were doing and applauded her, too. The band took their seats, began a new tango, and it was up to Harrison and me to try to maintain the level of entertainment on our own. We stood apart and then turned our heads to each other and began the walk. Then came the embrace. Harrison had obviously worked a lot harder at mastering the dance than Kevin and I had, but all I to do was follow. As Harrison Ford led me around the room, a double spin here, a hooked leg over his, and a dangerously low dip there, I knew I would have followed him right through the gates of hell as long as they were playing a tango. I could feel my skirt swirl and the heat of his breath on my neck. The song was coming to a close and I noticed there was a flower on the floor and then another. People were so excited they were pulling flowers from my centerpieces and throwing them to us in appreciation. It was madness! In a grand dip, I picked up a rose—yes, a rose—and to complete the cliché, I put it between Harrison's clenched teeth. The camera was flashing again, our family and guests laughed, and Harrison and I laughed so hard, we had to stop dancing. Everyone clapped again for us as they had for Mother, and we camped it up, blowing kisses and taking bows. Then we tangoed off the floor to our table.

"God, that was better than sex!" Harrison said in an unguarded moment.

"I didn't know you could dance like that!" Liz said.

"It's all about the dress," Kevin said.

"You're probably right. How are you feeling, Mother? Are you all right?"

"I am perfectly fine. Anyway, every other person here tonight is a doctor or something, so this would be the perfect time to collapse, don't you think?"

Her remark was directed to Aunt Diana.

"What do I think? I think you and that girl of yours can *dance,* Miss Josie, honey! That's what I think!"

"I think dropping dead at your grandson's wedding would be bad news, Mother. Memorable, to be sure. But not great."

"Don't make me cut a switch," she said, and laughed.

The band had resumed dance-party music and my eye caught Judith dancing with one of Charles's younger associates. She had removed her jacket and you could see that she wasn't wearing a bra, since the back of her dress was cut low almost to that part of her backside one dreads viewing when the plumber is working under your sink. This crack in the wall, so to speak, led me to assume, as did all others who were held hostage by the raunchy spectacle before us, that she was sans panties as well.

"She must be drunk as a skunk," Liz said.

"Completely toasted," Kevin said.

"Ladies don't dance like that in Kingston," Diana said.

"Especially if you're the stepmother of the groom!" Mother said.

"Her maternal instincts aren't exactly top-of-the-line," Harrison said, and we all snickered.

There were a lot of people dancing, so I imagine it took Charles a while to see what was going on and to decide how to react to it. Judith and her partner had now moved on to the Doggie Dance, which is so popular with today's trashy young people. It's a dance that resembles an imitation of the act that leads to bringing puppies into the world. With a look of great disappointment on his face, Charles worked his way through the crowd with Judith's jacket folded over his arm and interrupted them. I could not hear what was said, but I saw, as did everyone else, Judith take her jacket, return to her table for her handbag, and walk out.

"Looks like trouble in paradise," Kevin said.

"Water seeks its own level," Mother said.

"You lay down with dogs, you get up with fleas," Liz said.

"Stupid people do stupid things. By the way, Mellie, do you waltz?" Harrison asked.

"Do I waltz? What kind of a question is that?" I couldn't waltz worth two hoots, but it was a chance to smell him some more. "Our Jamaican visitors are horrified by Judith."

"She should have learned to tango," Harrison said.

Chapter Twenty

ALABAMA BLUES

It was Sunday morning and you could have believed that my house was north on the compass, as everyone drifted in for one last impromptu dose of festivities and farewells. We all said to one another that if there was anything we could have done to make Charlie and Priscilla's wedding weekend more wonderful, we couldn't think of it. They thanked us all over and over. Except for the scandalous Judith episode, which left us wondering on what kind of quicksand Charles's marriage stood, all else had been a dream.

Just those few days together had been so surprisingly profound and deeply gratifying. A wedding. The bonds of my two sons and their wives were strengthened and mine with all of them, especially my precious grandchildren. I had another grandchild who would be born in December. Another heart to love was coming into the world and I would not miss a minute of it. Wasn't it amazing what could happen when you laid down your sword and opened your arms?

The day had begun early again. At seven-thirty that morning, the seemingly indefatigable Kevin and his team of wizards had zoomed downtown to collect the decorations and oversee the pickup of all the rentals. Liz took Harrison out for a neighborhood stroll to buy the Sunday *New York Times,* fresh bagels, smoked salmon, and all the other traditional fixings along with a cinnamon coffee cake for the children, brought home still warm from the oven. Mother sat between Penn and Mary on the sofa, reading children's books to them, and they read back to her. Charlie was right there, too, teasing the children, tickling them, and doing the old trick of making quarters magically appear from behind their ears.

Knowing I didn't have a housekeeper, Nan

and Dan packed all their belongings and stripped the beds and threw the towels in the wash. Without asking, Priscilla pitched right in to set up a breakfast buffet on the dining-room table.

By the time Harrison and Liz returned, Allison, Diana, David, and Joseph rang the doorbell, I scrambled two dozen eggs and made a pot of grits, and we were all gathered in my house again, pouring coffee and tea, serving food, laughing, and swapping more stories.

Priscilla and Charlie were talking about taking a honeymoon in August when things in New York were quieter because, they joked, the sick people were out at Fire Island and in the Hamptons. That wasn't exactly true because there were always more sick people than there were doctors, but they wanted and needed to take a vacation at some point.

Mother invited them to come to Sullivans Island. Priscilla's eyes twinkled with excitement and she said she would love it if Charlie would love it and Charlie said he loved anything Priscilla loved. It was, after all, only day two of the marriage. But when it was decided right then that Mother would be their honeymoon hostess, Mother was thrilled to pieces.

"Wonderful! This gives me something grand to look forward to!"

Between bites and sips of every goodie I could find left in the refrigerator, Diana, David, and Joseph insisted that we visit them in Jamaica.

"We'll show you all about Jamaican hospitality!" Diana said.

"Me, too!" Allison said. "My family would love y'all, too!"

"I can't think of a thing I would enjoy more," I said. Hold the roasted goat, I thought. "I've heard wonderful things about your country, seen a thousand pictures, but I've never actually been there."

"As much as you love that little island you hail from," Joseph said, "I can't believe you've never been to Jamaica! You should come and visit *all* the islands in the Caribbean. One is more beautiful than the next!"

Harrison said, "Joseph? You don't understand these people from Sullivans Island. When that sun goes down, they fall under some kind of spell and you can't get them over the causeway!"

Joseph slipped into the manly Jamaican accent you hear in travel ads. "Harrison, mon? You bring them down to Jamaica and we'll have them all dancing in the moonlight, drinking some very nice rum, some island romance . . . you know what I am saying?"

I wanted to say, Do I have to bring my own sombrero? Instead I said, "I think that sounds like a fabulous idea, so we'll have to just pick a date and plan it!"

We hugged like old friends, promised to stay in touch, and Charlie and Priscilla took them all outside to hail a cab to the airport.

Harrison and Mother were the next to depart. Because of my concerns for her health, it upset me terribly to see her go. I knew that Harrison was going to be watching over her and that was reassuring, but I could just feel her slipping through my fingers and didn't know how to stop it. Maybe it was just that we were aging and that was what truly bothered me.

"It was a beautiful weekend, sweetheart," she said to me. "I'm so proud of you."

"I'm so proud of you, too, Miss Josie, and I'm going to miss you like mad!"

"Then come to the island. Come as soon as you can."

"I will. I promise." I hugged her like it was for the last time. Somehow, I knew it wasn't the last time but that *time itself* was the point.

I had yet to say good-bye to Harrison.

"Okay, you. Thanks for coming and bringing Mother. Stay out of trouble."

"Yeah. Thanks for having me. I don't want to hear any wild tango stories about you." He hugged me and kissed my cheek. It wasn't much but I wasn't expecting more.

"That goes double for you. See y'all! Call me when you get back home so I know you're okay?"

When I closed the door, I leaned back against it and sighed. I was spiraling down from preparty jitters to postparty blues. All the anticipation, all the work and details, and it was over so fast! But at least there would be pictures and I had trips to plan and practically a new life lay ahead with my grandchildren.

Kevin breezed in, and just as I was serving him the last scoop of eggs and a slice of coffee cake, the phone rang. It was Charles.

"I'm calling to apologize," he said.

"For what?" I was thinking the list of things for which he owed apologies was so long, I couldn't imagine where he would begin.

"Well, first of all, for Judith's behavior . . ."

"Charles, you can no more control Judith's behavior than I could yours."

"I deserve that. Anyway, we're separated . . . as of last night. I left. Seems that she's, um, been fooling around with one of the junior partners . . ."

"The fellow she was doing the nak-nak dance with?"

"Um, she says it's called the grind and that's how everyone dances these days. But yes, he's the culprit."

"Let me just assure you that not everyone dances like humping doggies." What goes around comes around, I thought.

"I'm sure you're right. Anyway, I'm staying at the Athletic Club and I've been up all night thinking about things and what a fool I've been."

Now, just what was I supposed to say? "Gee, big surprise your slut turned out to be a slut"? This was news to whom? Or how about "Oh, poor Charles, come home to me, all is forgiven"? In a pig's eye, honey, or better yet, a goat's! All weekend I'd enjoyed a house filled with happy people and now Mr. Misery was on line one. But I, or the Buddha within, tried to be nice.

"Charles? Listen to me. I have everyone here and I'm sort of in the middle of cleaning up brunch and saying good-bye and this just isn't the best time for me to talk."

"Oh, I didn't realize that, but of course, that's what you would be doing now. Why don't I call you another time, then?"

"Sure." In an act of supreme charity that put me on the level of, say, Mother Teresa of Calcutta, I added, "Any time. Like tonight or tomorrow."

"Thanks. Okay, then. Bye."

Kevin was standing there listening to my end of the conversation. "Let me guess . . . that was Charles on the phone and his wife wasn't pretending last night?"

"You got it. I always did try to tell him that those oranges weren't worth the squeeze."

Dan, Nan, and the children were getting ready to make their exit and I welled up with tears.

"Gosh! Look at what a sentimental old fool I'm becoming!"

"Oh, Mom!" Nan said, and put her arms around me, and yes, she called me *mom* and that really turned on the waterworks.

I reached in my pocket for a tissue.

"I just hate to see y'all leave! I mean, I feel like I am just getting to know you all over again and now it's time to say good-bye, and well, I just hate it."

Dan cleared his throat, and to my utter

surprise he said, "So do we. But we're going to do better about staying in touch and visiting each other, Mom. Nan and I talked about it. Expect a package in about a week. Zillions of pictures and your very own laptop—simple to use, I promise!"

"My sweet son! And lovely Nan! Please take care of yourself, sweetheart." She had had such trouble conceiving and carrying pregnancies to term, I hoped she would not do anything too strenuous that could bring on any problems.

"Don't worry, Momma Mellie, this baby's as healthy as a horse! I can feel it."

I nodded to her and kissed her cheek. Then I knelt down to hug Mary and Penn.

"My sweet darling grandchildren! Oh! How I'm going to miss you all so!"

"But you're taking us to that magic place, aren't you?" Mary said.

"Mango Island?" Penn said.

Dan laughed, ruffled the hair on his son's head, and said, "Yes! That is a splendiferous idea! Let's all go together! Miss Josie would love it and so would we!"

Splendiferous? See? I wasn't the only nerd in the family.

They finally made it out the door, which left

Kevin, Liz, Priscilla, Charlie, and me to do the postmortem. Charlie and Kevin went to retrieve Harry from Liz's apartment and Priscilla and I put away so many things I couldn't count them. Liz had decided to commandeer the laundry and was busy transferring towels from the washer to the dryer and folding sheets. This may seem trite but I can't begin to tell you how it filled me with pleasure to have Liz and Kevin, but especially Charlie and Priscilla, pitching in as though it was their home.

Finally, the dishwasher hummed and I put the kettle on for tea. I was so bone tired that I knew a shot of strong caffeine was in order to keep me awake until bedtime.

"Hot tea, anyone? Coffee?"

"Great idea," Charlie said.

"I'll take a gallon of coffee," Kevin said.

"You earned it!" I said, and everyone agreed.

I had washed and dried my own tea service three times that weekend. As I reached for the teapot and coffeepot again, it dawned on me that I had not given Priscilla and Charlie their wedding gift.

"Charlie? Do you have the strength left to do your poor mother one small favor?"

"You just name it!"

"On the floor of my bedroom closet is a huge package from Bergdorf's. Will you bring it to me, please, dear? And there's another one on the top shelf."

A minute later he stood there with the tea-service box, which was large enough to hold an air conditioner.

"What's in here, bricks?"

"What in the world?" Priscilla said.

"If you can believe this, I forgot to give you your wedding gift."

Charlie said, "Mom! We can't take another thing from you! It's too much! The ring! The dinner? All the flowers? All that you and Kevin did? Seriously!"

"Oh, hush up and open it!" I said. "Just remember to be generous to your children someday! This is from Miss Josie."

I thought Priscilla would faint as she unwrapped each piece. At the end, when it was all set up on the tray on the coffee table in front of her, she was absolutely flabbergasted.

"I do not know what to say. This is a treasure that I never would have even had the nerve to dream of owning. I promise you. I will take care of it so well."

"Jackpot!" Harry said from the kitchen. Priscilla was startled.

"That's his opinion, Charlie," Kevin said, "and he's usually right."

"I'll say!" Charlie said, and laughed. "That bird is so great."

"Charlie? I'm the one who taught him to say jackpot," Kevin said.

"Charles is a horse's ass!" Harry said as loud as he could.

"What?" Charlie said. "What did he say?"

Priscilla covered her mouth, hiding giggles.

"Not you. Your father. He likes you."

"Well, he's right about the old man. But I'm just wild about Harry."

"I feel a song coming on," Kevin said.

"WAH wah," I said to Kevin. "And you think I make stupid jokes?" Then I turned to Charlie. "Good. I'll leave Harry to you in my will. He's only eleven. They live for eighty years sometimes!"

"Seriously?"

"Yes, anyway, this tea service belonged to an old aunt of mine. And I have sterling flatware for you, too! Bring the other box, sweetheart."

When Priscilla opened it, I thought she might faint.

"What? Charlie?" Here came Priscilla's first example of her thousand-miles-an-hour talking speed. "We need to *move,* and I mean, *tonight! Because* we can't take this back to *our* neighborhood. I'd have to hide it under the bed and get under there with it! Don't you know some *crack-head* will cut our throats for it? *No, sir! We're moving!"*

That was the speech of the weekend and we laughed until we thought we would collapse. Even Charlie agreed. It was probably time for them to move to a lower-risk neighborhood.

"You can leave it right here until you think it's safe to take it," I said.

"Well, praise God, because I ain't *ready* to die tonight!" Priscilla said, and laughed, too.

We were all draped around the living room in various stages of exhaustion, drinking coffee and tea, picking on leftover cake, saying that Charles got his but wasn't it a great weekend? Not one of us wanted to bring it to a close.

But as fate would have it, the party was

definitely over a few minutes later when Liz's cell phone rang.

"Who in the world wants something from me?" she said, and answered it. "Hello?" Her face became very serious and she said, "Hang on. Y'all, I'm gonna take this outside."

"Sure, sweetheart, go in the garden, if you'd like."

She did. Well, we couldn't imagine what it was about, but we were too tired to give it a lot of thought, so we made small talk until she returned. The news had been catastrophic. Her face was drenched in tears, her shoulders were shaking, and she stood there in the middle of the room, arms crossed and gasping between sobs. Priscilla hopped up from the sofa, left, and returned with a box of tissues from the powder room.

"Honey?" I got up and put my arms around Liz and led her to my favorite chair. "Sit. Tell me. Whatever is the matter?"

"It's my momma. She's dying. She got in a horrible car wreck and there are all kinds of terrible complications. She called to ask me to forgive her. My stepfather . . . he died about six months ago. She didn't even tell me. Not that I care, but I could've done something for her, right? What am I supposed to do now, y'all? This had to happen *now*?"

I wasn't sure why she thought the timing had to do with anything, but my Charlie was already trying to come up with a solution.

"We could bring her up here," Charlie said. "I know a bunch of guys at Columbia who specialize in trauma—"

"It's too late. They have her in intensive care but she's lost so much blood and has so many broken bones and she's having trouble breathing . . ."

"Oh, Liz, honey, I'm so sorry," Kevin said.

"I think you *have* to forgive your mother, Liz," I said.

"Mean as she was to me? All the things she accused me of doing? Blamed me for? She ruined my whole childhood with all her lies and games."

"Perhaps, but, Liz, sweetheart, listen to me. My mother told me all about it. This might sound like Miriam and not Mellie or Mom or your friend talking, but I'm going to tell you something now that I want you to remember all your life. Are you listening?"

She sighed, shook her head, and looked up at me. "Yes. What?"

"When someone's dying and they ask

your forgiveness, it is a greater sin to with-
hold it. This is no small matter. You have to
put your own anger aside and think of her.
No matter how she may have hurt you with
her own misguided judgment, and I know
some of it was terrible, you have to forgive
her so she can die in peace. She's your
mother, hon."

"So she waits until *now*? Wouldn't it have
been nice if she had told me when *my stepfather died*? We could have had six months
to talk about *all of this*."

"May I say something?" Priscilla said.

"Of course," Liz said. "Why not?"

"Get on a plane and go to her," Priscilla said.
"Tonight or tomorrow. But go right away."

"And just *why* should I rush to her side?"

"Because when she dies, you don't want
to live with any regret. And secondly, it will
make it easier for her to die. Do you think I
would lie to you?"

"No, of course not."

Priscilla continued. "Well then, believe this.
I see people pass every day, and the ones
who have family around them go a lot easier.
Mom is right. I don't think you want it on your
conscience that she called for you and you

turned away from her. That will haunt you until the day you die yourself."

"Liz?" Kevin said. "Personally, I agree. She absolutely should've told you about your stepfather's death. But from what you've told me, she probably thought you would have unleashed the hounds on *her* while she was trying to bury *him*. Anyway, Priscilla and Petal are right. You have to go to her."

Liz looked to Charlie.

"Hey! I'm not going to start disagreeing with my wife at this point!" Everyone smiled at that, even Liz. "Anyway, I think she's right, too. Ya gotta suck it up for this one, kid. You have to be the bigger person."

Liz pulled out her cell phone and dialed.

"Hey, this is Liz Harper calling. Can I speak to my momma?" While she waited she looked from one of our faces to the next. "Momma? Hang on. I'm coming to Birmingham." They exchanged a few more words; Liz hung up and said in a southern drawl, "Sheeeeeit. Pardon me."

"You said it. Now come on," Kevin said. "I'll call the airlines and you pack. See you later, Mellie Puss and Drs. Swanson! Or is it Dr. Swansons?" He pulled Liz to her feet and to the front door. "I swear, I can't get a day off for love or money!"

It was just a little over three weeks until Liz's mother passed away finally, from a bout of pneumonia. We talked every day and Liz admitted that everyone had been right to encourage her to come home.

"It must have been a terrible thing to be my momma," Liz said. "She had so much guilt over so much. But what I've learned is that you never let anything or anybody come between you and your kids."

"You're telling *me* this?"

"Anyway, I just sit with her and read to her and all that stuff. She kept telling me she's sorry and that she's so proud of me and all. If she knew about Truman Willis, she probably would have got herself out of bed and beat me with a stick."

"Listen to me. That's a canceled check and the lesson has been learned."

"We're all still learning lessons, aren't we? Like when do you finally get it right?"

"That, my dear, might be one of life's most perplexing questions."

Kevin and I had already decided that we were going to the funeral, and Charlie and Priscilla had already agreed to take care of

Harry when the moment arrived. We made the phone calls and the arrangements and the next thing I knew we were changing planes in Atlanta. We always said that if you die and go to hell, you would still have to change planes in Atlanta. For my money, one plane ride was enough, but Kevin booked the flights and I didn't want to argue about it.

Kevin could see that I wasn't a happy traveler, especially when the plane we had to take from Atlanta to Birmingham had propellers. Big, ugly, loud propellers. Giant food processors. The airline wasn't even trying to hide the antique death trap at the end of a Jetway. We had to walk down the Jetway, down steps and across the tarmac, and willingly board. I needed five milligrams of something in the worst way. Or a double something.

Don't you know that because the flight was so short there was no beverage service? So Kevin had a white-knuckled partner for the duration. He decided chitchat would relieve my nerves and it helped a little.

"Petal? I think Priscilla and Charlie are getting along well, don't you?"

"Yes. I think they're perfect for each other."

"So? Did Charles ever call you back?"

"No. Who cares?"

"Think they're getting divorced?"

"Think I care about that either?"

Blah, blah, blah. Despite Kevin's best efforts, I was scared to death.

The plane began its descent and I grabbed the ends of the armrests, clenched my jaw, and closed my eyes, squeezing them together as hard as I could.

"This thing is like a giant slingshot," I mumbled.

"No, it's not. It's actually safer than a jet."

"Whatever. I finally get my life like I want it and now I'm gonna die like this."

"No, you're not."

To my complete shock, we touched down and glided along the landing strip like we were sliding on silk and came to a gentle halt. I opened my eyes and looked over at Kevin.

"What?"

"Petal, Petal . . ."

"That was the finest landing I have ever had and I intend to write the airlines a thank-you note."

"Look out, Continental, here comes Miriam, out of retirement! Fountain pen and all!"

There was just no getting away with any-thing with that man.

Because it was already night, we decided to check into a Ramada Inn after we went to the funeral home where we knew we would find Liz. The nice gal at the Avis counter gave us a map and directions, highlighting every-thing with a yellow marker.

"It's only about thirty minutes from here."

"Thanks," we said, and were on our way.

We found the funeral home easily enough, parked, and went inside. The room where her mother's wake was in progress was crowded. I was glad that we had wired flow-ers ahead of time because the arrange-ments her mother had received so far were scant and unimpressive. It was understand-able. From all Liz had told us, her mother's friends were hardworking farmers, lived strictly by the Good Book, and flashy funeral flowers might have been considered an ex-travagance. But they had turned out in droves to comfort Liz and that was what mattered most.

We spotted Liz right away at the back of the room, talking to some people around her age.

"Probably childhood friends," I said, and Kevin nodded in agreement.

We went right to her side and Liz hugged us and introduced us to them. They all seemed nice enough, especially one handsome fellow whom Liz introduced as James. James had the eye for Liz and it seemed to me it was mutual. He was the right age, polite, good-looking, and very personable.

"He used to be Jimbo when he was in high school, because his name is James Robert. But when he went off to Harvard Law School, he became James."

We all shook hands, and James said, "Yeah, but then I got tired of the big-city rat race and decided to come on back home and set up shop where I really wanted to be."

"James is gonna help me figure out what to do about Momma's farm because it's mine now."

"Excellent," Kevin said, and whispered to me later, "He's not wearing a wedding ring."

"I'll bet he will be soon."

Strange as it may seem, Liz and James were a natural fit. You would've thought they had been a couple for years.

The funeral service at her family church the next day was lovely. We went to the cemetery for the burial, thinking not many people would. It was bad enough to lose a parent, but then worse to lose one with whom you had unresolved issues. It seemed to me, though, that whatever the relationship had been, there was still nothing more numbing and horrifying to endure than watching the body of someone you had loved being lowered into the ground.

We stood with her in the bright sun of the late morning together with a surprising number of friends and family members who *had* come, and Liz cried like a baby on Kevin's shoulder. And James, who held her hand, offered her a handkerchief. I liked his gesture very much. Afterward, we all went back to Liz's childhood home and the farm she had inherited.

The house was bustling with members of her mother's church who had delivered enough food to feed an army. Casseroles of string beans and others of macaroni and cheese, platters of sliced turkey and ham, cakes and pies, baskets of bread, and all the condiments needed to round out a meal covered the dining-room table while more waited in the kitchen.

The way Liz had described her home, you would have thought she had grown up in a shanty with newspapers stuffing the walls for insulation. That was not the case. It wasn't Tara, to be sure, but it was a nice typical clapboard house with a front and back porch, an old tin roof, and working shutters on the windows. In front of the house were enormous hydrangeas and azaleas. Behind the house was a pecan grove and there were probably a dozen peach trees. What was she talking about? I thought the landscape was absolutely beautiful. On the other hand, it would be easy not to love a place where you had known so much pain.

The kitchen was from the time of Noah and the bathroom that I used had seen better days, but it wasn't anything to be ashamed of and nothing was wrong with it that a moderate amount of money couldn't fix.

I was very proud of Liz. She was composed and surprisingly in command, given the gravity of the day. She thanked each person and listened attentively as her mother's friends told a special story about her mother and as they offered their condolences. James remained at her side. Kevin and I liked James more and more.

Later, when everyone was gone, Kevin and I stayed to chat a little.

"So, who's this James?" Kevin said. "Has he ever been married? Kids? Visible means of support?"

"Oh, Kevin," Liz said. "He's the older brother of one of my high school friends and I've known him all my life. He's got a small law practice and he does just fine."

"And?" I said, just like a Nosy Nellie/Mellie would.

"No, he's never been married and there are no children that I'm aware of."

"Well, you should ask him that because these days people go around having babies without a thought of marriage or a home . . . I'm just looking out for you, that's all," I said.

Of course, throughout the day and last night as well, I couldn't get my own mother off my mind. I was worried sick about her.

"How far is the drive to Charleston?" I asked.

"About seven hours, depends on traffic, of course," Liz said.

"Hey, Kevin? Want to go to Sullivans Island with me and surprise Miss Josie?"

"You only have to ask me once! Of course! Want to join us, Liz?"

"No, but thanks. I'm exhausted. Besides, I

have to stick around here and see what I have to do to settle Momma's estate."

Kevin said, "I take it you don't want to fly, Mellie?"

"You're a regular mind reader, Kevin. Do you know that?"

Kevin made arrangements to drop off the car at the Charleston airport. I called Charlie and he said it was no problem for them to house-sit for as long as I wanted, so we changed our tickets. At nine the next morning we left a stoic Liz, handsome James, her new farm, and the state of Alabama in the rearview mirror of our rental car.

We made our way through Georgia talking about everything in the world except the obvious, that it was Liz's mother's death that had been the trigger for me to go see my own mother.

"Think we'll ever see Liz again?"

"Of course we will, Petal! Even if they discover oil on those ten or twenty acres of hers, she has to come back to rescue all those stuffed animals and her Lava lamp!"

I laughed at that and said, "I suppose you're right. I'm so glad I brought the pictures from the wedding with me. Now I can show them to Mother."

"Yeah, somehow we never got around to showing them to Liz. Didn't seem like the thing to do, did it?"

"No, it didn't. Well, they're in that thing called PowerPoint, and if I can ever figure out how to get them out, I could print them. If I had a printer, that is."

"Not to worry, we will get it all sorted out. Given *our* history together, that's an *easy* one to solve."

We drove and drove and I slept for a while and finally we passed the sign that said WEL-COME TO CHARLESTON.

"Pull over at the next gas station," I said.

"Why? Little girls' room?"

"No, I want to drive so you can look around."

"Oh! Great idea. Thanks!"

We had our Chinese fire drill and minutes later the expected oohs and ahs spilled forth from my friend interspersed with reverential silences and sighs.

"For all the years I spent in Atlanta, I can't believe I never came here! I've never seen anything so beautiful," Kevin finally said. "It gives *breathtaking* a whole new meaning, doesn't it?"

"Leave it to you, my poetic friend, to aptly describe the indescribable."

"Gosh! I want to see everything! What all is there to do here?"

"It depends on what you are interested in. History? Parasailing? Gullah culture? Food? Catching fish? Catching the breeze?"

"I think I've got the picture, Mellie. But just promise me we'll take a few hours to go downtown to the historic district."

"Absolutely!"

Maybe Kevin had the picture, but nothing could have prepared me for what I saw when I laid eyes on my mother.

She was as thin as a blade of marsh grass, fast asleep in a chair on the porch, and covered in a blanket despite the warm temperature. Purple half-moons hung under her sunken eyes and her complexion had a pronounced tone of jaundice. I didn't want to startle her, so I motioned for Kevin to follow me around the porch to the other side of the house.

"Something is very wrong here," I said. "She looks like death warmed over."

"Get Harrison on the phone."

I dialed his cell and he answered.

"Harrison? Hey, it's Mellie. Do you have a moment?"

"Well, hey yourself! Where are you? Blowing bubbles on top of the Empire State Building?"

"No. Actually, I'm on Mother's back steps wondering if there's anyone who wants to tell me the truth about her health."

There was a pause and I could hear him breathing.

"I'll be right over," he said.

Chapter Twenty-one

SANDS OF TIME

"How long did y'all think it would take for me to find out?" I asked my mother. "And exactly what are we dealing with here?"

We were in the living room. I was reeling inside, terrified, brokenhearted, and knew that it was only the beginning of the roller-coaster ride. Harrison was leaning against the fireplace mantel. Kevin was staring out the sliding-glass door that looked out over the marsh, giving us some space. My mother was seated on her favorite club chair and I was sitting on the edge of the ottoman opposite her. She took my hands into hers and smiled a kind of an apologetic smile as she looked in my eyes.

"Well, my darling girl, it appears that I don't have a lot of time left on this earth. I have fully metastasized cancer."

I burst into tears and Harrison put his hand on my shoulder.

"Please, no," I said. "Please tell me this isn't true."

"I'm so sorry that we didn't tell you before now, but your mother wanted to be the one . . . to say it . . . I mean, it just wasn't my place." Harrison stepped away to the powder room and brought me a handful of tissues.

He was right of course. It wasn't his place to deliver that kind of news. I looked to my mother for some explanations.

"Why? Why didn't you tell me?"

"Because the right moment never came around. There just wasn't a right moment. When? At the wedding?"

"No, of course not."

"To tell you the truth, that's why I went organic. Or tried to live on all organic foods. I thought I might prolong my life, and I did! I have already beaten the predicted odds by over two years. I was feeling really fine, robust in fact, until just recently. I mean, didn't I tango at Charlie's wedding?"

"Yes, and you were fabulous!" Kevin said.

"Well, thank you, but now I think the nasty monster is finally going to get me after all."

"I'm so sorry, Miss Josie," Kevin said. "What can I do?"

"You can roll me a big fat doobie, if you know how to do that. It helps the pain."

"Pain! Oh, Mother! Is that why you're smoking pot?"

"Why else would I? You think I want to be all doped up on morphine? That stuff is addictive!"

"Um, where might I find . . . ?" Kevin said.

"It's in the freezer, Kevin. In a plastic bag that once held frozen corn. Rolling papers are in there, too."

"Right! In case the corn police show up . . ." Kevin said, and Mother smiled.

"Oh, my girl! It makes me laugh to think that you thought I was turning into a hippie or something! We laughed about that, didn't we, Harrison?"

"Yes, ma'am, we surely did."

"But I don't understand how this happened. I mean, don't you get regular physicals, Mother?"

"Yes, but I would always skip two of the tests. Listen to me, this is what happened. I felt absolutely fine. I very foolishly didn't get a mammogram for a few years because the radiation frightens me and we don't have it in our family history. And I did the monthly self-exam and never felt a thing."

"Mother? One in eight women is diagnosed with breast cancer. It's not about family history anymore. I know at least ten women who have had it and never had a single case in their families and never smoked and don't drink!"

"Personally, I think it's because of environmental toxins, but I'll get to that. And yes, I know that the whole mammogram procedure is different now and no longer considered dangerous. But anyway, I had microcalcification, which I never could have felt anyway. And, to add insult to injury, I didn't get a colonoscopy either."

"Oh, great."

"You're telling me? So the oncologists weren't even sure what the primary site of the cancer was. My legs were killing me, so I finally went to the doctor about it, and by the time I gave in and had a complete physical, I had a body full of demons. Stage-four everything. Chemo and radiation weren't going to save me, would have made me sick as the devil, and I would have been dead in a year or less anyway. So I decided to take my chances with some alternative treatments. Lucky for me, my cancer has been slow to spread, probably because I'm older and also because I drastically changed my diet. And I was in very good shape when I was diagnosed. All the farming exercise has helped me a lot, too."

"Oh, Mother. So what are you thinking now? I mean, do you have a plan?"

Kevin had rolled Mother a fat joint that was as neat as a pin. He handed it to her.

"Miss Josie? I went to Woodstock, you know," he said.

"Oh, sure," I said, "you would've been about four years old."

"I went with my parents," he said.

"He's a big liar, Mother."

Mother and Harrison chuckled.

"Well, I watched the video," he said.

"Whatever! So, Mother? What about you? A plan?"

Harrison gave Mother a light and she inhaled deeply.

"No, baby. I think we are just coming to the end of the road. Right now smoking this crazy weed helps, but if and when my symptoms

get too bad, I guess I'll call somebody . . . maybe take an aspirin . . ."

"Aspirin? You're not even taking aspirin?"

"That was a joke, Mellie. Do you want to
know something? Being happy and laughing
boosts your immune system."

"Yes. I've heard that. I realize I need to
work on my sense of humor."

"Yes, you really do."

The conversation went on for as long as
Mother wanted to talk about it and then I
helped her up to bed. She was worn out.

It was the end of the day and I went outside with Harrison and Kevin to watch the
sunset.

"I'm just absolutely heartbroken," I said. "I
knew something was wrong."

"Yes, you said that on the way here," Kevin
said. "God, look at that sun just hanging there
like a ball of fire."

"Your mother is one helluva great lady,"
Harrison said. "Anybody want a glass of
wine?"

We said that would be great and Harrison
returned with a bottle and three glasses
within minutes.

"Scuppernong?" I asked.

"Actually, this particular variety is called

Noble, appropriate for the occasion, don't you think?"

"What *is* this?" Kevin said, giving it a smell and pursing his lips.

"It's a local wine," Harrison said, "and I think you'll find that it stands up to ice very well."

"Just drink it, Kevin. To Mother!" I said, and we touched the edges of our glasses.

We were quiet as we stood there watching the sun slip away, each of us keeping our own thoughts to ourselves. Then, in the fading light, the sky painted itself with great streaks of sheer rose and lavender. I would never forget one detail of this day.

We left Birmingham after helping Liz bury her mother, and soon, if she could, I suspected Liz would be coming here to help me bury mine. I just hated the fact of it and the coincidence made it all the more terrible.

How brave my mother was, I thought. How brave to thumb her nose at modern medicine and to do all she had done to fight her disease. Now I understood why she had Cecelia, and why she went to all the lengths, transporting her to visit organically fed gentlemen goats, to keep her lactating most of the year—so that she could always have milk and yogurt that was free of chemicals. It was why Mother kept all those nasty chickens and tilled her vegetable garden, fertilizing with her own compost.

I suspected that the initial efforts came from her simply trying to heal herself. But those efforts led her to fall in love with the recycling, save-the-world, live-green movement in the first place. It was never about the bomb dropping and blowing up the grocery stores. That was her cover story. Knowing her, she enjoyed the challenge.

I still wrestled to understand why she had not told me she was so ill. Maybe she didn't believe it herself. Maybe she didn't want to admit it. Perhaps she thought I would badger her into all the chemo and radiation that she knew couldn't really help at her stage. I probably— no, I *definitely* would have. Or maybe she just wanted to live her life this way—collecting old eyeglasses and toothbrushes and making plates and bowls from potato starch. Yes, she had probably fallen in love with the lifestyle because it was the absolute opposite of how she had lived with my father.

If she could lengthen her life, feel well, and do something good for the planet along the way, it had certainly been so much the better. It was one reason why people called her

Miss Josie after Daddy died instead of Josephine. She had transform herself. Unconsciously or not, I had taken my cue from her by allowing Harrison to baptize me Mellie.

One thing was certain then. I wasn't leaving Sullivans Island until Mother went to her Great Reward. As of that moment, there wasn't anything more important to me than her comfort and her care. I wouldn't let her suffer for a minute. Not for a minute.

All right, I figured I could rise to the feeding of her goat and the chickens. I could tend a vegetable garden with the best of them. However, I couldn't see myself actually milking a goat named Cecelia and I had no intention of gathering eggs and being pecked to death by a bunch of filthy chickens. I was sure I could hire someone to do that part of the job. There had to be someone somewhere in the area who had a kid who wanted to earn some money to buy beer with a fake ID or whatever they did in this neck of the woods with a few extra dollars. I would make that a high priority.

Now that I had a laptop I could get on the Internet and see what I could find out about palliative care. In the meanwhile, gentle massages or herbal baths might help. Who knew? Maybe someone who practiced kinesiology could do something to alleviate pain or improve her state of mind if she became depressed. Acupuncture? I would make a list and go over it all with her.

Yes, I would do every single thing I could because plain and simple, I loved her so much. Yes, I had a sense of duty to her but that was not why I was staying. It was because I really loved her and everything about her. Every quirk, every peculiarity, the way she could change her lifestyle and embrace something new, how empowered she was, and the way she loved. The way she loved was a mighty force. And she loved me so much sometimes it scared me. I knew by the way her eyes were almost backlit with affection when she saw me coming up her stairs and the way her voice was raised an octave when she heard my voice on the other end of a call to her. There was nothing she would not have done for me all my life and now there would be nothing I would not do for her. Sure, she had given me the dickens for mourning Charles's departure and because I was so judgmental and unforgiving, and because I expected too much from other people sometimes. But I *was* stuffy and prudish and a social climber. She had been right to point out these shortcomings to me because if your mother can't help you to shape up, who will? And there is no one more entitled to telling you where you are lacking in your character than your own mother.

As long as she was ambulatory, we could walk together and I would show her how I had changed and tell her that she had been right all along about so many things. I would make sure I got her out of the house once a day at least. We could take the golf cart down to the beach and look up at the stars. I could read to her. Maybe she could help me conquer the late-week crossword puzzles in the *New York Times.* She could sit on a kitchen stool and tell me how to make the yogurt we both loved so much, courtesy of Cecelia.

If she wanted to, she could tell me everything she had never told me as though I would write her memoirs. It was strange to realize how much I *didn't* know about my mother. Her favorite movie? Her first kiss? Her favorite place in the world? The funniest joke she had ever heard? So many details to discover, and how long did we have together?

I knew that the day she finally closed her eyes that my sorrow would be unspeakably devastating, but there were minutes, hours, and days in between now and then. I would take full advantage of them.

I needed to call my children and tell them, and Liz should know, too. Even that stupid Charles probably deserved a call. But I decided I would wait until I had come to grips with the news myself. Perhaps I would call them tomorrow or the next day. I still needed time to absorb it.

"I'm starving," Kevin said, breaking the quiet. "And I think I might like a vodka martini."

"Why don't we walk over to Station Twenty-two Restaurant?" Harrison said. "We can bring your mother back some shrimp and grits. She loves that."

"Excellent idea," I said. "I'll just leave her a note."

We ordered a bottle of wine, a martini for Kevin, and I told them over dinner that I was staying.

"I wouldn't leave my mother either," Kevin said. "If you want I can send you clothes and whatever you need."

"Clothes, yes. I don't need anything else."

"I'm glad you're staying, Mellie," Harrison said. "It's going to do a lot to boost her spirits."

Kevin left so early the next day, the sun wasn't even up. But I got out of bed to make him some coffee and a piece of toast but mostly so that we could have a last word together. Walking out to the car, he said, "I'm so sorry, Petal."

"I know. Thanks."

Cecelia wandered over to the edge of her fence, bleated, and looked at us as though she expected us to make polite conversation with her. It wasn't happening.

"Have you thought about a milking ensemble? Something Swiss with puffy sleeves and a crinoline? Or shall I check the Armani department when I get back to work?"

"Somebody should give you a good pinch," I said. "If you think I'm touching that goat, you're cracked."

"I'll send a film crew if you do," he said, and laughed.

"Have a safe trip," I said, "and thanks, Kevin. I love you, you know."

"As you should!" We hugged and sighed. "I love you, too. Call me every day."

"I will." I watched him drive away, and bravery, loyalty, and love put aside, I knew I was in deep manure, or I certainly would be if I stepped in the chicken yard.

First, there was the issue of the eggs to be dealt with. Next, Cecelia probably needed a squeeze or I imagined her milk would begin to dry up. We had to keep the old goat producing because Mother loved her milk.

Maybe Mother would be up to the task for today and I could ask Harrison to help me find someone quickly.

It was too early to call anyone and I checked to see that Miss Josie was still fast asleep. It was almost dead low tide, so I decided to go for a walk on the beach. I left Mother a note and took the golf cart over to Station Twenty-six. There was a nice walkover there and I wanted to check its condition to be sure that Mother could navigate it. It was in perfect shape with a handrail and there were several benches thoughtfully positioned either for a resting place or as a place to lean or to remove your shoes.

One of the many things I loved about Sullivans Island was that you could leave your shoes on the walkway or down on the beach and they would be there when you got back. If I left a pair of shoes, even my ratty oyster-roast sneakers, on the front stoop of my town house in Manhattan, they would be scooped up in two minutes flat. Once, during a sanitation workers' strike in New York, people joked that they gift wrapped their garbage, left it on the curb or on the trunk of a car, and it disappeared almost immediately. What does that tell you?

It was going to be a beautiful day. Hundreds of tiny sandpipers were all over the shore, digging for breakfast in the mud with their needle-nosed beaks. As I approached them, they would scatter, fly low over the water, and then return as soon as they sensed it was safe. I looked out toward the horizon and the shrimp boats were there, their nets lowered as they moved slowly across the water. A European container ship was rounding the far end of the island headed into port. It looked for a moment like it was going to slam into the island and run aground, but of course that was an optical illusion.

I breathed deeply and wondered what really lay ahead of me. The first person I would call would be Charlie. After I told him the news, I would ask him and Priscilla to stay in my house, pay the bills or send them to me, and most of all, take care of Harry. Maybe I would ask him to call his father so that I could avoid the attack of acid reflux I would surely get if I had to hear a shred of disingenuous pity or sympathy come from Charles's mouth. Yes, I would ask Charlie to make the call.

Next, I would call Dan and Nan. And then Liz.

I would start cooking for Mother that very day, under her supervision of course. I would put her juicer on the counter and have it going all day long. Consumer that I was, even *I* knew that fresh vegetable juices were like a transfusion of energy. But rolling her a joint? I didn't have any expertise in that department whatsoever. Maybe I would buy her a pipe. I wondered where or who she bought the pot from. Did she get it delivered like pizza? Was there some sleazy drug dealer who would sneak up our porch steps after dark with her new supply? Maybe I would ask Harrison to handle that. Yes. That was a good idea.

I turned around and began walking back. It was almost seven o'clock and time to begin the day. I thought about the yoga studio at Station Twenty-three and it occurred to me that it might not be a bad idea to look into it. I was going to need something to help me deal with the stress, and maybe meditation might be a good idea for Mother *and* me. Every step of the way up and down the beach, that little voice in the back of my head wanted me to throw myself on the sand and weep. There was no time for that. In fact, I was determined not to cry at all. I swung by the yoga studio, noted the name and phone number, and went on home.

Mother was on the porch in her bathrobe, having a cup of tea. "Good morning, sweetheart," she said. "Did you sleep well?"

"All things considered, I slept well enough. You?"

"I have a hard time staying awake! Get yourself a cup of tea then come out and join me. I'm just watching the birds."

There was a container of green tea spiced with orange on the counter. I was an English Breakfast kind of gal, loving my caffeine, but I thought, Oh what the heck, green tea is supposed to be so good for you, so why not? It was aromatic and tropical and tasted delicious without a single thing added to it.

I went back out and sat in the chair next to her. "So how are you feeling, Miss Josie?"

"You want the truth or what you hear on the news?"

"I'm not sure."

"Okay, here's the straight skinny. When I wake up, I feel like a poopy doodle."

"Mother? Is that a tired snack food or is it related to actual poop?"

"Both. As I move around, have my tea, and

force myself to make something to eat that I don't feel like eating . . ."

"Appetite not so good?"

"Yes. Because I am nauseated all the time and nothing appeals to me."

"Maybe we should switch to vegetable juice. A small glass. What do you think? Carrot and apple? Maybe a thin slice of twelve-grain toast with a dollop of jam?"

"Ugh. But I'll try it."

"Listen, I decided I'm staying."

"For how long?"

"For as long as you need me."

She got very quiet and I knew she was thinking that I thought she would be gone in only a few weeks and she was still holding out hope against hope that she still had months or years.

"It doesn't matter how long it is, Mother. What did I leave in New York anyway? And if you're doing well, I can make a fast trip to check on things and come right back here, right?"

"Really? Would you really do that for me? What about your house and your bird?"

"Charlie and Priscilla are going to stay there and they've got Harry covered. Besides, Priscilla's not happy with their neighborhood, so I'm sure she's thrilled. Anyway,

Kevin's there, too, and Liz will be back soon."

"Poor Liz. How's she doing?"

"Liz is something else. She and her mother had a terrible relationship, as you know. I think she mourns the relationship they never had more than the fact that she's gone. She said they reconciled and I hope she believes it."

"Still. Whether she was a witch or a saint, she's lost her mother. I remember the day I buried mine. It was the worst day of my life."

"Well, unless I get hit by a truck, it will no doubt be the worst day of mine, too. But I don't want us to have a lot of morbid talk, Mother. Let's just take one day at a time."

"Mol-asses. When did you turn into such a grown-up?"

"Me? Honey, I'm just like everybody else. I grew up when I had to. And I'm taking over your kitchen, with you still in command of course. I just don't think cooking is the best use of your energy."

"Well, Dr. Mellie? What do you think *would* be the best use of my energy?"

"I just want you to talk to me. We'll take a walk every day. I'm going to start a journal. I want you to give me your recipe for yogurt.

There are a million things, Miss Josie. I've been thinking about it."

"Are you going to tell the children?"

"Unless you want to. I mean, I don't think it would be fair to tell Charlie and not Dan."

"And you have to tell Charlie right away." She was quiet for a minute or two and then she said, "You can tell them. No point in keeping secrets now. They might want to visit before I drop. This stinks, right?"

"It stinks in the extreme. I'm going over to Whole Foods and stocking up on organic whatever they have."

"Do you trust them? I mean, there's organic and there's organic, you know."

"Yes. I do know and I trust them."

"Well, then get me a chocolate cake."

We laughed at that and the many things it meant.

I came in later with bags and bags of groceries and it was plain to see Cecelia needed attention, which meant the eggs were probably still there, too. Mother was dressed in her farmer clothes but asleep in her chair by the fireplace. She stirred when she heard me unpacking and putting away all the things I had bought.

"Need a hand?" she said. Her voice was so weak it frightened me.

"No, that's okay. I can handle this."

"I was going to go milk Cecelia and gather the eggs, but I just don't have the strength."

I looked to the ceiling, hoping it would open and somehow I would be delivered by a miracle. Seeing none, I took a deep breath and said, "Don't worry about it. I can do it."

"Thank you, sweetheart."

I put on my oyster-roast sneakers, a pair of jeans, and a long-sleeve denim shirt. I got a basket and gloves to avoid pecking and went outside to try and figure this out. Inside Cecelia's shed was something that resembled a small stage. A bucket was there and a stool was on the ground next to it, so I figured it must be the scene of the crime. There was a trough at the end with a kind of a guillotine contraption to hold her head still but not hurt her neck. If I put some grain in the trough and led Cecelia up there, she might be distracted enough by the food to let me do the foul thing I had to do.

Suddenly the egg gathering seemed like the more desirable party to attend.

Mother had smartly designed her chicken yard so that it was movable. When a patch of yard had been grazed to bits, she could move the fencing to another spot. And the coop wasn't so big and heavy that two healthy men couldn't lift it and reposition it. She had wire mesh over the top to keep out the hawks and the other predators and to keep the chickens in. It seemed to me that the whole enterprise was more trouble than it was worth, but I knew Mother would have sternly disagreed.

I stood there with my basket, looking at the chickens for a minute or two. They didn't seem so horribly threatening, so I opened the gate and slipped inside. They were pecking around the yard and didn't attack me, so I thought things might go well. I opened the small door on the side of the coop that con- cealed the nesting box and looked inside. There were several eggs there that I reached over and took as quickly as I could. I did not see the hen that flew at my arm with her dag- ger beak. Well, she didn't fly but she sure came out of nowhere and stabbed me. I pulled my arm out of there as fast as I could. My arm wasn't bleeding but my heart was racing. I had three eggs. Okay, I got out of there alive with mission one accomplished.

Cecelia was staring at me. She was smart enough to know that the person who dealt with the chickens would most likely be the same person who dealt with her. I thought about it for a minute. Compared to Harry and that pack of wild birds I had just visited, Cecelia was downright docile.

"Come on, girlfriend, this is our big moment."

She actually followed me and I put the egg basket on the table in her shed. She looked at me and I looked at her. I filled her trough with feed and looked at her again. She did not appear to be any happier about this than I was.

"Okay, onstage! This is your cue." Nothing. "Let's go, Cecelia!" No movement.

I noticed that she had a collar and approached her slowly. Cecelia wanted the feed but she was as unsure of my abilities to perform this dastardly assignment as I was. This was not a dumb goat. She began to retreat and back out into the yard. I knew I had to catch her. She had somehow intuited that I had formula-fed my sons. Additionally, in her Nigerian-dwarf-goat brain she calculated that her own udder relief—another bad joke— would come at too high a price. The chase began and for the next fifteen minutes she escaped every attempt I made to grab her by the collar. I was sweating and out of breath and I wondered how Mother had the stamina for this, all for some milk and yogurt.

"Not worth it!" I said out loud.

"Sure it is." I turned to see Harrison standing outside the fence, laughing so hard I thought I might have to kill him. "I wish I had a camera."

"Harrison?" I was not laughing. I returned to the shed, picked up the egg basket, and stomped over to the gate where he stood. "This is not going to work. We have to hire someone today. I can't do this. End of story."

"Oh, Lord! I'm sorry to laugh but watching you chasing that goat was about the funniest thing—"

"Just stop, okay? I'm a failure. I can't even get a couple of eggs without being attacked and the goat doesn't want to know me."

"Let me show you how to do this, Mellie."

He went to the shed, got a leash that I didn't know was there on the hook, cornered Cecelia, clipped on the leash, and led her to the milking stand. He led her up the step, pulled her head through the holder, secured it, and rubbed her nose or snout or whatever you called it.

"Good girl," he said.

"Waaaah!" Cecelia bleated, and began to eat.

He sat on the stool and milked her like he had done it a thousand times.

"How's our Miss Josie today?"

"Not worth two hoots. Maybe we should call the doctor and ask for a house call or something. I can tell she's in pain and she doesn't want to eat."

"That's not good."

"No, it's not good at all."

It was the beginning of the end and we knew it.

I called Charlie and had spoken to him, telling him everything I knew. Priscilla called me and asked if there was anything they could do. Should they come? What were her symptoms? When I told her she was very quiet. I did not ask her how much time she or Charlie thought Mother might have left. I did not want to know. And besides, who could really say? It was all in God's hands.

When I told Dan and Nan, they cried. It surprised me, but apparently they had fallen in love with Mother all over again at Charlie's wedding and their children were completely infatuated with her. How much longer did she have? I could not answer them either.

When I called Liz, she was incredibly sad to hear the news. She was still in Alabama and intended to return to New York. But she had good news. She was pretty smitten with James, spending a lot of time with him, and each day it was more difficult to see herself in Manhattan anymore. She promised to be there if I needed her. She said she understood how I felt. All I had to do was whistle and she would drop everything and come. I thanked her and told her I would call.

Harrison found someone to care for the chickens and for Cecelia. He was a student from the College of Charleston who'd grown up on a farm near Orangeburg.

One day I said to him, "How do you keep the chickens from pecking you?"

"Ya gotta show 'em who's the boss. Plus I use a garbage-can lid as a shield."

"Now why didn't I think of that?"

I spent my days seeing to Mother's comfort and adjusting myself, or so I thought, to how life would be without her. I asked her every day how it was going for her. Was she afraid? No, she said she was not afraid. Afraid of terrible pain, perhaps, but she was not afraid to die. I spoke to her doctor and he said that whenever she felt she needed serious pain management, we only had to call and he would be there.

Kevin called almost every day to check on Mother and then one day he said, "Listen, I'm a little worried about Harry."

"Why?"

"I went downstairs to check on him yesterday and he's losing feathers." Kevin said he had asked the vet and his reply was that Harry missed me. "So I'm thinking I might put the old boy in his cage, rent a van, and drive him down to you. What do you think?"

"He's not happy with Charlie and Priscilla?"

"Of course he is but he's *attached* to you! That's how these birds are!"

"Then bring him on down."

Kevin arrived with Harry on Saturday and unfortunately had to leave the next morning.

"Duty calls, Petal. How are you holding up?"

"Okay. I mean, I'm incredibly grateful to have this time with her, but it's so sad to see Mother, you know, just fading away. Harry? What's up?" Harry looked like he'd been plucked.

"Pretty Miriam," he said, and I knew he was happy to see me.

"Everything's okay, baby." I let him crawl

out of his cage and onto my fingers and nuzzled him.

"It's worse than having kids," Kevin said.

"Close. At least kids become independent or useful at some point."

"True."

Harrison came to sit with Mother, and Kevin and I went over to the Water's Edge on Shem Creek for dinner.

"So what's up with you and Harrison?"

"Zero. Look, romance is the last thing on my mind right now."

"Understood. But do you think that at some point there might be something?"

"Who knows? I think he's got commitment issues. And to be honest, I don't know how I feel. I mean, he might be the most wonderful man I've ever met—besides you, of course—but I wouldn't trust my judgment about that kind of thing at this point."

"So, tell me how it's going with Miss Josie."

I told him that Mother and I would walk a little each day for the first few weeks but then it was less and less until now it was all I could do to get her to bathe and dress. She was drinking small amounts of my vegetable juices and chicken broth and occasionally she would ask for ice cream or some chocolate. On a rare day I would manage to get her to eat the yogurt she had taught me to make or a soft-boiled egg from one of the chickens.

"Loss of appetite is a bad sign."

"I know that. She doesn't even want her marijuana anymore. She says the pain lets her know she's still alive and she wants clarity so she can tell me things. She's told me stories about her parents that I had never known and things about my father that I had forgotten. She showed me her favorite book of poetry and read her favorite lines to me. I mean, Kevin, it's like trying to stop the tide. It's going to come and go just like we are. What can I do?"

"She's so sweet, Mellie. She really is. Just do what you're doing. And you should probably call hospice."

"I agree. I think it's time."

Harrison was always nearby if I needed him and I did. All the time. I was in this weird place where all I wanted to do was talk to my mother and then I wanted to run to him to repeat what she had said and to cry that I had not known this or that.

Finally, when we had hospice nurses and volunteers coming and going and Mother had agreed to take morphine injections, things fell into an organized routine.

But soon it seemed to me that Mother was sleeping almost all the time and refusing all food. She drank water but that was all. Basically, she was starving to death while she slept and I couldn't stand it. I felt wretched and horrible guilt about it, but I couldn't stand to see her this way and I wanted it over. At night when I would pray I would ask God to be merciful and to let her suffering end. And mine. Then I would beg forgiveness for my selfishness and cry myself to sleep.

One evening around seven I was on the porch reading the newspaper and the hospice nurse came to me.

"Your mother is out of the bed and asking for you," she said.

"What? How could that be?"

I raced upstairs to find her on the balcony, staring at the sunset, the time of day she loved most.

"I wanted you to watch this with me," she said as though she were perfectly fine.

I put my arm around her waist and she leaned into me for support. We stood there for the fifteen minutes or so it took the sun to go from glaring, screaming white to that fabulous red orange that was so sensual and undulating.

"I love you, Miss Josie. You know that, don't you?"

"And I love you, my precious girl. Don't ever doubt that for a moment. And I am so proud of the woman you have become."

"Mother. You're the one who saved me. How will I get along without you?"

"You'll be fine, sweetheart. Every time you see the sunset like this, you think of me and I'll be thinking of you."

"Okay. That's a deal."

When the sun was all gone I put Mother back in her bed with help from the woman from hospice and she drifted off to sleep. I sat alone in the room with her, next to her bed for a long time. Around nine or ten the nurse came in to say that Mr. Ford was there. I went downstairs, looked at Harrison, and knew that Mother had died the second I walked out of the room. I could feel it in every cell of my body. Then a tail of light raced right through the living room, in the space between where we stood facing each other. We both watched it go through the open sliding-glass door, out and up into the sky.

"Mrs. Swanson?" the nurse called out to me.

Harrison put his arms around me and I began to sob. No one had to tell us what we had just seen and what we already knew.

Epilogue

It seemed that my world came to an end the day we buried my mother, and part of it did. But now it had been almost a year. For the first six months I missed her with a ferociousness that would have me convulsing in tears in an instant. All I had to do was look at a picture of her or hear a certain song. Or write a thank-you note for yet another donation that someone made to fight breast cancer or colon cancer. Mother had more friends who honored her life than I ever knew.

But as my mourning subsided I would smile instead of cry on her birthday or Mother's Day or when someone, an old friend visiting the island from Charlotte or someplace else, stopped by unannounced and told me a wonderful story about her. I would invite them to have a cup of green tea spiced with orange that I had come to love. You see, I never left the island after Mother died, except for very short trips. As long as I stayed, people she knew might continue to drop by the house, and in my mind that kept Miss Josie alive.

Nan had delivered an eight-pound baby girl whom they named Josephine, and it thrilled me no end to hold that child in my arms when I went to the christening. After great discussions with Charlie and Dan, I made some powerful decisions. Charlie and Priscilla would continue to live in the town house. Rental income combined with their own earnings gave them more than enough money to maintain it. On my death, they would have it appraised and either buy Dan's share or sell it and split the money. Priscilla was happy beyond words. So was Charlie. Priscilla and Charlie would have no trouble renting Liz's apartment, as they knew many residents and doctors who would love to live in that house.

It should come as no surprise that Liz moved home to Birmingham and didn't sell the farm. She was hoping something permanent would develop with James. And Kevin? Well, since I abandoned him, he teasingly said, he finally decided to take a job in Paris to style a chain of fifty department stores. He had been offered the job over and over.

"It's not the same without you, Petal. I mean, I adore Priscilla and Charlie, but it's not the same."

"Go for it, Kevin, but you had better swear to visit me once a year!"

"Or you come to Paris . . . when you get rid of that goat?"

"Watch it or I'll bring Cecelia with me!"

I would miss him like crazy but he was going off to have an adventure. It was time for him to have a change of venue.

When Charles got wind of Mother's death and that I was staying permanently on the island, he tried to buy the town house from me for such a paltry sum that I laughed in his face.

"What's so funny?" he said. "I think that's a very fair offer."

"Charles? In real life or on the screen or in any book I have ever read, *never* have I encountered someone like you."

"So I'll take that to mean you don't want to sell it to me?"

"Yes, because it's worth almost three times as much as you're offering and we both know it. And Charlie and Priscilla are living there. Charles? Did you send flowers when Mother died?"

"Um, I heard about it too late."

"Okay. Did you send a card to me or the children? Call them? Say you were sorry for their loss? Did you make a donation to any of Mother's favorite charities?"

"All right, all right. That's enough. I was uncomfortable with it, okay? Death makes me very squeamish."

We wouldn't want Charles to feel squeamish or uncomfortable, would we?

In a very calm voice I said, "Well, what do dial tones do for you?" And I closed my phone.

Harrison had witnessed this and he high-fived me with a burst of laughter and pride.

"Take-no-bull Mellie is on the job!" he said, and laughed.

Yes, Harrison and I had finally found our way to each other's heart but not to the altar. I was in no rush, and besides it was more fun to make him worry and wonder about the depth of my commitment to him. Recently, he gave me a toe ring that absolutely symbolized nothing more than my transformation to a woman who would wear one. Or maybe it didn't.

"What's this supposed to mean?" I said, recognizing it wasn't for my finger. "I mean, if I wear it on my left foot, does it mean we're serious?"

"Why don't we call it a starter ring and see where things go?"

"You mean, like, you're working your way up from my feet to my hands?"

"Come on, Mellie. You know me."

Harrison's issues with commitment were his problem, not mine. He would either overcome them or he wouldn't. But honestly, I was satisfied with my toe ring and the relationship we had. We saw each other every day and night and were all but inseparable. Like Kevin had always been, he was my best friend except there were other meaningful benefits.

All right, I know nobody's going to be happy until they get the scoop on our sex life. Here's the deal. We have one. It's gorgeous and tender and delicious and he sends me right through the Milky Way. Satisfied? No? You want a full report? Well, I think it's in pretty bad taste to kiss and tell, but just this once, I will.

Here's how it started. One morning, I was in the kitchen washing the breakfast dishes and he showed up with an enormous bouquet of flowers, wrapped in cellophane and dripping with ribbons. This was an unprecedented event. He was just standing there on the other side of the glass sliding door instead of just walking right in, like he usually did.

So, recognizing his behavior as slightly strange, I opened the door and said, "Hey! What's up?"

"Today Miss Josie's been gone for six months and I thought maybe some flowers might, you know, cheer you up. You know, girls like flowers."

"So do women," I said, teasing him a little. "Thanks! They're gorgeous."

"Well, actually that's what I wanted to discuss with you."

"What?"

"The fact that you're a gorgeous woman . . ."

"And that you're a gorgeous man? I've noticed that, actually."

"Well, and there's something else."

He put the bouquet on the counter and gave me the come-hither hook with his finger. I followed him outside to the bottom of the steps, where a leafy sapling stood in a two-foot-tall plastic planter.

"It's a mango tree," he said. "They're not supposed to grow here but I thought maybe Miss Josie's oversight from wherever she is and ours, of course, might make the impossible happen."

That was when I thought my heart would burst. I threw my arms around him and hugged him with all of my might.

"You wonderful man!"

He hesitated for a moment and then he put one arm around my waist and ran his other hand down the back of my head, his fingers pulling through my hair. He put his mouth next to my neck and said, "I'm in love with you, Mellie, and I don't know what to do about it."

"Just love me, Harrison. I've been in love with you from the moment I saw you." Here came the tears, but this time they were different. I was finally safe and there was no doubt that Harrison was the man with whom I was going to spend the rest of my life.

"Why didn't you say something?"

"Because I thought you were my mother's boyfriend? Weren't you?"

Harrison stepped back from me and started laughing, the deep kind of laugh that comes from the bottom of your throat in a burst and continues until there are tears and you have to rush to blow your nose or else you will never be received in polite company again.

"Tissue?" I reached in my pocket and handed him one.

"No, you silly goose! Don't you know that your mother had chosen me for *you*? Why do you think I was here every time you came to visit?"

"Oh, come on. You don't think she was just a little sweet on you?"

"Sure, maybe I do. But, Mellie, by the time I met her, she was sick as a dog. I took care of her because I liked her. It was the most natural and comfortable friendship with a woman I had ever known. Better than my own mother—what I can remember of her and certainly more than I've ever had with my daughter. And, I *never* in a million years ex-pected to feel this way about you or about *anybody* for the rest of my life."

"Well, here we are. Now what? Plant the tree?"

"I think we're supposed to kiss now and

plant the tree later. I thought six months was a respectable amount of time to wait to give you this news. About the way I feel, that is."

"Yeah, six months was good. I'm ready. I mean, I think I can handle this now."

So, right there, at the bottom of the steps on the pathway to my driveway, we kissed. At first it was tentative and then it became clear to both of us that we were five minutes away from scandalizing the neighbors. It was, after all, not even ten o'clock in the morning.

By the time we got inside, the mood was broken a little because the impulse to launch ourselves into a full-blown sexual encounter right then and there suddenly seemed capricious.

"Do you think maybe a little more cat and mouse is in order?" he said.

"Yes, I hate it, but I do."

The rest of this may seem a little stupid to some, but you have to understand that we were both nervous. It's one thing to have a, pardon me, *screw* with a dope like Manny Sinkler. I mean, sure it was immoral, but it wasn't going anywhere. *This,* however, was the *big one.* What if we were horribly incompatible?

It was best to learn these things after dark.

For the rest of the day we puttered around talking about things like finding someone to take Cecelia and the chickens off my hands for good. I wanted to plant lots of flowers and a vegetable garden just for my grandchildren, who would be four in number very soon, as Charlie and Priscilla were also expecting a blessed event. Harrison said he thought we should just deliver them to Manny Sinkler's house and let him deal with it. I said it wasn't worth the effort because who cared about him?

We found a corner of the yard with the best possible sunlight, wind protection, and drainage for the mango tree. We planted it together and sneaked another kiss in the process. Finally, the day was winding down to a close.

"So what do you want to do for dinner?" he said.

Screw, I thought. But I said, "Why don't we cook at your house tonight?"

We grilled some tuna steaks and nothing happened except some heavy necking until Harrison changed his mind, that is. I was loading the dishwasher and he had the brilliant idea to scoop me up off my feet and carry me to his bed. Now this would be very romantic except that he tripped and dropped me, falling

himself and throwing out his back in the process. I put his bruised ego on his couch with
an ice pack, kissed him on the head, and said
I would call him in the morning.

I drove his car home, poured myself a
nightcap, and said to Harry, who had grown
back his feathers, "No sex. I thought it was
gonna happen and then he dropped me on
the floor. So, no sex tonight."

Harry looked at me this way and that and
then he said, "No sex tonight!"

Great, I thought. Hopefully, he'd forget it
by tomorrow.

Well, he didn't.

Harrison, who felt much better the next
morning, arrived that night for dinner with a
bottle of scuppernong wine, which I was actually becoming accustomed to drinking and
enjoying. I had made some thick crab cakes
and a salad.

Harry made his announcement after dinner that the dessert wasn't me, and Harrison
said, "The hell you say, bubba."

I looked at Harrison and didn't know what
to say.

"Come on, Mellie. We're going upstairs.
You talk to that bird way too much."

"Yeah, and he's not discreet."

We went to bed like a married couple of twenty years and I assumed he was planning to stay the night. He was. When the lights were out, he found me in the darkness and pulled me to him. All I've got to say about what happened next was it was how it's supposed to be when the man's a real man who loves women and who has a healthy appetite for them. Every time we have been together since that first night, it's been fabulous. And over the next six months, which brings us up to now, there wasn't a hair on his body I didn't know and adore. I was pretty sure he felt the same way. And there were tiny mangoes, too many to count, dangling from the branches of our tree.

We were standing on the driveway watching Priscilla push a stroller toward us with my lovely infant granddaughter named—can you believe it?—Miriam Elizabeth, and next to her was Nan with her three in a wagon. They were coming back from the beach for tomato sandwiches and naps for the children. No doubt they had built sand castles and jumped the waves.

"We can't keep playing house like this, Mellie. It's a bad example for the grandchildren."

I put my arm around his waist and squeezed

him. That may or may not have been a marriage proposal.

"Whatever you say, baby. The children are still young."

You see? Everything happens for a reason. My father's death brought my mother back to Sullivans Island. Charles's stupidities sprung me from a terrible marriage and have given me Kevin, one of my greatest friends, and Liz, who had given me all the subtle clues on how to love my daughters-in-law. My mother's love for me had brought me to Harrison. And the island. It was all about the island. The tempo of the life, the sweet salty air, had even healed Harrison of his fear of love. And me of mine.

If you had told me five years ago that this was the life I would be living, I would have said you were insane. I was the city slicker with cynical opinions for every occasion. But now there I was in the evenings, all my rocking chairs except one filled with loved ones of every age, watching the sun go down. The empty one, her favorite, I reserved for the spirit of Miss Josie.

Sometimes Harrison and I would dramatically tango the length of the porch to make the children laugh. Penn and Mary would swing in the hammock and I would tell them stories, the same ones of my childhood.

"This is truly a special place, Mom," Priscilla said, and Nan agreed.

"It's unbelievable! Moving here and bringing us together was such a wonderful idea," Nan said.

We all agreed wholeheartedly to spend Easter, Thanksgiving, and a week together during the summer on Sullivans Island every year. At Christmas I would alternate between New York and California. Harrison was invited to everything.

Perhaps I could persuade Liz to come from Alabama or Kevin to visit from Paris for a few days to take care of Harry when I had to leave. I would entice them for a visit, to arrive a few days before I had to depart, feed them steamed vegetables from my magical garden and grilled fresh fish that had been swimming that day, caught from the dock out near Awendaw where the ferryboat sails to Bull's Island, and where Harrison most loved to drop a hook.

We would catch up over dinner and into the night, rightfully reclaiming our special and chosen familial positions with one another over as many varieties of muscadine wine as we could find and pour—Darlene, Pam, Hunt, pineapple, and of course, scuppernong—along with a perfectly ripened organic goat cheese, spread on delicious organic crackers, topped with my own miraculous mango chutney.

Tonight, when my sons and their wives and children were asleep in their beds, and Harrison was gently snoring in his recliner chair in the den, I would slip out to the porch for a dose of my mother's spirit. I would sit in the rocker next to her favorite, breathe deeply, and just as I would at sunset, I would feel her all around me.

Her breath would be sweet and I would almost hear her whispering right into the center of my heart. *My darling girl,* she would say, *bringing your family together to love each other is all that matters.* In the next instant I would think of how much I missed her and then I would be reminded beyond a doubt that she had never left me at all. I would reach over, touch the arm of her chair, and give her a little push to rock in time with me.